Mrs. Henry Wood

Lady Adelaide

A Novel

Mrs. Henry Wood

Lady Adelaide
A Novel

ISBN/EAN: 9783337001568

Printed in Europe, USA, Canada, Australia, Japan

Cover: Foto ©Andreas Hilbeck / pixelio.de

More available books at **www.hansebooks.com**

CONTENTS.

iv CONTENTS.

LADY ADELAIDE.

CHAPTER I.

HARRY DANE.

On a somewhat wild part of the coast of England, between one and two hundred miles distant from the metropolis, lies a small town or village called Danesheld. The land on either side of it rises high, and overlooks the sea, whilst the descent of the rocks, in places perpendicular, is not so in all. There are parts where they slope back so gradually that a sure foot may descend with ease: and in such places the hard nature of the rock appears to have softened with time, for grass, and even wild flowers, grow upon the surface. In ancient times it was a settlement of the Danes: and the name now corrupted into Danesheld, was formerly written Danes' Hold. To the right of the village, as you stand facing the sea, the land is wild and rugged, and without a sign of human habitation. To the left, towards the east, may be seen some scattered houses of a superior description, two or three of them handsome mansions; and behind, lies quite a colony of poor cottages and fishermen's huts, older than the mansions, older even than the village. It should be noticed that all these houses face the sea, the high road running immediately before some of them; and the green heights extending between the road and the rocks.

Beyond all, still towards the east and about a mile distant from the village, rise the conspicuous towers of Dane Castle; a long, but not high building, its red stone dark with age. There is a tower at either end, and a square turret surmounts the great gateway in the middle: from which turret

a flag is always floating when the chief, Lord Dane, is
sojourning at the castle.   Like the rest of the dwellings, it
faces the sea, a narrow strip of greensward intervening
between the gates and the high road.   Beyond the road,
which has neither hedge nor boundary wall, the grassland
stretches out smooth and flat to the edge of the heights.   It
is broad too just here, nearly a quarter-of-a-mile intervening
between the castle and the sea.   Opposite the extreme end
of the castle, and very near to the brow of the heights, are
the ruins of what was the chapel in the days of the monks.
Its walls still stand, and its casements, from which the glass
has long since gone, are sheltered by prolific ivy, a darker
screen than any glass could be.   The lords of Dane would
cause this ivy to be trimmed occasionally, but it grows in
clustering profusion.   Traces of the altar and of ancient
gravestones may be seen inside still, but no roof remains : it
is open alike to the calm and the stormy sky.   A picturesque
sight does that old ruin present in the beams of the rising
and the setting sun ; still more so in the pale, mystic beauty
of a moonlit night.   In this part the rocks are perpendicular,
and not very high ; somewhat farther on they recede greatly,
and some rude steps are cut in them to the beach below.
The young Danes in their boyhood, the present lord's two
sons, would run up and down these steps with impunity,
to get to their boat, which they kept moored below them.

Behind the castle there is a small garden ; flowers and
fruit do not seem to flourish here ; and between the castle
and the village may be seen the signs of husbandry—
ploughed fields, grass-lands, with here and there a farm-
house, surrounded by its ricks and barns ; all, or nearly all,
belonging to Lord Dane—village, houses, lands ; the various
tenants paying rent for their occupancy.

It was a sunny day in spring.   Perched upon a gate that
led into a clover field, within view of the castle windows at
the end facing Danesheld, within view also of the high road
and the green plain before it, there sat a gentleman doing
something to a fishing-rod.   He looked about eight-and-
twenty ; a tall, slender man, with good, though somewhat
thin and sharp, features, and with dark eyes.   His velveteen

shooting-coat was thrown back, for the day was really warm; and he was whistling softly at his work. Hearing footsteps, he lifted his eyes, and saw advancing from the direction of the village, a middle-aged man, a stranger, who wore the attire of a gentleman-sailor. As the stranger neared the gate he lifted his glazed hat from his head; but, whether in courtesy, or whether merely to wipe his brow with his handkerchief, was not clearly obvious.

"Is that Dane Castle?" asked the stranger.

"Yes."

"I thought it must be," was the comment of the sailor spoken in an undertone. "Are the family at the castle now?"

The gentleman with the fishing-rod pointed towards the flag. "There is the sign. When his lordship of Dane is at home you see the flag waving there; in his absence it does not show."

"But why so?"

The young man shrugged his shoulders; his manner of speaking was idle, characterized by a certain equanimity almost bordering on ridicule; not ridicule of the stranger, but of the Danes he was speaking of. "Because it's one of the old Dane customs. They have some queer ones. Those scrolls and crosses you see on the flag are the Dane arms."

"Are both the sons at home? Pardon my questions," continued the stranger; "I made acquaintance with one of them abroad, some years ago."

"The younger one is at home—the ex-captain," replied the young man, equably, as though to answer questions on the Dane family were as much his business in life just then as splicing the fishing-rod. "The heir is in Paris. He is a fast man, and a continental life suits him."

"Are the brothers still at variance?"

"They are, and always will be."

"Some dispute about fortune, is it not?"

"Some ill-blood, but no dispute. There might be dispute if that would alter the existing state of things, but it won't. Not that the ill-blood is on the captain's side; I'll give him his due there: the fault is the heir's."

"Is there not a young lady staying at the castle?" resumed the stranger, after a pause. "I forget her name."

"Adelaide Errol," was the answer, given with the same coolness of tone and manner; but this time the young man lifted his eyes, and scanned the sailor. "A wild Scotch lassie is what Danesheld styles her."

"I have heard her called an angel," returned the sailor; "nothing less laudatory."

"Then," and the dark eyes were fixed on the stranger as though they would read him through and through, "if you have heard that, I'll wager it was from no other than Harry Dane."

"From William Dane."

"William Henry, it is all one; we dub him Harry here. The old peer is fond of the name, so also is my lady; and they have rarely called him anything else."

"And the name of the elder one is Geoffry, I remember. He——"

"You wouldn't find the heir to Dane named anything but Geoffry," came the interruption. "Another of their superstitions."

"Indeed! Is William Dane to marry Adelaide Errol?"

The gentleman raised his eyebrows. "Well, people say so. The captain, gallant son of Mars though he be—or was—has singed his wings in the brightness of her fascinations. He——"

"I wish you'd talk plain English, sir," cried the stranger, a little testily: upon which the other accorded him a prolonged stare.

"What else am I talking? Dutch?"

"Rhapsody: and it is a language I never understood. Is Captain Dane to marry the young lady, or is he not?"

"What a very unreasonable man you seem to be!" was the rejoinder, accompanied by a half laugh. "Don't I tell you it is said that he will? Captain Harry worships the very ground she treads on. You'll call that rhapsody again perhaps; but it is fact."

"And she?"

The young man drew down his lips with an air that

seemed to intimate that it was no business of his. "How do I know? there's no answering for women. Perhaps she returns his love; perhaps she does not. My Lady Dane impresses upon her the fact that the Honourable William Henry, although he may be getting on towards middle-life, is no bad match for a portionless damsel."

"William Dane is rich," remarked the stranger.

"I wish I were a tithe as rich. Some arrangement exists in the Dane family by which the younger branches step into their fortune as soon as they are of age; and Harry, who comprised all the branches in his own person, took possession of his. It was fifty thousand pounds. To that there was another fifty thousand; more—for it had been accumulating some few years—left him by his uncle, William Henry Verner. And the captain can't be spending half his income. Just now, visiting at home, he is spending nothing."

"How long does he intend to remain at home?"

"You had better ask that of Adelaide Errol. When he arrived at home, he said he had come for a week or two——"

"You mean when he landed from the States?"

"I mean when he landed from the States. And what the deuce brought him wandering so long in the States has always been a mystery to me. He must have turned into an American! He came home, saying he should remain a week or two: that's six months ago: and he's here still, fooled by this mad passion for the—— But it's no business of mine," broke off the young man. "He once talked of repurchasing into the army; for my part, I can't think why he sold out of it."

"Why do you call it a mad passion?"

The young man took out his penknife, and leisurely scraped a spot off the fishing-rod.

"Random figures of speech slip from us at times which frequently have little meaning."

"I beg your pardon. That may be the Dane family."

The young man turned his head. A group had appeared on the greensward near the chapel, the most prominent object amidst it being an invalid chair, in which reclined a fine-looking old man, whose gray hair was fast turning to white. It was propelled by a man-servant in the Dane livery—purple velvet waistcoat and breeches, and a white coat laced with silver. A tall, fine, very handsome old lady accompanied the chair. Behind came a man of noble features, who might be approaching his fortieth year, upright and stately, slender still, and far above the middle height. A fair girl of nineteen walked by his side; now before him, now behind him, chattering to him, and putting forth all her attractions, as it was in her nature to do. She had a very brilliant complexion, blue eyes, and a profusion of fair hair—a lovely vision undeniably, taken altogether; but the features were not especially good, and the eyes roved about too much for true ones. Behind all, came another footman in the same livery.

"You are right," was the answer; "it is the Dane family. They have been taking my lord for his morning airing. The two servants relieve each other in wheeling the chair."

"Is Lord Dane an invalid?"

"An invalid!" echoed the young man, as he hastily put his fishing-rod together. "It is to be hoped neither you nor I will ever be such a one. Lord Dane had a dreadful fall with his horse last autumn, when out hunting, and has become paralyzed in the lower limbs. There is no cure for him, the doctors say; it will only go on from bad to worse. And now, sir, I must wish you a good-morning."

"I thank you for your courtesy in answering my questions," said the sailor.

"Sir," rejoined the young man, in deliberate tones, "I have told you nothing that you might not have heard from any man, woman, or child within the dominions of my Lord Dane. The politics of the family, so far, are patent to the world."

He sauntered away as he spoke with that indolent languor we are apt to associate with the idea of a gentleman; perhaps because it belongs so exclusively to the upper classes. The sailor looked at the distant group; he had no difficulty in divining that the tall old lady must be Lady Dane; the young and pretty one Adelaide Errol. Captain Dane he knew.

At that moment another person came up, walking along the road from the direction of the village; a dark, short, thick-set man, dressed in the plain black attire of an upper servant. The sailor—as we have been calling him, though he was nothing of the sort—went forward and accosted him.

"Can you tell me who that gentleman is?" he inquired, pointing to the one with the fishing-rod.

"It is Mr. Herbert Dane."

"Not a son of Lord Dane?" cried the other, seeming puzzled.

The man threw back his head. "Oh dear, no; he is nothing but a relative. *That* is Lord Dane's son, the Honourable Captain Dane."

He was moving on, after speaking, but the sailor once more arrested him.

"Ravensbird, I think you have forgotten me."

The man turned and stared, and then touched his hat with respect.

"Colonel Moncton! Indeed, sir, I beg your pardon. I don't think I had looked at you; I was watching the family. We often see strange sailors about here, and I took you for one of them."

"Tell your master I am here, Ravensbird. Stay; don't say who it is before them all. I have no time to call at the castle. Tell Captain Dane that a strange gentleman wishes to speak to him."

The servant touched his hat and hastened forward. Herbert Dane had joined the party then: they were just entering the castle gates. Ravensbird spoke to Captain Dane, whose servant he was, and the latter turned.

"A gentleman wants me? What gentleman, Ravensbird? Where is he?"

"Down there, sir. He wishes to see you very particularly."

Captain Dane felt annoyed, and walked away impatiently. That fair girl by his side was more to him than all the gentlemen in the world. She looked after him, and then threw her eyes—rather self-willed eyes, and not always pleasant in expression, in spite of their bright azure—on the servant.

" Who is it, Ravensbird ? "

" A stranger, my lady."

" And a Yankee," added Herbert Dane, " as I'll protest, by his accent."

They were under the great gateway now, and the young lady at once put her arm within Mr. Herbert Dane's, and began to pace it with him, whilst the servants were occupied in taking Lord Dane home. Herbert told her of the stranger's questioning, and they laughed together.

The account given by Herbert Dane of the family was a correct one, so far as it went, and was patent, as he had observed, to the world—that is, the world of Danesheld. Lord and Lady Dane had only two sons, no other children ; and since the two grew up, had not derived much comfort from either. The heir, Geoffry, was a spendthrift, passing his time chiefly away, and when at home, making it disagreeable by reason of his temper. Nevertheless he was the favourite, and had been indulged to excess. He was envious of his younger brother ; envious of his popularity, his good looks, and, above all, of his fine income—a far larger one than *he* enjoyed, for Lord Dane had heavy expenses, and could not give him an exorbitant allowance.

An enmity grew up between the brothers—" bitter blood," Danesheld called it—and there seemed every prospect that it would be lasting. The chief offender was undoubtedly Geoffry. He flung scorn and insult upon Harry ; and Harry, hot-tempered, retorted in kind. Nor could there be a doubt that Harry Dane in his heart resented the love and favour lavished at home on his brother.

When Captain Dane was three-and-twenty, he accompanied his regiment to Canada, from which, after a few years' stay there, he came home an invalid, and then sold out. After a year or so of home sojourn, he went again to America ; and from that period he had chiefly lived in the New World, travelling about to different parts of it, and paying a visit to England only on rare occasions. Now his stay in the old home promised to be a longer one, for he had fallen in love with the Lady Adelaide Errol. He spoke already to her of marriage ; he spoke fondly of taking her

out to America afterwards, to introduce her to his friends
there; and then he proposed to return to England and settle
down for good. Herbert Dane was not far wrong when he
said the captain worshipped the very ground she trod upon.
The chief pleasure of his existence seemed that of being ever
with her; and there is no doubt that he imparted to her in
confidence much of the history of his past life.

And the Lady Adelaide? She was one of the veriest,
vainest coquettes that ever secured the love of man. People,
looking fondly on her winning ways, were apt to say what
a warm-natured, sweet girl she was. They were entirely
mistaken. Few girls were so innately selfish, though as yet
she herself was unconscious of it. She had come to Dane
Castle two years ago, and was the daughter of the deceased
Earl of Irkdale, a very poor Scotch peer. Adelaide Errol,
on the death of her mother (sister to Lady Dane), found herself without a home; for that of her brother, the wild young
earl, was not a desirable one. So Lady Dane sent for her
to Danesheld, where she arrived with her French maid,
Sophie; and had been turning the heads of the neighbourhood ever since.

Captain Dane walked quickly up to the stranger, and
their hands met in a warm clasp. Colonel Moncton was an
American, and they had been close friends. They still
corresponded, and it was in Captain Dane's recent letters
that the colonel had read of Adelaide Errol. Nothing could
exceed Captain Dane's astonishment; he had supposed him
to be safe in New York.

"Where in the world did you spring from?" he exclaimed.
"Have you taken a tour through the bowels of the earth,
and come up on this side?"

Colonel Moncton laughed. "I was tempted into buying
a yacht, and must needs try her at once, like a child with a
new toy. The wind was fair and wafted us to England.
We put in at Plymouth, and there—— "

"And thence you came round to Danesheld, like the good
fellow that you are!" interrupted Captain Dane, in a glow
of gratification. "I heard an hour ago there was a large
clipper-built yacht in the bay, sporting the stars and stripes,

but I never thought of you. I was going down to have a look at her; the passion for yachting was a passion of my own once."

"I was about to say," continued the American, gravely, "that when we reached Plymouth I found that the last mail had brought over letters for me. Dane, they are letters of recall. My wife has been seized with sudden illness, and we are putting back again with all speed."

"But you will surely stay a little time with me—at least a day or two?"

"I cannot, indeed. Pardon the seeming discourtesy, Dane. As the yacht had put in here, I would not leave without trying to see you, but——"

"Then you did not put in on purpose?" cried Captain Dane, in tones of reproach.

"The master of the yacht put in because he could not help himself. We ran foul of a stupid barge last evening, and received some slight damage; nothing to speak of—a few hours will repair it. Walk down with me and look at her."

"But you will come into the castle first, and be introduced to my family?"

"This afternoon," answered the American, as he linked his arm within his friend's, and led him towards the village, just beyond which was situated the small bay. "You have Ravensbird with you still, I see?"

"Oh yes, he's a fixture. They don't like him at the castle; he's too independent for them. He suits me; and he is in my confidence, besides."

. "Who was that bright-looking girl you were walking with, just now?"

The red rose actually dyed the captain's cheeks, as though they had been a schoolgirl's. His love was powerful within him.

"That was Adelaide Errol."

"I thought so. And when are you to take possession of her? as we say of other things."

"It is impossible to know with certainty," answered the captain, his lips parting with a fond smile. "She is a capricious little beauty; as capricious as your yacht, Moneton; and plays fast and loose. It will be some time this year."

"And shall you never visit the New Country again?"

"Once more; and bring her with me, I hope. I must make arrangements, you know, for having my——"

At that moment Mr. Herbert Dane overtook them, his fishing-rod still in hand. He strolled by their side, speaking a few idle sentences, but Captain Dane did not appear to encourage him, neither did he introduce him to his friend. So Herbert Dane walked on.

"That gentleman is a relative of yours, I believe," observed Colonel Moncton.

"A cousin. His father was the Honourable Herbert Dane, Lord Dane's brother; but the Honourable Herbert got out of his money, and has left his son and daughter almost penniless. But for an income secured to Miss Dane, they wouldn't have enough to live on. I don't think it will be of much consequence to Herbert in the long run. He has the same talent for spending, and would inevitably have got through all, if his father had not done so before him. A mine of gold, more or less, would be nothing to him."

"Does he live at the castle?"

"Certainly not. I'll show you where he lives directly. The worst thing his father ever did for him was to bring him up to no profession. The Church, the Bar, the Civil Service, all are legitimate openings for a poor man of family. The Army scarcely so, because you can't get along in that without a private income. I'm sorry for Herbert, on the whole, though I don't like him."

Turning down a green lane on the right as he spoke which led to three or four houses, Captain Dane halted before one of them; a small, low dwelling, covered with ivy. It was a pretty place, though little larger than a cottage; a lawn in front, with beds of unpretending flowers.

"That's his house, and there Herbert vegetates, doing no earthly thing in life except a little fishing or a day's sporting. The house is his, and he and his sister live there—a fond, foolish girl, who thinks him perfection. She has three

hundred a year of her own, and Herbert has about one, and
so——"

A summary end was put to any further revelations Captain
Dane might have made. A young lady, with a profusion of
ringlets and very pink cheeks, came running down the
garden path, threw open the little iron gate, and caught
hold of his arm. She was in a thin, airy dress, and had the
most childish manner in the world.

"Oh, Harry, I'm so glad to see you! I'm going away
this afternoon, you know, for a week or two. You said
you'd come last night and wish me good-bye."

"But I was unable to come, Cecilia.—Colonel Moncton,
Miss Dane."

Miss Dane curtsied, and simpered, and blushed, and put
her hands to the tips of her ringlets, and was altogether
abashed at the sight of the stranger. But Captain Dane
had no time to waste on her this morning. He wished her
a pleasant visit, and walked away.

"Poor Cecilia!" he laughed, as he put his arm within
his friend's. "She's a good-hearted little soul, but has not
a particularly large share of brains."

They went on through the town and reached the small
bay—so small as to be unavailable for large craft—where
the yacht was lying. A beautiful vessel was this American
yacht. She was named the *Pearl*, and was at the present
moment the pride of Colonel Moncton's life. He was fond
of fresh pastimes and new toys; and, being a man of good
fortune, could afford to indulge his fancies.

Meanwhile, Mr. Ravensbird had entered the castle, and
sought a companionship he was fond of, that of Lady
Adelaide's French maid, Sophie Deffloc. He was a dark,
sallow, stern-looking man, ugly at the first glance. Nevertheless the face was an honest one, and there was a kindly
expression in the penetrating black eyes. The castle
wondered what pretty Sophie could see in Richard Ravensbird: but ugly men often find the greatest favour with women,
as all the world knows. He had been into the town on an
errand for her now, and she would only abuse him for it.

"There's your commission, Mam'selle Sophie," said he,

putting a small paper parcel on the table. "I hope it's executed to your mind."

Sophie unfolded the paper, and took out its contents, three or four yards of narrow ribbon. She was an exceedingly neat, trim damsel, dressed to perfection in her quiet attire. Her features were saucy, her eyes dark gray, and her head and hair might have made the fortune of any hairdresser's window. She stamped her foot petulantly as her eyes fell on the ribbon.

"If ever I saw the like!" she exclaimed—and she spoke English with great fluency, though with a foreign accent. "I send you to buy me four yards of blue ribbon, and you bring purple! I have told you, fifty times, that you have not the eye for colours."

Ravensbird laughed. Her grumbling was sweeter to him than others' praise, and Mademoiselle Sophie knew that it was so, and presumed accordingly. "I did my best, Sophie; won't it do?"

"Do! It must do. If I order you back you might bring gray; but don't think you are going ribbon-buying for me again. You need not expect it."

"You sent me, Sophie."

"And if I did? Did I expect that you would be more stupid than a camel? Hand me my workbox, monsieur. It is on the table there. Who was that sailor-gentleman you were talking to, by the swing-gate?"

Ravensbird handed the workbox, throwing his keen eyes on her as he did so. "How did you know I was talking to any one by the swing-gate, Sophie?"

"I stand at the tower-window in my Lady Adelaide's room; I look out for you and the ribbon. 'He is taking his time,' I say to myself, 'standing there to talk.' Who was it?"

"A friend of the captain's; a gentleman we used to know in America."

"What did he talk about?" inquired Sophie, who had all the insatiable curiosity of her nation and sex.

Ravensbird laughed; he generally answered her questions with the same sort of condescending pleasure as that we use in answering an attractive child. "He did not talk of much, Sophie. The chief thing he asked me was whether Herbert Dane was my lord's son."

"Ah," responded Sophie; "if he were my lord's son, things here might go a little smoother."

"What things?" inquired Ravensbird, opening his eyes.

"What things?" repeated Sophie, ironically. "I say to myself this long while that you and your master are the only blind ones in the castle: except, perhaps, my Lord Dane. You think my young lady has love for your master; he thinks so. Bah!"

"What is up now?" cried Ravensbird, after a pause of astonishment.

"There is nothing up that there has not been all along," returned Sophie, with cool equanimity, "if you had but looked out to see it. My young lady is a flirt; she's vain; she likes all the admiration she can get, whether it is from Captain Dane or whether it is from Squire Lester; but in a corner of her heart there is one more precious than either. He was there a long while; long before your master came home and put the upset to things by wanting her for himself."

"What *do* you mean?" exclaimed Ravensbird.

"I mean that there's love between those two, Mr. Ravensbird. Have you no wits that you should stare so?"

"Can you allude to Herbert Dane?"

Sophie nodded, as she bit off an end of cotton. "They love each other to folly."

"Then, if so, how dare she delude my master by her false smiles?" cried Ravensbird indignantly.

"She does it for a purpose," was the cool answer. "Just about the time that your master came home, my Lady Dane began to suspect that she and Mr. Herbert cared for each other, and she spoke about it, and my young lady was sick to death with fright, lest he should be sent away, or they be otherwise separated. So when Captain Dane came forward with his grand offers, she made a show of accepting him to blind my Lady Dane. She makes a show of accepting his love to blind *him*, because she will not let the truth be

known, for Mr. Herbert's sake. As to her marrying the
captain, I hope my head won't ache till that time comes."

Richard Ravensbird, standing against a side-table, felt
like one who was listening to some awful plot, some wicked
conspiracy. Had Fieschi's infernal machine been pointed
at his head, he could not have shrunk from it as a worse
danger than the one he seemed to shrink from now. As he
looked at Sophie with bewildered eyes, much of the past
seemed to grow suddenly clear to him. He remembered
how often he had seen the Lady Adelaide lingering with
Herbert Dane; he remembered how, many a time, he had
seen her exercising some little ruse to avoid his master.
And he had set it all down to the natural coquetry of
woman.

"Do they meet in private?" he asked.

"When they can; just once in a way. She runs out now
and then on a fine evening, to take a little walk with him.
My lady drops asleep after dinner in the drawing-room; my
lord keeps Captain Dane with him at the dinner-table; and
she slips on her gray cloak, putting the hood over her head,
and goes out. Mr. Herbert is waiting for her, and they just
take one turn across the heights by the chapel ruins, and
back again. She dare not stay many minutes for fear of
being missed."

"Treacherous she-serpent!" muttered Ravensbird, whose
amazed ears were tingling with indignation. "Why,
Sophie, it—it—it's a shocking thing for her to do! It's not
respectable."

"It's not what?" shrieked Sophie. "It's not what?"

"Well, and it is not," persisted Ravensbird; "not for a
young lady like her. She is engaged to my master, and she
goes out with a hood over her head and meets somebody
else! At any rate, it's not seemly."

"You want a hood for your head," cried Sophie, treating
him to a specimen of her woman's tongue. "Is not Mr.
Herbert Dane my lord's nephew, and is he not to be trusted
to take care of her? She's to be trusted herself, for the
matter of that, for there never was one less likely than she
to run into danger. She's giddy and thoughtless in trifles,

but she's as wise as you are, mon ami, in great things. What do you fear for her?—that the sea will rise and swallow her up? If she walked out with Captain Dane, or with Mr. Lester, or with my lord himself, would you say it was 'not respectable?' Go along!"

"But look at the treachery!" cried Ravensbird. "My master is honourable, unsuspicious, as open as the day, and he ought to know of this. It's shameful treachery, I tell you, Sophie. If nobody else enlightens him, I will."

"My friend," interrupted Sophie, emphatically, "you just take my advice, for it's good—*don't you interfere.* Folks that tell unpalatable truths never get thanked for them. Let things take their course. When Captain Dane presses for the marriage, as he'll do soon, then she must speak out herself, and that will be best. Perhaps, after all, she may take him—I should, I know; at any rate she'll have to choose between them. But don't you go and break your head against a wall."

Metaphorically speaking, Mr. Richard Ravensbird was breaking his head against one then; he had never felt so puzzled, so indignant, in all his life. He made no opposition to her advice, thereby allowing her to suppose that he fell in with it.

"Herbert Dane!" he repeated, all the scorn of his nature concentrated on the name. "If she must have been false to my master, I could better have supposed it was that she loved Squire Lester."

Mademoiselle Sophie Deffloe lifted her eyebrows in pity. "That shows what you know about such things," was her retort. "Mr. Lester is twice as old as she is. What does she care for Mr. Lester? He is the handsomest man in Danesheld, and so she listens to his galiant speeches, and likes him to be her slave. If you were a gentleman, she'd square her elbows at you to keep you off, because of your ugliness."

"She'd be welcome," returned Richard Ravensbird.

He was too much incensed at the duplicity practised on his master to heed the shafts launched by Sophie on himself. He was deeply attached to Captain Dane. Clenching his hand as he stood, he felt that he should like to deal out her deserts to the Lady Adelaide: a rare feeling for the generally phlegmatic Richard Ravensbird. But his nature could, on occasion, be aroused into fierce passion; and in that respect he exactly resembled his master, Captain Dane.

a.

CHAPTER II.

TURNED OUT.

THE door on the left hand of the gateway of Dane Castle opened into what was called the hall; an apartment that for its capaciousness and splendour was the boast of the country. Its walls were hung with pictures, no carpet was allowed on its pavement of rich mosaic; its furniture was massive rather than elegant. In the old days, when Lord Dane was in health, and there were large dinner gatherings at the castle, this hall was used as the reception-room and the withdrawing-room. It communicated with the dining-room by folding-doors, a fine apartment also, but not of the large proportions of the hall. Both these rooms looked on to the front of the castle, facing the sea; the hall extended itself the whole depth of the castle, saving for a wide stone passage that ran along behind, and into which it also opened; the dining-room and a smaller room behind it, used now as Lord Dane's sleeping-chamber, which chamber also opened into the passage. Above were the drawing-rooms and the principal bedchambers.

On the other side the gateway the rooms were of less importance; those to the front were little used; the kitchens and servants' sitting-rooms were at the back. The stone passage just mentioned ran along nearly the whole length of the house—a gloomy passage at the best, and dimly lighted. A staircase wound up from it at either end—the one was used by the family, the other chiefly by the servants. Two or three uninhabited rooms opened from it towards the back of the castle, of which one was notable, if only from its appellation—the death-room. Other passages, curious odds-and-ends of intricate places, abounded in the castle; some converging to an entrance-door at the back, which was kept locked by Lord Dane's orders, and of which the butler, Mr. Bruff, had charge of the keys, so that the only entrance and exit made use of was by the great gateway.

Evening came on—the evening of the day above noticed—and the party assembled in the drawing-room before dinner was a small one: consisting of Lady Dane, Adelaide, and a guest, Mr. Lester. Mr. Lester, generally called Squire Lester—must have been eight or nine and thirty, but he did not look it. He was a gay, fascinating, very handsome man, of middle height, with dark hair, and eyes of violet blue. Daneshold was beginning to say that his attraction at the castle was the Lady Adelaide—that he was hoping to win her for his second wife, in spite of Harry Dane's open claims.

She stood against the window now, talking to him. He was bending his head as he 'listened, and his violet eyes were fixed on her with an admiration that told its own tale—a tale that Lady Adelaide was little loath to listen to; for she only lived in this species of flattery. She wore a white dress without ornaments, save that it had a bow of pink ribbon in front, enclosing a knot of pearls. A pearl necklace was round her neck, and pearl bracelets were on her arms just above the gloves. Harry Dane came in, and Mr. Lester drew a little away.

" I thought you were gone," exclaimed Lady Adelaide.

" I am later than I ought to be," he answered. " I have been looking for some papers that I want Moncton to take over for me."

" I understood that your friend was to call and see us to-day, Harry," observed Lady Dane.

" He will come to-morrow instead. The skipper finds he can't get out before to-morrow evening; so it gives Moncton another day here."

" The skipper !" echoed Lady Dane. " That's one of your Americanisms, Harry."

"Indeed, no. I assure you it is plain English," was the laughing answer. "Good-bye, Adelaide."

"A pleasant evening to you," she rejoined, allowing her hand to rest for an instant in his.

Just then the butler appeared and announced dinner. Captain Dane held out his arm to Adelaide.

"My tardy departure has brought me some reward at least," he said, as he led her away in the wake of Mr. Lester and Lady Dane.

"A fine reward!" she said, slightly throwing back her head with a laugh.

"A sweet reward!" he murmured in her ear. "Adelaide," came the impassioned addition, "to have you on my arm like this, though it be but for a minute, imparts a thrill of joy to me for the whole evening."

They descended the handsome staircase, threaded the spacious hall, and entered the dining-room. There he left her, bowing over her hand, which he held again in his, with something of chivalrous courtesy. He was on his way to dine on board the yacht with Colonel Moncton, who had declined an invitation to the castle.

Lord Dane was already at the head of the table, seated. He was always in his place, as now, before the guests came in. A fine host still, of commanding presence. Nothing of his malady was apparent now: he enjoyed his dinner; he was full of wit and repartee—and Lord Dane had the reputation of being a man of brilliant conversation. None, seeing him thus, could suspect he had not the full use of his lower limbs, or that he was kept up by mechanical support. Lady Dane took her seat opposite to him, Mr. Lester and Adelaide on either side, and the dinner began, Bruff and two servants being in attendance.

It was a lovely night, almost as bright as day; and Richard Ravensbird, somewhat later in the evening, was standing at the castle gateway, enjoying the moonlight. Before him stretched the smooth, green table-land; the sea beyond it almost as smooth and calm. Standing where he did, however, he could only see the distant sea, not the waves under the heights. On the right were the scattered

villas : farther on, the village and its lights; almost opposite him the old chapel ruins, their casements and ivied
walls, broken in places, ghostly and weird-looking as the
moonbeams fell on them.

Mr. Richard Ravensbird contemplated the scene to his
satisfaction, and then strolled across the road, over the grass,
and went inside the ruins. There was an aperture at either
end, each serving for a doorway, so that you could walk
right through. Grass grew in places; the grave-stones, still
discernible, cold and gray, covered the remains of those who
had for centuries been dust of the dust. Pieces of the
marble flooring were left still, and traces of niches, and
hooks, and miniature altars, peculiar to places of Roman
Catholic worship. Such relics had no attraction for Richard
Ravensbird, and he quitted the ruins and walked to the
edge of the heights. In this one part the rocks were not
very high, nor at all formidable; and Mr. Ravensbird looked
down at the strip of land beneath which formed the beach.
It was very narrow here, and for about two hours at high-
tide was covered by the water, when it was of course
impassable. At other times preventive-men paced it—a
warning to smugglers.

These preventive-men had each his defined beat, extending a nominal mile in length, but it was a very short
one; and their pacing was so timed (or ought to have been)
that they met at the given boundary at a certain moment,
exchanged the signal "All well;" and then turned back
again. Scandalmongers said they lingered sometimes in
each other's company at these meeting-points; had been
seen to light pipes, and produce black bottles from holes
in the rocks, and make themselves altogether comfortable.
The supervisor heard the rumour, and said they had better
let *him* catch them at it.

A sad event had occurred on the beach a week previous to
this. The man on this portion of the beat sat down, as was
supposed, and fell asleep, and the tide overwhelmed him
and carried him out to sea. The body was washed ashore the
next day, and a subscription was now being raised for the
wife and children, which Lord Dane had headed with a

donation of five pounds. The next sum on the list was twenty-five. It was recorded under the initial " H," and was suspected (and with truth) to be from Harry Dane, who would not openly put himself down for a larger sum than his father.

As Ravensbird stood looking down, the preventive-man on duty that night came slowly round the point, a little higher up, where the rocks projected and shut out the view beyond. Ravensbird waited until he was underneath, and then called to him.

" Is that you, Mitchel ? "

The man looked up. At first he could not distinguish who was speaking.

" Don't you know me, Mitchel ! It's light enough. Take care you don't go to sleep, as poor Biggs did."

" Oh, it's you, Mr. Ravensbird. No, sir : I'll take care of that. We think it must have been just above this very spot that he sat down and yielded to drowsiness, if he did yield to it. And we have been talking pretty freely amongst ourselves, saying what nonsense it is to make us pace this strip of beach. Why, in some places—round that point, for one—it's not a foot broad that we have to wind round! Biggs is just as likely to have slipped off, and got drowned that way, as to have dropped asleep."

" If you can make the revenue officers think it's nonsense, and take you off the duty, the smugglers will be obliged to you."

" Not at all, sir. They could move us to the heights, and there we should be out of danger. There's not many smugglers left nowadays."

" You must be timid men to fancy danger where you are. A child might keep himself out of it."

" Being on the watch constant, perhaps he might : but one gets off the watch sometimes."

Ravensbird laughed. "Thanks to what you take to warm you on a chilly night, Mitchel."

" No, indeed, sir, you are out there. We take nothing, and dare not ; it would be as much as our places are worth. I say, Mr. Ravensbird, don't you lean over so far ! You might be attacked with giddiness,"

"Not I," answered Ravensbird. "I like looking over heights; my nerves are steady."

"It's more than I like," was the answer. "And that would be a nasty fall; it would be sure to break limbs, and might cost life. Good-night, sir."

"I don't covet the fall. Good-night, if you are going on. I suppose the tide will soon be up."

The preventive-man passed on, and Richard Ravensbird strolled back to the ruins. Barely had he entered them, when he saw some one approaching from the direction of Danesheld, and recognized Herbert Dane.

"Then Sophie was right!" he exclaimed. And up to that very moment there had been a grain of willing doubt in the man's mind.

Mr. Dane advanced, whistling; he leaned against one of the ivy-covered window-frames, and looked out in the direction of the castle. In this position there was no fear of his being discovered by any stray passers in the road.

She came up presently, enveloped in a cloak, her feet swift. Herbert Dane hastened forward to meet her; and Mr. Ravensbird, safely ensconced within the ruins, called down something that was not a blessing on all treachery. Herbert Dane took her on his arm, and they walked quickly through the chapel to the open ground beyond it—almost ran, indeed, for the young lady seemed impatient. Mr. Ravensbird hid himself in the darkest nook as they passed, and then quietly followed them, and peeped out as they paced about between the chapel and the heights, she hanging lovingly on his arm.

"Is the gallant captain at home this evening?" Ravensbird heard him ask.

"No, he is gone on board the American's yacht. Squire Lester is dining with us. Oh, Herbert," she added with a gay laugh, "I think, what with one admirer and another, my head will be turned. The squire is growing more demonstrative."

"Squire Lester's nobody, Adelaide. The only one to be feared is nearer home."

"You need not fear," she impulsively answered. "I hate him! I despise him! He may be one that men esteem and women admire, but he has set his unwelcome love upon me, and therefore I hate him!"

"He is the Honourable Harry Dane, and his purse is weighty," remarked Herbert bitterly. "No despicable rival."

"If you begin like that I shall go back again," she returned, with a pretty affectation of childishness. "You know that he is nothing to me; that I shall never marry him, though I am obliged to let it be thought I will. Why he—but I must not tell that; I gave my promise. Do you fear I would marry him, Herbert, when I—I care only for you?"

"What is it that you may not tell?" inquired Herbert Dane.

"Oh, nothing; only something he said," she answered carelessly; "it does not concern either you or me. You are cross with me, Herbert: you think I ought not to encourage him, but how can I help myself? If my aunt suspected that I cared for you, or you for me, we should be sent flying to opposite corners of the earth."

"Adelaide, this deception cannot go on for ever; an explanation must come."

"I suppose it must, some time."

"And when it does?"

"Now, please don't worry me about the future, Herbert! When it does come, I dare say I shall see my way out of it. Do you know what idea floats sometimes through my mind? That I will tell Harry the truth—how we love each other—and throw myself on his generosity, and get him to keep the secret."

"Don't talk nonsense, Adelaide."

"Why are you so cross to-night?"

"I am not cross, only pained. My life seems like one long painful dream now, and at odd moments I think you do not really care for me."

The accusation was unfounded, and Adelaide Errol looked up at him in reproach, her eyes filling with tears which he could see in the moonlight. He murmured a word of contrition, bent down, and pressed a kiss upon her lips. Mr. Richard Ravensbird, in his hiding-place, rather wished that it had been anything else.

For a few minutes Ravensbird heard no more; they were standing side by side on the brow of the heights, looking out on the sea. Then Lady Adelaide seemed to turn in a hurry.

"No, don't write to me," she was saying, when they came within Ravensbird's hearing again; "we must chance it. I am not sure that it would do to entrust notes to Sophie: she and that ugly servant of Harry's, who is as dark as his name, are great friends. It's a shame you can't run in and out of the castle at will, as you used to do; but what you say is true,—that they all look coldly upon you. I must go, indeed, Herbert: suppose my aunt were to wake up and know that I was here! Oh! what a scene there would be!"

"Where's the harm?" hotly returned Herbert Dane. "You are as safe with me, I hope, as you are indoors with her."

"But you are the very one she does not choose me to be with, don't you see!" said the girl, laughing. "She'd think there was treason concocting against Harry. Has Cecilia gone on her visit?"

"She went this afternoon. You are in a hurry!" he said, speaking as if excessively aggrieved. "It's not often you come out here, goodness knows. And I have told you I cannot be here to-morrow night."

"It's not often we have these lovely nights. You would not have me come out on a dark or a wet one. Not through the chapel, Herbert," she added, for he seemed bearing towards the entrance door. "I never go through it but I think of ghosts. You must have an affection for them."

He laughed; and Ravensbird watched them slowly pass outside, obtaining a clear view of their features through the apertures of the ivied casements.

Herbert Dane did not go far; he was afraid, possibly, of being seen. They stood a moment to shake hands; she ran swiftly away over the turf, and he came back and propped his back against the wall, as before, whilst he watched her enter the castle. Then he took his way towards Danesheld at a swift pace; and Mr. Richard Ravensbird, emerging from the ruins, cooled his indignation by a walk on the heights before he returned home.

The morning rose as lovely as the night had been : not quite so calm, for a slight breeze appeared to be getting up. "All the better for Moncton's yacht," observed Captain Harry Dane, as he sat at breakfast, with his mother and Lady Adelaide, the sunbeams falling on the table, and causing the white cloth and the silver to glitter. "The wind is fair, too, for her; she'll go out with a run."

"When does she go out?" asked Lady Dane.

"To-night."

"You stayed late on board last night, Harry, did you not?"

"Yes. I think it was past twelve when I left her. I and Moncton were talking of old times. He is anticipating the pleasure of welcoming you some time to his home, Adelaide; he has a charming place at Washington."

Lady Adelaide threw back her head, and there was incipient defiance in her tones as she spoke.

"It may be that he will not have the pleasure. Washington is a long way off, Captain Dane."

"Captain Dane!" he echoed, not pleased at the title.

"Harry, then," she rejoined good-humouredly, for Lady Dane was turning upon her a disapproving eye; "if you are ashamed of the other name."

"I am not ashamed of it, Adelaide," he quietly said ; "but I like a different one from you."

"Oh dear!" sighed Adelaide, petulantly throwing herself back in her chair; "how crooked and contrary things go in this world!"

"What things?" inquired Lady Dane.

"Many things, aunt. Sophie was as cross as two sticks this morning, and that beautiful bird Mr. Lester gave me is drooping its wings. I think it is going to die."

As Captain Dane quitted the room after breakfast, he was

met by his servant Ravensbird, who craved five minutes'
speech of him. They ascended to a small apartment in the
turret that the captain made his sitting-room, and were shut
in. Lady Dane ordered the breakfast things away, and
opened her prayer-book to read the psalms for the day. She
was a thoroughly good woman. When Adelaide Errol first
came, her aunt had caused her to join in the exercise; but it
had been done with an ill grace, an impatient manner; and
Lady Dane at length told her, gently, to wait until her heart
was more attuned to it. Poor Adelaide, who had never been
trained in such habits, thought them a weary task, and Lady
Dane had the good sense to remember that none should be
forced into religion. She sat in her easy chair near the
fire, whilst Adelaide, in her pretty peach-coloured muslin
dress, her fair hands peeping from beneath its lace cuffs,
her cheeks as pink as the muslin, with some mental excitement, stood at the window.

The room was near the drawing-room at the end of the
house; one window facing the sea, another overlooking
Danesheld. It was a glorious spring morning. The sky was
blue, with a few fleecy clouds upon it; the sun was shining
brilliantly; the hedges were putting forth their tender
green, and the early flowers were opening. Not on any of
these, pleasant objects though they were to the eye, gazed
Lady Adelaide: she did not give a thought to the beautiful
expanse of sea stretched out in the distance, or to the stately
vessels sailing slowly along; she saw nothing of the pretty
villas near, nor of the labourers at work on the farm lands;
no, her attention was absorbed by something else.

Astride upon the same gate where you saw him yesterday
sat Herbert Dane. He might be seen there often, for it was
within view of the one window of the morning-room and of
a charming young face that was wont to appear at it. He
had discarded yesterday's fishing-rod; but held instead a
silver-mounted riding-whip, with which he switched, now
his boots, now the bars of the gate, all in his usual listless
manner. Think you the Lady Adelaide could have eyes for
other sights when he was there? He took off his hat to her
once when she first appeared; and a stranger would have

seen nothing in the action beyond the ordinary courtesy of a gentleman. She probably saw much more.

"Aunt," she cried, suddenly breaking the silence, and it seemed, to her impatience, that half-an-hour at least must have elapsed since Lady Dane had held her prayer-book, though in reality it was barely ten minutes: "is it not time, think you, to get ready to go out with my uncle?"

"Not yet, Adelaide. It is only—What's that?"

Loud and angry tones, as of voices in dispute, arose suddenly from the floor above. Lady Dane started from her chair in alarm, and Adelaide went to the door, and opened it.

Captain Dane and his servant Ravensbird were on the stairs; the captain held his servant's collar, and was propelling him downwards in fierce anger. Both of them seemed in a state of ungovernable fury. They stumbled down to this, the first landing, and then Captain Dane, with a push and a kick, sent his servant whirling down the lower staircase.

Lady Dane, utterly aghast, gazed over the balustrades at Ravensbird. The man righted himself, looked up, and shook his fist at his master. But he appeared not to see the ladies.

"Take care of yourself, Captain Dane," he said, the words coming forth in malignant, hissing tones. "I shall never lose sight of this insult until I have repaid it."

"Good heavens, Harry!" exclaimed Lady Dane, as Ravensbird disappeared amidst a group of gaping servants, whom the noise had caused to gather below, "what does all this mean? What has Ravensbird done?"

"Never mind, mother. He will not disturb the peace of the castle again. I have discharged him."

"Discharged Ravensbird?"

"The hound!" burst forth the captain, who could not in the least get over his fury.

"But what had he done?" reiterated Lady Dane.

"He attempted to impose on me with lying tales, and when I would have forced from him his motive for the villany, he —— But there, I can't go over the matter; I shall kill him if I do," broke off the captain.

And turning round, he stalked back to his room again, leaving Lady Dane and Adelaide to any conjectures they might please to form.

Mr. Richard Ravensbird, vouchsafing as little explanation as his master, strode past the wondering servants in the small stone hall, which must not be confounded with the great hall before mentioned, and down the stone passage. He never spoke a word; his face was livid; his nostrils were working. Only as he was turning towards the gateway, did he look back, and ask one of the footmen to gather his clothes and other property together, and despatch them after him to the "Sailor's Rest." At this juncture Sophie appeared on the scene, demanding an explanation; but Ravensbird waived her off. With the persistency of her sex she laid hold of him, and then Ravensbird said she should hear from him in the course of the day, as he shook himself free. Nothing more could she obtain from him, though she followed him beyond the great gates, and stood there until he was out of sight.

Herbert Dane was still astride on the swing gate, almost tired, it must be supposed, with his want of occupation. The appearance of Mr. Ravensbird, with a peculiarly enraged expression of face, was a welcome divertissement.

"Halloa, Ravensbird! What's up?"

The man stopped as he answered, looking into the face of his questioner, and giving each word its full force.

"I have been kicked out of the castle, sir."

"Kicked out of the castle!" echoed Herbert Dane, in astonishment. "By whom? Not by its lord?" he added, with an attempt at a joke.

"I have been ignominiously thrust forth from the castle and from my long service; kicked downstairs in the sight of my Lady Dane and of the domestics," repeated Ravensbird. "He who did it was my master. But let him look to himself, for I swear I'll be revenged. There are some insults, sir, that retaliation alone can wipe out. This is one of them."

"And what was it all for? How did you offend him?" reiterated the wondering listener.

"I was endeavouring to do him a service; and my friendly words—friendly I meant them to be—were taken up in a wrong light. I say, let him take heed to himself."

Ravensbird strode on, waiting for no more. Herbert Dane gazed after him, unable all at once to recover his surprise. The silver-mounted riding-whip was at rest now.

"Ravensbird looks a queer customer to offend, at the present moment," quoth he to himself. "What a livid face of anger it was. I think Mr. Harry *had* better take heed to himself."

Meanwhile, Lord Dane, to whose ears the scandalous sounds had penetrated, summoned his son to his presence, and demanded an explanation. But Captain Dane wholly declined to enter into details. "Ravensbird had behaved infamously, and had received his deserts," he said; and nothing more could his lordship get from him.

Colonel Moncton called in the course of the morning, and remained to luncheon. The *Pearl* was ready to go out now, and was waiting for the evening tide. Lord Dane inquired what time she would sail, and the colonel replied he believed they should get away by about nine o'clock. He asked Captain Dane to dine with him on board at seven, and the captain promised to do so.

The two friends went out together after luncheon; and Lady Adelaide, standing listlessly at the drawing-room window, watched them as they strolled about. Captain Dane was showing his friend the few points of interest within view. He took him into the chapel ruins; he showed him the steps of a descent a little higher up, with the small landing-place below, where he and his brother used to moor their pleasure-boat. They descended these steps now, and continued their way to the village by the narrow path chiefly used by the preventive-men, parting when they reached the yacht, for Captain Dane pleaded an afternoon engagement.

And the day passed on to evening.

There was no guest at dinner that night at the castle.

Lord Dane, his wife, and Adelaide were seated at the table, when somewhat to their surprise, for they had heard the promise given to Colonel Moncton, Captain Dane entered and took his place.

"Is it you, Harry?" cried Lord Dane. "I thought you were dining on board the yacht."

"I changed my mind afterwards, sir, and sent a message to Moncton. Perhaps I may go down to see him off."

The words were spoken in short, strange tones. Lord Dane saw that his son was suffering from inward annoyance.

"You are allowing that affair with Ravensbird to vex you, Harry," he said, looking at him.

"It has vexed me very much indeed, sir; more than I care to speak about."

"Harry, you must take care of that man," said Adelaide, who was this night attired in a blue silk, shot with white, that shone and glimmered in the gaslight. "I hear he meditates some vengeance upon you."

Harry Dane's only answer was to draw down his lips in contempt for Mr. Ravensbird and his vengeance; but Lord Dane inquired of Adelaide where she had picked up that piece of news.

"I happened to meet Mr. Herbert when I was out this afternoon," she said; and anyone hearing her answer, and seeing the composed expression of face, might have deemed Mr. Herbert some remote elderly connection whom she hardly presumed to speak to, or to know by sight. "He said Ravensbird passed by him on leaving the castle this morning, vowing he would be revenged; and he thought Harry had better have such a man for a friend than an enemy."

A smile of irony, mingled with almost implacable anger, crossed the face of Captain Dane. "Let Ravensbird be left to me," was all he said; and after that, throughout dinner, he spoke only in monosyllables, and Lord Dane noticed that he sent nearly everything away untouched.

CHAPTER III.

THE FALL FROM THE CLIFF.

"SHALL I, or shall I not go?" debated Lady Adelaide, as she stood in weary impatience at one of the windows of the drawing-room, looking out between the muslin curtains at the lovely night. "Herbert said he could not come up to-night, and that's a great shame. Tiresome people! And such a night as it is! I think I *must* go," she added, after a pause. I don't know what it is that makes me like this freedom of running out alone, unless it is that they taught me to be self-dependent as a child. How bright the moon-light is as it glistens on the water! I will go for five minutes. I think my lungs are exacting, and require fresh air after the heat of the dining-room."

She turned and looked at Lady Dane. Yes, there was no impediment there; her ladyship was fast asleep in her easy-chair. It was, indeed, a most charming night—the sea calm, the air genial, the moon bright as day. The promised breeze of the morning had subsided into one barely sufficient to carry out the fishing craft and Colonel Moncton's yacht. Adelaide Errol quitted the room on tiptoe, put on her gray cloak with its hood, and stole forth through the great gateway. Had any one preached to her of imprudence touching these short moonlight excursions, she would have laughed at them, and said she was as safe from harm out of doors as within. Perhaps she was; for a cry might have brought forth the whole castle to her rescue.

Lady Dane slept on—the more soundly, perhaps, because she had been longer than usual to-night in dropping off, to the secret annoyance of her impatient niece. Could she only have discerned the young lady at that very moment, tripping with light steps over the grass! Lady Dane had been greatly put out with the chief event of the day—the quarrel with Ravensbird. Harry had never been her favourite son—but he was her son; and any grief or annoyance to him found its echo tenfold in her breast. Ah! if these careless sons only know the pain they bring!

Suddenly, as it seemed, Lady Dane began to dream. She thought the encounter was being renewed—that Harry had seized hold of Ravensbird and was striking him in the face, causing the man to utter a succession of screams. So vivid was the scene that Lady Dane awoke.

She awoke to find that the screams were real. She sat up in her chair, bewildered for a moment, wondering what was the matter and where every one was. But the screams were not those of Ravensbird; they were the shrill screams of a woman, and they came from the greensward. Lady Dane went to the window, threw it open, and looked out. A gray object was flying over the grass towards the castle. Not at first did Lady Dane recognize it, though the hood was flung back from the fair young face, and the elaborately-dressed hair was distinct in the moonlight. Then she saw Bruff, followed by other servants, run across the road, and the young lady fall into their arms. Lady Dane clasped her hands in an impulse of astonishment and fear. It was her niece, Adelaide!

She went down as quickly as her age allowed, into the great hall, and met Bruff bringing in Lady Adelaide. Panting, trembling, crying still, unable to support herself, the girl was evidently under the influence of some great terror. Lady Dane's questions were utterly useless, for Adelaide was not in a state to answer them. She fell into a chair in strong hysterics. The wondering servants removed her cloak; ran for smelling-salts, for water; Lady Dane chafed her hands, and altogether there was great commotion. In the midst of it the voice of Lord Dane was heard calling for Bruff. The man hastened into the dining-room, and Lord Dane, who still sat at the head of the table, the bell-rope attached to his chair by means of a silken ribbon, angrily inquired what all that unseemly noise meant.

"My lord, the cries are from Lady Adelaide. She seems to be taken ill."

"*Seems* to be taken ill! What d'ye mean?"

"She was outside, as it appears, my lord. She was

running home from the heights and screaming, when we got out. Something must have frightened her."

" Lady Adelaide shrieking like that ! Lady Adelaide on the heights at this hour ! " reiterated Lord Dane, in angry disbelief. It is not likely, Bruff."

" But, my lord, it *is* so," persisted Bruff. " Those cries you hear now are Lady Adelaide's. She is in the hall, and my lady is with her."

" Undo this," said Lord Dane.

He alluded to the silken ribbon attached to his chair. The butler obeyed; and Lord Dane, touching a spring, propelled the chair gently forward over the carpet. Bruff threw open the folding-doors, and Lord Dane went on to the hall, bringing his chair in front of Adelaide. Hysterics are not so uncontrollable as some people imagine; and the presence of Lord Dane put an end to these. But Lady Adelaide trembled all over, as if in a fit of ague, and her face was white as death.

" What is all this, Adelaide ? " he inquired. " Have you been frightened ? What is it ?" he added, rather sharply, turning to his wife, for Adelaide suddenly flung her hands up to her face as if refusing an answer. " Bruff says she was out on the heights, and came screaming home again. I don't understand it."

" I'm sure I don't," returned Lady Dane. " It's true she was on the heights, for I saw and heard her. She must have been frightened in some way."

" But what brought her on the heights ? "

" That is just what I want to learn. When I fell asleep after dinner she was in the drawing-room, reading. It seemed to me that barely five minutes had elapsed, when she came back from the heights crying in the way you must have heard. I have asked her ten times what brought her out; but she does not answer me."

Lady Dane was cross also. She thought the young lady might answer if she would. Lord Dane, choleric as ever was his second son, and unused to contradiction, wheeled his chair a foot closer, and laid his hand upon her shoulder. Some of the servants were standing round, but he was unmindful of them.

"Now, Adelaide, this won't do. I want to know what it is that is the matter with you, and I will know. What brought you out?"

"I don't know," she answered, shivering. visibly in her strong emotion.

"But you must know; you did not walk out in your sleep. Adelaide, understand me—I am asking *to know*. Did you go out to meet any one?" he continued, a shrewd suspicion arising in his mind.

"Oh, no, no ; indeed I did not; indeed, Lord Dane, I did not," she replied, with what seemed very unnecessary vehemence.

"I thought it possible you might have gone out in expectation of meeting Harry, or with him. Very foolish of you both if you had, when you can walk out together as much as you choose in the daytime. But Harry went down to the yacht, I think. Your explanation, Adelaide?"

"I will tell the truth," she said, with a flood of more silent tears. "I stood at the window after my aunt went to sleep, looking out on the lovely night. I never saw a night more beautiful, and it came into my head that I would run across the heights and back again, and I put on my gray cloak and went out. I meant no harm."

"And a very wild-goose trick it was!" interposed Lady Dane. "Young ladies don't run out alone at night in this country, Adelaide, however bright the moon may be."

Adelaide did not care for the reproof; her aunt might reproach her with being a "wild-goose" for ever if she pleased; what she did care for, was the penetrating look of my Lord Dane, whose keen eyes were fixed on her face.

"You have not told us what alarmed you," he quietly said.

"And I don't know what alarmed me; I don't, indeed, uncle. I was so foolish as to think, in a spirit of bravado, that I would run through the chapel ruins, but no sooner was I in them than a horrible fear came over me, and I ran home screaming. I could not have helped screaming had it been to save my life."

"Poor child!" spoke Lady Dane in compassion.

"I can't bear the ruins even in the daytime," she resumed,

with a shudder; "and at night they seem full of nothing but ghosts. Oh, aunt! I will never run out alone again."

Lord Dane felt unconvinced. As to ghosts, he had hitherto believed the young lady to be one who was no more amenable to such fear than he himself was.

"Adelaide," he gravely said, "did anything else frighten you? Did any one accost you on the heights?"

"Not any one indeed," she answered, earnestly; "no person whatever saw me or knew I was there. No one ever is on the heights at night."

"Had a mad bull strayed on to them?" cried his lordship, in an access of anger. "Nothing less than a raging animal of some sort ought to call up such senseless terror as this."

"Poor child!" again whispered Lady Dane in her increasing compassion, fully believing every word her niece had said. "She has told us the truth, I am sure, Geoffry. Don't you remember how frightened I used to be of ghosts myself when I was young; how I would fly past the death-room with my face hidden, if ever I had to pass it, and how you used to laugh at me?"

"There, dry your tears," cried Lord Dane, accepting the position, though there was still a corner of incredulity left in his heart. "You had better come into the dining-room, and take a glass of wine. And don't go running out again at night, lest you meet real ghosts instead of fancied ones."

Lord Dane touched his chair and went slowly away. Lady Dane followed. Adelaide was rising from her seat, passively obedient—as she would have been at that moment had Lord Dane invited her to a glass of opium instead of wine—when her glance happened to fall on her maid. The French girl's eyes were fixed upon her with so strange a gaze that Lady Adelaide recoiled in a second attack of terror.

"What is it, Sophie?" she gasped.

"Nothing, my lady. I have no fear of those revenants for my part. I did not think your ladyship had."

But the tone was curiously bold; almost covertly insolent. And the Lady Adelaide, instead of checking the freedom, looked as if she could have fallen at the maid's feet and implored her to be silent.

It was about this same hour, or a short while before it, that Mitchel, the coastguardsman, came winding round the point, on his beat, near Dane Castle; just as on the previous night when he had been called to from the heights by Richard Ravensbird.

He came quietly round the point—where the rocks projected so much as scarcely to leave a foot of beach to walk upon—his monotonous steps a shade quicker, it might be, than usual, for this was his last turn ere the tide should come up; and Mitchel, never a strong man, was always eager for the time of rest. His thoughts reverted to the great event of the day—the dispute between Ravensbird and his master—which had become known all over Danesheld an hour after it had taken place. It is possible that the recollection of the colloquy with Ravensbird the previous evening, on that same spot, brought the subject of the quarrel to his mind then.

Suddenly, before the point was well rounded, a sound of angry voices arose in the still night air. They seemed to come from the heights, in the direction of the chapel-ruins, just where Ravensbird had been the past night; and Mitchel naturally looked up. He could see nothing—the rocks rose too perpendicularly; but in another minute two men—as they looked to him in the moonlight—appeared on the very ledge of the heights, engaged in a sharp scuffle. The voices had ceased then: the struggle seemed to be for dear life: and Mitchel, full of horror at the danger, stood still and gazed.

An instant of suspense—it was not longer—and one of them fell over the cliff, or was thrown over; immediately following upon which, shrill cries of terror, evidently not in the voice of a man, arose faintly beyond, in the distance.

Mitchel stood in dismay, his heart leaping into his mouth. As may have been gathered from the short conversation with Ravensbird just alluded to, he was not of a brave nature; few men of permanently weak constitution are so. Mitchel managed to keep up and go about his duties, but he was always ailing, and earlier in life he had been subject to epileptic fits. He had really to take heart and courage before he could advance; the sight of a dead man to Mitchel would have been as bad as that of a ghost to a school-girl, and he had little doubt that the unfortunate victim before him was dead—killed by the fall. In breathless trepidation he at length ran along the beach to the spot, and stooped over the man lying there.

Dead he appeared to be. The face was upturned in the bright night, the eyes were closed, the mouth was slightly open, and the skin wore a blue and ghastly look in the moonlight. Mitchel recognized the features, and recoiled as he did so; if anything could have augmented his terror and dismay at the moment, it was that recognition: for they were the features of the Honourable William Henry Dane.

The first thought that came into the coastguardsman's brain was, that the other man must have been Ravensbird; the second was to wonder what he should do. He was ignorant of what he ought to do; or indeed of what he *could* do. Impulse led him to lift his head and shout, hoping he might be heard on the heights; but there came no answer. Little chance was there that the assailant would respond; and no one else was likely to be abroad there at night.

The faint cries in the distance had soon died away, and Mitchel began half to doubt whether he had really heard them. Mitchel took off his own coat, folded it, and laid it under Captain Dane's head; he rubbed his hands, he sprinkled water from the sea on his face, and he rubbed his heart.

But Captain Dane never moved, or gave the faintest sign of life. Not a vessel happened to be within hail at the time, or Mitchel in his desperation would have shouted to that. Again he raised his voice to the heights—a poor voice at the best of times, not as strong as most men's—but the echoes died away into silence, and there was no answer. Suddenly he was seized with terror—partly at finding himself helplessly alone with the dead, partly at the recollection that the tide would soon be up and overwhelm the body, partly at the horror of the situation altogether.

Mitchel was one of those who become hopelessly incapable on a sudden emergency; he knew no more than a child what was best to be done. The nearest way off the beach was round the point he had just traversed, and up the steps a very little higher, the same steps which poor Captain Dane descended in the morning with his American friend. It would have been Mitchel's proper course to take, for he could soon have obtained assistance at the castle. But, Mitchel argued, if he ran along the beach the opposite way, towards Danesheld, he should meet, almost immediately, the next preventive-man, the boundary-point not being far distant. Two vague ideas were floating hazily in Mitchel's mind, prompting him to the latter course; the one was, that it would be terribly lonely to go by way of the steps and across the heights with the certainty of never meeting a soul; the other was, that he could bring back his comrade, the preventive-man, and between them they might manage to bear Captain Dane's body from the advancing sea.

Standing in lamentable indecision, his brain confused, Mitchel stooped again over Captain Dane. The face had not been injured in falling. He pushed the hair from the cold brow; he took up one of the hands intending to feel for the pulse, but in his tremor he let the hand slip, and it fell a dead weight. Mitchel's terror came on again with twofold violence, and hardly knowing what he did, he tore away at his utmost speed, his heart beating wildly against his side. You need not ask which way he went; in these moments of terror, reason yields to impulse: and Mitchel's face and steps were turned towards Danesheld, his eyes strained for the welcome view of his comrade.

But he did not meet him. Whether the man had stolen a march upon time (as was most likely), and gone away too early; or whether (as he afterwards declared) he was perched upon a ledge that was partly sheltered in the rocks, looking at what he called a "suspicious craft" lying off the coast, never was satisfactorily settled. Certain it was, the two men did not meet, did not see each other, and Mitchel went tearing on all the way to Danesheld, the beating of his heart growing louder, and now and then impeding his progress, in a manner that Mitchel scarcely liked, and did not understand.

The first place he came to was the coastguard station—a low building close to the beach. Outside, it looked just like a barn; inside, it consisted of two rooms and a sleeping closet. As Mitchel neared it, he was conscious of a sense of great relief from two causes: that he was within hail of living beings again, and that there would yet be time to rescue the body of Captain Dane.

The outer door of the station opened into a good-sized room. In this, round a blazing fire, were gathered four men, comfortably gossiping as they sat: the supervisor, whose name was Cotton, two friends who had dropped in, and a preventive-man. This coastguard station, having little to do with its time, possessed the character for keeping up any scandal that might be current in Danesheld. It was some time since a dish had been served up to it equal to the one afforded them that day—the quarrel of Captain Dane with his servant, and his expulsion from the castle. Nothing else had been talked of in Danesheld since the morning, and it formed the topic of conversation now in the station as the men sat round the fire, each of the four offering his own conviction as to the origin, or cause, in contradiction to the rest. Exceedingly astonished were the disputants to find the door open with a burst, and a coatless man bolt in upon them in what seemed to be mortal terror. They recognized Mitchel: his eyes seemed starting from his head, and his face was in a white heat.

"What on earth's the matter with you?" wrathfully demanded Mr. Supervisor Cotton, who came to the conclusion that Mitchel had been drinking.

Mitchel could not answer. His heart was beating as he never remembered it to have beaten before. He laid both his hands upon it, and staggered against the wall; his lips were turning white, great drops of water were coming out on his brow. Mr. Cotton began to doubt whether there might not bo some other cause for these strange appearances than the one he had hastily assumed.

"Why have you left your beat? What brings you here in this state? Where's your coat?" he reiterated in wondering wrath, finding Mitchel did not speak.

"He is dead; he is dead!" gasped Mitchel at length. "I must have assistance for him. If——"

Mitchel did not go on; apparently his breath would not let him continue, or perhaps it was his heart. Mr. Cotton and his friend stared.

"Who is dead? what are you talking of?" cried the supervisor.

Mitchel opened his lips, but no words came forth, and he suddenly threw up his hands. But for their springing forward and catching him, he had fallen to the ground.

"What is it?" cried Mr. Supervisor Cotton. "He looks as if he was in a fit. Lay him down here; and, Sims, you run for the doctor."

Mitchel was in a fit. The fright he had experienced on the beach, or the prolonged and violent exertion of running, or perhaps the two combined, had brought on a similar fit to those he had been subject to in early life.

CHAPTER IV.

RAVENSBIRD'S ARREST.

THEY were gathered together in the coastguard station, their faces bent over the prostrate man, Mitchel; the doctor present now, and Mr. Supervisor Cotton himself holding the light. Sims, the preventive-man, despatched in search of the surgeon, had not been able to find him immediately; he met him at length in the town, walking arm-in-arm with Mr. Apperly, Lord Dane's solicitor; but some time had then been lost. Sims told of Mitchel's attack, which he called "queer," and the two gentlemen turned their steps to the station. Mitchel was insensible still, and frothing at the mouth.

"Just move away, will you, and give elbow room," said the doctor, whose name was Wild, to the spectators. "Do you know what brought this attack on, Mr. Cotton? I suspect the man must have been unduly excited."

"He came banging in here in a fine state without his coat," was Mr. Cotton's answer. "I never saw a man so upset: all his breath was gone; and his speech too. I thought he must have been drinking!"

The doctor, a thin active man, with black curly hair, made no observation. He was busying himself with Mitchel. The supervisor resumed:

"After an effort, Mitchel got out some words about wanting assistance for somebody who was dead; so far as we could understand them. For my part, Mr. Wild, I think he was moonstruck."

"I don't, sir," dissented Sims, turning to his superior. "I think he must have had a fright. Mitchel's a quiet, steady man, not given to drink, or anything of that sort, but he's a regular coward."

The only way of arriving at a solution of the mystery was to wait until Mitchel himself revived to tell it. Mr. Wild remained with the man, and he grew better, but it was nearly an hour before he was able to speak. They placed him in a chair in front of the fire, and gave him something to drink.

"Now, Mitchel," began the doctor, "let us have it out. What caused this attack of yours?"

Mitchel did not answer. He was probably diving into his memory for the various events of the evening.

"What's the hour?" he suddenly asked, attempting to spring up to get a view of the clock behind him.

"Hard upon ten. You'd better sit still, Mitchel."

But instead of sitting still, Mitchel staggered a few paces forward, and had to sink back again. He was weak yet.

"Then it's too late!" he exclaimed in excitement, "The body will have been already washed away!"

He told the tale as well as he was able; his sentences
were disjointed still.   There had been a scuffle on the brow
of the heights between two men, and one of them was flung
over, or fell over.   It was Captain Dane.

The name startled them all. Mr. Apperly was still
present, and lifted his legal face with a sharp suspicion.

"You say a man was scuffling with Captain Dane, and
eventually pitched him over, Mitchel?"

"As it seemed to me, sir.   That they were quarrelling
and struggling is certain; and Captain Dane would not be
likely to fling himself down."

"I fear, then, his assailant was the man Ravensbird,"
gravely observed Mr. Apperly.   "He was heard to utter
threats of revenge against his master to-day."

"It was him, sir, safe enough!" cried Mitchel, speaking
in accordance with his assumed conviction.   "I'd never
have thought it of him, though.   But what is to be done?"
added the man, in more energetic tones.   "The tide is safe
to have carried away the body."

"Are you *sure* he was dead, Mitchel?" asked the surgeon.

"Stone dead, sir.   It was nothing but that which
frightened me so."

What was to be done, indeed!   They might well ask it.
Without more delay, they all, with the exception of Mitchel
and a man who stayed behind to take care of him, started
off to the spot by the land way: the beach, they knew, was
then impassable, for the tide was up.

Gaining the heights by the chapel, they looked down.
The tide was nearly at its full height, and the beach covered
with it.   Not a trace, above or below, could be seen of the
calamity, as described by Mitchel, and there was every
chance that the body had been carried out to sea.   Satisfy-
ing their curiosity to the full, by gazing down at the water,
bright in the moon's rays, they took counsel as to what
should be the next step.   Someone must break the news
to Lord Dane; and the two professional gentlemen, as the
most fitting, undertook the task.

"I don't like to do it," abruptly exclaimed the doctor, as

they walked across the greensward, the castle and its lights in front of them. "Harry Dane was not the favourite son; but still—a son is a son."

"I'm sure I don't," returned Mr. Apperly. "It strikes me, do you know, that you and I are not the proper people to do this. I think it should fall on Herbert Dane."

Not a more welcome suggestion could he have made. The surgeon gladly caught at it, and they left the castle for the present, and bent their steps to Herbert Dane's residence. The modest household of that gentleman and his sister consisted of only two servants, a maid and a man. The latter came to the door and said his master was at home.

Mr. Herbert Dane was making himself comfortable. He sat on a sofa before the fire, a cigar in his mouth, and some glasses at his elbow. His back was towards them as they went in.

"This is your promised nine o'clock, Harry!" he cried out. "A pretty long time to keep a fellow waiting! I suppose you have been dancing attendance on that yacht."

"Mr. Herbert——"

Herbert Dane turned short round at the surgeon's voice, and rose. "Oh, I beg your pardon!" he said, with a half laugh. "I thought it was Captain Dane: I am expecting him."

They did not take the offered chairs. They waited until the servant had closed the door, and then looked gravely at Herbert, in the vain hope that their countenances might in a degree prepare him for the news. It was again the surgeon who spoke.

"Mr. Herbert, we have a most unpleasant task to perform, and we have come to you to help us out with it. We were on our way to the castle, bearing evil tidings to Lord Dane. An accident has happened to his son."

But Herbert Dane was more intent on hospitality than on taking in the meaning of the words, and was placing spirits on the table, and ringing the bell for more glasses. Only one gas-burner was alight, and that dimly; but the fire was blazing. He pushed the sofa aside, and extended his hand to turn the gas on, instead of which he turned it out.

"A plague on my clumsiness! I never do know which way these screws ought to go. Gentlemen——"

"Mr. Herbert, you did not hear me, I think," interposed the surgeon. "Never mind the gas. A dreadful accident has happened to Captain Dane, and we want you to break the tidings to his father."

"To Captain Dane! What is it?"

"He has fallen, or been thrown, over the cliff by the chapel. There is little doubt it has killed him."

Herbert Dane had twisted up some paper, and was putting it between the bars of the grate, intending to relight the gas. He dropped it from his hand, and turned his dismayed face, on which the firelight played, towards his visitors. They noticed how pale it was becoming.

"Fallen over the cliff?" he uttered. "When? How? How did it happen? I have been expecting him here since nine o'clock."

They told him all they knew, and asked him to be the one to break the news to Lord Dane. Herbert Dane looked blank at the request. He would go a hundred miles rather than do it, he said presently. He had not been in favour latterly at the castle, and his uncle might receive it worse from him than from any one else. He would go with them and help, but he would not be the chief spokesman. It seemed to him a very horrible addition that the body should have been washed away: Harry might not have been dead. "The preventive-man was certainly a fool," he continued with emphasis. "He ought to have gone up the steps and got assistance at the castle. Which of them was it?"

"Mitchel: I said so," replied Mr. Wild. "And a thousand pities it should have been Mitchel: any of the other men would not have lost their senses over it. To think he should have fallen into a fit, and been unable to speak until it was too late!" continued the surgeon, resentfully.

Herbert Dane tossed his hair from his brow. He was leaning his forehead on his hand, his elbow on the mantelpiece. "Does Mitchel say that he could not distinguish who the other one was, struggling with Harry—with Captain Dane?" he asked.

"Fast enough," cried out the lawyer, before his friend could speak. "Who should it be but the discharged man, Ravensbird."

"Ah!" ejaculated Herbert Dane, a glow flashing into his pale countenance. "I told Harry, when I met him this afternoon, he must take care of that man. Not but that my warning was spoken as much in jest as in earnest," he added, in a dreamy tone.

"We are wasting time, Mr. Herbert," said the surgeon. "Unless we see Lord Dane at once, he may hear of it in some abrupt manner: and that would not be desirable. Besides, it is already late."

"But won't you take something first?"

They declined; and Herbert Dane followed them from the room, taking his hat from the little hall as he passed through it. The servant was opening the door.

"Am I to ask Captain Dane to wait, sir, when he comes?" inquired the man.

"Captain Dane?" mechanically repeated Herbert, looking at the servant as if half bewildered. "No."

The first person they saw at the castle was Bruff. Lord Dane was in the dining-room: his usual sitting-room at all times of late. Lady Dane was with him. Bruff thought they were expecting Captain Dane home every minute. The gentlemen could go in.

The two went in, ushered through the hall by Bruff. Herbert Dane walked half-way across it, and then turned round. When Bruff came back, he found him standing under the large gateway.

"I declare I don't like to face them, Bruff," he exclaimed. "Telling ill news used to make me shiver as a boy. It will be an awful shock, especially for Lady Dane."

"What has happened, Mr. Herbert? They whispered something about the captain as they went in. He was quite well when he went out from dinner."

"I really cannot tell you what has happened; I don't understand it," was the reply of Herbert Dane. "They came to me just now with a tale that he had fallen over the cliff, here, near the ruins, and asked me to come up and help them to break it to Lord Dane. Let us go on the heights, Bruff, and see if we can discover anything!"

Bruff took his hat and went after Mr. Herbert, feeling stunned and bewildered, but incredulous on the whole. Herbert told him what he had heard: and Bruff audibly wondered whether Mitchel was a "born fool."

Meanwhile, the two gentlemen were imparting the tidings to Lord and Lady Dane. Things are often mercifully softened. It was the case here. Mr. Apperly happened to say that the supervisor, Cotton, entirely disbelieved the story, judging it to be a chimera of Mitchel's brain induced by the man's approaching illness: and if Lord and Lady Dane did not entirely rest in this hope, they at least found considerable comfort in it. Mr. Wild allowed that Mitchel's brain, if excited by the account of Captain Dane's quarrel with Ravensbird, might have actually imagined the scene of the scuffle between them on the heights; and the tale he told be altogether a delusion.

But Lord Dane did not sit still under the hope and do nothing. He had not the use of his legs himself, but he speedily set in motion those who had. Some of the servants were sent flying for the man, Mitchel, some for the police, some across the heights, and some to the bay to see whether the *Pearl* was gone out. · Herbert Dane came back with Bruff, and agreed with his uncle that the tale was incredible.

"I have been waiting at home for him all the evening," Herbert said. "I met Harry this afternoon, and he said he'd come in at nine o'clock, after the yacht was off, and smoke a cigar with me. He had promised to do so last week, and never came."

"It is not *possible* that Ravensbird should dare to attack him!" exclaimed Lord Dane, his haughty face flushing crimson.

"My lord," spoke up Bruff, "a note was left here for the captain about an hour ago. Mills, the sailmaker, brought it up. He has been at work on board the yacht, and said the American gentleman gave it to him just as they were putting off."

"Then the yacht has gone!" cried Lord Dane. "Bring me that note, Bruff."

Lord Dane opened it at once; he was a man given to act promptly and decisively, and he considered the circumstances justified the measure. The note was addressed to the Honourable William Dane, and contained but a few words:

On board the Pearl: half-past eight o'clock.

"Dear William,

"What has become of you? I received your message, declining dinner, but have been expecting you since. It is not kind; though I conclude that something has unexpectedly detained you. We are off in five minutes. I shall look out for you to the last.

"Ever yours,
"C. Moncton."

"Why, when Harry left the dinner-table he said he was then going to the yacht," cried Lord Dane, giving the note to Mr. Apperly.

"What time was that, my lord?"

"What time was it, Bruff?"

"I think it must have been half-past eight, my lord," replied the butler; "or close upon it."

"I daresay it was. He lingered on in a brown study at the table, drinking nothing. But he told me he did not think the yacht would go out before nine or half-past."

The serjeant of police answered to his summons, and came up to the castle; not so Mitchel, the preventive-man, who was too ill to do so. Mills, the sailmaker, came, sent for by Lord Dane; and he proved that Captain Dane did not go down to the yacht. Colonel Moncton, he said, was looking for him till the last moment, but the captain did not come. At the instant of their putting off, the colonel gave him the note, and asked him to bring it up to the castle.

At length the bustle of inquiry was over and the castle cleared, the police having received Lord Dane's orders to apprehend Ravensbird. The old Lord and Lady Dane sat up the livelong night, losing hope with every passing

moment. The tide receded from the strip of beach, leaving
no signs that anything, dead or alive, had been there, leaving
not even Mitchel's coat. And at length the morning light
dawned, and the morning sun shone out to gladden the
world, but no trace had been found of Harry Dane.

Just before entering Danesheld, standing in an obscure
spot, halfway between the first house in the village and the
sea, was a small inn, called the Sailor's Rest. It was kept
by a man of the name of Hawthorne, who had once been
gamekeeper to Lord Dane. A well-conducted inn, rather
better than a common public-house, affording good bed and
board to travellers, and having also its share of bar and
parlour custom. The men-servants from the castle were
fond of dropping in, to drink their glass of ale with the
landlord; and it was at this house that Ravensbird had
taken up his sojourn, when turned out of doors by his
master.

On the morning after the calamity, which was not yet
generally known, the landlord was in the bar alone; or, at
any rate, he thought himself alone. He was busy polishing
his taps and setting things straight, according to his custom
before breakfast, when one of the preventive-men, on his
way to the beach, came up the passage and entered.

"Half a gill of rum, landlord; the morning air's chilly
like."

"We shall have a fine day again," observed the landlord,
as he handed what was asked for.

"It's to be hoped we shall, for the work that's got to be
done in it," replied the customer. "They are going to drag
in shore for the body; and I suppose all Danesheld will
turn out to see."

"Drag for what body? Has any one been lost?"

The man was in the act of putting the glass to his lips.
He put it down again, and gazed at the landlord.

"Do you mean to say that you have not heard of the
misfortune that has overtook the castle? Captain Dane's
murdered."

"Captain Dane murdered?" echoed the landlord, doubting
whether his ears played him false.

"He was assaulted on the heights last night, just opposite the castle, and flung over the cliff," explained the man, "Mitchel was on his boat underneath and saw it all. When he came to examine the fallen man, he found it to be Captain Dane; and he was stone dead."

Mr. Hawthorne fell back amongst his taps, feeling not far from "stone dead" himself.

"And Mitchel came running up to the guardhouse at the pace of a steam-engine, which set his heart beating, and threw him right into a fit, so that he never spoke for an hour or more. The consequence was not a soul knew of it in time, and the tide came up and washed the body away. Sickly fellows like Mitchel are never good for much."

"And who was it attacked him?—who threw him over?" asked the landlord, when he could recover his speech.

"Nobody need ask that twice. It was his servant, Ravensbird."

Once more the landlord backed, and a brass ladle, which he happened to have in his hand, fell to the ground.

"Ravensbird!—*Ravensbird*, do you say? Why he has been staying here since yesterday! I couldn't have slept in the house with him last night if I had known this."

"'Twas Ravensbird done it, and nobody else. He wasn't long in carrying out his threats of revenge. The most curious part is, how he managed to entrap Captain Dane on to the heights; to their very edge. Some say——"

At this moment an interruption occurred which nearly made the speaker (as he phrased it afterwards) jump out of his skin. Over the high wooden screen which ran partially across the bar, facing the fireplace, appeared the head of Mr. Ravensbird, who had been quietly seated there all the time.

"Your name's Dubber, I believe," he said, glaring indignation at the preventive-man.

Dubber was taken back. He stood in silence, too much confused to make any reply.

"How dare you stand there and traduce me?" demanded Ravensbird. "By what authority do you accuse me of the crime of murder?"

"Well now, Mr. Ravensbird, if it is not true, and you are innocent, I'm sure I beg your pardon," spoke the man, gathering his wits together, and making the best of the situation. "As to telling Hawthorne—if I had not told him, the next comer would; the wonder is, he didn't hear it last night. If you were not a party concerned, you'd be the first yourself to talk of it. I didn't speak in ill-nature."

"Did I understand you to say that Mitchel affirms I pitched Captain Dane over the cliff?—that he saw me do it?"

"It's what Mitchel says."

"Did he say so to you?"

"Not to me; I haven't seen him since. Sims. told me about it, and he was in the guardhouse when Mitchel got in."

"Is it true that Captain Dane is dead?" continued Ravensbird, after a pause.

"*That's* true enough; and the tide carried his body away. They are getting ready the drags now. Lord Dane has had the police up at the castle half the night, they say. But I must be off, unless I want to get reported; my time's up."

He turned with the last sentence and went out hastily, glad to be away from the sallow face and stern eye of Ravensbird. Mr. Ravensbird descended from the seat of the screen on which he had been standing, and came round to the landlord.

"What do you know of this business, Hawthorne?"

"If you were sitting inside the screen, Mr. Ravensbird, you must know as much as I do," answered the man, feeling by no means secure that Ravensbird was not going to attack him. "I never heard a word of it till Dubber came in. You did startle me, putting your head up like that. I thought you were in bed."

"I have been down this half-hour. What do you think of this tale?"

"I don't know what to think of it. Who would harm Captain Dane? He had no enemies, and was a friend to us all. I'm sure the quarrel with you was quite unlike him."

" Unlike his general nature. He was put out—and so was I. Where's my hat? Upstairs, I think. I shall go and ascertain the truth of this business."

He left the bar to go to his chamber, and almost at the same moment the sergeant of police entered. He gave a quiet glance round, and then nodded to the landlord.

" Good-morning, Hawthorne. You have got Master Ravensbird lodging here, I believe. Is he up yet?"

" He was here in the bar not an instant ago, Mr. Bent. He's gone to his room now to get his hat. He wants to go out and learn particulars of this sad affair about Captain Dane. Dubber has been in, telling about it. I'm sure you might have knocked me down with the click of an empty gun."

The sergeant withdrew to the passage, and there he propped himself against the wall. The position commanded a view of the back door of the house as well as the front.

" A fine morning, Mr. Ravensbird," cried he, as the latter appeared.

" Very; I am going out to enjoy it."

" An instant first. I want to say a few words to you."

" Not now," returned Ravensbird, impatience in his tone.

" No time like the present," was the reply of the sergeant, as he laid his hand on the man's shoulder. " Don't be restive. I *must* detain you."

Ravensbird turned his sallow face on the officer, his eyes flashing with anger. " By what right? What do you mean?"

" Now, Ravensbird, don't be unreasonable. Take things quietly. You are my prisoner, and all the resistance you can make will not avail you."

Ravensbird's answer to this *was* resistance. A slight scuffle, and he suddenly found a pair of handcuffs on his wrists.

" The most senseless thing a man can do is to attempt to resist an officer in the execution of his duty," observed the sergeant in a tone of pleasant argument, as though he were discussing the point with a knot of friends. " Lord Dane gave me orders last night to arrest you: I might have knocked the house up and taken you then; but I thought I'd do the thing politely and wait till morning. I put a man or two on outside, back and front, to make sure."

"How dare Lord Dane order me into custody? He has not the right to do it. He is not a magistrate."

The sergeant broke into a little amused laugh. "A stipendary magistrate, no; but he is lord-lieutenant of the county. Don't you question Lord Dane's *rights*, my good man."

Ravensbird was cooling down. "Understand me," he began;—"your name's Bent, I think?" he broke off to say.

"Bent, it is."

"Understand me, Mr. Bent: I do not wish to resist any lawful authority, and if I were free as air this moment, I should stay and face the charge out. What I am annoyed at is this: I was on the point of going out to inquire into the attack on Captain Dane, and to pick up what I could; for, by fair means or foul, I intend to sift it out. I have a motive for so doing that you know nothing about; and I would rather have given a ten-pound note from my pocket than been stopped in it."

The sergeant coughed incredulously. There was not a shadow of doubt in his opinion, and he did not suppose there could be in any one else's, that Captain Dane's assailant stood before him.

"I'm sorry I can't spare you. It's all very plausible, Ravensbird, this show of wanting to learn particulars, but you have an old hand to deal with."

Ravensbird looked steadily at the sergeant, never quailing. "You may be an old hand; experience has made you so; but you have taken the wrong man in taking me. I did not know that any accident, any ill, had happened to Captain Dane, until Dubber just now told it; I did not know but that he was alive and well. And that I swear."

"Now don't take and swear any nonsense, or it may be used against you," was the sharp retort. "It's not my way to make bad worse for those who come into my custody; but when they will get slipping out all sorts of admissions in their folly, why I'm obliged to take note of it. The best thing you can do is to sew your mouth up until you are before my Lord Dane. And that's friendly advice, mind."

Possibly Ravensbird felt it to be so. And he relapsed into silence.

CHAPTER V.

TAKING THE OATH.

AMIDST the surmises, doubts, and suspicions, that were troubling the breast of my Lord Dane, equally with that of every inmate of the castle, two convictions stood out clearly from the general obscurity: the one was, the certain guilt of Richard Ravensbird; the other, that the extraordinary behaviour of Lady Adelaide Errol on the previous night must have had reference to the calamity.

Lady Adelaide denied it. Lord Dane called for her the first thing in the morning, and put the question to her in his straightforward manner: "Did she witness anything of the struggle, and was it that which had terrified her?" With many tears and protestations, and apparently in much terror still, for her frame trembled and her face was white, she totally denied it. But it must be confessed that Lord Dane retained his suspicions.

About ten o'clock, Ravensbird was marshalled to the castle. Lord Dane sat in his state chair in the great hall. Mr. Apperly was with him: and the lawyer—though not there professionally, for this was no official investigation, simply what Lord Dane called a private inquiry—had pen and ink before him, intending to take down, for his own satisfaction, any point that struck him. Vigorous in mind, if incapable in body, was Lord Dane. He had not yet seen Mitchel, but the man was expected up. Squire Lester was near Lord Dane, not in his magisterial capacity, but as a friend. Supervisor Cotton was also there. All doubt as to the fate of Captain Dane was over; the morning tide had washed his hat ashore, and a fishing boat picked up Mitchel's coat at sea. A feeling was gaining ground that the fall was not the result of accident, or a blow given in the heat of dispute, but was deliberate murder. Never was the guilt of a prisoner more positively assumed than that of Ravensbird, not only by Lord Dane and his family, but by the police. The sergeant had made his own inquiries amongst the household, and his opinion was conclusive. No little sensation was created when Ravensbird appeared, not in handcuffs —those had been removed—but guarded officially by the sergeant.

" You bad, wicked man ! " burst forth Lord Dane, in anguish, forgetting the dignity of his position in the feelings of a father. " Could nothing serve your turn but you must murder my poor son ? "

" I did not murder him, my lord," respectfully answered Ravensbird.

" We don't want useless quibbling here," interrupted Lawyer Apperly, before Lord Dane could speak. " If you did not deliberately kill him with a knife, or a club, or a pistol, or any weapon of that sort, you attacked him and threw him over the cliff. I don't know what else you can call it but murder."

" I never was on the heights at all last night. I never saw Captain Dane after he turned me out of doors in the morning," quietly responded Ravensbird. " Who is it that accuses me ? "

" Now, my good man, this absurd equivocation will not avail you, and you only waste breath, and my lord's time in using it," impetuously cried Mr. Apperly, who was of an excitable temperament, and given to putting himself into a heat. " You have brought enough sorrow upon his lordship, without seeking to prolong this trying scene."

" I asked you, Mr. Apperly, who was my accuser, and I have a right to be answered," said the prisoner in rather dogged tones, for he saw that his guilt was taken for granted by all present.

" Circumstances and your own actions are your accusers,

and Mitchel the coastguardsman is evidence," explained Mr. Apperly.

"Where is Mitchel?" feverishly interrupted Lord Dane. "Could he not have been here before this?"

Supervisor Cotton had thought he would have been: he went out of the hall to see if there were any signs of his coming.

"Does Mitchel say that it was I, my lord, who struggled with Captain Dane—and that he saw me?" questioned Ravensbird.

"Of course he says it," interrupted the lawyer before Lord Dane could answer. "Do you hope he would conceal it, prisoner?"

"Then he tells a malicious, gratuitous lie, Mr. Apperly," was the prisoner's rejoinder, as he turned and faced the lawyer. "And he must do it to screen the real offender."

Lord Dane inclined his head forward and spoke.

"Ravensbird, as Mr. Apperly says, this line of conduct will only tell against you. Had no person whatever witnessed the act, there could have been no reasonable doubt in regard to it; for who else, but you, was at variance with my son? Of the nature of the quarrel between you and him yesterday morning I am ignorant, but it is certain you must have provoked him grievously; and you left the castle uttering threats against him."

"My lord, so far that is true," replied Ravensbird, calmly and respectfully. "I gave Captain Dane certain information, by which I thought to do him a service, but he received it in quite an opposite spirit. It was connected with his own affairs; was not pleasant information; and it aroused his anger towards me. Smarting under the unmerited treatment—for it was unmerited—I grew angry in my turn, and I confess that I answered my master as I ought not to have answered him. This vexed him further, and he said some harsh and bitter things. We were both in a passion; both excited; he beyond control; and he ordered me out of the house on the instant, and kicked me down stairs. I ask you, my lord, whether it was likely I could take it calmly, without a retort? I had been a good servant to my master;

had served him faithfully for years; he had reposed confidence in me; had grown to treat me almost as a friend; and that made me feel the insult all the more keenly. I left the castle overflowing with wrath, and for the next two hours all I did was to give vent to it in harsh words—"

"You were heard to say you would be revenged," interrupted Lord Dane.

"Ten times, at least, I said it, my lord, and many heard me; but by the end of the two hours my anger was spent. Threatening words they had been, but idle as the wind. I never seriously entertained the thought of taking vengeance on my master. I liked him too well. I had only spoken in the heat of passion; and before the day was over I actually began in my own mind to find excuses for him."

"You forget that your struggle with him was witnessed by the preventive-man," spoke Lord Dane, who had listened impassively.

"It never was, my lord, for no struggle with me took place. What Mitchel's motive for accusing me can be, I cannot tell: either his eyesight must have deceived him, or he is screening the real offender at my cost. But I don't fear: the truth is sure to come to light."

"The truth has come to light already," sarcastically interrupted Mr. Apperly. "But all this is waste of time. My lord, can we ask no questions of any one else whilst we are waiting for Mitchel? Sergeant Bent here craves permission to make some inquiry of Lady Adelaide Errol. He has heard that she was a witness to the struggle."

"She says she was not," replied Lord Dane, while Mr. Lester lifted his head in surprise.

"How was it possible that Lady Adelaide could have witnessed it?" asked Mr. Lester.

Lord Dane explained. Tempted by the beauty of the night, Lady Adelaide had foolishly run across the heights. She came back at once, crying out, evidently frightened. He himself thought she must have witnessed something of it, but she denied it.

"Pardon me, my lord, if I put in my opinion," said the sergeant: "her ladyship is but a young and timid girl, and would doubtless shrink from acknowledging she had been a witness to anything so dreadful. From what I have heard your servants say, the French maid especially, I feel sure she did see something of it. If you will allow her to come in, I will put a question or two to her."

"Have her in if you like," said Lord Dane, adopting the view taken by the officer, and thinking that if she did know anything she should be made to speak.

It was Mr. Lester who went for her. And it is probable that Lady Adelaide did not dare to disobey the summons, for she came in leaning on his arm. As she stood near Lord Dane, in her white morning dress with its blue ribbons, she seemed a very vision of loveliness. The sunlight played on her fair hair, and her colour went and came fitfully. Mr. Lester had placed a chair, but she did not accept it; she seemed only eager to get away again, and stood before the table, both her hands resting on it.

"Your ladyship witnessed the struggle last night on the heights," began the sharp police-sergeant, speaking very blandly, but in a perfectly assured tone. "Will you kindly tell me how much of it you saw?"

The confident tone deceived her. She assumed something or other had come out to betray her, and that further denial would be useless. Glancing round the room in terror not to be mistaken, the expression of her eyes not unlike that of a stag at bay, she caught the penetrating gaze of Sophie Deffloe. Why had *she* come in? A faint cry escaped Lady Adelaide's lips.

"Had your ladyship any motive in going on to the heights last night?" proceeded the officer, who had no suspicion that it was not quite an exceptional occurrence. "You could not, I presume, have known that any quarrel was about to take place there?"

"Oh no, no," she vehemently answered, bursting into tears.

"The affray took you by surprise, then? as we have been assuming. Will your ladyship relate what you saw?"

Her ladyship glanced round the room, the expression of her face not to be mistaken. She sought for sympathy, and she sought for escape; she gazed pitifully up to Lord Dane's eyes, into Mr. Lester's, and then she turned and caught the stern ones of her maid.

"Why does Sophie stand there?"

The appeal was made to Lord Dane. He had seen the girl, and supposed she was there in attendance on her mistress. The police-officer thought Lady Adelaide was trifling with him.

"It may be better that your ladyship should declare now what you saw and know, or you may be called upon to do it more publicly."

"Speak out, Adelaide," said Lord Dane, sternly, feeling there was more behind than she had confessed to, and angry at her previous denial. "If you don't, I'll have you examined upon oath. You told me you ran inside the ruins and began thinking of ghosts, and that the thought frightened you."

"Oh no, no, uncle, not upon oath!" she broke forth, the one word seeming to drown all others. "I will tell you the whole truth at once; I will, indeed," she added, turning from the keen gaze of the sergeant. "It is true I did begin to think of ghosts, as I ran through the ruins, and I was turning back in my fear, when I heard voices outside, near the edge of the cliff. I felt glad of it, because it took from the loneliness of the place, and I went to the opening and peeped out. Two men were on the very edge of the cliff— struggling, fighting; and in another moment one of them disappeared—had fallen over. It almost frightened me to death. I flew back through the ruins, across the grass to the castle; and I believe I screamed, though I don't think I was conscious of it at the time. Bruff came out and met me; and that's all I know or can tell you."

"Why did you not state this at the time?" cried Lord Dane, his brow darkening.

"I was too frightened," she murmured. "Besides, I thought my aunt would be angry enough with me for having run out, without confessing what I had seen."

"Had you spoken then it might have saved Harry's life," said Lord Dane, in low tones of pain. "Did you recognise him?"

"Oh no, uncle," she wailed. "How can you ask it?"

"Did you recognise the other man?" asked the officer.

"I did not recognise either."

"Not at all? Not in the least—in any sign? Surely your ladyship could see whether he was a tall man or a short one?"

Never had Lady Adelaide betrayed greater terror than she was betraying now. Her lips were white, her hand trembled. Twice she essayed to speak before words came.

"I don't know what either looked like; I don't know whether they were tall or short. It all passed in a moment."

"Did no idea, ever so faint, convey to your ladyship's mind a suspicion of who either of them might be?" came the persistent question.

"No; unless I thought that they were robbers attacking one another."

"Nor the voices either, my lady? Did you not recognise them?"

"I did not hear the voices, except in that first moment when I was inside the ruins," she answered, shivering. "They were not speaking at the last, in their struggle; or, if they were, I did not hear them."

"Then you positively recognised neither Captain Dane nor his assailant?"

"Why can you not believe me?" she retorted, in a tone of anger, of wild pain. "Was not Captain Dane my cousin? Had I recognised either him or the other, should I not be ready to avow it? Let me go back," she added imploringly to Lord Dane. "If I remain here for ever I cannot tell you more."

"An instant yet, my lady," persisted the sergeant. "Did the other—the one who did not go over the cliff—attempt to follow you when you ran away?"

"Not that I know of. I did not look round to see."

"I do hope and trust your ladyship has told all," was the comment of the police-sergeant, as she moved towards the door, waiting for no further permission.

Mr. Lester advanced, and led her from the hall, Sophie Deffloe slowly following. "How *cruel* they are!" she said,

the tears running down her cheeks. " As if I should not
be too glad to tell anything that I know. I wonder you
allowed that man to pursue me with his questions!"

"In the presence of Lord Dane, on an occasion such as
this, I am no one," whispered Mr. Lester, his tone betraying
the warmest, tenderest sympathy. "I felt for you more
than I can express. But, Lady Adelaide, don't run out
at night alone again."

"Never, never!" was her vehement answer. "This has
been a life's lesson to me. But I thought not of harm."

. "Harm!—no," murmured Mr. Lester, as he bowed over
her hand at the drawing-room door and resigned her,
Sophie Deffloe having halted at a distance to watch her in.

"What are you staring at, Sophie?" inquired Mr. Lester,
as he passed the girl on his return to the hall.

"That regards me," she replied, translating her thoughts
more literally than she generally did.

Lord Dane grew impatient in his chair of state, waiting
for the appearance of the preventive-man. There seemed
to be some unusual delay. The most unconcerned individual present appeared to be Richard Ravensbird, and his
cool, independent bearing rather irritated Lord Dane. That
there was not a loop-hole for his possible innocence, all
Danesheld would have testified to.

A murmur, and Mitchel came in at last, under the wing
of Mr. Cotton. The man looked pale and ill, and Lord
Dane ordered him a chair whilst he spoke to what he had
seen and heard. He described hearing the voices in dispute,
seeing the struggle on the edge of the heights, and the fall
of one, whom he found to be Captain Dane.

"Thrown over by Ravensbird," cried excitable Lawyer
Apperly.

"Yes," assented Mitchel.

"Were there no signs of life whatever in my son?" inquired Lord Dane, suppressing, as he best could, all show
of feeling.

"None, my lord: he was dead beyond mistake. I wish
I could have carried him away in my arms, my lord, instead
of leaving him there to be washed away by the tide!"

fervently added the man, in an accession of regret and remorse. "But it was beyond my strength. If I had not fallen into that fit, there'd have been time to get to him."

"You could not help it, Mitchel," replied Lord Dane, in sad, kind tones. "Did you recognise it to be my son on the heights, before he fell?"

"No, my lord," replied Mitchel, shaking his head. "The moon was bright, but moonlight isn't daylight, and I couldn't get a clear view above, from the place where I stood. The scuffle did not seem to last a moment, either, before he was over. It was only when I got to him, trying to lift him up, that I saw it was Captain Dane."

An interruption came from Ravensbird. He had stood with his stern black eyes fixed on Mitchel ever since the man's entrance; they seemed to devour every turn of his countenance, every word that fell from his lips.

"My lord," said he, turning to Lord Dane, "if I were before a regular court, undergoing a formal examination, I should be allowed an advocate; the worst criminal is not denied as much as that; but here I have none to help me; I stand alone. I should like to ask this man a question, my lord."

"Ask it," said Lord Dane.

Ravensbird turned and faced Mitchel. "You have just said you could not recognise Captain Dane on the heights, not getting a clear view of him. If you could not recognise him, how could you recognise me?"

"I did not recognise you," replied Mitchel.

A pause. Richard Ravensbird spoke out eagerly—passionately:

"Then why did you say you did?"

"I didn't say it."

"You did. As I am told."

"No, I did not say it. My eyesight did not carry me so far. It——"

The words were interrupted by the sergeant. "Do you mean to deny, Mitchel, now that you are before my lord, that it was Ravensbird who flung over Captain Dane?"

"I couldn't say that it was, sir, or that it was not. It

might have been him, or it might have been anybody else, for all I saw."

The sergeant looked at Lord Dane. "I understood your lordship, last night, that Mitchel had recognised Ravensbird as the offender."

"I understood that he had done so" replied Lord Dane. "You told me so, Apperly; as did Mr. Wild."

Mr. Apperly brought his spectacles and his red face down upon Mitchel, and spoke in sharp quick tones:

"What do you mean by this denial, Mitchel? You know you said last evening it was Ravensbird; said it in the guard-house."

"I said it was sure to have been Ravensbird on account of the quarrel he had with his master in the morning," answered Mitchel. "Everybody else said so too. But I never said it from my own knowledge; my own eyesight."

"Then, are we to understand, Mitchel, that you do not know positively who was engaged in the conflict with my son?—that you do not recognise the person?" asked Lord Dane.

"I did not, my lord. I surmised it to be Mr. Ravensbird, of course, because of the quarrel we have heard of; but I could not see the two who were struggling on the heights; that is, not to recognise them. I should not have known the one to be Captain Dane but for his falling on to the beach where I was."

The whole room felt non-plussed. Every one in it, including the usually keen and correct police-officer, had understood that Mitchel was ready to swear, by the evidence of his own eyesight, to Richard Ravensbird.

"It does not make a shade of difference," cried Mr. Apperly, over-zealous in the Dane interest and his own conviction. "Richard Ravensbird was heard to utter threats against his master—"

"I beg your pardon, Mr. Apperly, it makes every difference," sharply interrupted Ravensbird. "For a credible witness to say he saw me commit the murder, is one thing; but when he says he did *not* see me, it's another."

"Perhaps you can account for your time yesterday, Ravensbird, hour by hour, until ten o'clock at night?" cried the lawyer.

"Perhaps I can, if it's necessary I should," retorted Ravensbird. "After I was turned from these gates, I went straight to the Sailors' Rest, and the landlord 'can tell you so."

"But you may not have stopped at the Sailors' Rest?"

"I did stop at it: and twenty people going in and out saw me there. I did not stir out all day. I dined and had tea with Hawthorne and his wife."

"What did you do after tea?"

"After tea I sat with them for some time, and then I went out for a walk."

"I thought so!" cried impetuous Mr. Apperly. "Where did you walk to? Which road?"

Ravensbird paused in hesitation, and the fact could only tell against him.

"I don't know that it matters to any one which road I went," came the tardy answer.

"It matters to every one. Perhaps you took this road? Why bless me!" added the lawyer, jumping up with the suddenness of the recollection, "I met you myself, Ravensbird! I was on my way home from a client's, and I met you coming in this direction; towards the castle. It was about seven o'clock."

"I did not see you," said Ravensbird.

"Perhaps not. I saw you, and that's more to the purpose. Where were you going?"

"That's my business," answered the man. "I was going about no harm, and I did none. I was not out long; I was soon back at the Sailors' Rest."

"What time did you get back?" quickly asked the lawyer.

"Mitchel," as quickly rejoined Ravensbird, "what time was it when you saw the struggle and the fall?"

"It was between half-past eight and a quarter to nine," replied Mitchel. "Hard upon the three-quarters I should say."

Ravensbird drew back with the air of a man who has vanquished his adversaries and done with contention. "That settles the question so far as I am concerned, my lord. I was back in the parlour at the Sailors' Rest by twenty minutes past eight. I remember hearing it strike a quarter past by the church-clock just before I got in, and I took out my watch to see whether it was right. I did not stir out again all the evening."

Lord Dane felt amazed at the man's confident manner; he did not believe a word of his assertion.

"Mitchel," he said, "are you sure as to the time yourself?"

But even as Lord Dane spoke, he remembered that his son was indoors with him, sitting at the dining-table, until half-past eight, or close upon it.

"I am quite sure, my lord," was Mitchel's answer. "It's not often we preventive-men are mistaken as to the time; we've nothing to do, marching about there, but listen to the quarters and the hours as the church-clock gives them out. Besides, there's the tide to guide us; it's quite an amusement to note the tide and the time keeping pace together. I should think the exact time that Captain Dane fell was about twenty-two minutes to nine. It went the three-quarters soon after I left him, when I was running along the beach."

"I suppose you could swear to this, Mitchel, if required?" cried keen Lawyer Apperly.

"Yes, I could, sir; it's the truth."

The answer went for little. Mr. Apperly felt quite certain that there was a mistake somewhere.

"Perhaps, Ravensbird," he suggested, "you will inform Lord Dane what you were doing with yourself during that interval of absence from the Sailors' Rest, and where you passed it. According to your own account you must have been away pretty nearly an hour and a half."

"I respectfully submit to my lord that where I was matters not to this inquiry," was the reply of Ravensbird. "Mitchel declares the murder must have been committed—"

"Stop a minute. This is the second time you have called it 'murder.'"

" Well ! " cried Ravensbird, " it is what other people are calling it."

" Not in the confident tone you use. Go on."

" Mitchel says it took place at about twenty-two minutes to nine. I was back at the Sailors' Rest before twenty minutes past eight. Even had I gone direct from the heights to the inn (but I was not on the heights at all last night), I must have left them at eight o'clock, or thereabouts, to get down at the time I speak of. I was in by twenty minutes past eight, and I did not go out again. If this is proved—and you can call a dozen witnesses to testify to its truth, by sending to the Sailors' Rest—then I submit, Mr. Apperly, that you have no right to inquire into my actions. Once establish that I was not, that I could not have been Captain Dane's assaulter, and I am as free and independent as you are. Why, I was playing dominoes with one of the customers at half-past eight, and I played with him till ten."

The most obvious course at this stage of the proceedings was to send to the Sailors' Rest, that the prisoner's words might be confirmed or refuted. The sergeant himself went down, and Lord Dane waited with ill-concealed impatience. As before, the only man in the room perfectly at his ease, to all appearance, was Ravensbird.

Mr. Bent came back again. He returned with a crest-fallen expression of countenance, and acknowledged himself " floored." " Floored for the present." Hawthorne and his wife, with two or three other credible witnesses, declared that Ravensbird was back at the Sailors' Rest by twenty minutes past eight. They were able to fix the time from the fact that Ravensbird had called their attention to the clock in the parlour, saying it was " just right" with the church. And it was certainly true that he did not leave the house again, and that he was playing at dominoes until nearly bed-time.

In the teeth of this evidence there could be no pretext for detaining Ravensbird in custody, and Lord Dane unwillingly ordered him out of it. Unwillingly, because from the depth of his heart he still deemed the man to be guilty.

" You are at liberty to go, Richard Ravensbird."

" My lord," said the ex-prisoner, walking slightly forward to confront Lord Dane, " I think, even yet, in spite of testimony, you believe me to have been the assailant of my master. Once more let me assert the truth : I never saw him after I left this castle in the morning."

" I do believe it to have been you—you, and no other," replied Lord Dane, bending forward his severe face. " You have triumphed for the moment; but I would have you remember, Richard Ravensbird, that crimes such as this are sure to come to light sooner or later."

Ravensbird's only answer was a bow, respectful enough. His manner to Lord Dane throughout had been characterized by marked respect. Indeed, it could not be said that he had been disrespectful to any one, only fearlessly independent. He passed out of the hall without another word. Bruff was standing in the gateway, but Ravensbird brushed past him without speaking, and turned towards Danesheld, followed by Mr. Cotton and Mitchel.

Lord Dane, Squire Lester, Mr. Apperly, and the police-sergeant remained in the hall. The two former were talking together. Mr. Apperly was in a reverie, and the officer was pencilling down some memoranda in an old note-book he had taken from his pocket, his countenance very thoughtful.

" You look puzzled, Bent," observed the lawyer, rousing himself.

" It's what I am, Mr. Apperly. Out and out puzzled."

" You still think him guilty ? "

" I'm sure he's guilty," was the emphatic answer.

" Well," said Mr. Apperly, whose opinion had somewhat veered round after so decisive an alibi, " I don't feel sure of it now. One can't shut one's eyes to facts. If the man was really back at the Sailors' Rest by the time he mentions ——"

" I tell you he was not back," interrupted the sergeant; " or else Mitchel is mistaken as to the time. There's not an earthly thing you can be so deceived in as evidence given to establish a fact resting upon time. Look here ;

you noticed, didn't you, what I stated : that Mr. Hawthorne said he had called their attention, when he got in, to the fact of its being twenty minutes past eight ? That very circumstance was enough, in any experienced mind, to prove his guilt. He did it with a motive, rely upon it. Some craft had been at work : probably he had contrived to put the clock back. It's not *that* that's puzzling me. Ravensbird's neither more nor less clever than others of his stamp, and we shall catch him yet. As to an alibi, I've known the hardest counter-swearing as to time ; and both sides honest in what they swore to, only they were mistaken. Their clocks and watches were wrong ; or the sun was too fast ; or the coaches, that never were out by so much as a minute before, were out then. *I* know what alibis are worth."

"What is it, then, that's puzzling you?" asked Mr. Apperly.

Their tones had been low ; but the sergeant dropped his voice almost to a whisper, as he answered curtly :

"The young lady. She puzzles me altogether. That she knows more than she has told, I'm sure : that's nothing ; folks often give us only half evidence, and the short-coming lies light enough upon their conscience."

"Don't you believe her?"

I don't say that I entirely disbelieve her. But look here,"·added the sergeant, using again his favourite phrase, as he was given to do when very much in earnest, "I can understand her having been frightened at the time : any young girl would be, witnessing a scene such as that: *but what is it that's frightening her now ?*"

Mr. Apperly seemed struck with the question. "She did seem to be in fear as she stood there, there's no denying it," he remarked.

"Ay ; mark me, sir, if there's any one, besides himself, that could establish the guilt of Ravensbird, it's the Lady Adelaide. She——"

The sergeant stopped, arrested by a look of Mr. Apperly's. Turning, he saw the fine old face of Lord Dane extended in rapt attention. He had spoken louder than he thought for,

"What is that you are saying, Bent?"

The sergeant explained. He had really no particular wish to keep his suspicion from Lord Dane, and he avowed a belief that the Lady Adelaide could, if she chose, speak to the guilt of Ravensbird.

"And her motive for not doing it—her motive?" questioned Lord Dane, hotly.

"Ay, my lord, I can't fathom it; that's where I'm puzzled. That favourite French maid of hers is Ravensbird's sweetheart; perhaps for her sake she is screening him. She looked afraid of the Frenchwoman as she stood here."

Of all the various incidents, aspects, and doubts by which the affair had been surrounded since its occurrence, this new suggestion was about the most objectionable to Lord Dane. He was very much given to jumping to conclusions upon impulse, and he did so now. From the first he had felt a latent conviction that Adelaide Errol had not told the truth: he had felt it that morning in the hall as she stood under the informal examination. This suggestion offered a solution to the mystery, and he adopted it with almost measureless anger, and with deep, deep pain. *She* to screen the destroyer of his poor son, her betrothed husband!

"Thank you for speaking of this, Bent," he said, his tone one of concentrated passion. "No doubt you are right; as you were before to-day, when you expressed an opinion that she must have seen something, which she had persistently denied to me. I remember the mention of the oath startled her in a strange degree: we will see what she says to it now."

A peremptory message brought the Lady Adelaide again into the hall: Lord Dane's mandates in his own home could not be disobeyed. She appeared to have called up a little bravery for the occasion; but it was a shallow pretence, and her very lips turned white as she walked up to Lord Dane. Mr. Lester rose to assist her as before, but Lord Dane checked him.

"*I* will deal with Lady Adelaide this time, Mr. Lester."

She stole a glance at the different expressions on the faces of those present—the curiosity of Mr. Apperly's, the impassiveness of the sergeant's, the compassion of Squire Lester's; but as she met the severity of Lord Dane's, a faint cry escaped her. He laid his hand upon her wrist, and spoke slowly:

"We have reason to think that your recent denial was false, Adelaide Errol; we believe that you did recognize the assailant of my son. Who was it?"

"I don't'know," she answered, an ashy hue overspreading her face.

"You *do* know: as we believe."

"I have said I do not know. It was too dark to recognize him," she added, scarcely able, as they all saw, to speak the words with her dry and bloodless lips.

Lord Dane would not put to her the leading question—Was it Ravensbird? He waited, never taking his stern gaze from her face.

"Once more: who was it that struggled with my son?"

"I do not know. Indeed, I do not."

"Then, if that be in truth the case, you will have no objection to testify to it on oath. Mr. Lester, will you officiate?"

Her face became scarlet; and a startled glance of terror —a silent appeal for mercy, rather—went up from it to those merciless ones around. The magistrate took a book from its place: he would have liked to refuse to act, but Lord Dane was resolute. And Mr. Lester thought little of the ceremony: he, at least, ever believed her to be true.

"It is a mere form," he gently whispered. "Nay, do not tremble so."

She turned and looked behind her, as if wondering whether there might not be some escape yet. Surely none. And there, in the background, stood Sophie Deffloe. If ever despair shone from hollow eyes, it shone then from Lady Adelaide's.

With hands that shook as they were raised, with words that trembled and faltered on her tongue, with cheeks that were fading again to the hue of the dead, she, Adelaide Errol, spoke the solemn oath before Heaven—that she had recognized neither Captain Dane nor his adversary.

And Lord Dane's suspicions of her truth, and almost
every one else's suspicions, had any entertained them, were
set at rest. But the suspicions of Sergeant Bent still
lingered.

CHAPTER VI.

ANOTHER PHASE OF THE NIGHT'S STORY.

RICHARD RAVENSBIRD, meanwhile, in returning to Danesheld, had encountered Herbert Dane. The gentleman was
at his favourite spot, the gate, where you have already seen
him more than once. Not perched upon it whistling, as
was his wont in gayer times, but leaning against it in
melancholy sadness. No fishing-rod to be spliced was in
his hand to-day, no light silver-mounted whip switched
time to his opera tunes. That the untimely fate of his
cousin was giving him true and lively concern, there could
be no manner of doubt. Exceedingly surprised he looked
to see Ravensbird approaching, unaccompanied by those
attentive guardians of the law.

"What! have they let you off, Ravensbird?"

"Could they do otherwise, Mr. Herbert?" was the response of Ravensbird, facing his questioner, as though he
disdained to shun inquiry.

"Do otherwise!" echoed Herbert Dane. "Well, I don't
know, Ravensbird. If Mitchel saw you throw my poor
cousin over——"

"But Mitchel did not see me," interrupted Ravensbird,
his piercing black eyes fixed full on the face of Herbert
Dane.

"I heard that he said so last night; said it in the hearing of several people. Has he eaten his words to-day?"

"No, sir, he has not. Mitchel never spoke the words;
it was a misconception altogether. _I_ also heard that he
had said so; and I thought he was trying to screen the real

offender. He has just now testified to my lord that he could not distinguish who the strugglers were. He would not have known Captain Dane but for his falling at his feet."

"How came the report to get about, then, that he recognized you?"

"Chiefly, I expect, through Mr. Apperly. He was more set against me than any one."

"And so, on the strength of the non-recognition, they have given you your liberty? My lord's grief must have made him lenient. I suppose you will hasten now to put the sea or some other formidable barrier between yourself and Dancsheld?"

"Why should I do that, sir? An innocent man does not fly like a craven."

"Innocent!" repeated Herbert, in a tone of ridicule, if not of scorn.

"Yes, sir; innocent."

"Ravensbird," said Herbert Dane, quietly, "it is of no use keeping on the exalted ropes before me. The words you spoke on this very spot yesterday morning, threatening vengeance on your master, would be enough to hang you. But——"

"Do you believe me guilty, Mr. Herbert?" interrupted Ravensbird, drawing nearer with those penetrating eyes of his.

"I was about to say, Ravensbird, that you are safe for me," proceeded Herbert Dane, unmindful of the interruption. "I saw that you dropped the words in the heat of passion, hardly conscious, if I may so express it, that I was within hearing to take cognizance of them. I was sorry for you at the time, feeling that Captain Dane's conduct was unwarrantable; and I shall certainly not array myself amongst your accusers. Moreover, were you gibbeted on that oak-tree there, it would not bring your master back to life."

"Sir," repeated Ravensbird, his tone very matter-of-fact, "I asked if you believed me guilty?"

"What a superfluous question! Do you suppose there's

a soul in the place that does not believe it, although you
have contrived to escape from your bonds."

"Pardon me, sir; I ask you whether *you* believe it?"

Herbert Dane felt annoyed at the persistency of the man.
"You ask me if I believe you guilty, when I have just said
I could hang you. I do."

"Then why don't you hang me?" returned Ravensbird.

"I have told you why. I don't care to go out of my way
to do you harm; and also because it could not benefit the
dead. But guilty, in a degree, you certainly are. Not,
perhaps, of wilful murder; it may be, that in struggling so
close to the edge, the fall was accidental."

The way in which Ravensbird stood his ground before
Herbert Dane—hardy, self-possessed, not a muscle of his
face moving, not a tremor in his voice, and his searching eyes
never once relinquishing their independent stare—astonished
that gentleman not a little.

"Then allow me to tell you, Mr. Herbert, that I am *not*
guilty. Let me tell you something more, sir. Shall I?"

"Well?" responded Herbert, lifting his questioning eyes.

"I believe I could put my finger on the guilty man. As
certain as that you and I are face to face, sir, I believe it."

"What do you mean?" asked Herbert Dane, after a pause
of blank surprise.

"I mean, sir, what I say. I may be wrong—I have no
proof; but I am content to wait for that. I know some
one besides myself who owed Captain Dane a grudge."

Herbert Dane stared at the speaker from head to foot,
uncertain what to make of his audacious words, his still
more audacious manner.

"You are thinking me too bold, I see, sir. But when an
innocent man is taken up on a charge of wilful murder, some
freedom of speech may be excused him."

"Freedom is one thing, Ravensbird; falsehood is another.
I believe you are telling me——"

"I am telling you the truth, sir," boldly interrupted
Ravensbird. "I believe I know who it was struggling on
the heights with my master, just as surely as if I had
witnessed it."

"Oh," said Herbert Dane, and he was quite unable to conceal the sarcasm of his tone, "then you were not a witness to the struggle?"

"No, sir, I was not; and for the best of all reasons—I was not within a mile of the place at the time. It has been proved, sir, that when that assault took place, I was at the Sailors' Rest, playing at dominoes—then, and for some time before it; and my lord and Mr. Apperly released me from custody because there was no pretext for keeping me in it."

"If it was really not yourself, and you do know who it was, you should say it," cried Herbert Dane, slowly.

"I judge otherwise, sir. I have no proof, and might not be believed. I prefer to bide my time. Do you still believe me guilty, Mr. Herbert?"

"Ravensbird, I do."

For a full minute Ravensbird gazed at him, as if unable to credit the avowal. Then his eyes fell, and he turned away.

"It may be that you do believe it," he said, speaking as it seemed more to himself than to Herbert. "In that case, all I can say is, that the time may come when we shall both be undeceived. I have sworn to my lord that I am not guilty, that I was not the assailant; I swear it again to you. Good-morning, Mr. Herbert."

Herbert Dane was still looking after the man as he disappeared in the distance, when Mitchel and the supervisor passed on their way from the castle. Herbert Dane accosted the former.

"So, Mitchel, after all the reports current last night and this morning, I hear that you now deny having accused Ravensbird!"

"It was a mistake, sir, people saying that I accused him. I thought it was sure to be Ravensbird—I believe I said as much, but I never said that I saw him, or that I recognized him. That was impossible by moonlight, standing where I did. It appears now that it could not have been Ravensbird, and I am vexed that he should have been subjected to any unpleasantness through me."

"Then you did *not* recognize Captain Dane's adversary?"

" I did not, sir."

" Mitchel's coat has been fished up this morning, Mr. Herbert Dane," put in the supervisor, desiring a little talk on his own score. " The waves must have left it high and dry on the beach last night, and Bill Gand's boat picked it up as he was coming in with the early tide. Captain Dane's hat has been washed ashore too; but perhaps you've heard that."

Herbert Dane nodded. He did not appear inclined to pursue the conversation; and the two men continued their way.

" I'll know, at any rate, what grounds they have for letting the fellow off," he said in soliloquy, as he turned his steps to the castle. " Every one said it *must* have been Ravensbird."

He had reached the gateway, when the hall door was suddenly opened by Bruff, who was showing out Mr. Apperly and Sergeant Bent. Herbert - accosted the lawyer; the sergeant walked on.

". We must wait a bit, Mr. Herbert," spoke the solicitor, in reply to a question; and his tones were excited and his face was red, for he had again taken up the idea of Ravensbird's guilt. " I can't question the good faith of the witnesses—I believe them to be honest; and Hawthorne and his wife, at all events, would be true to the Dane family; but that there's trickery at work is as sure as that you and I stand here. Bent knows it, he says. The hands of Hawthorne's clock were surreptitiously put back, or some other devilry."

" Ravensbird has just told me, with the coolest equanimity, that he was in the Sailors' Rest at the time of the fall; that it has been so proved to the satisfaction of Lord Dane," said Herbert.

" The insolence of the man! " apostrophized Mr. Apperly. " He boasts of it, does he ? In a manner it has been proved, and Lord Dane could only release him from custody; but our business will be to disprove it again. There are two fearfully suspicious facts against him; Bent has been noting them. One is, that he particularly called their attention to

Mrs. Hawthorne's parlour clock, with a secret view, of course, of getting them to observe that he was back at the inn by twenty minutes past eight; the other is, that he had been then away from the place for an hour and a half or so, and he refuses to state where he went to, or what he was doing. Let us wait awhile, Mr. Herbert?"

With a significant nod that spoke volumes, the lawyer hastened after Sergeant Bent. Herbert turned to Bruff, who had stood by during the conversation.

"What do you think of it, Bruff? Ravensbird asserts his innocence most positively."

"Well, sir, we don't—as upper servants—know what to think. If appearances had not been so much against him —that is, the quarrel with his master and his revengeful threats—Ravensbird is about the last we should have suspected. He never seemed a revengeful man. Then, again, the evidence has posed us: if he was at the Sailors' Rest, he could not have been on the heights."

"Very true," replied Herbert Dane, speaking in a mechanical sort of manner, as if his thoughts were elsewhere. "Apperly talks of a suspicion that the clock might have been put back—but I don't know."

Bruff shook his head. "If it was put back at all, it must have been put back a good three-quarters of an hour; allowing that Ravensbird tore back at top speed after doing his work on the heights: and I don't see how all of them could have fallen into the trap; one or two were safe to have detected it. Three-quarters of an hour is a long time to be mistaken in, sir."

"Of course it is," replied Herbert. "It appears to be a mysterious affair altogether."

"Did you hear, sir, that my Lady Adelaide was a witness to the scuffle?" asked Bruff, who loved to talk of marvels as well as most people.

"No."

"It is true, sir. You knew about her having run in from the heights last night, screaming. Up to this morning she denied that she had seen anything; but when she was had into the hall before them all—my lord, and Squire Lester,

and Bent, and them—she couldn't hold out, and told the
truth. She had seen two men struggling, and one of them
fall, and it nearly terrified her to death."

" Did she recognize them?" inquired Herbert Dane,
some eagerness in his tone.

" No, sir, she did not. They have just had her in again,
and put her upon her oath as to the point."

" Put her upon her oath!" repeated Herbert Dane.

" They did, indeed, Mr. Herbert," replied Bruff, dropping
his voice. " It was quite cruel, I think. By what I can
gather, Sergeant Bent asked that the oath should be admin-
istered, for he had got it into his head that she did perhaps
recognize the captain's assailant, and was afraid to confess
it. I hope they are satisfied now. "

" Did she take it ? "

" Oh, yes, sir. Knowing that she had not recognized the
man, she made no objection, I believe. Sophie has been
telling me about it. Her ladyship just saw the outlines of
two forms, and that one of them fell ; but she saw no more :
and they might have known that, without troubling her to
swear to it. She was only in the ruins, peeping out."

Herbert Dane lifted his head with an aspect of relief.
" I am heartily glad she did not. It is not well that ladies—
girls—should be brought into these things. What a pity
they troubled her ? If the scuffle took place at the edge of
the heights—as we have unhappy evidence that it did—and
she was in the ruins, it is scarcely possible that she could
have recognized them. However, it may be a good thing to
have set the doubt at rest."

Bruff looked at him ; he was speaking with so dreamy an
air, as if his thoughts were far away.

" Open the door, Bruff. I am going in to my lord."

In his chair of state still, but alone now, sat Lord Dane.
He welcomed his nephew with more cordiality than he had
evinced to him of late. Great grief softens the heart.
Herbert sat down and listened patiently to the heads of
evidence which Lord Dane began to recount. He told it
all, even to his having caused Lady Adelaide to take the
oath, and Herbert did not interrupt it by a word.

" Do you think Ravensbird can be guilty ? " inquired Herbert, when it was over.

" Ravensbird is guilty," was the peer's emphatic reply. " Every probability points to him. Put Ravensbird out of the question, and who else can we suspect ? Harry had not an enemy in the world. All Danesheld loved him."

" True," replied Herbert, in the same mechanical tone he had once or twice used to Bruff.

" It is a most unfortunate thing that Adelaide did not take better notice, as she was there," resumed Lord Dane. " Bent thought she had recognized Ravensbird and was afraid to say it, or else was screening him for that French-woman's sake. A ridiculous notion, and I am sorry I took it up. The fact is, the poor child was so utterly terrified last night, that she could not get over it, and denied she had seen anything, which made me suspicious."

" In one point of view it is a good thing Lady Adelaide did not recognize him," observed Herbert. " It would have been most disagreeable for her to have to give evidence in a court of justice."

Lord Dane assented ; and the interview was interrupted by the entrance of Mr. Lester, who had been sitting with Lady Dane. Herbert left the hall and went upstairs, hoping to find Adelaide.

She was not in the drawing-room, neither was Lady Dane. He was looking about, when he saw Sophie passing in the corridor.

" C'est toi, Sophie la Belle ! " exclaimed Herbert, who had been a little given to decorous flirtation with the waiting-maid, and to making use of his stock of French. " Where's Lady Adelaide ? "

" I have no time for your nonsense this morning, Mr. Herbert," crossly responded Sophie. " My young lady's ill."

" Ill ? "

" Ill, and lying down ; and I am going to the kitchen to make her some herb tea—which the English know nothing of doing, poor ignorants. My Lady Dane is with her now, gone to have her scold out."

" A scold for what ? "

"And my young lady deserves it," added the girl in her
national freedom of speech. "Why does she go and upset
herself and the house for nothing? If she didn't see anything beyond just the scuffle, why she didn't; she need not
have made all that fuss. Allez!"

Sophie disappeared, diving down the stairs towards the
domestic regions. And Mr. Herbert Dane, seeing nothing
to be gained by remaining at the castle, took his departure
from it.

But another phase of the story was about to arise. As
Herbert Dane was strolling along with the listless air of
one who has nothing on earth to do, he encountered a man
well known in the locality—better known indeed than
trusted. His name was Drake, and his ostensible occupation
was that of a fisherman, to which he added as much petty
smuggling as he could accomplish with impunity; his boat
being given to hover round foreign vessels, and bring away
anything in a small way that it could. He touched his blue
woollen cap, made in the form of a nightcap, by way of
saluting Mr. Herbert Dane.

"A fine horrid tale I've been hearing of, sir, since our
boat got in!" he began. "Folks be saying as the captain's
murdered, and his body gone floating out to sea, Davy Jones
only knows to what latitude. Be it true, sir?"

"It is an incomprehensible affair altogether, Drake," was
the answer, "but I fear it is only too true. The body has
not been found. They have been dragging for it all the
morning."

"I saw 'em," responded Drake. "Who was it attacked
him?"

"Ah, that's the question."

"They be saying down the village yonder, that it turns
out not to have been the captain's servant, who was first
took up for it."

"I make no doubt they are."

"Well now, master, perhaps I can throw a bit of light
upon this here matter. 'Twon't be much, though."

"You!" returned Herbert, gazing at Drake.

"Yes, me. I had been up to Nut Cape, for I wanted to

have a talk with old—that is—that is, I had been up the road past the castle——"

"Never mind; speak out, Drake," interrupted Herbert Dane significantly, in reference to the man's hesitation. "You had been up to Nut Cape to hold one of your confabs with that old sinner, Beecher; that's about the English of it. But if I saw the pair of you running in a boat-load of contraband goods under my very eyes, you might do it for me. I am not a preventive-officer, and I concern myself with no one's business but my own."

"Well, I had been up to old Beecher's," acknowledged Drake, "but only for a yarn—indeed, sir, for nothing else. I stopped there longer than I thought for, and was coming back full pelt, afraid my boat might put off without me, when I heard voices a-quarrelling. I was on the brow of the heights—I mostly goes and comes that way, instead of the road—and was just abreast o' the chapel ruins, when my ears caught the sound. They come from the direction of the castle, and I cut across to see what the row might be. Standing on the grass, midway between the ruins and the castle, were two men—the one was speaking in a loud angered tone, and I had got almost close to him, when I saw it was Captain Dane. Seeing that, of course I cut away again."

Herbert Dane paused for some moments. "Where do you say this was?" he resumed.

"Between the ruins and the castle, a trifle nearest the castle, maybe. The other man was a stranger."

"A stranger!" involuntarily repeated Herbert Dane, who had probably been expecting to hear that it was Ravensbird.

"Leastways he was a stranger to me; I'd never seen him before, to my knowledge. A big, hulking sort of fellow, with a pack in his hand."

"What sort of a pack?"

"Well, I don't know; it might have been a box or a parcel. 'Twas dark and biggish. It had been on the ground before I got to 'em, but the man swung it up in his hand, and then on his back. I didn't stop to take much notice, seeing the other was the captain. The captain was blowing him up."

"In what terms?" cried Herbert, with eagerness. "Can you remember?"

"'How dare you, fellow?' I heard him say, and that was all I caught distinct. But I heard 'em both at it, railing like, as I steered off."

"What time was this?"

"Well now, I can't be positive to five minutes," was Drake's answer. "Half-past eight, maybe."

"Drake, are you, sure that it was a stranger, and not Ravensbird?" impressively questioned Herbert Dane, after a pause.

"Have I no eyes to see with?" was the retort. "'Twas no more like Ravensbird than 'twas like me or you. 'Twas a chap rising five foot ten, with long arms and broad shoulders."

"You must speak of this affair before Lord Dane."

"I was on my way to the castle now to do it. I knows my duty. Not but what I'd rather go ten miles t'other way than face his lordship."

A smile crossed Herbert Dane's otherwise perplexed face. "He is not so indulgent to you suspected smugglers as you would like, and you fear him. But if you can help his lordship to trace out this assaulter of his son, it will no doubt atone for some old scores, Drake."

"Anyway it's my duty, having seen what I did see, and I'm not going to shirk it, sir," was Mr. Drake's reply.

He touched his woollen cap, and proceeded towards the castle. Herbert Dane continued his way to Danesheld, with a view to inquiring whether any later news had turned up. Perplexed, indeed, he was, and he could not divest himself of the suspicion that the man whom Drake had seen in dispute with Harry Dane *was* Ravensbird, in spite of the present different description and of the pack.

"One's eyes get deceived in the moonlight," he soliloquized. "As to the pack Drake speaks of, it may have been a small valise that Ravensbird had been to the castle to fetch away. On the other hand, Drake may of course be correct in saying that it was a stranger. In that case, Ravensbird——"

Herbert Dane's reflections were brought to a standstill. Turning a sharp bend in the road, he came upon Mr. Ravensbird himself, seated upon a milestone that lay back from the path. He was in deep thought and did not look up.

"You are in a brown study, Ravensbird."

The man turned abruptly at the salutation. "Oh, it's you, Mr. Herbert Dane! I was lost in last night's work, sir; and did not hear you come up."

"Ravensbird," returned Herbert Dane, a whole world of candour in his voice and countenance, "I consider myself bound to mention that your denial of having attacked your master has been possibly in a degree confirmed. Observe, I say possibly."

A peculiar smile, somewhat cynical in its aspect, flitted over the features of Mr. Ravensbird.

"It appears that another man attacked Captain Dane on the heights last night; at any rate, Captain Dane and another were having a quarrel there together; and if the description given to me of this other be correct, it was not you."

The smile on Ravensbird's face changed to a look of astonishment. He did not reply: only fixed his questioning eye on the speaker.

"Now, it's only natural to infer that whoever that man might be, he caused the catastrophe. A stranger, tall and broad, he has been described to me, carrying a pack on his back. Possibly a travelling hawker, who may have importuned Captain Dane to make a purchase, and was roused to anger on refusal. One fact appears to be indisputable: that they were contending angrily, and such men, loose characters often, have been known to commit evil deeds on very slight provocation."

"Who saw or heard this?" asked Ravensbird. "You, sir?"

"I!" haughtily returned Herbert Dane. "What a very senseless question! Should I, or any friend of Captain Dane's, keep such a thing secret? The man who witnessed it was Joe Drake. Not a very reliable gentleman in a general way, but I think he speaks the truth in this instance. I met him a few minutes ago, and he stopped me to tell it. He was on his way to the castle to inform my lord."

"He has been tardy in declaring this," was the sarcastic comment of Ravensbird.

"Not at all. He could not declare it at sea, where he had been all night. He knew nothing of the accident to Captain Dane until he came in just now with the last of the tide. He was on the heights last night, coming down from Beecher's, and witnessed the dispute or whatever it was. The time tallies pretty well; he thinks it was about half-past eight."

Ravensbird made no immediate reply. His eyes were fixed on vacancy. Herbert Dane resumed:

"When you told me that you could place your finger upon the offender, I assumed it to be spoken in vain boast, if not in deliberate deceit. It has now struck me that you also may have seen this encounter. Was it so?"

"I—I was not aware—that Captain Dane—I did not know of any encounter of his with a stranger," replied Ravensbird, his tones full of hesitating uncertainty, and his eyes still wearing the look of a man in a dream.

"Possibly this man was no stranger to your master?" said Herbert Dane, scanning him searchingly.

"Possibly not," was the reply of Ravensbird, waking from his reverie. "It is not probable that a stranger would attack him to his death."

"Still less probable that a friend would do so, Ravensbird. What is perplexing you?"

"That, sir, is a question that you must pardon me for declining to answer. The more I hear of this business the more it does perplex me; I'll say that much. Daneshell may make very sure of one thing—that I will not leave a stone unturned to unravel the mystery. It has accused *me* of being the offender, Mr. Herbert Dane; I'll try and make it eat its words before I die."

Drake's story, in so far as that such a man as he described

had been in the neighbourhood at the time, was corrobo-
rated in rather a remarkable manner by Squire Lester.
That gentleman had been riding home from a distance, and
passed the castle about the hour named by Drake, half-
past eight, or a little before it. Only a few yards past the
castle he met a man walking in the middle of the road, and
his horse shied at him. "A big ill-looking man, with a
flat box strapped on his back." Mr. Lester said he took
particular notice of him, and should know him again, he
was sure, for the moon shone full on his features. He
turned and looked after him, and saw him quit the road and
go on the heights. This was close to the castle.

Every possible search was set on foot to discover this
packman. Lynx-eyed Lawyer Apperly turned Drake inside
out, metaphorically speaking, and Squire Lester's description to the police was elaborately minute. But the man
could not be found or heard of.

Neither was the body of Captain Dane. The drags did
their work effectually, but they brought forth nothing from
the covetous sea. There could not be a doubt that he was
indeed dead ; and the Dane flag floated in sadness half-mast
high above Dane Castle.

CHAPTER VII.

MORTALITY.

MISFORTUNES seldom come singly. If a trite saying, it is a
true one.

A telegram was despatched to Paris acquainting the
Honourable Geoffry Dane with his brother's death, and
more explanatory letters followed it. But when the mis-
sives arrived they did not find their owner. The Honourable Geoffry had departed from Paris, nobody knew exactly
whither ; he had spoken of Italy, of Malta, and of other

places. Upon this information reaching Lord Dane, he
wrote to the family bankers, who were generally kept cognizant by Mr. Dane of his movements, desiring them to
forward to his son the letters he enclosed, which was done.

Herbert Dane meanwhile was taking advantage of this
distressing calamity to renew his former friendly intercourse with Lord Dane; to make good, once again, his old
footing at the castle. He had done nothing in particular to
forfeit it. Lord Dane had acquired a habit of finding fault
with him on the score of his idleness; Lady Dane had
suspected that her niece Adelaide might be growing to like
him too well, and both had simultaneously discouraged his
visits. Lord Dane had offered to procure him an appointment abroad. Herbert Dane declined to go abroad, and this
gave some offence. Altogether, his visits of late had been
rare and his welcome cold.

But in this sad event minor interests and animosities were
forgotten. Herbert Dane brought to the castle any scrap of
news he could pick up, and he was eagerly looked for and
welcomed. He it was, apart from the police, who exerted
himself to gain tidings of the man with the pack, and though
he was unsuccessful, Lord Dane did not the less appreciate
the efforts. But the one great reward that Herbert Dane
sought, he had not yet obtained—the sight of Adelaide Errol.

She kept her room for days; pale, wan, timid; starting,
as it seemed, at shadows. Lady Dane thought the fright
that night on the heights had in some way affected her
nervous system, and she called in Mr. Wild. Mr. Wild
thought the same, and in addition concluded that she was
grieving for her betrothed husband, Harry Dane.

It was no affectation, no imaginary illness: they could
see that. She was ill in mind, and ill in body. But how
greatly she strove against it, was known to herself alone.
Adelaide Errol possessed a stronger mind than most persons
of her sex and age, and a more indomitable will; and when,
after the seclusion of a few days, she forced herself to
appear downstairs again, the household noticed no difference
in her, except that she looked wan and was unnaturally calm
—a calmness that was rudely disturbed at a word spoken by

Mr. Wild. Adelaide was sitting on a sofa near the surgeon and Lady Dane; she had been answering the doctor's questions, saying that she felt "quite well" now, when he inadvertently mentioned the name of Captain Dane. As though it had been the signal for some feeling, pent up within her, to give way, she burst into a violent flood of tears; all her self-possession had deserted her, her assumption of coldness was gone.

Mr. Wild drew his chair closer to her. He waited until she was calm, and then laid his fingers upon the black crêpe at her wrists to give impressiveness to his words. Lady Dane, from her seat on the other side the hearth, looked on in silence.

"There is some great and secret grief upon you, Lady Adelaide. Take an experienced man's advice, my dear young lady, and *disclose it*. When once these sorrows are spoken of, they lose half their sting."

Her only answer was a movement of pain. She flung her thin hands before her eyes in very tremor.

"And when any self-reproach is mingled with the grief, it should above all be told, for it is in the nature of self-reproach to exaggerate itself; let silence be kept long enough, and it will become a very vulture preying on the vitals. Come, let me make a guess and help you. The severe reflection cast on you by Lord Dane has sunk into your conscience to the point of torment. Is it not so?"

He alluded to certain words spoken by Lord Dane in his pain and anger, when he first became aware that her denial, of having witnessed anything on the heights, was false. He reproached her with having been in a secondary degree the destroyer of his son. Had she confessed what she had seen, so that rescue and help might have hastened to Harry, perhaps his life had been saved.

"You are right," replied Adelaide, the tears streaming through her fingers; "in a secondary degree I am the cause of Harry's death, for I might have sent assistance to him in time, and I did not. It will be a burthen on my conscience for ever. How shall I bear it? I could not *live* if they took me up and tried me for it."

" *Tried* you for it ! "

She took her trembling hands from before her face, and then saw that an additional auditor was present whom she had not expected. It was Herbert Dane. He had come in unheard during her burst of emotion, and was leaning over Lady Dane's chair in mute astonishment. As if his presence recalled her to her senses, she turned to Mr. Wild with an intimation that the subject was at an end, smoothed her face to composure, and sat calm as a statue.

"I shall be all right soon, Mr. Wild. Don't talk about my health again, please; and Geoffry Dane will be at home in a day or two, and the house won't seem so dull. He—oh, is it you, Mr. Herbert Dane? I beg your pardon."

She half rose from her seat to return his greeting; rose in too great a flurry, as it seemed, to see his outstretched hand. The interview was broken up. The surgeon, her curious expression "tried" still echoing in his ears, went downstairs to pay his daily visit to Lord Dane—who had never ceased to be a patient, and was in a more precarious state of health than the world suspected—and Lady Dane descended with him.

"I am so glad to see you better, Adelaide," began Herbert Dane, when they were alone; and he took her unwilling hand, but she drew it from him again. "My darling, what has been amiss with you?"

"Please not to talk," she answered, in quite a tone of affectation. "Mr. Wild says I ought not to exert myself."

. It struck Herbert Dane, as he retreated, that she was under the influence of some inward and violent agitation; and that this assumption of what might almost be called childishness was only put on to conceal its signs.

"It is the first time we have met since that fatal night, Adelaide," he resumed, his voice full of tender confidence; "let me now say how deeply I felt for the terror to which you were unhappily subjected. You must try and forget it; time is a great healer of all things. And oh! Adelaide——"

"I asked you not to speak to me, please," she interrupted, in the same tone as before, but there appeared to be something the matter with her breathing, though she was doing her best to conceal it. "I am sorry you came up."

Herbert Dane look at her keenly. He crossed to the sofa and sat down by her side and essayed again to take her hand. But she rose at once and went to a distance.

"Adelaide! do you wish to avoid me?"

"I should like to avoid every one,—especially you, if you begin to talk of the past. I have taken a draught of the waters of Lethe; when it has quite done its work, I shall begin a new life, and never, never recur to the past again."

"Will you tell me what you mean?" he asked. He had risen and would have stood by her side; but she immediately went from him to her seat on the sofa. He put his elbow on the mantelpiece, and followed her with his questioning eyes. She bent her head downwards for a moment, and then raised it with what looked like a sudden resolution, and there was a pink flush upon her cheeks.

"Indeed, I am not equal to saying much to-day. You heard what Mr. Wild accused me of being—a sort of accessory to Harry Dane's death. Whether I was that, or not, can never perhaps be decided; the fall itself might have killed him. But of one other thing my conscience most bitterly convicts me—cruel deceit. I must try and atone for it."

"In what manner?" inquired Herbert, after a pause.

"Well, I shall see—I scarcely know yet; real atonement, of course, there can never be. I hope you will forgive me for what you may deem caprice or unkindness; but, to begin with, I must request you never again to speak to me of—of love."

"Adelaide!"

"It is all over. In these few days of seclusion and sorrow I have formed resolutions, and nothing can shake them. I will at least not continue the deceit to Harry now he is dead, though I was heartless enough to do it when he was living. I shall see you often, no doubt; you will be here as a relative of the family; but I pray you henceforth to forget the past."

" I think this shock must be turning your brain," was his reply.

"Not so. My brain is as clear as yours. Do not come nearer, please; you cannot alter my resolution."

" What have I done to offend you ? "

" Nothing personally. But I will not be false to Harry Dane. I could not be so from very fear; I should think his ghost would haunt me. He was my betrothed husband."

" You did not care for him," returned Herbert Dane, regarding her curiously.

" There it is. Had I cared for him I might regret him less—if you can understand the feeling. I do care for him now."

" But not to wed yourself to his memory. Surely you do not mean that ? "

" Perhaps not. I feel so miserable in this house that I think if any one came and asked me to leave it with them I would go. Stay! not with *you*—you joined with me in practising that deceit on Harry. I beg your pardon for saying this, Mr. Herbert Dane: I am afraid you will not understand my feeling, but indeed I cannot help myself."

" Adelaide, my darling, I think I do understand your feelings, and allow for them and pity them ; they will wear away, as the nervous shock you have experienced wears away. Not at present will I tease you or press you : I know that you love me ; that you love no one else in the world ; and I am content to wait my time."

He spoke with tender consideration. Adelaide flung her hands before her eyes: she did indeed love him, and no other. He took a step towards her, when in a sudden access of what might be called fear, as if doubting her own firmness, she rose from her chair and fled from the room, almost upsetting Lady Dane who was entering it.

" Mr. Wild finds my husband not so well this morning," she remarked to Herbert. " I think he is vexing himself, Herbert, at not hearing from Geoffry."

Lady Dane was correct in her surmise. Lord Dane was not only vexed, but angry ; there had been ample time, as ho believed, for the Honourable Geoffry to have received the news and respond to it.

" Geoffry might have written at least, if he did not choose to come," he observed that same evening to his wife ; " it's just like him."

Alas ! Geoffry Dane came all too soon. Not himself, but what remained of him. He had travelled to the neighbourhood of Rome, and on his arrival had been attacked by the malaria, and in three days he was dead. The letter written by Lord Dane, and duly forwarded by the bankers, was not in time to reach him, and he died in ignorance of his brother's fate. His personal attendant, Wilkins, sent the unhappy news to Lord Dane. Even as he, the bereaved father, held the letter in his hand, the body was already on its way home for interment, having been embarked at Civita Vecchia.

How strangely solemn were the tidings to the neighbourhood ! The death of the one brother following so closely on that of the other, seemed to bring with it they knew not what of superstition. Still more grievously did it strike on Dane Castle. Almost before the half-mast flag had been lowered for Harry, it was lowered again for the heir, Geoffry. Lord and Lady Dane were bowed to the very earth with grief : those they had lost were their only children, and whispers went abroad that neither would long survive them. Upon Lady Dane, especially, the tidings seemed to tell with terrible effect ; the servants gazed at her in fear, and said they could see the " changes for death " in her face.

On a gay morning in May, a hearse, whose sable hue and mournful plumes contrasted unpleasantly with the earth's sunny brightness, arrived at Dane Castle, having travelled from Southampton attended by the valet, Wilkins. The burden it bore was taken out, and deposited in the castle death-room.

Why was it called so gloomy a name ?—a question frequently asked by strangers. Simply because the room was consecrated to the dead. When a member of the Dane family died, the body was placed within it to await interment, to lie in state, it may be said, and the public were admitted to the sight. The apartment was never used for any other purpose; a cold gray room, perfectly empty, with a stone floor, and narrow windows, which were too high for the tallest man to look through, and which were not made to open. Tradition went that when any one of the Danes was about to leave the world, that floor would become spotted as with great patches of damp, remaining perfectly dry and unstained in others.

The trestles were brought from their closet and set up in the middle of the room, and the coffin was placed upon them. Lord Dane was wheeled in in his chair, Lady Dane glided in and stood by his side, both struggling to suppress their grief until they should be alone. One or two of the upper men-servants were present, and certain workmen, who had been waiting in attendance, prepared to unseal the coffins.

At that moment Wilkins, suddenly becoming aware of what was intended, stepped forward, arrested the workmen by a motion of the hand, and addressed Lord Dane.

"My lord—I beg your pardon—but is it a safe thing to do, think you? May there not be danger? He died of malignant fever."

A disagreeable feeling fell upon all, and some involuntarily drew a step back. Lord Dane reflected.

"I do not fear infection," he presently said. "Let those who do fear it retire; but I will see the remains of my son. Stories have been told before now of—of—others being substituted for those supposed to be dead."

Wilkins turned to Lord Dane, astonishment on his face and tears in his eyes.

"My lord, is it possible you can suspect——"

"No reflection on you, Wilkins," interrupted his lordship; "I did not mean to imply any. There is a difference between satisfaction from mere conviction, and satisfaction from ocular demonstration. I have no moral doubt whatever that my dear son Geoffry lies within that coffin; nevertheless, I choose to be indisputably assured of the fact. Retire," he somewhat sharply added to the servants; "and do you," nodding to the mechanics, "proceed with your work. Had you not also better leave us?"

The last words were addressed to Lady Dane. She simply shook her head, and waited.

It was a long process, for the lead had to be unsoldered. But it was accomplished at last. The domestics had quitted the room, all except Bruff.

Lord Dane looked at him in a questioning manner.

"*I* have no fear, my lord. Allow me to see the last of poor Mr. Geoffry."

Geoffry Dane it was, unmistakably ; and less changed than might have been expected. A long, yearning look from all, a few stifled sobs from the childless mother, and the coffins were re-closed for ever. Then they left the room, and the public, those who chose to come, were admitted.

An incident took place that night in the house, that caused some unpleasant commotion. It happened that Sophie was suffering from a cough ; it had clung to her some weeks, and was very troublesome at night. She was in the habit of taking a soothing decoction for it, made of herbs—tisane, as she called it ; and this she carried regularly upstairs when she went to bed. On this night she forgot it, or it may be rather said that she would not go down for it, she felt nervous at passing through the long corridors, remembering what was in the house. She had been kept late with Lady Adelaide, and knew the household would be no longer below. But no sleep could she obtain. Her cough proved unusually severe. At length, out of patience, she rose from her bed, determined to brave ghostly fancies and lonely corridors, and fetch her tisane.

Wrapping herself up, she started, carrying a hand-lamp. Her way led her down the best staircase, for she slept in a room adjoining Lady Adelaide's, and through the long dreary stone passage, past the death-room. How Sophie scuttered along, how her heart beat and her skin crept as she passed the door, she would have been ashamed to acknowledge in broad daylight. In common with the generality of the French of her grade and class, she was superstitiously afraid of being in the presence of the dead—and they are more so I think than are Englishwomen—although she had boldly avowed to Lady Adelaide her disbelief in "reve-

nants." But there is an old proverb, "More haste, less
speed," and poor Sophie received an exemplification of its
truth; for so great was her haste, that in passing the
very spot, the dreaded door, she lost one of her slippers.
With a little cry of terror at the stoppage *there*, Sophie
snatched it up in her hand, did not wait to put it on, but
tore on to the housekeeper's room.

The tisane was inside the fender, where it had been
placed to retain warmth. Sophie took up the jug and put
it on the table for a moment whilst she drew breath, after
the running and the fright, and put on the refractory slipper.
She was stooping to accomplish the latter, when a noise
close above her head interrupted her.

It was nothing but the time-piece on the mantelshelf
striking the half-hour after midnight. But Sophie's
nerves were unhinged, and it startled her beyond self-
control. She shrieked, and grasped the nearest thing to
her, which happened to be a chair; she hid her face upon
it, and wondered how in the world she could muster
courage to get back to her room.

Back she must get, somehow; for the longer she stayed,
the worse she grew. "If ever I leave my tisane downstairs
again," quoth Sophie, "may a ghost run away with me,
that's all!" She took up the jug, drew her cloak round
her, and began to speed back again; not very fast this time,
for fear of spilling the tisane.

Poor Sophie! the real fright was coming. As she gained
the corridor in which was situated the death-room, her hair
nearly stood on end. A perfect horror seized her in that
moment of passing the dreaded door. If you ever experienced the same uncontrollable midnight terror, reader,
you will understand Sophie's. Her eyes irresistibly, and in
spite of her will, turned to the door, fascinated as by the
averted power of the basilisk; had her very life depended
on it, she could not have averted them. In the same
instant, a hollow, wailing sound, as of a groan, broke from
within the stillness of the room.

Almost paralysed, nearly bereft of her senses, Sophie
fell against the door, and the movement caused it to open,

as though it had been imperfectly latched; yet Sophie knew that the door had been securely locked the previous evening at dusk. There came another groan, and what looked like a flood of white light from the room; and the miserable Sophie, breaking into unearthly shrieks, fled along the corridor, dropping the jug and the tisane with a crash and a splash! That those hermetic solderings and fastenings had come undone, and what they confined had risen, and was pursuing her, was the least of her imaginings.

Her cries ascended through the broad open well, as it was called, where a staircase had once been, to the floors above, and echoed through the length and breadth of the house. Out came the terrified servants, and a peal rang from the bell of Lord Dane; Lady Adelaide, a bad sleeper now, opened her door and stood at it, her face as white as her maid's.

When they gathered the account of the trembling Sophie, some of the braver of the domestics proceeded to the death-room, and there the cause was made clear.

Kneeling on the stone floor beside the coffin, lost to all outward things save her grief, a white dressing-gown only thrown over her night-clothes, was Lady Dane. The sounds of pain and sorrow had come from her; and the "white light," as Sophie had described, from her lamp. Not for a long time could they prevail upon the unhappy lady to return to her own chamber. In vain they urged upon her that she would surely catch her death of cold. "What matters it?" she murmured. "Harry first, Geoffry next; both gone, what signifies death, or anything else, that may come to me?"

Geoffry was buried in the family vault, amidst much pomp and ceremony, as befitted, according to the world's usages, the late heir of the Danes. Lord Dane was too feeble to attend the funeral, the recent events had greatly increased his bodily illness, and he seemed as a man shattered. The new heir attended as chief mourner, accompanied by hosts of friends.

The new heir was Herbert Dane. He it was who had stepped into the Honourable Geoffry's place, and become the presumptive successor to the title, the rich and wide

domains. Not less to his own astonishment than to that of
his neighbours, was he there. He could not realise his
position; could scarcely believe in it. Was it he himself?
he would ask, when he awoke in the morning; was he
really a man of importance, the future Lord of Dane, or
was he the obscure young fellow who used to sit on the
gate mending his old fishing-rod, without a coin to buy a
new one? At odd moments, a question stole over him,
whether his heirship was safe and sure. Every probability
pointed to the fact that Harry Dane must be dead; but it
had not been indisputably proved. Lord Dane said he had
heard of such frauds as one dead man being buried surreptitiously for another. Herbert Dane knew that it was no
very uncommon case for a man supposed to be dead, but of
whose death there was no certain proof, to return to the
world's stage again. It was a notion that did not appear
to cross the mind of Danesheld, but it certainly did that of
the heir; unpleasantly so; and it seemed to him that he
would almost have forfeited his new heirship to set the
doubt at rest, one way or the other. Lord Dane retained
not a grain of hope—he believed his younger son to be as
surely dead as he knew the elder one to be—Herbert Dane
was now his indisputable heir, and from henceforth he was
to be called by his second name, Geoffry. Geoffry was a
favourite name of the Danes. From the creation of the
barony, more than two-thirds of the lords had borne it, and
it was held (another of their superstitions) that those who
did so bear it were more lucky and reigned more happily
than the rest. Herbert Dane had been christened Herbert
Geoffry, his friends calling him Herbert, not to interfere
with his cousin Geoffry, the heir. Now that the succession
had lapsed to him, he was never more to be Herbert, but
Geoffry.

The words heedlessly spoken by the servants, that their
lady might be catching her death, when they found her on
the floor by the coffin, were destined to be borne out more
literally than such words usually are. Whether it was the
kneeling so long on the cold stones in the chilly night, or the
scantiness of the apparel she had thrown on, or the change

from the warm bed she had been lying in, certain it was that a violent cold, accompanied with inward inflammation, attacked Lady Dane. Mr. Wild said it was pleurisy; the physician, summoned in haste from the county town, called it by a more scientific name; unlearned people supposed it to be inflammation of the lungs; and it matters little what it was called, Lady Dane was in imminent danger.

She lay in her spacious and most comfortable bedroom. The servants, moving softly, were anxious and attentive; the doctors unremitting; the neighbourhood concerned. Could life have been kept in Lady Dane by earthly means, they were not wanting; but when the time comes for its departure, who may prolong its stay? Lady Dane was dying, and she knew it.

On the third morning, when the physician paid his visit and was gone again, a rumour went through the household that the great man had said, in confidence to Mr. Wild, that it was a hopeless case.

"*She'll* make the third then," observed Sophie Deffloe with equanimity. "I thought it would have been my lord."

"What's that?" cried the butler, turning to the Frenchwoman.

"Why, when two die close together in a family, it's well known there'll soon be a third. I've remarked it scores of times in my own country."

"What a marvellous country it must be!" sarcastically rejoined Bruff, who was sincerely attached to his lord and lady, and could not bear the possible death of either alluded to without pain. "A nice place to live in!"

"Nicer than yours," retorted Sophie. "You may sneer as long as you like, Mr. Bruff, but you only observe. The captain was the first; Mr. Dane was the second; and her ladyship will be the third. Wait and see."

"Perhaps there'll be a fourth," said Mr. Bruff, aggravatingly. "My lady's a trifle better to-day than she was yesterday; let me tell you that, mam'selle."

Bruff should have said a little easier, not better. Better, Lady Dane was not; easier, she was; but it was in the relief from pain that mercifully precedes death.

Adelaide Errol was sitting alone with her aunt in the afternoon; the once careless girl seemed more fitted now for a sad room than a gay one. How changed she was since the night that had brought to her such terror, even strangers were beginning to see. Her brilliant colour had faded, her rounded form had grown thin; her spirits were unequal, her step was languid, her manner subdued. She sat in her aunt's invalid chair, her cheek pressed upon her right hand, her eyes fixed vacantly on the fire. Lady Dane was speaking to her in her weak voice of the future; but Adelaide, at the best, seemed indifferent to it.

"Come here to me, Adelaide," at length said the invalid. "Why are you so sad?" she asked, as Adelaide stood at the bed, a vivid blush dyeing her cheeks at the question.

"Child, I shall not be long here, and I would ask——"

"Oh, aunt!" interrupted Adelaide in a tone of pain.

"Do not distress yourself, my dear," was the calm rejoinder. "It causes me no distress. I have a Friend in heaven, Adelaide, and I know He will welcome me to His Father's home. The world has become to me too sad to live in. I shall be *glad* to go from it; and my husband will, I am certain, very speedily follow me. He, in his bed below, Adelaide; I, in this one; and neither of us can see the other for a last farewell."

"Yes you will," said Adelaide, the tears raining from her eyes. "Lord Dane is up, and they are going to bring him here this evening."

"Can they do it? Thank Heaven for that comfort. But whence arises this strange sadness of yours? I do *not* think it is caused by Harry's death."

"It was a dreadful death, aunt," shivered Adelaide, shunning the question.

"Ay, a dreadful death," murmured Lady Dane. "Child! let there be neither concealment nor equivocation between us in these my last hours. I believed that you did not love Harry; that you would have loved Herbert had you dared. If you do love him, there is nothing now to prevent your marrying him; and in that case, you need not go to Mrs.

Grant's, which would be a poor home for you after this. Tell me the truth."

Adelaide Errol was visibly agitated as she bent over her aunt, who had taken her hands and held her there. Speak she must, there was no escape; but even Lady Dane, dying as she was, observed how violently her heart beat.

"I do not wish to marry Herbert Dane."

"He is Geoffry now, Adelaide. He will succeed his uncle; he will be Lord Dane."

"I know. But I did not like Harry so much as I have done since his death. And I—I will not yet put another in his place. Herbert—Geoffry, I am forgetting too—I shall never put there."

"Then shall you make up your mind to go to Mrs. Grant's?"

"I suppose so. It will be very miserable, no doubt; but —oh aunt, I wish Harry was back in life again! I would marry him the next hour."

She drew away from the bed in a fit of hysterical tears as she spoke. Perhaps the contrast between the vision of being mistress of Dane Castle as Harry's wife, and the home of discomfort offered to her at Mrs. Grant's, caused the emotion quite as much as any other feeling.

The excitement was not good for Lady Dane. Not that it could much affect her now. A few short hours, and all of emotion, whether for good or ill, was over for her in this world.

CHAPTER VIII.

MARGARET BORDILLION.

ABOUT half-a-mile from Dane Castle, standing almost at a right angle between the castle and the village of Danesheld, was the dwelling of Mr. Lester. It was a substantial red-brick dwelling, known by the name of Danesheld Hall, and

but for its size might have been mistaken for a farm-house,
surrounded as it was by outbuildings, barns, sheds, rick-
yards, and other appurtenances that a large farm generally
possesses.   Its site was somewhat solitary, no houses being
in the immediate vicinity, whilst the wild wood at the back,
ranging out and extending to some distance, did not render
its aspect more cheerful.   The wood belonged to Lord
Dane ; it joined his shooting preserves, and was a favourite
resort of poachers.

Mr. Lester's property was not entailed.   It had come to
him by bequest, not inheritance ; and a large portion of his
income was derived from his dead wife.   A distant relative
of his was the former owner of Danesheld Hall, and he made
George Lester his heir upon condition that he should take
up his residence on the estate, and make the Hall his home.
George Lester was a dashing young guardsman then, rather
poor, and very fond of life, and he knew not whether to be
pleased or annoyed at the bequest.   The fortune was most
welcome, but to vegetate in the country and be dubbed " the
squire "—at that he winced.   However, we grow reconciled
to most things with time, and so did George Lester to this.
He sold out, married, and took up his abode at Danesheld.
But he still resentfully called it a " bleak place," " the fag
end of the world."

His wife was a Miss Bordillion.   That he never loved her
very passionately, was known to herself as to others.   He
had engaged himself to her in the old days on account of her
" expectations " ; and with his own accession to fortune,
though his heart might have prompted him to wish the
engagement cancelled, he did not allow himself to dwell on
any suggestion so dishonourable, but married her.   After
all she brought with her no fortune.   In her own right
Katherine Bordillion possessed none.   She was of a good
but poor family ; there was a saying in the locality, " poor
and proud as a Bordillion."   She had been brought up by
Mrs. Hesketh, a wealthy lady, who was herself childless.

The marriage was a happy one, Mr. Lester making a kind
and excellent husband.   Two children were born of it, a son
and daughter.   They were still young children when Mrs.

Hesketh died. Her will was a somewhat curious one. To
Mrs. Lester she bequeathed unconditionally twelve hundred
a year, funded property; of course it became virtually Mr.
Lester's, and was at his disposal. It almost doubled his own
income: but he derived other benefit also. To the little
daughter Mrs. Hesketh left a sum of fourteen thousand
pounds; the principal was invested at large interest, and
this interest was to be enjoyed by Mr. Lester so long as the
child remained unmarried. There were other legacies,
amidst them one to the son.

After a few years, Mrs. Lester began to droop. During
her last illness, a distant cousin was staying with her, Margaret Bordillion. They had been girls together, close and
tried friends since, and Mrs. Lester besought a promise from
her that she would remain at the Hall after her approaching
death, to watch over and train her little girl, Maria. Margaret Bordillion was a delicate-looking woman of two or
three and thirty, and the pink hue came into her cheeks as
she thought of what the world might say, if she remained
an inmate of the gay and attractive George Lester's house.
But when death is brought palpably before us—and
Margaret Bordillion knew that it was very close to that
chamber, as she held the damp hand and gazed at the
wasted face of Mrs. Lester—minor considerations are lost in
the vision of the solemn unknown future upon which a soul
is entering, upon which we must speedily enter ourselves,
a little sooner or a little later; and we feel far more anxious
to fulfil our duty in the sight of God, wherever it may lie,
than to care about "what the world will say." Mrs. Lester
received the promise she asked—that Margaret Bordillion
would remain at the Hall to take charge of Maria, at any
rate for the present.

"And remember, Margaret," Mrs. Lester had whispered,
drawing Margaret's face down that she might catch unmistakably the low accents, "should any warmer feeling
arise hereafter between you and George, should he ever seek
to make you his wife, remember that I now tell you I should
be pleased at it."

"How *can* you contemplate such a thing! how can you

speak of it at this moment?" interrupted Miss Bordillion,
aghast, drawing up her tall, slender form. "You, his wife,
can calmly entertain the idea that he may marry another!"

"The world with its passions are fading away from me,
Margaret," was the reply of Mrs. Lester; "it almost seems
as though I had already left it. George is almost sure to
marry again, and I would rather that he made you my
children's mother, than any other woman.".

Mrs. Lester died. It was two years ago now, and Miss
Bordillion had remained at Danesheld Hall. But she kept
very much in the background, more as though she were
only Maria's governess, wholly declining to preside as the
Hall's mistress. She partially regulated the domestic affairs,
and gave her gentle orders to the servants in a timid, suggesting sort of a way, not assuming authority over them.
She never officiated at table in the place of Mrs. Lester;
when Mr. Lester had visitors, she did not appear at all,
remaining in private with the child; and she more often
passed her evenings in her own sitting-room than joined
Mr. Lester. Maria was only eight years old at the time of
her mother's death; had she been grown up, Miss Bordillion
would not have felt the awkwardness of her position so
much. Some women might not have felt it awkward at all:
but Miss Bordillion was of a modest, sensitive temperament,
exceedingly alive to the refined proprieties of life.

What had these two years brought forth for her heart?
Love. Thrown into daily contact with George Lester and
his attractions, influenced possibly by the dying words of
Mrs. Lester, Miss Bordillion had allowed herself, though at
first in all unconsciousness, to become deeply attached to
him. And when a woman's love has lain dormant for over
thirty years of her life, and is then awakened, it bursts into
a strength and depth of passion that the young little dream
of. Timid, modest, retiring, Margaret Bordillion nourished
it in secret, gradually giving way to the hope that she
should be made what Mrs. Lester had suggested—his second
wife. The hope grew into intensity, nay, to expectation;
and her days became as a dream of paradise. Better for her
that she had seen the truth from the first—the dark cloud,

ominously near, might not have poured forth its wrath so
mercilessly on her unsheltered head.

One morning, only a few days after the death of Lady
Dane, as Mr. Lester rose from breakfast, he remarked that
the summer heat appeared to be coming on early, and they
had better change their breakfast-room. It was their
custom to do so during the hot months, for the one generally used faced the morning sun.

"I will tell the servants to-day," said Miss Bordillion.

When the son, Wilfred, was at home they generally all
breakfasted together—as on this morning. Miss Bordillion's
niece, Edith, was staying with them. She was the only
child of Major Bordillion, and had just been sent home
from India, where the major, a widower, was stationary.
Miss Bordillion received her at the Hall, and was looking
out for a suitable school for her.

The two little girls, both very lovely children, ran out to
the lawn through the open window. Wilfred vaulted after
them; like a genuine schoolboy, he delighted in teasing
them. Wilfred was fourteen years old, Edith Bordillion
twelve, and Maria ten.

Miss Bordillion sat down in a remote window-seat to
read a letter that the post had brought her, when she was
aroused by the voice of Mr. Lester calling to her. He was
in the adjoining room, standing at a window that faced the
south.

"Margaret, I want your opinion," he said, as she put her
letter down, and advanced. "Has it ever struck you what
a famous conservatory might be carried out from this end
window?"

"It would be an excellent spot for one," she answered.

"The idea has been floating in my mind for some time.
If I ever carry it out, it must be now."

"Why now?" questioned Miss Bordillion.

Mr. Lester laughed, and his beautiful face wore an
unusual air of embarrassment. The term beautiful sounds
wrong when applied to a man; it was not so to him.
His face was almost delicately beautiful; so much so that
only the depth of passion, gleaming from his deep-set

violet eyes, redeemed it from effeminacy. Margaret Bordillion's love stirred within her as she gazed at him, standing there in the rays of the morning sun. He turned his eyes full upon her, shaking off the embarrassment under a frank smile.

"It is two years now since Katherine died," he said, dropping his voice to the low tender tone that it always seemed to wear to her ear. "Should you be very much shocked, Margaret, if I were to begin to wish for some one to supply her place?"

How wildly her heart beat at the words, she alone knew. Mr. Lester's smile increased.

"And in that case, you know, we ought to have the old house brightened up beforehand. It wouldn't do to leave alterations until afterwards. What say you, Margaret?"

Say, poor thing! nothing. Margaret Bordillion stood with her face bent down and her cheeks glowing. She was altogether mistaken. Certainly she did not construe the words into an offer: she had better sense than to do so; but she believed that, so far as they went, they pointed to herself. George Lester was one of those men whose manner to women is naturally soft and tender, conveying unintentionally more than he meant by it. Margaret Bordillion may be forgiven that *she* so understood it; his slight embarrassment, a thing she had never remarked in him before, aiding the misapprehension.

Mr. Lester waited for her answer, but none came. He saw the marks of confusion, of shyness; it was impossible to conceal them, facing him as she did in the bright morning light, and he also jumped forthwith to a wrong conclusion. He attributed these signs to displeasure, and thought she was feeling pained at the idea of a successor to Katherine.

"Margaret," he said, his tone persuasive, and he laid his hand gently on her shoulder, though neither tone nor action was born of tenderness for *her*, "I am so tired of my widowed life. Katherine is gone, but we who are living should not be wedded to the dead. Think upon this matter; and try and overcome your distaste to it."

Mr. Lester stepped outside and joined the children,

Having broached the subject, he would not say more until she should have had time to grow reconciled to it. And Margaret Bordillion? She remained standing, as he had left her, the day's radiance a type of the radiance that was overspreading her whole soul.

" I shall be his wife at last?" she murmured to herself: " his wife! How have I deserved so intense a happiness?"

But alas, Mr. Lester has not spoken of *her*. Had he been told that Margaret Bordillion had applied his words to herself, he would have gazed out amazement from the very depths of those dark-blue eyes. He had been thinking of one younger, if not fairer than she—the Lady Adelaide Errol.

On terms of close intimacy at the castle, running in and out with the freedom of a son, far more freely than its new heir, Mr. Lester had almost made it his home during the day or two that had elapsed since Lady Dane's death. He took all the arrangements upon himself to relieve Lord Dane; he spared him every possible care. This had brought him into frequent contact with Lady Adelaide; and they had spoken together of her future plans, and what this change must bring forth for her.

To say that Mr. Lester had become attached to Adelaide Errol would be a slight phrase to express his feeling for her. He loved her with that passionate love he had never felt or pretended to feel for his first wife; she had become the angel of his hopes, the day-star of his existence. During Harry Dane's life this love had not been entirely kept under; it had been allowed to show itself to her at times. With the keen discernment of love in all that regards the beloved object, Mr. Lester had detected that she did not care for Harry Dane; he fully believed that she intended to reject him, and was contented to wait for that time to press his own suit. The bare sight of her was as heaven to his soul. He knew nothing of any regard there might have been between her and Herbert Dane: that they had cared for each other never entered his imagination.

Lady Dane had foreseen the probability that after her death another home might be desirable for Adelaide. She could think of none but that of a distant relative, Mrs. Grant, a widow lady who lived in a remote part of Scotland, who was very poor, and had a number of young children. This lady would only be too thankful to receive Lady Adelaide and the liberal remuneration she would bring with her. To Adelaide herself it seemed a terrible prospect ; purgatory would be nothing to it, she said confidentially to Sophie ; but necessity has no law. The castle would no longer be a home for her. Lord Dane was confined to his room, and she was, it may be said, its sole inmate.

"But surely you will not like going to this Mrs. Grant's, Lady Adelaide ?." Mr. Lester had observed to her on the day following Lady Dane's death.

"Like it! I shall hate it beyond any earthly thing. But what am I to do, now my aunt is gone ? "

George Lester's heart leaped within him. The barriers of silence were flung down, and he there and then poured forth his tale of love, beseeching her to become his wife, the mistress of his home. She was a little taken by surprise, and her first impulse was to reject the offer, for she cared for Mr. Lester no more than she had cared for Harry Dane. But she thought of Mrs. Grant's remote home, full of children and discomfort, and checked the denial upon her lips.

"Will you give me a day or two for consideration, Mr. Lester ? "

He would have been happy to give her a month or two, so that she did not reject him at the end. And for two days he said no more. On the third evening she spoke to him of her own accord, accepting his offer ; spoke so calmly and quietly that Mr. Lester might have known she had no love for him, but that a man in his position is blind.

"But you will not exact the fulfilment of my promise yet," she added. "In a year's time, perhaps. As your affianced wife, I can remain at the castle so long as Lord Dane is spared, and we shall meet constantly."

Mr. Lester was all too thankful for this. And he lay awake three parts of the night, projecting alterations and improvements in his dwelling, all for her happiness and welcome. His children, his friends, had dwindled down to

a very small place in his affections; there was no room for
them beside Adelaide; she was all in all. No wonder he
suspected not the true cause of Margaret Bordillion's confusion. He was going forth again presently to bask in the
sunshine of her presence. But not until after the burial of
Lady Dane, three days to come yet, was the news to be
confided to Lord Dane.

And Margaret remained on in her dream of happiness, in
the spot where Mr. Lester had left her; how long she
scarcely knew. The voices of the children, outside on the
lawn, were as music to her ear; the tones of Mr. Lester as
he spoke to them, were as the sweetest melody to her heart.
The entrance of a servant with some household question
aroused her to realities.

Let us take a glance at this servant, who rejoices in the
name of Tiffle—Miss Eliza Tiffle. She is the upper servant
at the Hall, and its ruling power; fair and deceitful in
speech, and very crafty. A little stealthy woman, with a
sharp, thin, red face, and small sly ferret's eyes of a light
green. She assumes airs, and is dressed in an old silk gown,
dyed brown, and a white muslin apron. You might take her
for any age from twenty to forty: perhaps she was about
midway between the two.

Tiffle had begun life as a kitchen-maid, had risen to be
cook, had taken service with Mrs. Lester during her last
illness as cook and housekeeper. So efficient did she prove
herself, that her poor invalid mistress looked upon her as an
invaluable treasure, and bade Mr. Lester keep her always if
possible. She was made housekeeper only, and a fresh cook
was engaged under her. "Let her superintend all," said
Mrs. Lester. But when that lady died, and it was found
that Miss Bordillion was to remain, Tiffle went straight to
her master and gave warning; there was nothing Tiffle
hated so much as what she called "them half-and-half
mistresses." Mr. Lester would not take the warning; he
fancied that the house, deprived of both lady and housekeeper, would inevitably come to grief; and he raised Tiffle's
wages, and told her she must remain. Tiffle consented to a
three-months' further sojourn, graciously enough in appear-

ance, but rebelliously at heart. But when the three months came to an end, and Tiffle found how very little Miss Bordillion troubled her—that she had, in fact, more unlimited sway than in the life-time of her late mistress—she said no more about leaving. Truth to say, Miss Bordillion let her alone from simple dislike; she doubted her instinctively, and felt rather afraid of her. One of the sourest of virgins was Tiffle in her sway, liking to rule with an overbearing hand; she was neither of a desirable temper nor a kindly disposition, and the servants called her "cross-grained." Tiffle, in her turn, hated Miss Bordillion. As a rule, she hated most people, but Miss Bordillion especially, for that lady was her ostensible mistress, and Tiffle saw that she was not trusted. Tiffle was one who could hate to some purpose, with her apparent fairness and her real cunning.

"I thought I'd come to you, ma'am," began Tiffle: "might you be forgetting the orders this morning?"

"In truth I think I forgot the time, Tiffle," said Miss Bordillion, rousing herself; and her cheeks were so bright, her soft dark eyes so radiant, that the observant housekeeper gazed at her with interest, apparently looking all the time the other way. "Mr. Lester was speaking this morning about making some alteration in this room, and I had lost myself in plans."

It was no evasion. Her blissful thoughts had roved even to that, and when Tiffle came in she was really planning the conservatory in her own mind, with the way in which it might be best carried out.

"The butcher has been kicking his horse's heels at the door these ten minutes, and old Gand has come to say he has a lovely John Dory," proceeded Tiffle, sourly, for Miss Bordillion's neglect had not pleased her.

"Get what you like from the butcher, Tiffle; take Gand's John Dory: for the rest, arrange the dinner yourself," joyfully answered Miss Bordillion in gladness of heart.

Tiffle growled a surly acquiescence. Even this little command did not please her. She made a show still of deferring to Miss Bordillion, but that lady for the most part replied by leaving all arrangements to her.

" Does master take his lunch at home? " she asked.

" I don't know. He has not done so generally of late, you know; but perhaps—perhaps he will to-day. Let the young ladies have mutton for their dinner, Tiffle."

"Master Lester won't eat mutton," said Tiffle, fiercely. " He told me in his insolence yesterday that he got enough of that stuff at Rugby."

Miss Bordillion laughed. " You can get him something else, Tiffle. He is not often at home."

Tiffle would have liked to give him dry bread; and her fierce rejoinder was not caused by resentment at the order to send up mutton for the young ladies, but at the thought of him, that the mention of the mutton had called up. He was a generous, high-spirited boy, but very aggravating where he took a dislike; and he and Tiffle had owned to a mutual antipathy from the first hour they met. That a certain innate repulsion to each other existed, not explainable by any law except that of instinct, was all too evident, as the numerous contests proved when Master Lester was at home. Sometimes the aggression was on his side, sometimes on Tiffle's; Miss Bordillion kept herself aloof from the arena, and the servants invariably took the part of the boy.

Tiffle, her business over with Miss Bordillion, made her exit, not by the door, but by the window—a French one that opened on the ground. She went about the house just as if she were its mistress, paying scant deference to any one, except her master. Miss Bordillion supposed she was going out to inquire of Mr. Lester, who might be still there, what his plans were for the day in regard to meals; but the truth most likely was that she meant to fling a passing lance at Master Lester.

This she did, to her heart's content. Mr. Lester was not there; and something she said, in reference to the boy's distaste to mutton, something especially provoking, caused that young gentleman to follow her to her own precincts and " have it out." Tiffle retorted again, and the contest grew hot. So loud did it become, that Miss Bordillion was aroused, and thought it best to hasten to the scene of action,

It might have made a subject for Wilkie. They stood in the middle of the back-yard, between the servants' outer gate and the kitchen entrance. Tiffle, red, furious, loud, her little frame quivering with passion ; the boy standing before her in a provokingly cool attitude, saying all the insolent things a schoolboy can say when he chooses. He was a slender boy, tall for fourteen ; his face one of delicate beauty, his eyes blue as his father's. The servants had come out and were gathered in an admiring group; the butcher-boy and Bill Gand looked on, and enjoyed the contest with a broad grin ; and the two little girls, drawing a doll's carriage, had followed in the wake of the boy and Tiffle : Maria Lester, a sweet child with timid manners, the same delicate features that characterized her father and brother, soft brown eyes and silky brown curls ; Edith Bordillion, a graceful fairy, with light eyes, a laughing face, and fair hair. But the face was not laughing now; both of them were terrified, and Maria began to cry.

" Wilfred, Wilfred, what is this ? " cried Miss Bordillion. " Tiffle——"

She was too late. Tiffle, with a shriek, flew up to him and gave him a smart blow on the cheek. Wilfred Lester did not strike again : he seized both her arms firmly, and held her there powerless, gave her a slight shaking and a great deal of impudence. Tiffle was half mad: she had always mastered him hitherto, but the boy was now growing beyond her.

Miss Bordillion parted them. She touched Wilfred, and insisted on his releasing the woman ; and she kept him by her side whilst she inquired into the cause of the dispute. So far as she could discover, Tiffle was in fault; certainly she was the aggressor : and Miss Bordillion, really scandalized at the scene, gave her a quiet but most decisive reprimand. Possibly the foreshadowing of the full authority she might soon be vested with in the house, imparted to her the courage for it. Tiffle was utterly astounded, and an evil gaze went out from her little sly half-closed green eyes—eyes that Master Wilfred was in the habit of openly likening to a cat's,

"Her fault, Margaret! of course it was her fault," denounced Wilfred, boldly. "She can't let me alone. I shouldn't have interfered with her if she had not interfered with me. She came shuffling up to me with those cat's feet of hers, and attacked me sneeringly about my not choosing to eat mutton: the children can tell you so. I'm not likely to stand that. She's not going to regulate what I eat: it lies with papa to do it, or with you. My opinion is," boldly added the lad, "that you have been here too long, Tiffle."

Miss Bordillion drew the boy away. Tiffle's tongue followed him with loud abuse. She was in truth in a frightful temper; and a slight murmur of applause that arose amongst the servants at the boy's concluding opinion, did not tend to calm her.

"Yes," she said to the domestics in her passion, "you'd like to get rid of me, wouldn't you? but you can't do it. Neither you nor that saucy reptile."

Driving them right and left, dismissing the grinning butcher-boy with an order to come again in half-an-hour, snatching the John Dory from the quiet fisherman's hand, she went indoors, and flung the fish to the cook. Mr. Lester's butler, a silent, civil man, the least aggressive of all, and who got on pretty well with Tiffle, followed her to the housekeeper's room.

"I wouldn't let my tongue run on so freely if I were you, Mrs. Tiffle," said he in a friendly tone, "especially before Miss Bordillion. You might find yourself the worst for it. It strikes me there's going to be a change in the house."

"What change?" snapped Tiffle.

"Well—though I'm not sure that I ought to talk of it—from a word the squire let drop to me this morning, I think he is going to marry again."

"Going to—marry again!" echoed Tiffle, her voice subdued to something very like fear, in the excess of her consternation.

"Yes, there's not the least doubt he is; but that's between ourselves as yet, mind."

Tiffle turned cold all over; a conviction that the man spoke truth seemed to settle down upon her suddenly and

hopelessly. She pushed back her red hair from her bewildered forehead.

"Then it is to that animal, Miss Bordillion!" she exclaimed wrathfully. "The designing, crafty witch! making
bones about sitting with him, and keeping herself away
with the children, as if afraid he might eat her."

The butler only smiled. He had no idea Tiffle would do
what she did do. But when Tiffle was exasperated she did
not stand on trifles. Quitting the butler, she proceeded in
search of Miss Bordillion, and found that lady in the breakfast room applying herself to the final perusal of the letter
which she had laid down that morning in obedience to
Mr. Lester's call. To see Tiffle with her shrivelled face
scarlet was nothing; but to see her come in with a bold
step and her elbows squared was a different matter.

"I have lived in the family before ever you came near it,
Miss Bordillion," she began, panting with passion; "and I
think that if this change was in view I might have been
injected into it."

Miss Bordillion was accustomed to Tiffle's singular use
of words, a peculiarity of Tiffle's that afforded perpetual
amusement to Wilfred Lester. She supposed this outbreak
had reference to the recent quarrel; but did not in the least
understand it.

"Explain yourself, Tiffle."

"I say it's a shame for them servants to have been in-
lightened, and me, their head, who ain't a servant in the
strict sense of the word, to have been kept in the dark,"
continued Tiffle. "But when things is set about in this
kivert way, they don't bring much luck with 'em."

"Explain yourself, I repeat," interrupted Miss Bordillion.
"What are you speaking of? You forget yourself, Tiffle."

"It have just been told me by Jones that you and
Mr. Lester are going to make a match of it," shrieked
Tiffle. "He says his master told him so: and, I repeat, I
think *I* might have been made a confidence of, instead of
him. It's not ways that I've been accustomed to, Miss Bordillion, I always had respect paid to me in all my places,
and I mean to have it."

Never in her whole life had Margaret Bordillion been so completely taken aback. Tiffle's insolence, Tiffle's passion, all faded into nothing at the woman's news. It was *that* which robbed her of her self-possession, and covered her with confusion. She blushed, she stammered, she faltered ; bringing out some disjointed words that she "did not know," she "was not sure." It never occurred to her to doubt the suggestion that Mr. Lester had himself informed the butler, and in her innate adherence to truth she would not attempt to deny the fact.

"And so, as I've not been used to this sort of under-handled treatment, and can't stomach it, I'll give warning to leave when my next quarter's up, ma'am, which will be just four weeks to-morrow."

Tiffle turned and flounced out of the room, having read the signs of love all too correctly ; leaving Miss Bordillion with a rosy hue on her delicate face, and lost in the sweet mazes of her delusive dream.

CHAPTER IX.

BROUGHT IN BY THE FISHING-BOAT.

THIS day was to bring forth an event, beside which the morning quarrel between Wilfred Lester and Tiffle, or that spotless domestic's subsequent onslaught on Miss Bordillion, faded into insignificance. As if to put a final and decisive close to any latent hope Lord Dane might inwardly cherish, and to set at rest the secret, tormenting doubts of the heir, the body of Harry Dane was found, and brought to the castle.

Adelaide Errol was in the drawing-room with Mr. Lester in the afternoon. He was talking to her about the very project he had alluded to in the morning to Miss Bordillion, a new conservatory, and she listened with an absent, listless air, as if she cared not for conservatories or for anything else in life. Suddenly she lifted her head and listened. A sound in the road, unnoticed at first during their conversation, had been gradually advancing nearer; it was as the tread of many people, and was now within the castle gateway.

Strange to say, there was a prevision within her mind of what it really was. She stood with her hands clasped before her, the colour fading from her face. Nothing was to be seen from the window but a number of people staring into the gateway. Without a word to Mr. Lester, she glided down the stairs into the very heart of the commotion. A dozen fishermen, or so, were congregated in the gateway, the outer gates of which had been closed hastily, to keep out the crowd. They had carried up a sort of hand-barrow to the castle, on which lay a body, covered from view. It had been picked up some miles down the coast, and they brought it to Danesheld in their boat, scarcely looking at it, and never giving a thought to its being the body of Captain Dane. It happened, however, that Ravensbird was strolling on the beach when the boat came in, and he immediately, at the first glance, pronounced it to be that of his late master. The features were unrecognizable, but he knew it by the teeth, and by a mark upon the right arm. Harry Dane's teeth had been of great beauty, white and regular.

Adelaide was unnoticed in the confusion. Several of the servants were gathered in the gateway; the fishermen were gesticulating and talking loudly in their rude dialect: Lord Dane, who was up that afternoon, had caused himself to be wheeled to the scene, and sat in his chair looking on from the hall door. Ravensbird stood before him, telling how he had recognized the body, and by what signs. If anything could have surprised Adelaide at the moment, it was the sight of Ravensbird. The fact was he had entered with the fishermen, and Lord Dane chose to hear what he was saying before he ordered him forth.

What motive impelled Lady Adelaide to go forward to the barrow she could not have told: possibly, in that moment of agitation, of terror, she was partially unconscious of her actions. That she was under the influence of some all-powerful emotion, none who saw her blanched face, her wild eyes, could doubt. She reached the barrow, and was lifting its covering, when one of the fishermen unceremoniously interposed.

"It's no sight for my lady," he said, appealing to Lord Dane. "It's no sight for women, young or old. You may judge, my lord, that it is not."

"Go away," said Lord Dane to her, sadly but imperatively, after a moment's pause, as if convincing himself that it was really Lady Adelaide. "What brings you here?"

"You'd never get it out of your sight all your life after, young lady," spoke up another man, who had drawn close to the barrow to guard it from her, for he had daughters of his own.

"Quit the scene, Adelaide; are you mad?" sternly reiterated Lord Dane.

"I think I am mad," she murmured, as recollection came to her mind and a flush of crimson to her cheeks. Turning hastily to obey Lord Dane, she caught the eyes of Ravensbird riveted upon her.

"Is it indeed Captain Dane?" she asked, in agitation, halting near the man whilst she spoke.

"It is, my lady, all that's left of him. I should know him amongst a thousand."

She burst into a passionate flood of tears, and hastened to her own chamber. Squire Lester, having no conception of what was passing below—he had taken it for some petty commotion—waited her return to the drawing-room; and waited in vain.

An inquest was called with due speed. It was little more than a form, just to satisfy the requirements of the law. Ravensbird testified to the remains being those of his late master; Mitchel gave his evidence; also the man Drake. An extensive fracture of the skull, at the back of the head, was discovered, more than sufficient to cause death. The verdict returned was, "Wilful murder against some person or persons unknown;" and this proved that public opinion did not, as at first, wholly condemn Richard Ravensbird.

The episode related by Drake had been gradually making its way with the more reasonable portion of Danesheld. Ravensbird's alibi was also so decisive, excepting to the prejudiced, that suspicion had been lifted from him, and the man with the pack was almost universally looked upon as the criminal. Somewhat curious to say, his non-appearance told conclusively against him in the public mind. Unless he was in hiding, the efforts to find him must have been successful. The question now was, where was he concealed? and how should he be tracked when he came out of his lair?

Lady Dane and her son were buried together. And there was more true mourning for William Henry Dane than there had been for Geoffry. Again was Lord Dane unable to attend, and the chief mourner, as before, was the new heir.

On his return from the funeral Herbert Dane—but we must do as the rest do, and change the name—Geoffry Dane was met by a message at the castle entrance, summoning him to the presence of the lord. Handing his hat, with its crape, to Bruff, he went in at once, and was shocked at the change he saw in the fine old face looking up at him from its pillows.

"Are you worse, uncle?" was Mr. Dane's involuntary greeting.

"I suppose I am, Geoffry. I feel very ill. They got me up: I was hoping to go where you have just been; but I fainted, or something of that sort, and had to be laid down again. I want to talk to you, Geoffry. I have a charge to leave you: a charge above all other charges. You will fulfil it?"

"I will, indeed; to the utmost of my power."

"According to the arbitrary decrees of fate — how capricious, how unlooked-for they are!—you will be the seventeenth Baron Dane. Geoffry,"—and the old peer laid his hand impressively on his nephew's wrist, and gazed at him from his anxious face—"I charge you, by all your hopes of happiness, to endeavour to bring to light the destroyer of

my son! Spare no energy, no trouble, no cost; let no idleness overtake you at your task; be not tempted by want of
success to relinquish it. Never take your surveillance from
that man. Do you hear me, Geoffry?"

"But he is not yet found, sir."

"Not found! What do you mean?"

"You are speaking of the packman, are you not?"

"The packman!" ironically returned Lord Dane.
"Pshaw! That tale has never, in my opinion, been worth a
rush. You have heard me say so, Geoffry. Some travelling
bagman, who encountered Harry as he was leaving the castle,
and followed him on to the heights to induce him to purchase
a cotton handkerchief or a horn knife from his store; and
Harry rode the high horse at being importuned, and abused
the fellow. That was nothing more, rely upon it. No;
whoever dealt out death to Harry that night did it with
premeditation. It was Ravensbird, Geoffry; and I charge
you to look to him."

A shade of annoyance passed over the face of Mr. Dane.
"I don't like to differ from you, sir; but indeed I do not
think it was Ravensbird," he rejoined. "I accused the man
of it at first; but that was before the evidence came out of
his having been at the time at the Sailors' Rest. It could
not have been Ravensbird."

"I tell you, Geoffry Dane, it was Ravensbird, and no
other. Do not you rest until you bring it home to him: it
is my great charge to you. And now to another matter.
Where's Cecilia? Has she come home yet?"

"No. I had a letter from her this morning. She tells
me she cannot be home for a week or two. Mrs. St. Aubin
is ill, and Cecilia is staying longer in consequence.".

Lord Dane looked disappointed. "I wanted her to come
and stay at the castle until Adelaide quits it for Scotland."

"Is it decided that she goes to Scotland?"

"Quite so. What else can she do? She can't stay on
alone here. I wanted Cecilia to be with her until she went.
Not that she's much more staid than the other. Adelaide
came down amidst the crowd the day they brought Harry
home, and lifted the tarpaulin to look at him. She's as

wild as a March hare. Think of her running out on the heights that night!"

"She will not like to go back to Scotland."

"Necessity has no law," observed Lord Dane. "Mrs. Grant is a relative, and will take care of her. Were Irkdale married he might give her a home; but he is not."

"I think—I think, uncle," stammered Geoffry Dane, the flush of love dyeing his brow—"I think she would be happier with me. If you will sanction it, and pardon my speaking of it to-day."

"In what way happier?"

"As my wife."

"Geoffry, I had better be explicit with you," said Lord Dane. "You cannot suppose that since the death of my sons I have not cast my thoughts to the future of those who are left. My wife gathered an idea some months ago that Adelaide cared for you more than she did for Harry; but she said nothing to me of this until after Harry's accident. For my part, I deemed Lady Dane must be mistaken. Unless she cared for Harry, why should she have engaged herself to him? But Harry went; Geoffry went, and you stepped into their place as my heir. In the last interview I held with my poor wife I spoke to her of this, for I knew that leaving Adelaide alone was her great trouble. I said that if you and Adelaide cared for each other, the marriage would be a suitable one. And, to tell you the truth, Geoffry, I would give her to you more cordially than I would have given her to Harry; for I don't like the idea of cousins marrying, and to you she is no blood relation."

"Well, sir?" said Geoffry, for Lord Dane had paused.

"Well, Lady Dane then told me that she had spoken to Adelaide, and found she was mistaken in her suspicion. That it was Harry to whom Adelaide had been really attached, and she wholly declined to be addressed by you. Therefore I imagine, if you are indulging dreams of Adelaide, you are nourishing a chimera."

A proud, self-satisfied smile parted the lips of Mr. Dane. "At any rate, I have your permission, sir, to win her if I can."

"You have that. But there were other things I wanted to talk to you about, and I find I am getting exhausted. You will come in again this evening, Geoffry."

Mr. Dane quitted the room and went straight to the drawing-room in search of Adelaide. He found her in the smaller room, from the end window of which she had so often looked out for him in happier times. She was standing at it now in her deep mourning, sad enough—not looking out—the blinds were drawn to-day. She turned with a start when he entered, and would have passed him.

"Am I scaring you away, Adelaide?"

"Oh no," she answered, with a confused blush, and took her seat in Lady Dane's large chair.

"I hear it is in contemplation that you should return to Scotland, to be with Mrs. Grant."

"It was in contemplation," she answered.

"You might just as well bury yourself alive, as become an inmate of Mrs. Grant's uncomfortable home."

She made no reply. She had her jet chain in her fingers, and seemed to be counting its links. Mr. Dane stood whilst he talked to her.

"Adelaide," he resumed, his voice sinking, his face a little bent in his earnestness, "will you pardon the apparent unseemliness of my speaking to you on this day, at this hour?—your uncle has excused it. It is only a single word I would say. You will let *me* welcome you to a home, instead of Mrs. Grant. As my wife——"

"It is impossible," she interrupted.

"How impossible?"

A moment's struggle with herself, and then she let the jet chain fall from her fingers, and raised her head in sudden resolution. All her self-possession had returned to her, and her tones, though low, were firm as a rock.

"Because I have promised to be some one else's wife."

Geoffry Dane turned sick at heart. He loved this girl with a passionate, enduring love. The change in his countenance struck her with keen pain.

"I would soothe it to you if I knew how," she said, in an impulse of kindness. "I would, indeed, Geoffry."

" What has changed you?" he asked. " The time was,
not so long ago, when we were scheming and planning how
we could contrive to pass our lives together. You said that
if I had only a few hundreds a year you would risk it."

" Don't talk of it," she interrupted. " The past is gone
for ever."

" And the present is with us. I can now offer you what
I could not then; what I never—I solemnly declare—so
much as glanced at. I can make you—all too soon, I fear—
mistress of this castle and of these broad lands."

" You need not enlarge upon it; I perfectly understand.
You would make me Lady Dane."

" I would make you Lady Dane and my dear wife," he
replied in tones of the deepest tenderness. " Oh, Adelaide,
why do you look at me so? What misery has come between
us?—what has changed you?"

" But I cannot accept the offer," she said, with measured
coldness. " Geoffry, indeed all is at an end between us; at
an end for ever."

His face was working sadly; he could hardly subdue his
emotion sufficiently to speak. " At least you can tell me
the cause of the change. *Why* is it at an end? Oh,
Adelaide, my darling——"

" Hush!" she interrupted. " Such words are treason, now
that I am engaged to another."

It may be that he questioned whether she was dreaming,
or whether she was only playing with him. That she was
in earnest he did not believe, and she saw that he did not.

" It is the truth, Geoffry. I am engaged to Mr. Lester."

Was his face turning to stone? It looked so in its pallor.
Hers was flushing.

" Mr. Lester!" broke derisively from his lips. " Marriage
with him will be, for you, worse than a mockery. You do
not care for him."

" What was I to do?" she rejoined, in momentary self-
abandonment, her brow knitting with pain. " It was my
only alternative. At Mrs. Grant's I should have become
melancholy mad. Are you about to abuse me, Geoffry?
For mercy's sake don't look at me like that."

"It was not your only alternative. Had you not me to fall back upon?"

She shook her head. "The fate of Harry Dane lies as a weight upon my heart," she whispered; "the deceit we practised towards him is ever before my mind. I told you this once. Were there no other man left in the world, Geoffry, I would not be your wife."

"And you have no pity for me!"

"Yes I have. I have some pity for myself also," she added, holding out her thin wrists. "It has told upon me."

"Adelaide, I would far rather you had killed me."

"There are times when I wish we had all been killed together," she answered, rising. "Fare you well, Geoffry. Do not come upstairs to me again, for indeed this emotion is neither good for you nor me."

"A moment yet, Adelaide. Nay, you shall stay whilst I warn you. If you marry George Lester you will commit as great a mistake as any woman ever committed in this life."

"I think not. At least I shall risk it."

"As surely as that you and I are standing here, you will do so. You love me; yes, you do—this is no time for conventionalities, and I tell you so openly. A life with George Lester will be, for you, one long unsatisfied yearning."

"Yearning! For you!" she retorted, drawing down the corners of her lips, the words not pleasing her. "You are mistaken, Mr. Dane."

"A yearning for escape from the existence you have imposed upon yourself," he said with some sternness; "and there will be none."

"I will not hear this. The discussion is altogether unseemly now. You have but returned from leaving my dear aunt and Harry in their grave. You——"

Whether it was the awakened grief this thought occasioned or that the interview was becoming too painful for her feelings, she burst into a flood of tears. Mr. Dane would have taken her hands in his, but she drew them away.

"No, Geoffry, it is better not. I *cannot* be anything to you again, therefore do not tempt me by so much as a touch of the hand; it would only make my task the harder; we

will not meet again until I am Mr. Lester's wife, danger
will be over then. Forgive me for all," she sobbed, "and
think of me as kindly as you can : you see that I suffer too."

He might have caught her to his breast, but she was
wiser than he. Given the absolute necessity of parting—
which he, at least, could neither see nor understand—and
she was acting as she ought to act. Before he could arrest
her by so much as a look, she had escaped from the room.

And what of sunshine was left in Geoffry Dane's heart
went out of it.

He sat awhile in the darkened room, his face buried in
his hands, and rose up at length with a groan of pain. De-
scending the stairs, he went mechanically into the presence
of Lord Dane, and told him what he had just heard—that
Lady Adelaide was about to marry Mr. Lester. He never
glanced at the fact that it was not his place to inform Lord
Dane : he was past sober reflection ; minor considerations
were utterly lost in the tumult of his great misery.

Lord Dane was greatly astonished. About to marry
George Lester ! "Well," he said slowly, after some minutes'
consideration, "it may be good for Adelaide that it should
be so. She will want a curb-rein, unless I am mistaken—
she is careless and full of folly—and George Lester is of an
age to hold it judiciously. *You'd* have given way to all her
whims and caprices, Geoffry."

There was no reply. Lord Dane looked round for his
nephew, and was startled by what he saw on his countenance.

"You love her !"

"I never thought she would reject me," broke painfully
from his lips.

"Be a man, Geoffry," said Lord Dane, in some wonder ;
"if she won't have you, if she prefers George Lester, you
can't alter it ; but don't sigh after her as if you were a love-
sick school-girl. She's very pretty, and that's about the
extent of her good qualities, in my opinion. *I* shouldn't
like to choose her for a wife ; she's unsteady as the breeze.
Harry the other day, George Lester now ! Forget her, and
look abroad for some one better."

It was good advice, if Geoffry could only have taken it.
Ah, what to him were the honours, the wealth that had
so strangely come to him; what mattered the envy, the
congratulations of the world, so freely lavished on him,
when the capricious conduct of one woman was breaking his
heart?

But another's happiness was to be shattered. How contrary
do things run in this life! Of the four concerned, the only
one whose heart lay at rest was George Lester; he thought
in his blindness that Paradise had fallen on him. Better
for him that he had chosen Margaret Bordillion!

Miss Eliza Tiffle bottled up her wrath for a day or two
after her onslaught on Miss Bordillion. Tiffle was quite
capable of bottling it up for a month or two, if revenge
needed. She never opened her lips until the Monday of
the following week, and then it was incidentally.

She and the maids under her were at issue upon some
point, as was frequently the case. Tiffle insisted on her
will being obeyed, and a scene of domestic rebellion ensued.
The butler spoke to her in private; it was ever his way to
make peace: would she give in to them? No, said Tiffle;
as long as she was at the Hall she'd let them know who was
mistress; when she left they might do as they pleased; it
was under four weeks they'd have to wait. The butler was
surprised, and an explanation ensued. She told him she had
spoken her "free mind" to Miss Bordillion, and the man
stood aghast.

"You surely did not speak of it to Miss Bordillion!" he
exclaimed. "You did not accuse *her* of being about to
marry the master!"

"I did, and that you had said it," returned Tiffle triumphantly. "I told her that I was not accustomed to such sly
goings-on in a house, and gave warning on the spot."

"But," said the perplexed butler, "it is not Miss Bordillion that Mr. Lester is going to marry."

"Not Miss Bordillion!"

"Certainly not. *You* have gone and put your foot in it."

Tiffle's green eyes glared. She thought Jones was deceiving her.

" Who is it, then ? "

" If I tell you, it must be in strict confidence, Mrs. Tiffle.
When I spoke before, I did not know, though I guessed :
but I have heard for certain now. It is the pretty girl at
the castle, Lady Adelaide."

Tiffle did not like making an idiot of herself, as she found
she had done, and she flounced away to her own parlour and
shut herself in.   Down she sat for half-an-hour, reviewing in
her mind the points of the case ; and then she proceeded
with meek steps into the presence of Miss Bordillion, who
was at work in the breakfast-parlour.

Very different was this Tiffle from the outrageous Tiffle of
the other day.   She stood in quiet, humble deprecation,
smoothing her hands one over the other, as was her custom
when in a particularly deceitful mood, her false eyes shooting
out quite affectionate glances at Miss Bordillion.

" What is it, Tiffle ? "

" Oh, ma'am, I hope you'll pardon me, and I've come to
apologise humbly for what I said a morning or two ago.
That Jones led me into the misapprehension, and I should
like to turn him away for it. If the whole lot went, it
wouldn't be a loss.   I find there was no grounds for
kippling your name with my master's."

" Your words took me so entirely by surprise at the time,
Tiffle, that I did not meet them as I ought to have done, or
reprove you," was the quiet reply of Miss Bordillion. " Mr.
Lester entertains no intention of changing his condition
at present, so far as I know. Do not take up groundless
fancies again."

" You see, ma'am, I was mistaken in the party," returned
Tiffle, standing her ground.   " I thought it had been you—
for which I am here to beg a humble parding—whereas I
find it's somebody else. But, Miss Bordillion, master *is*
going to marry, and I'm glad to be able to tell it you,
ma'am, if you don't know it."

Slowly Miss Bordillion gathered in the words. Had
they any meaning, or had they none ? Her heart beat
wildly as she gazed at Tiffle.

" I'd not have said anything to offend you for the world,

ma'am; and a regular soft I was to think as you and master
could have an idea of one another," went on the affectionate
woman in, a frank tone, the corner of her eye turned
stealthily on Miss Bordillion and her changing face.
" Over young she'll be for him, prudence may say; but none
can't say she's not lovely; and Squire Lester—as is well
known—has an eye for beauty.   Not but what her hair has
a cast of the reddish over it; maybe you've remarked it
yourself, Miss Bordillion."

" I don't know what it is you are talking about," was the
poor lady's murmured answer.

" Not know, ma'am! why, of the Lady Adelaide Errol.
It's her that master has fixed his choice on."

Margaret Bordillion's pulses stood still, and then coursed
on with alarming quickness.   Outward objects were growing
dim; her senses seemed to be losing themselves in a faint-
ness.   But for a desperate effort, she might have lost
consciousness.

And Mrs. Tiffle, after a consoling expression of sympathy,
closed the door on the misery of the ill-fated lady, and went
down the passages in the joy of a gratified revenge.

CHAPTER X.

THE LEASE OF THE SAILORS' REST.

To say that the news had stunned Miss Bordillion would
feebly express the terrible blow dealt out to her by Tiffle.
At the very instant that that estimable waiting-woman
entered into Miss Bordillion's presence, the unhappy lady
had been buried in a dream of the sweetest fantasy, pictur-
ing to herself the words that George Lester might even that
night say to her.   Since the morning when he broached the
subject of the conservatory, he had said no more, but she

had thought nothing of it; a great deal of interest and com-
motion had been excited by the recovery of the remains of
Captain Dane, and Mr. Lester was full of nothing else.
And there had been the double funeral.

She sat on, when Tiffle left her; her sewing fallen on her
knees, her scissors on the ground. Her whole mind was a
chaos, conscious of nothing save the one fact that it was not
to her George Lester's love was given, but to another. The
rubicon was passed—it has to be passed by most women
once in their lives—and Miss Bordillion found its waves
all the worse to battle with from her tardy crossing. She
had entered on a new life, a new way, and must henceforth
traverse it. Behind her were sweet and sunny Arcadian
plains; stretching out before her were rude rocks and sharp
thorns, a rugged, toilsome, endless road, and a lowering
sky. She would do well not to look back whilst she toiled
wearily along it.

To doubt the news never occurred to her; she felt sure
that it was true. It explained various little items she had
observed lately in the conduct and movements of Mr. Lester,
which had rather puzzled her. Even then, in the first dawn
of her agony, she looked the matter full in the face, shrinking from it, it is true, but persevering with the scrutiny.
Better for her that she should do so. Her own plans would
have to be decided upon, for if the young Lady Adelaide
was to be brought to the house, his wife, she must quit it.
She thought of it for the whole of the remaining day, giving
no sign of her pain, save that now and then a suppressed sound
of agony broke from her. The children inquired if she felt
ill, but she answered no. Mr. Lester did not come home to
dinner, and she supposed that he had remained at the Castle
with Lord Dane, as he did sometimes, without warning them
at home. Ah! she knew now what his attraction was there.
She sat up until he came home; not in her own sitting-
room, as was her usual custom, but in the library, waiting
for him.

It was striking eleven when he entered. He came in,
saying something about the warmth of the evening, calling
to the butler to bring him in a bottle of soda-water. Then

he caught sight of Miss Bordillion, and greeted her with a gay laugh.

"Why, Margaret, this is dissipation! Eleven o'clock, and still sitting up!"

She could not answer. The task which had seemed tolerably easy in prospective, the very words which she had conned over and over to herself in the last hour, was an almost impossible one now. She sat close to a small shaded lamp, away from the glare of the chandelier, and was ostensibly sewing. That was nothing unusual; some work or other, generally plain useful work, was generally to be seen in the hands of Miss Bordillion. As yet she kept silence, striving to school her manner to indifference, collecting her energies to speak with calmness. Mr. Lester continued, noticing nothing:—

"I'm sure this is much more sensible of you than dancing off to bed with the birds, or shutting yourself up in your own sitting-room, leaving an empty room to welcome me. I can't think why you should do so, Margaret; just as if you were afraid of me."

Speak she must: yet how subdue the agitation that gained upon her? How hide it? Her heart was beating wildly against her side; her face was white, her lips were dry. Suddenly she rose from her seat and went to a side-table, on which was a little workbox of Maria's; she stood there rummaging its contents, her back to Mr. Lester. And then she managed to bring out the words she wished to say, or others that did for them.

"I have been hearing some news to-day; and I thought I would wait up to ask you whether it was true. On these warm evenings, too, it is agreeable to sit up late. The heat appears to be coming in early."

"What momentous news have you been hearing now? That the Thames has taken fire?"

"Something nearer home," she answered, shrinking with pain from his light, careless manner: it seemed as a very mockery to her own misery. "I have been told that you are going"—a sudden cough seized her and she had to pause—"to marry Lady Adelaide Errol."

"Now who in the world could have given you that piece of news?" demanded Mr. Lester, his tone full of banter still.

"It came from Jones."

"From Jones!"

"At least, I think so. Tiffle mentioned it to me, and I think she said Jones was her informant. I am not sure, but she said"—poor Miss Bordillion was confusing the two interviews, Tiffle's first news and the second—"Jones had it from you."

"The idea of Miss Bordillion's listening to the gossip of servants!" was his laughing retort. "I thought you were a wiser woman, Margaret."

Margaret stood over the workbox still; she seemed to be dropping no end of things, and picking them up again. She did not dare to turn her face round in its terrible agitation. At that juncture the butler came in with the soda-water.

"So, Jones," began Mr. Lester, "you have been making free with Lady Adelaide Errol's name, I hear, in conjunction with mine."

Jones nearly dropped the waiter in his consternation. The bottle and the glass clashed together as he laid them on the table. He stared at his master, and turned crimson and purple; but not a word of excuse or denial could Jones bring out.

"Pray from whom did you receive your information?" continued Mr. Lester.

"Sir, I'm sure I beg your pardon if it is not correct: or if I ought not to have mentioned it; but I only did so to Tiffle in strict confidence. I had it, sir, from Mr. Dane."

"From Mr. Dane!" repeated Squire Lester, surprise causing him to echo the words.

"From Mr. Geoffry Dane, sir. Yesterday evening I was near the Castle and met Mr. Dane. He stopped to speak to me; he's always affable, sir; and just then Lady Adelaide, in deep mourning, passed us on her way from church, her maid and Bruff behind her. It was the first time she had been out, I fancy, since the commencement of the troubles. 'She's a winsome young thing, sir,' I said to Mr. Dane, when he was putting on his hat, which he had taken off to her; 'as good as a sunbeam.' 'It's a sunbeam you'll soon have at home, Jones,' said he: 'in a short time she leaves the Castle for your master's house, changing her name to his.' Mr. Dane looked quite queer when he said it."

Squire Lester turned his gaze on his servant. "Queer! How 'queer?' What do you mean, Jones?"

"Well, sir, I can hardly describe. There was a curious look in his face, and the corners of his lips were drawn down. I certainly did speak of it this afternoon to Tiffle, but I cautioned her not to mention it again," went on Jones. "I know I ought not to have repeated it, sir, and I am very sorry; but Mr. Dane spoke of it quite openly to me. Shall I contradict it, sir?"

"Oh dear no," carelessly replied Squire Lester. "Leave the soda-water. I'll help myself."

"The tale-bearing ferret!" said Mr. Jones, as he withdrew, anathematizing the offending Tiffle- in his rage. "Many a master might have turned me away for it. If she stops here, I won't."

Miss Bordillion had been gaining some composure during the colloquy. She turned to Mr. Lester.

"It is true, then?"

"Yes, it is true, Margaret," he answered, his manner changing to seriousness.

"I think you ought to have told me."

"Of course I ought. I meant to tell you to-morrow morning. What I said the other day was intended as a herald of the news. I have lost no time, for it is only to-day that things have been settled with Lord Dane, and how Herbert—Geoffry I mean—came to know it, I can't tell. It does not matter."

"Is the marriage likely to take place soon?" she asked in a low tone.

"That I cannot tell you. Adelaide said something about waiting a twelvemonth, but when I spoke to Lord Dane to-day, he expressed a wish that it should take place as soon as possible. Some compromise will be effected, I suppose, between the two."

" At any rate, you will give me notice of the time as soon as you know it yourself? " she rejoined. " But I can begin forming my plans at once."

" What plans?"

" For quitting the Hall, and finding another residence."

Mr. Lester paused: there was a blank look upon his face.

" What are you thinking of now, Margaret? You need not quit the Hall."

" Nay, I should rather ask what you are thinking of," she rejoined. " I shall certainly leave the house quite free for Lady Adelaide."

" The house is large enough for you and for Adelaide. She will not be putting you out of your place as mistress, because you have never assumed it. You can remain here precisely as you have hitherto done."

" No, Mr. Lester; it is impossible. Before you bring home your wife, I shall make room for her."

" Margaret," he said in a low tone, " I do not forget that you promised Katherine to supply her place to Maria; to be in a sense the child's second mother. Are you forgetting it?"

A flush of pain dyed her face, called up by the association the words conveyed. She laid her hand upon her bosom to still its beating.

" You are bringing home Maria's second mother in Lady Adelaide."

" Nonsense, Margaret! Adelaide is little better than a child herself; how could she fulfil the duties of a mother to a girl of Maria's age? I should not think of saddling her with the charge of a child for whom she does not as yet care. When she shall have children of her own, experience will come with them. Margaret, how can you talk of parting with Maria, loving her as greatly as you do?"

That it would bring her more grief than she was prepared to acknowledge, Margaret Bordillion knew. Mr. Lester resumed:

" By your own desire, you have been taking the place of governess to Maria; for the last two years it is you alone who have instructed her, assisted by her masters. You must remember, Margaret, that I did not fall in very readily with the plan; I thought it was a task that ought not to be imposed upon you. You met my objection with certain arguments: one was, that you were perfectly competent to instruct her, and possessed an innate fitness and liking for the employment: another was, that you objected to a young girl's being consigned to strange governesses, of whom we knew nothing; a third was, your promise to Katherine personally to watch over Maria. Do you follow me?"

"Perfectly."

"Then I would remind you that those arguments are still in force. By leaving the Hall, you would abandon Maria to a hired governess, you would forfeit your promise to Katherine. Margaret, dear Margaret," and Mr. Lester took her hand in his, "do not think of this: at any rate for the present. It will be time enough after Lady Adelaide comes home, if you then find that you do not care to remain. I ask you for Maria's sake, be not hasty in this. Remember how Katherine left her to you."

She withdrew her hands, calmly and quietly, though her chest was heaving, her face working: and Mr. Lester saw the emotion. But he was still under that misapprehension of his: he thought she was vexed and agitated at his replacing his first wife with a second.

"We will talk further of this another time," she said: "it is getting late now." And rolling up her work as if she had not a minute left to spare, she hurried from the room.

"Plenty of time," repeated Mr. Lester to himself, as he took up the bottle of soda-water. "And I'm not at all sorry that those meddlers paved the way for me. The idea of Margaret's taking it up in this light! I never saw her so ruffled. It's just like women and their romance, to fancy that when a man loses his wife he should remain wedded to her grave: they've no common sense. And in my case— when Margaret knows I had no love for my wife, but only esteem—pshaw! she'll come to her senses. I think I'll have a dash of brandy in this soda-water," he concluded, ringing the bell for Jones.

Miss Bordillion went straight to her chamber, and sat down to think. What should she do? What ought she to do? She was a woman greatly alive to the dictates of conscience; one who was most anxious, even at a self-sacrifice, to faithfully perform whatever duty fell to her. And the appeal from Mr. Lester in regard to Maria had touched her conscience.

"I did promise Katherine. I said I would never abandon the child to a school, or a governess, without my supervision. Should I place my own pain, my chilled feelings, in comparison with this?" she continued, deliberately questioning herself. "I deserve this punishment. What right had I to assume he was going to ask *me* to be his wife, because I had madly suffered myself to become attached to him? Yes, I deserve it! Let me take it upon me, and bear it in silence as I best may."

She sat on to the small hours of the morning battling with her trial. Before she rose, she had made a sort of compromise between her feelings and her conscience. She said to herself that she would not hurry away at once, as she had thought to do. She would remain in the house until the marriage. And then, whilst Mr. Lester and his bride were absent on the customary tour, she would quit it. It is possible that the holding back from entering upon a distasteful change, which we all are apt to feel, insensibly induced her to this compromise. And Margaret Bordillion was very poor, knowing not, in truth, how she could live when she quitted the Hall.

Lord Dane took a turn for the better, to the secret surprise of Mr. Wild. That gentleman at least knew that his life could not be very much prolonged. But medical men assume that it is not in their province to proclaim this to their patients, and the surgeon of Danesheld was no exception.

A wonderful turn for the better. He was helped up now in the morning early, as he used to be ere his troubles fell upon him; he was even taken out in his chair in the charming weather. Squire Lester would walk on one side of it, Adelaide on the other. Occasionally he would be

accompanied by Geoffry Dane; and at those times Lady
Adelaide was never there. But this improvement lasted
only a week or two; Mr. Wild could have told it was
deceitful from the first.

He took to his bed, from which he was destined never
more to rise. In common with most chronic invalids, he
did not seem to anticipate death. That death would lay
its cold hand upon him at no distant period, he knew quite
well; but he did not think that it was so very close to him.
For the matter of that, neither did the surgeon; his malady
was such that he might be taken off at any minute, or live
six months yet. He strongly urged upon Adelaide that her
marriage should take place; the castle would be Geoffry
Dane's home the moment the breath left his body, he said,
and no longer a suitable residence for her. Mr. Lester did
his part towards seconding the mandate; he had a special
licence in readiness; he besought Adelaide to waive form
and ceremony, and to accede. It was of no avail; Adelaide
would not listen, and he might as well have talked to the
wind. She was in deep mourning, she objected, and her
aunt and Harry were only just buried.

" You will go to church and give her away, Geoffry,"
Lord Dane said to his nephew. " She is holding back now;
but it won't last long. It's all mock modesty."

Geoffry Dane's face flushed with some indescribable
feeling. He passed his hand across his brow carelessly to
hide it from Lord Dane.

" No, I would rather not," he answered, in low, firm tones.
" If she marries George Lester, why—let her marry him;
but I will not take act or part in it."

" You are very foolish, Geoffry."

" I dare say I am. Let her send for Lord Irkdale."

" That's easier said than done. Irkdale dare not put his
foot in England on account of his debts. Never mind, we
shall find some one else."

One day Lord Dane sent for the lawyer, Apperly. He
had several things to speak to him about; but he had been
putting it off from time to time, as he would *not* have put it
off had he suspected that death might be very near. Still

no long time had elapsed, and Lord Dane probably thought none had been lost.

First of all, Lord Dane spoke of his will. He wished a fresh one made. The death of his sons enabled him to bequeath legacies to whom he would; and he directed that such should be left to Lady Adelaide, to Cecilia Dane, to his servants, and to others. But they were not of great value; for, of available property, Lord Dane had little; nearly all went with the entail.

Mr. Apperly listened to his instructions in silence. "Have you forgotten, my lord," he asked, "that you are heir to your son, Captain Dane? He must have left a great deal of money."

Lord Dane shook his head. "We shall not one of us here benefit by that, Apperly, however much it may be. One day when we were speaking upon money matters—it was the day he told me, poor fellow, of his love for Adelaide Errol, and his wish to marry her—I asked him if it had ever occurred to him to make a will. I think you knew all his money was invested in different securities over in America?" broke off Lord Dane.

"Yes, I know that."

"Ay; he replied to me that his will had been made long ago, and was in safety in America. All he possessed he bequeathed to American friends, he added; and I could not help telling him he might have been more brotherly and remembered Geoffry. But they were never cordial with each other, as you know. No, Apperly; if I were starving for want of a pound, it could not come to me now from Harry's funds. I shan't live to want any of them, and Geoffry's dead: otherwise it would worry me enough that so much money should go out of the family."

"But had he lived to marry Lady Adelaide, he would surely have cancelled this will?" cried Mr. Apperly.

"Of course he would. He said so. But he did not live to marry her, and it was never done."

The lawyer took his instructions home with him. The next day, somewhat to Lord Dane's surprise, he was up at the castle again.

"Already!" cried his lordship, who seemed unusually drowsy. "Is it ready? There was no such hurry. I'm not likely to go off like the snuff of a candle."

"It will be ready this afternoon, my lord, and I will bring it up for execution whenever you please. But I did not come about the will now," continued Mr. Apperly; "I came about another matter. Hawthorne wants to quit the Sailors' Rest."

"What does he want that for?" questioned Lord Dane.

"You may remember that his two brothers went over to Australia some three or four years ago. It seems they have done very well there, and they want Hawthorne and his wife to join them. The man has been shilly-shallying over it these several weeks past—I will and I won't—and now he has made up his mind all in a hurry, as is generally the case in these matters. He would like to be off at once; next week, if possible, and——"

"A man and a woman can't get off on a four or five months' voyage to take up their abode in a new country, without more preparation than that," interposed Lord Dane.

"They are not going to sail quite so soon," explained Mr. Apperly. "Hawthorne's sister, Keziah, once nursemaid at Squire Lester's, married a London tradesman, as your lordship may remember. A baker, he was, I think. They are going; and they want Hawthorne and his wife to join them in London as soon as may be, that all may make their preparations together. Hawthorne has been to me about it, asking whether your lordship will absolve him from his lease."

"I don't know about that," said his lordship, who had never been a particularly easy man with his tenants.

"He'll do little good stopping," returned Mr. Apperly. "Since the letter came from Australia, enlarging on the fortune his brothers are making, Hawthorne's brain has been so filled with golden visions, that he knows not whether he stands on his head or his heels. But he came to me again this morning saying he had a tenant for the Sailors' Rest."

"Ah," said Lord Dane, "it's a good house, and twenty

will be after it as soon as the news got wing. Any steady man may make an excellent living there. Hawthorne will do well to think twice before he gives it up."

"I have told him so. But you see that sun, my lord, up in the heavens; you might just as well try to turn that in its course as to turn Hawthorne from his new project. His wife is more wildly bent on it, if possible, than he. She has her boxes ready packed, to be off to London as soon as they obtain their release, leaving Hawthorne behind her to wind things up."

"What would they do with their furniture and fixtures?"

"Whoever takes to the house must take to them. He puts the value down at six hundred pounds altogether; furniture, fixtures, stock, lease, and goodwill; and it's not too much. One man is after it who would make a good tenant— Mitchel."

"Mitchel!" echoed Lord Dane. "What could he do with a public-house? And where's his money to come from?"

"Your lordship is thinking of the preventive-man. I allude to his brother—John Mitchel."

"Oh, ay, I forgot him. Yes; he would be a good tenant, and could pay Hawthorne money down. Well, I leave it to you, Apperly. If Hawthorne finds me a suitable tenant, why, I'll release him."

"Very good, my lord."

"Before the bargain is actually struck, that is, before anything is signed, let the name of the new tenant be submitted to me formally. I like to approve of my tenants."

"It shall be so," said Mr. Apperly. "But I suppose I may allow the negotiations with John Mitchel to go on? Hawthorne and he can do nothing until they know whether Mitchel would be acceptable as a tenant."

"Yes, yes; they can go on. I shall make no objection to Mitchel. A respectable man is John Mitchel."

"That's all right then, so far," remarked the lawyer. "At what hour shall I come up with the will? Three o'clock—four o'clock?"

"Any hour. You'll not find me out," added Lord Dane with a faint smile.

" Then I'll say three o'clock; and bid your lordship good-day now, hoping my visit has not fatigued you."

He had quitted the room, when Lord Dane's bell rang a hasty peal. It was to recall him.

" Apperly," cried his lordship, " I feel somewhat fatigued; not as well as I did early this morning. I don't think I'll trouble you to come up again to-day."

Some instinct within the lawyer's breast rose against this.

" Is it well to procrastinate, my lord ? " he asked. " Won't it be a good thing over, and off your mind ? "

" I don't care to be more fatigued to-day than I am," was the reply of Lord Dane. " Come up to-morrow at eleven o'clock. Tell Hawthorne I should like to see him before he leaves; we shall not meet again in this world."

The lawyer bowed his acquiescence, and went home quickly, conscious that many clients must be waiting to see him. Amidst them was John Mitchel.

" Hawthorne and I have come to terms, sir," was his greeting to Mr. Apperly. " We shall want you to make out the agreement and transfer. I don't care how soon it's done."

" All very fine, my good man," returned the lawyer, who, being a lawyer, of course threw difficulties in the way, though none really existed; " but there's a third party to be consulted in this affair, besides you and Hawthorne. And that's Lord Dane."

" I feel sure his lordship will accept me readily," returned Mitchel. " He could not find a surer tenant; you intimated as much yesterday, Mr. Apperly."

" I have nothing to say against you, Mitchel; there's no doubt his lordship might get many a worse. Well, I'll see about it in a few days."

" But, if you could manage it, sir, we should like the deeds drawn out immediately. I wish to take possession next week, and Hawthorne wants to be rid of it."

" Pooh, pooh ! " cried Mr. Apperly, " you can't take a bull by the horns in that way. Some men are six months getting into a house. I am busy to-day, and I shall be busy to-morrow; but you may come in again the next morning. Meanwhile, I'll contrive to see Lord Dane."

"I dare say, sir," returned John Mitchel, looking hard at the lawyer, "you might accept me now if you would. It's not altogether that I am in so great a hurry to get into the house; it is Hawthorne who is in haste to get out of it, as you know: but what I want is to make sure that I shall have it—that I shan't be put aside for another. I'd pay this freely to secure it, sir."

He laid down a ten-pound note. Ten-pound notes had charms for Mr. Apperly, as they have for most men, for lawyers in particular, according to popular belief. He looked at it complacently; but, true still to his craft, he would not speak the affirmative word.

"I have some power vested in me, Mitchel, certainly: I believe I can promise that you shall become the tenant. Subject, you understand, to the consent of Lord Dane."

"Of course, Mr. Apperly. Then it is a settled thing; for I know his lordship won't object to me. So I'll say good-morning, and thank you, sir."

"And step in the day after to-morrow, in the forenoon, Mitchel. Meanwhile I'll be drawing up the necessary papers. As to this," added the lawyer, carelessly popping the note inside his desk, "it can go into the costs."

CHAPTER XI.

UNEXPECTED.

BUT things were not to be quite so smooth and straight as the lawyer assumed. There was to be acting and counteracting. Somewhere about the same hour that John Mitchel was paying his visit at Mr. Apperly's, Ravensbird paid one at Mr. Geoffry Dane's. And Mr. Dane's servant looked exceedingly surprised at the presumption.

"Well he *is* at home," acknowledged the domestic, in

answer to the inquiry pressed upon him. "But I shouldn't think he'd see you."

"Suppose you ask him?" rejoined Ravensbird, coolly walking indoors. "Say I have come on business."

The servant might have refused positively in the old days, but his master was a great man now, soon to be chief of Danesheld, and he did not dare do so. "I'll tell Mr. Dane what you say," said he ungraciously.

Geoffry Dane was in the small sitting-room where you once saw him, not enjoying himself now with a cigar and glasses, but seated in a chair doing nothing, his elbow on the table, his face bent upon his hand. He was often so seated now—in the same attitude—as befitted a face in which the lines of some great care were rapidly gathering.

"It's that Ravensbird, sir," said the servant, interrupting his reverie. "He has come into the house as bold as brass, and is asking to see you. On business, he says."

"I'm sure I don't know what business he can have with me," returned Mr. Dane, a shade of annoyance in his tone. "You can send him in, however."

"Sir," began Ravensbird, without circumlocution, when he entered, "report runs that my Lord Dane leaves many matters of business relating to the estate to you, now you are the heir."

"Well?" said Mr. Dane.

"I have therefore come to ask your interest and influence with his lordship, to get me accepted as tenant of the Sailors' Rest, or to accept me yourself if you have the power."

He spoke fearlessly; not at all as a petitioner, more as though he were making a demand. Ravensbird had always been remarkable for his independence of manner, but since the accusation it had increased fourfold. And it is probable that this helped on the reaction that was setting in in his favour: Danesheld could not connect that freedom of bearing with a guilty man.

"What! are you after the Sailors' Rest?" exclaimed Mr. Dane. "I have heard a dozen names mentioned, but not yours."

"I have not been after it noisily, as the rest have, sir:

but as soon as I found it was to be disposed of, I spoke
privately to Hawthorne. I must do something for a living;
I have been looking out ever since I left the Castle."

" Then you don't intend to go to service again ? "

"Service!" returned Ravensbird. "Who would engage
me after having been taken up on a charge of murdering
my former master? There may be some, Mr. Herbert—I
beg your pardon, sir, I ought to say Mr. Dane—who don't
yet believe me innocent. But I never did intend to enter
upon another service, if I left Captain Dane's. The Sailors'
Rest is just such a house as I should like. Will you help
me to it, sir ? "

" Ravensbird," said Mr. Dane, not replying to his request,
" it appears strange to me that you should remain at Danesheld. You have no ties in it; until you came here with
your master, indeed, you were a stranger to it, and had a
similar cloud fallen upon me, however unjustly, I should be
glad to get away from the place."

" No, sir," answered Ravensbird, in a quiet, concentrated
tone; " I prefer to stay in it."

" To enter upon the Sailors' Rest will require money,"
again objected Mr. Dane.

" I am prepared with that. I have not lived to these
years without saving money. *That* won't be a bar—as
Hawthorne knows. Hawthorne has been playing with me,"
continued Ravensbird. " I knew of his intention to leave
the house sooner than any one, and I said at once I would
take it off his hands. He quite jumped at it—was all eagerness to transfer it to me; but in a day or two his tone
changed, and he has been vacillating between me and John
Mitchel."

" John Mitchel would make an excellent tenant," remarked Geoffry Dane.

" Not better than I should," returned Ravensbird. " Hawthorne knows that: but a doubt arose in his mind whether
I should be acceptable to my lord, if he still wavers as to
my guilt or innocence; Hawthorne feared it might cause
delay, and so went over at once to the enemy, Mitchel."

" My lord does not waver: he believes you guilty,"

Geoffry Dane was on the point of saying; but he checked the words, and suffered Ravensbird to continue.

"It is not likely that Lord Dane can believe me to have been the assailant, in the face of the sworn alibi, though he was prejudiced against me at first; and it was only natural that he should be so. Will you accept me as a tenant, Mr. Dane?"

"I have no power to do so; you have taken up a wrong idea altogether. I certainly have transacted business for my uncle since I became his heir-presumptive; but he has not given me authority to let his houses."

"Will you speak to him for me, sir?"

Mr. Dane hesitated.

"I would speak in a minute, Ravensbird; but I am sure it would be doing no good. Apart from any prejudice he may or may not hold against you, he is one who will not brook interference, even from me."

"You might *try*," persisted the man, "whatever the result should be."

"Will you undertake not to be disappointed at the result? Did it lie with me, it would be a different matter; but it lies entirely with Lord Dane."

There was a pause. Ravensbird stood in silence, as if still awaiting an answer, his piercing eyes never moving from those of Mr. Dane.

"However, as you seem so set upon it, I will speak to his lordship," resumed the latter. "But I must choose my time: it is not every day that he will allow business matters to be so much as named."

"If it is not settled between now and to-morrow night, John Mitchel will have the place," rejoined Ravensbird.

"Then I will speak to his lordship between now and then," concluded Geoffry Dane.

A few hours subsequent to this, a junket was being held at Dane Castle by the upper servants. The sad events recorded had followed each other in quick succession, and the servants, as in decency bound, had secluded themselves so completely from society, that they were beginning to find the monotony irksome. They were holding, therefore,

a quiet soirée on their own account—a quiet little gathering of some half-dozen guests at most; and the housekeeper's parlour was decorated to receive them; and the
table groaned with a tea-feast.

Conspicuous amongst the visitors was Mr. Richard Ravensbird, who had been smuggled in surreptitiously, not to
interfere with the prejudices of Lord Dane. The servants
did not share in those prejudices: they believed his innocence to be an established fact, and considered him an ill-
used man, whom it was their bounden duty to honour.
Possibly the eloquent tongue of Mademoiselle Sophie
Deffloe had contributed to this opinion. Another guest
was a lady to whom you have had the honour of an introduction; no other than Miss Eliza Tiffle. It was the aim
of Tiffle's life to be "genteel," and she was got up accordingly—a flounced light muslin gown ornamented with primrose bows, and primrose streamers to her cap. Lord Dane's
valet, an old beau, who had been in search of a wife, as *he*
said, for twenty years, and had not found one to his mind
yet, was whispering soft speeches into Miss Tiffle's ear, as
he plied her with cake and wine and other good things.
The tea was over; but a splendid collation of what the
housekeeper called "sweets" had replaced it, and Mr. Bruff
had been liberal with his wine.

They were talking of no end of things—a very Babel of
tongues; of what concerned themselves and of what did not,
and especially of what concerned their masters and mistresses. The Lady Adelaide's proposed marriage to Squire
Lester was greedily discussed by Tiffle and Sophie—with
neither of whom did it appear to stand in any great favour
—and Mr. Bruff was eloquent upon the subject of the
departure of Hawthorne from Danesheld, and the new
tenant that would succeed him at the Sailors' Rest.

"They say it is to be John Mitchel," he observed to
Ravensbird.

"Do they?" returned Mr. Ravensbird, in answer. But
not a word spoke he that he was after it himself.

"Should you not just step through the passage into my
lord's room and see whether he is still sleeping?" cried

Bruff to the valet, heartlessly interrupting the flirtation between that gentleman and Miss Tiffle.

"My lord is sure to be sleeping," was the reply; "otherwise he'd have rung. He has been uncommonly drowsy all day. Lady Adelaide is sitting in the room. Let me alone for not neglecting my duty, Mr. Bruff."

"My faith!" ejaculated Sophie Deffloe, jumping from her chair by the side of Richard Ravensbird. "If my lady didn't bid me take her a shawl, for she felt chill, and that's an hour ago! What's my head worth?"

"I wonder the young lady likes to pass her evenings in a sick-chamber! I thought I heard she was not domestical inclined."

The remark was Tiffle's. Sophie had run out of the room to remedy her forgetfulness, and the housekeeper, Mrs. Corbet, a stout lady in a black paramatta gown very much trimmed with crêpe, took it up.

"She's lonely, poor young lady; and even the company of the sick is better than no company at all. You never saw anybody so changed as she is."

"She's moped to death, that's what it is," said the valet. "Half her time she has not a soul to speak to. I hope your master will soon take her away, Miss Tiffle, for her own sake."

"She's not well either, I'm positive of that," said the housekeeper. "Nobody in health, you know, could feel chilled on these warm nights: and she is always complaining of being cold now. So many deaths have been a great shock for her. First there was the Captain, then Mr. Dane, then——"

The housekeeper's enumeration was cut short. Sophie Deffloe burst into the midst of them in terror that had taken her breath away and turned her face white.

"Who is in the death-room?" she exclaimed.

"Not any one," said Mr. Bruff: "the death-room is locked up. Are we going to have some more of your superstitious fancies, Mam'selle Sophie?"

"It is not locked up; the door's open and the key is in it."

"It is locked up, and the key's hanging in my pantry," persisted Bruff.

"Then I tell you it is open—allez!" retorted Sophie, stamping her foot. "Have I eyes, Mr. Bruff? When I ran by to get the shawl, I think it must have been shut. I did not see, or I never should have the courage to go by it open; but when I came back, there it was—what you call ajar. I saw the key in the lock, and I saw the flags inside, and I thought I should have dropped."

Mr. Bruff turned into his pantry, muttering that she saw ghosts where none existed, intending to bring the key and confute her with it. The old valet spoke:

"Did you take the shawl into my lord's room, Mam'selle Sophie?"

"What should hinder me when I went to do it?" returned the saucy Sophie: and Tiffle peered at her from between the lids of her little green eyes, and thought how much she should relish the handling of Mademoiselle Sophie and her sauce, when she transferred her abode to the Hall.

"Was my lord asleep?"

"For all I know; I didn't look towards the bed," answered Sophie. "My lady was asleep. She had dozed off, leaning back in the great chair. So I threw the shawl lightly on her knees, and came away."

Bruff returned, with a softened step and a softened voice, his countenance a little perplexed.

"It's very odd," cried he; "the key is *not* in the pantry."

"So! it's Sophie that sees ghosts where there are none, and fancies doors open when they are not, and discovers keys in them that are safe in their pantries," retorted that demoiselle, turning upon Bruff. "Perhaps, if you'll walk as far as the death-room, you'll find that it *is* open, Mr. Bruff."

"I am going there," said Bruff.

Up started Tiffle, her primrose strings flying; her hands, which were elegantly cased in yellow gloves, clasping each other in simpering entreaty.

"Oh, Mr. Bruff, if you'd only illow me to accompany you, sir! I have so long wished to get a peep at the death-room of Dane Castle!"

"You are all of you welcome to come if you like," said Bruff to the company generally, as he took up a candle. "It's an empty room; nothing in it to be seen."

They followed in a body; every one of the guests. The scared Sophie, possibly feeling herself sufficiently protected when with Mr. Ravensbird, accompanied them. And her assertion was found to be correct—the door was ajar, and the key in it. Bruff inwardly vowed vengeance against the offender when he should pounce upon him. He had little doubt it must be one of the under-servants who had done it in the gratification of curiosity, or to annoy him. Taking the key from the lock into his safe fingers, he marshalled the company into the room.

"Why it's only a big, square, dreary barn of a place, with nothing in it!" ejaculated Tiffle, forgetting her gentility in her disappointment.

"I told you there was nothing in it," said the butler. "What did you expect to see?"

Perhaps Tiffle had expected to see something in the middle with black velvet over it, for she was looking excessively vexed and sour.

"I wouldn't mind going by this 'ere room fifty times over, when the bell was tolling midnight," cried she, with a contemptuous glance at the French girl. "There's nothing here to be frightened at. Where does that place lead to?"

"That's a closet," said the butler.

"What's inside of it?" demanded Tiffle.

"A pair of trestles," he replied in a low tone.

"Oh, could we have a look at 'em?"

"No, Mrs. Tiffle," was the grave answer. "That closet is never opened but when—when it's needful to open it."

"Well, it's a nasty, cold, dismal place, not worth the coming to see," retorted Tiffle. "Where's the good of having windows that you can't look out of? And how damp the floor is!"

The last remark caused them all to cast their eyes downwards upon the flags. They were certainly capriciously damp, stained and spotted in parts, dry and untouched in others.

"What sort of flooring is this?" inquired Tiffle, when her eyes had noted the effect. "Some stones give with the damp, and some don't—that is well known; but here the same stones—some are wet, and some are dry. And who ever saw flags damp on a hot summer's night, with the weather set in for a regular drought."

No reply was made to Tiffle. The servants were looking at the floor in dismay, for the superstition relating to it was rife amongst them.

The butler interposed. "It's nothing new," he said; "it is a state of things common to the flagstone with which the floor is laid. What were you looking at, Mr. Ravensbird?"

"It's very strange," exclaimed Ravensbird, who had been most attentively surveying the room in silence, since his entrance: "this place seems quite familiar to me, though I never was in it before. Where, how, and when can I have seen it?"

"In a dream perhaps," suggested Tiffle. "Odd sights do come to us in dreams."

"Likely enough," returned Ravensbird; and the butler turned and looked at him, surprised at the remark from so very matter-of-fact a man.

"As there's nothing particular here to detain us, and the flags may be cold for the ladies' feet, suppose we go back," cried the butler.

They filed out, nothing loath, and hastened along the passage with quick steps, Bruff remaining to lock the door. He had done this, and was putting the key in his pocket, when he was startled at seeing Lady Adelaide coming swiftly towards him. Startled, because it was quite unusual for her to be in that part of the Castle, and because her face was so white and scared. She laid hold of the butler's arm, as if impelled by fear.

"Bruff! something is the matter with Lord Dane," she shivered. "He looks—I don't know how he looks."

"Oh, my lady! you should not have given yourself this trouble. Why did you not ring?"

"I was afraid to remain alone," she whispered. "I

dropped asleep, and when I awoke I went to look at Lord Dane, wondering that he had not spoken or called. He was lying with his mouth open, and his face white and cold; it terrified me."

"Perhaps he has fainted, my lady. He did have fainting-fits at the commencement of his illness."

"Bruff," she cried, bursting into tears of nervous agitation, "it—looks—like—death. His face looks just as my aunt's looked when she was dead."

Without saying a word to alarm the rest, or to call attention to Lady Adelaide, Bruff went to Lord Dane's chamber, the terrified girl closely following him. Alas! Bruff soon found what had taken place: Lord Dane had died in his sleep.

Even then, Bruff, who was the very quintessence of order and decorum, made no fuss to disclose the calamity to the guests. He called away some of the servants, saying Lord Dane was worse, and despatched messengers for all whom it might concern. He could not send for Mr. Lester, because that gentleman was absent that evening from Daneshield.

Mr. Wild, Geoffry Dane, and Mr. Apperly, were soon round the bed. The surgeon said he had been dead more than an hour; considerably more. It caused Adelaide to shudder: he must have died then before she fell asleep: and she remembered, and an awful remorse sprang up within her at the thought, that she had sat buried in her own reflections until sleep stole over her, never giving thought to him, never once rising from her chair to look at him. He had died, the doctor believed, in his sleep, without stir or ·sign: and she was sitting within four yards of him! She stood shivering behind them now, listening to the comments and the sorrow. The household were half petrified: the poor old valet, who was really not very much younger than his master, shedding tears openly.

"Can *nothing* be done to restore him?" he demanded of Mr. Wild. "To think that this evening, of all evenings, I should not have gone in and out of the chamber every ten minutes, as was my custom!"

"Nothing whatever can be done, I tell you," replied the surgeon. "You may see that for yourselves. One comfort is, he went off quietly, without pain. I have thought this might be the ending."

"Then I wonder you didn't tell him so, Wild," came from Mr. Apperly, in a tone of reproof. "It was only this very morning his lordship said to me that he was not likely to go off like the snuff of a candle."

"And why should I tell him? He was prepared for death; he knew it was coming, and was very near; wherefore tell him that it might be sudden at the last?"

"No: he was not prepared for death," returned the lawyer, in a heat; not in one sense of the word. He had not settled his affairs."

The announcement took all by surprise. He, Lord Dane, with his protracted illness, not to have settled his affairs! Geoffry Dane smiled incredulously.

"It's true," said the lawyer. "After he lost wife and sons, his former will was cancelled, and I have been making a fresh one. Upon what pivots life's chances turn!" he broke off. "When I was with Lord Dane this morning, he appointed three o'clock this afternoon for me to bring the will up for execution; then, feeling fatigued, altered it to eleven to-morrow. And now he is gone! and the will is worth so much waste paper."

"Wanting the signature?"

"Wanting the signature," assented Mr. Apperly. "You will be the better for it," he added, looking at Geoffry Dane.

"No," quietly replied Geoffry.

They began to leave the chamber for the dining-room, into which it opened. He had died in the lower room, which had been his chamber since his accident. Strangers and guests filed out, with slow, uncertain steps, as if no one knew exactly what to do next.

"My lord, do you remain in the Castle from now?"

It was the housekeeper who spoke, and she was speaking to Geoffry, now Lord Dane. He was the new peer; the Right Honourable Geoffry, seventeenth Baron Dane.

"Yes; I suppose so," he replied. "It may be better that I should."

But as Lord Dane—we must begin to give him his title, too—spoke, his eye fell on Adelaide: and he recalled his words.

"Not to-night, however, Mrs. Corbet: the hurry is not so great as that. I will see about future arrangements to-morrow."

"As you please, my lord," replied Mrs. Corbet.

"Unless you would feel my being in the Castle a protection," he added, approaching Adelaide, and speaking in low tones. "In that case I will remain."

"Thank you, oh no! not on my account," she answered, a vivid blush dyeing her pale cheeks. "I shall have the servants."

"It shall be just as you wish. I will telegraph for Cecilia to-morrow. You may like her to be with you."

"Thank you," she repeated again. But both answers were given with a mechanical bewildered air, as if she did not know what she said or what she was about.

"I will wish you good-night then, Lady Adelaide."

"Good-night," she rejoined, holding out her hand. "You will—of course—please to—give the orders now."

"Yes, yes," he replied while her hand was in his. "I will see about everything: no trouble shall fall upon you."

She sat down in a corner behind the screen when he was gone, and burst into a flood of passionate tears. Sophie Deffloe looked round and saw her.

"I will not stop in the Castle another day now he is master of it," and her face as she mentally said it flushed painfully. "Were I to be with him again, I might forget my resolution, and give up George Lester; I might be persuaded to marry him after all, and then—what punishment might not heaven give me for my wickedness? Why did I ever love him? Why can we not forget each other? Where can I go?—Oh! where can I go?"

As Lord Dane turned out of the Castle gateway, Richard Ravensbird stepped up and accosted him: he appeared to have been lingering on the greensward.

"My lord, I must ask your pardon for interrupting you

at this hour. I would say just a word to you on business,
if——"

"It is not the time for it, Ravensbird," said Lord Dane
decisively. "I see by your address you know what has
occurred."

"I do, my lord; I was in the Castle at the moment,
spending an hour with the domestics; and very sorry I am
that the event should have been so sudden. I always respected Lord Dane."

"The servants have condoned your supposed offence, then,
though their lord did not," was the answering remark of the
new peer.

"I beg your pardon, my lord, but condoned is not the
proper term," readily returned Ravensbird. "To condone
implies that an offence has been committed. I committed
none."

"Well, what do you want with me?"

"It is about the lease of the Sailors' Rest. I find that
not an hour is to be lost, if I am to have it,—not an hour—
or I should not have attempted to speak to your lordship so
soon. Mr. Apperly has already begun to draw it up in
favour of John Mitchel, subject to the approval of Lord
Dane. My lord, *you* are Lord Dane now."

A pointed significance was given to the last sentence; a
free, independent, almost *demanding* tone, not pleasant to
hear. Was it possible that Lord Dane failed to remark it?
He did not appear to do so.

"And you think I can grant it to you?"

"I am sure you can, my lord; and I hope you will. Your
lordship will find me a good tenant."

"Enough discussion for to-night, Ravensbird," curtly
responded Lord Dane. "I have already said that it is
unseemly."

Ravensbird respectfully touched his hat and strode away
quickly towards Danesheld. Lord Dane proceeded in the
same direction, but at a slower pace. He was turning
towards his own house when hasty footsteps came up behind him, and he found himself joined by Mr. Apperly,
likewise on his way from the Castle.

"A dreadfully sad and sudden event," cried the lawyer. "I'm sure your lordship must feel it."

"I do indeed; it has shocked me much," replied Lord Dane, turning upon him his pale face—unnaturally pale it looked in the starlight. "We could not have expected him to be much longer with us; but at least I never anticipated this abrupt termination to his life."

"And to think that he did not sign the will! As I said, it will be all the better for your lordship; but for others——"

"Never mind that to-night, Apperly. I am not quite up to the mark. I loved my poor uncle, perhaps better than any one else who was left to him," added Lord Dane, his tone one of keen pain.

"Ay, I'm sure you did. When shall I meet your lordship for business. There are some things which must be seen to at once."

"You can meet me at the Castle to-morrow; I shall be there by ten o'clock. And meanwhile, Apperly, until I shall have looked into affairs, let any business matters you may have on hand rest in abeyance—granting new leases and things of that sort."

"Very good, my lord. But there's nothing much in hand just now, except the transfer of Hawthorne's lease to Mitchel. They both want to get it over sooner than pen can be put to parchment. The one wants to be off and away; the other thinks he is not sure of it till the lease is actually signed. I suppose I may go on with that?"

"No," said his lordship; "neither with that nor with anything else."

"But"—and the lawyer spoke as if taken by surprise— "Lord Dane had no objection to Mitchel as a tenant; he told me so this morning. I presume your lordship will have none."

"Lord Dane's death puts a stop to all such negotiations for the present," was the decisive and somewhat sharply-delivered answer. "Let them remain, I say, in abeyance."

Mr. Apperly nodded acquiescence and said adieu to the new peer, breaking out into a little explosion as he went on down the road.

"He'll be a martinet, as sure as a gun! We might almost as well have had the dead heir to reign here, the Honourable Geoffry. It's often the way with these men who unexpectedly come into power."

The new peer went home, and retired at once to his chamber. But instead of going to bed, as is the custom with ordinary folk, he paced his room until daybreak.

CHAPTER XII.

MARGARET'S CUP PRETTY FULL.

MR. LESTER returned home late, and was greeted by Tiffle with the news—Lord Dane was dead. He could not go to the Castle that night; it had struck eleven; but he was there betimes on the following morning. It was nearly midday before he saw Lady Adelaide. She came to him with her hands stretched out, her eyes wild, her cheeks hectic.

"Take me away, Mr. Lester! Oh! take me away! I will not remain here, the guest of Geoffry Dane."

Taken by surprise though he was, Mr. Lester was only too willing to echo her words. Indeed, he had been weighing possibilities in his mind all the morning, and he ventured to speak of one:

That she would marry him quietly and privately that day in the Castle, and come at once to his house.

The proposal startled her to tremor. She shrank from it, and Mr. Lester saw it with pain. What else, then? he inquired: any plan that she might suggest for her own comfort, he would help her to carry out.

What else, indeed! What other plan was there that could be suggested? She was fully determined—obstinately so, some might have said—not to remain another night in the Castle, although Lord Dane had telegraphed for his sister at the earliest moment. Mr. Lester rather wondered whence her wish for haste might proceed. It never occurred to him, unconscious man, that she feared companionship with the new peer might peril her promise to him.

In her dilemma, in her difficulty of devising any immediate home for herself, she gave some sign of relenting. Sophie Deffloe, happily or unhappily, suggested Mrs. Grant's, and that ended the contest. With a half cry, Lady Adelaide said she would not, could not go to Scotland; and Mr. Lester came again to the rescue, urging his suit by all the eloquence of which he was master. He reminded her that there would be no difficulty whatever in carrying out the arrangements with complete privacy; a special license was already in his possession, which allowed of the ceremony being performed in the Castle, and he begged her to bear in mind the fact that her uncle, Lord Dane, had himself urged their speedy union.

"It will look so strange, to be married whilst he lies dead in the house!" she said, with pouting lips. "What will the world say at our going away on a wedding tour, even before he is buried?"

"But I am not asking you to do that," said Mr. Lester. "I only say leave this home for mine. You shall remain there in privacy for a few days, and after the funeral I will take you anywhere that you may wish to go. You might, indeed, come to me as a visitor if you very much preferred it; Miss Bordillion is with me, you know; but I think, Adelaide, this would not be so pleasant for you. I am sure you would prefer to enter the Hall at once as its mistress."

"Yes; if I come," she answered.

There is no need to pursue the argument. It is sufficient to say that Mr. Lester obtained her consent, and he went forth to make the necessary arrangements.

Scarcely knowing whether he stood on his head or his heels, he halted outside the Castle. The Hall must be warned, and proper preparations made for the reception of this unexpected bride; the clergyman must be spoken to: which should he go to first? He dashed off to the clergyman's, whose house was at the other extremity of Daneshold, and, as it happened, he chose wrongly, whereby 'ensued some complication.

The Reverend Mr. James was out somewhere in the parish: he would be in directly to his two o'clock dinner. Leaving word that he would call again, Squire Lester bent his hasty steps towards his own home.

It seemed deserted; there was no echo of children's voices to be heard; there was no sign of living creatures to be seen. The remains of a repast, laid in the dining-room, alone greeted Mr. Lester. He rang a peal, in his impatience, that echoed through the house, and Jones came in.

"Where's Miss Bordillion?"

"She's gone, sir."

"Gone where?"

"Gone to Great Cross, sir, with Master Lester and the young ladies. They have been dining now, and will be home to a late tea."

Mr. Lester broke out with an impatient word. Great Cross was a large town some ten miles off by rail. How could proper arrangements be carried out for the hasty reception of his wife at the Hall, in the absence of its present mistress? There were five hundred things on which he wanted to consult Miss Bordillion.

"What on earth took her off to Great Cross to-day?" he exclaimed in his vexation.

"Well, sir," said Jones, who, if he ever condescended to a gossip with any one it was with his master, "I think she's chiefly gone to buy a doll for Miss Lester. Master Wilfred poked out the eyes of the old one yesterday, and melted its wax nose off. Miss Maria cried so that Miss Bordillion promised to buy her one to replace it."

"A new doll indeed!" retorted Mr. Lester; "she's getting too old for dolls. They have no business to go off in this manner for a day without consulting me."

"I heard Miss Bordillion remark to the children, sir, that she was sorry you went out so early this morning, before she could see you. If you had been home a quarter-of-an-hour earlier now, sir, you'd have seen them, for they have not long been gone."

"In that wretched omnibus, I suppose."

"No, sir, Master Wilfred's driving them in the pony-carriage. They were going by the half-past two train."

Mr. Lester pulled out his watch. Ten minutes past two. There would not be time for him to overtake them; though he might have done it had his horse been ready. The railway station was three miles off, and a public omnibus conveyed Danesheld passengers to and fro.

"What are they going to do with the pony-carriage?" he rejoined, quite savagely. "Leave it at the station?"

"Robert went over by the omnibus, sir, to bring it back," answered Jones, wondering much what could have gone wrong with his even-tempered master.

Mr. Lester really was in a dilemma. It was an unusual position to be in: that of having to tell a household that he was about to bring a bride home that day, and things must be in readiness to receive her. In his nature there was a certain reticence which rather deterred him from speaking; he knew nothing whatever about household arrangements, and would have preferred to turn over the whole thing to Miss Bordillion, rather than have to settle matters himself with his servants. And besides—and here lay the gist of the whole matter—he *owed* it to Miss Bordillion to make her acquainted with it at once. Short enough in any case would the notice have been, and he had an instinctive feeling that she would turn restive at the sudden invasion.

"Will you take any luncheon, sir?"

"Send Tiffle here," said Mr. Lester, allowing the question to remain in abeyance. But luncheon was a meal he rarely took.

Tiffle came in: her white muslin apron on; her hands, whilst she waited for orders, smoothing themselves one over the other—as poor Hood, who went from us too early, had it—"washing her hands with invisible soap and imperceptible water." Tiffle seemed to be always doing the same.

She waited, but no words came from Mr. Lester. He was thinking how much he should say and how much he should leave unsaid.

"Did you please to want me, sir?"

Mr. Lester spoke then rather obscurely; giving the woman a hint of the case, and that such and such a possibility might occur. Many maid-servants would not have understood his enigmatical language; but Tiffle's intelligence was of the sharper order.

"Rooms to be made ready for any contingency; Mr. Lester's own rooms; certainly, they should be set about at once. Should things be replaced as they were in the late Mrs. Lester's time? Should the pink silk toilette draperies——"

Mr. Lester lifted his hand in reproof. He did not want to be questioned about details of which he knew nothing. Tiffle, in the absence of Miss Bordillion, must take everything upon herself, and exercise her own judgment.

"It was very good," Tiffle answered. "Would dinner be required?"

But this, Mr. Lester was really unable to say. He supposed it would be: he would endeavour to send word later, and the hour. And Tiffle was to keep a silent tongue in her head, and not talk in the household.

He went up to his rooms, looking round him there, and putting aside various odds-and-ends of his own that were strewed about. A table in the room called his dressing-room, but which he had not used as one of late years, but as a smoking-room if anything, had sundry bundles of papers on it, letters, and other things; these he glanced over, threw some on the floor to be taken away, and the rest he locked up. It smelt of smoke, and he put down the windows and propped the door open. At length he took his departure, and sped back to the clergyman's.

It struck three. He had not thought it so late, and went along hurriedly. Soon he came to the clergyman's gate, and walked up the narrow garden path.

"Is Mr. James come in?"

"He has been in, sir, and is gone again," was the answer of the servant, who stood with the door in his hand.

"Been in and gone again!" echoed Mr. Lester.

"He came in, sir, not five minutes after you were here, and said that he must have his dinner directly. It was served, and I don't think he was ten minutes over it before he was out again."

"Did you give him my message?" inquired Mr. Lester.

ᶠ "Yes, sir. I said you wanted him upon business of very great importance; he replied that he was obliged to go out, but would be back again as soon as possible."

Mr. Lester looked around him in blank consternation. Any delay in the preliminaries, and Lady Adelaide might waver in her bargain, for she was capricious as the wind. Not to call her his own that day now that the cup of bliss had been brought so near him, Mr. Lester would have thought the greatest misfortune in life. Had he gone to his own home in the first instance and come here afterwards, he might have caught both Miss Bordillion and Mr. James. If he knew where to look for the reverend man, he would start off in pursuit; but Danesheld was a tolerably large parish, taking in the rural portion of it, and a very straggling one. Leaving a few pencilled words for Mr. James, he walked away towards the Castle.

The news on his arrival there both soothed and irritated him. Lady Adelaide was dressing for the ceremony. All very well, so far; but what if the clergyman did not make his appearance? Mr. Lester was as a man upon thorns. He saw Lord Dane and asked if he would give Lady Adelaide away. Very quiet was the reply, but it was in the negative; Lord Dane had business elsewhere; and a suspicion arose to Mr. Lester that the new peer was resenting the young lady's hasty departure as a slight upon himself.

It was past six when Mr. Lester again went home. He made some alteration in his dress, and took a mouthful of food as a substitute for dinner, for Lady Adelaide had declined to dine on her arrival. The clergyman had not yet turned up, and Mr. Lester was in a fever. He had been down again to the parsonage now; the servant said her master's tea was waiting for him, and he was sure not to be long.

What about Miss Bordillion? Mr. Lester had been in hopes that she also would be at home, but she was not. He sat down and wrote a note to her, telling Tiffle to give it her as soon as she came in. He then ordered his close carriage and went back in it to the Castle. The clergyman had not come, and he sent the carriage down to the parsonage to wait for him.

As ·Mr. Lester entered the great hall which had been hastily prepared for the ceremony, the late Lord Dane's official table serving for a temporary altar, covered with a gorgeous cloth—who should come fluttering up to him but Cecilia Dane. Lord Dane, as good as his word, had telegraphed for her early in the morning; and what with the hurried journey, and what with the news that greeted her, Miss Dane was more of a child than usual, and began asking him whether she could stand by Lady Adelaide at that altar in her heavy black gown, and whether there was time for her to go home and change it for a white one. Mr. Lester put her aside with a good-humoured word, as he went in search of one nearer and dearer. Black or white, what mattered such surroundings, if only that other one became his! There was a feeling on Mr. Lester, and had been all day, that she might yet slip through his fingers; there always is a fear of the sort, more or less, in regard to anything desired with intensity, when the time of fruition is at hand. And so the evening sped on.

It was getting on for ten o'clock, and Miss Bordillion was seated in an easy chair in the handsome drawing-room at the Hall. She and her charges had come home late, past eight, and glad enough she was, when tea was over, to despatch them to bed and be at rest. Even Wilfred was tired, and had made no demands to sit up later, as he generally did. Somewhat to her surprise, as she thus sat, the servant came in and began to light the large centre chandelier, which was not used in general.

"Why are you lighting that, Jones?"

"Tiffle sent me to do it, ma'am. She thought she heard the carriage coming down the road."

"Is Mr. Lester out in the carriage to-night?"

"Yes, ma'am."

"But why need you light the chandelier? There is sufficient light in the room without it," "

Jones could only repeat that he was doing it by Tiffle's orders. The man had not been made a confidant of by Tiffle, who had kept her information close. He knew there had been some unusual stir going on in the house, but never glanced at the real facts.

The carriage was Mr. Lester's. It slowly came round to the front, and Jones, his lighting finished, hastened out. Another minute and Mr. Lester came in, Lady Adelaide on his arm.

Had Miss Bordillion seen an apparition enter, she could not have been more startled and astonished. Lady Adelaide threw a rich cloak from her white shoulders as she entered, and stood revealed in her evening attire; a white silk robe adorned with costly lace, a pearl necklace, pearl bracelets, and white gloves. A small wreath was round her hair behind, from which fell a veil that looked very like a bridal one. Had Miss Bordillion entertained any suspicion of the truth, and looked closely, she might have seen that the wreath was composed of orange blossoms. But she was too bewildered to look or to think ; and stood with a petrified stare. What should bring Lady Adelaide to the Hall at this hour ? What should have caused her to deck herself out in that manner, with her uncle lying dead at the Castle.

"How do you do, Miss Bordillion ? It is scarcely fair to take the house by storm in this way, is it ? But I believe there was no help for it."

She advanced as she held out her hand, and it brought her under the blaze of light. Never had she looked more beautiful. Margaret Bordillion mechanically touched the offered hand, and glanced at Mr. Lester for an explanation, which he did not appear to see. He was looking at Lady Adelaide.

"Is tea ready, do you know, Margaret ? You would like some at once, would you not, Adelaide ? "

"Oh, yes."

Never had Margaret Bordillion been so scared out of her self-possession. Muttering some half-intelligible words about " telling the servants to bring it in," she escaped from the room. Ere she had gone half-way across the hall, she

remembered that the children had left some toys on the sofa
near the door, not particularly ornamental to a drawing-room,
and she turned back for them.

She opened the door softly, not caring that they should
notice her re-entrance, intending to scramble up the things
and escape again.   Better that she had not gone back!   Mr.
Lester stood with his back to her; he had gathered that fair
girl in his arms, and was whispering words of welcome with
his eyes and lips.   Margaret left the toys and went out
again, a dim suspicion, not of the truth, but of something like
it, beginning to make its way to her brain.

At the foot of the stairs she encountered Tiffle and Sophie
Deffloe.   The latter was without her bonnet, and looked as
much at home as if she had lived in the Hall for a year.
Tiffle was gorgeous in a stiffened-out old purple silk gown,
and white bows in her cap.

"I've been showing mem'zel her lady's rooms," said Tiffle,
her green eyes turned stealthily on Miss Bordillion's changing
face; "leastways master's rooms, which is the same thing
now.   But the luggage hasn't come down yet from the Castle,
and mem'zel can't unpack."

"Has Lady Adelaide Errol come to remain the night?"
inquired Margaret, more bewildered, more at sea than ever.
"Here, in Mr. Lester's house?"

"My lady's come for good, ma'am; come home," responded
Tiffle, winking and blinking as if the light of the hall lamp
dazzled her eyes, though in reality never taking them from
the face of Miss Bordillion.   "She and master have just been
married, and he has just brought her home.   Didn't the note
he left explain—Goodness me!" broke off Tiffle, diving into
her pocket, "to think that I should have forgot to give you
this, ma'am?   I'm sure I beg ten thousand pardens!   Mr.
Lester wrote it when he was at home this afternoon, and
charged me to give it you myself, and I put it in my pocket
for safety.   Out of sight, out of mind."

She had kept it there purposely, and she knew it.
Margaret did not faint: she only leaned against the wall
for a moment's support; her face was growing ghastly,
but she strove to carry it all off with an easy hand, and her

poor dry lips parted with a faint smile as she turned to Sophie.

"Married! Indeed?"

"But I surely thought it never would have got done to-night, miss," spoke up that self-possessed and voluble demoiselle. "My young lady has been sitting dressed since this afternoon, and the curé—what you call parson—could not be found. It was nine o'clock when he came, and we had nearly given him up. They were married in the great salon, the hall; and Miss Dane, she was maid of honour in a black robe. It was bad luck that, and I said so; but they would not listen. My lady's dress was all right; it was a new one made for her just before these troubles, and she had never worn it; and I went out and succeeded in getting the veil and the flowers in Danesheld."

Margaret Bordillion had heard enough. Tiffle began to tell of the confidence her master had reposed in her, and the bustle it had put her and the housemaids in; but she succeeded in passing them, and went up the stairs. The doors of Mr. Lester's rooms were open, and a flood of light came forth from them into the corridor. Margaret leaned her aching head against the wall, and opened the letter.

It contained only a few brief lines; explaining to her what was in contemplation, and the reasons for the haste—that Lady Adelaide had no other home to go to, and wished at once to leave the Castle, of which the new peer had taken possession. The words were penned with the utmost kindness, almost tenderness; and she stood looking at them she knew not how long, her sight dimmed by misery.

"Margaret."

The call startled her, for it was Mr. Lester's. Crushing the note into her pocket, and passing her hand across her eyes and brow, she moved to the head of the staircase and answered it.

"Yes."

"Do come down and make tea, Margaret," he said, running lightly up. "Poor Adelaide feels shy and strange; it is only natural she should do so, coming thus suddenly amidst us all. It is quite an exceptional case, you see."

" I—I cannot," gasped Margaret. " Indeed I cannot."

Mr. Lester took one of the trembling hands in his, and laid the other gently on her shoulder.

" Margaret, forgive me. I see that this is an awful blow to you, and can discern its source. You are thinking of the slight on poor Katherine. The feeling may be a just one ; but remember she is gone. Do not—do not let it prejudice you against my young wife, whom I have just sworn to love and cherish. Come down to her in your woman's pity."

Thinking of Katherine ! Well, better that he should have taken up the idea. Almost unconscious of what she did, she yielded mechanically to his hand, which grasped hers tightly, and drew her gently·after him.

" I did not know of it," she said. " Tiffle never gave me the note you left. Of course you took me by surprise."

" Tiffle's a fool for her pains then," returned Mr. Lester.

The tea-things were in the drawing-room then, and Sophie was taking off her lady's veil. Adelaide turned to Miss Bordillion.

" It was in my way when I sat down," she said, in a tone that sounded something like an apology. " It is a long one."

" You will not have the wreath off as well, my lady," asked Sophie.

" No. That does not trouble me."

Sophie retired, folding up the veil, and Lady Adelaide came and sat at the table by Miss Bordillion. With an action that seemed like the petulance of a spoiled child, she took her gloves off, and flung them on the table. It left the wedding ring conspicuous : she wore no other.

" I wonder how long it will be before I grow used to it ?" she said, glancing at Mr. Lester.

He only smiled in answer. Margaret was already making the tea. But how she got through the evening—and with a calm exterior—she does not know to this hour.

The next day she encountered them both : not by her own wish ; rather in express opposition to it. She remained in her own sitting-room all the morning, keeping the children with her, except rebellious Wilfred, who was off, she knew hot whither. After their morning lessons were over, they went out to play, Margaret with them. The fresh air might be good for her fainting spirit. "Come quietly this way," she whispered; and took them down the back stairs, and out by the back door, avoiding the ordinary passages in her dread of seeing Mr. Lester and his wife.

They went to what was called "Mrs. Lester's garden," a square piece of ground, close to the house, but well sheltered from view by trees and shrubs. Here Margaret sat down on a bench, and the two girls did what they chose. Both were very *young* children for their age; or, it may rather be said, for the present age. They were thoroughly natural, and simple: a few, let us say it in gratitude, are to be met with still, who are not women before their time. Maria had her doll's perambulator; the new doll, bought yesterday at Great Cross, was seated in it in state: a wondrous doll, as large as a baby, with blue eyes and flaxen hair, not unlike the new stepmother Maria had yet to see. Strange as it may seem, Lady Adelaide Errol and Mr. Lester's children had never met, although she had been so long at Dane Castle. But Mr. Lester was not one who liked to take his children out with him, or allow them to appear when he had guests at home.

A sudden noise caused Miss Bordillion to look up. Wilfred had appeared on the scene, was making a raid on the new doll, and the little girls began to scream. Margaret, anxious to avoid noise to-day, went towards them to end the disturbance by her authority, and found Master Wilfred holding the doll head downwards above their reach, and enjoying their distress. But the noise subsided before she was quite up with them: the girls ceased screaming and stood still; Wilfred, with a pleasant laugh, put the outraged doll back in its carriage; and Miss Bordillion found herself face to face with Lady Adelaide Lester.

"I think I have lost my way," she said, with a smile, holding out her hand in greeting to Miss Bordillion. "Mr. Lester came out with me, but stayed to speak to some man, and I walked on. Are you quite well this morning?"

"Quite well," murmured Margaret, whose colour went

and came to such a degree that it caught the observation of Master Wilfred, absorbed though he was. The boy had propped his back against a tree, and was staring at his new stepmother. She had resumed her deep mourning to-day, and wore a black burnous cloak of some thin material, with silken tassels; but there was nothing to protect her head except its abundance of bright flaxen hair, of the same colour as Maria's doll.

"And now I must know which is which," she said, with a smile at the two children. "This is Maria," she continued, pointing to Edith.

There was a laugh. Maria blushed and said no, she was Maria. Lady Adelaide looked at her for a minute, more critically than kindly.

"She is not like Mr. Lester."

"She's like our dead mamma," put in Wilfred; "only prettier."

Lady Adelaide turned upon him. "You are like Mr. Lester," she said. "I should have known you anywhere for his son. How old are you?"

"Fourteen."

"Fourteen! I had no idea the children were so old," she murmured, half to herself. "I don't think I ever asked, though. Is he always at home?" she added, looking at Miss Bordillion.

"Only in the holidays, in general. This is an exceptional time. He is at Rugby. Illness broke out in the school, and the boys were sent home."

"I shall not trouble you, Lady Adelaide," put in the boy, "if you are afraid of that. I can keep myself out of your way."

She looked gravely at him, as if she were weighing the words. In reality she was looking at the marvellous beauty of his face, of his blue eyes. Wilfred, of a touchy nature, hot-tempered and proud, thought she did not believe his assurance. It may be that the boy in his heart was resenting his father's second marriage just as keenly as was Miss Bordillion.

"Shall I take an oath to do so, Lady Adelaide? I will if you like."

What could have caused the words so to tell upon her? Her face became hot and cold, as one in terror; and she looked from him to Miss Bordillion; from Miss Bordillion to him again: a stealthy look of fear.

"Why do you say that to me?"

"I thought you seemed to doubt me," returned Wilfred, who was regarding his new stepmother as keenly as she was regarding him. "I don't suppose you will have anything at all to do with us; Miss Bordillion sees to Maria."

Lady Adelaide turned away with a laugh, and held out her hand to the little girls. "Which of you will show me the way to the rosery?" she asked. "Mr. Lester was going to take me to it, but I suppose I have caused him to miss me, by turning in here."

They both responded to the challenge and ran forward with her. Wilfred Lester followed them with his eyes.

"I don't like her at all, Margaret. She is not kind."

"Hush, Wilfred. You cannot judge of what she is, or tell whether you will like her or not, until you shall have seen more of her."

"Can't I?" answered the bold boy, "we shall see if we live long enough. Good-day to you, Margaret; I'm going for a sail with old Gand."

As he vaulted away in one direction, Mr. Lester appeared in another, looking for his wife. With almost feverish nervousness, as though she feared the moment for speaking would be lost, Margaret Bordillion went up and accosted him. She had lain awake the whole of the previous night, thinking of her plans, and she hastened to unfold them.

With rapid, eager utterance, — with words that were utterly unlike the usually calm tones of Miss Bordillion,— she poured forth her wish; nay, her prayer. She would hire that small house of his that was vacant, Cliff Cottage, if he would accept her as a tenant; there she would live and keep Edith with her and educate her; she had been thinking that perhaps he would allow her to have Maria also.

Mr. Lester laughed in answer.

"How can you be so foolish, Margaret? Cliff Cottage?

Why, it isn't large enough to swing a cat in. And where's
your income to come from to keep it up?"

"I have a hundred a year of my own, as you know. And
the money that Major Bordillion intended to pay for Edith's
schooling can be paid to me instead, if I educate her.
Perhaps you will also pay me for Maria?"

"Well, you have settled it nicely! What on earth is
running in your head, Margaret?"

"You will not want any of us now: you have your wife.
Wilfred is the greater part of his time at school; Maria
will be better with me than at home. As you once observed,
Lady Adelaide possesses neither the age nor the experience
to take upon herself so great a tie, even if she had the
inclination."

"But what I want to know is, why you need leave us at
all?" rejoined Mr. Lester. "You can be just as comfortable here as you have been. The house——"

"It could not be; it could not be," she interrupted, in
unmistakable agitation. Mr. Lester regarded her with
surprise.

"Why not?" he asked, after a pause. "That you have
some powerful motive for this proposed flight from the
Hall, I plainly see. Will you not tell me what it is?"

The painful crimson suffused her face and then left it
pale as marble. Did he suspect the truth then, as he gazed
upon her emotion? It cannot be said; Margaret never
knew, then or afterwards. He gave no sign, save that an
answering flush rose to his own brow and dyed it red.

"You shall have Cliff Cottage, if you wish it so very
much," he said, gently. "But as to Maria——we will talk
of that another time."

She bowed her thanks, and Mr. Lester turned away
abruptly in search of the Lady Adelaide.

CHAPTER XIII.

CHANGES.

HERBERT GEOFFRY, seventeenth Baron Dane, stepped into the honours of his ancestors, inherited and conferred. He set out with an intention to deserve them. The unsigned will of the late Lord Dane he carried out to the letter. Every wish stated in it he honourably fulfilled ; every legacy bequeathed in it he paid, just as though the deed had been duly executed. The Lady Adelaide's name was down in it for fifteen thousand pounds, and that sum was paid over to Mr. Lester.

But some great change had come over the young lord ; a strange sadness seemed to hang ever upon him. He confined himself very much to the Castle, paying few visits, and living as quietly as he could well do. The impulsive, careless spendthrift appeared to have taken another nature with his inheritance, and all at once to have become sober and prudent. Marks of this were daily apparent, and Daneshold looked on in wonder. Some of the domestics were dismissed with a year's wages, and the household at the Castle was re-organised on a small scale.

If there was one person not satisfied with the new peer, that one was John Mitchel : for he had been rejected as tenant for the Sailors' Rest. Mr. Apperly had gone on and completed the assignment of the lease to the man, in spite of Lord Dane's warning : he was destined to find the parchment useless ; and that the Sailors' Rest was to be given to Richard Ravensbird.

" To Ravensbird ! " he exclaimed in his astonishment when the news burst upon him—not that the word is quite appropriate, for Lord Dane spoke in a particularly unemotional tone. " *Ravensbird !* Surely your lordship does not intend to bestow it upon him ? "

" Yes, I do. Did you not know he was one of the applicants ? "

" Oh, I knew *that*, well enough. But I should have thought

your lordship would put him at the bottom of the list; or, rather, put him out of it altogether."

"Your opinion and mine, then, Apperly, are at issue upon the point," said Lord Dane pleasantly. "I cannot divest myself of the feeling that the man has had some injustice dealt out to him lately; and I think we Danes owe him a recompense. And, setting that aside, why should I not let him have the house? He is ready with the money, and will no doubt be a good tenant."

"Can your mind entirely absolve him from all suspicion —in regard to that night's fatal work?"

"It has absolved him long ago," was Lord Dane's reply. "I as fully and truly believe in Ravensbird's alibi as I do that you and I are talking face to face. I should not be likely, otherwise, to let him rent any house of mine."

"It will be a terrible blow to Mitchel," groaned Mr. Apperly, thinking of a certain bank-note that was lying in his desk.

"Not more than it would be to Ravensbird, if I chose Mitchel and rejected him. In common justice, I repeat, it is Ravensbird who ought to have it; he was the first to apply to Hawthorne, and he also came to me, asking my interest with Lord Dane."

"Lord Dane would never have given it him," said the lawyer testily. "He gave it to Mitchel. It was as good as giving it."

"At any rate, I elect in favour of Ravensbird," was the decisive answer; and the lawyer winced at the tone. "You can make out the necessary documents. It is exceedingly unjust, I know, to cast one man's sin upon another," resumed Lord Dane after a pause, "but, to tell you the truth, I can't bear to hear the name of Mitchel. Had his brother, the preventive-man, not lost his wits that night, Harry Dane might now be living amongst us."

"In that case your lordship would not be Lord Dane," was the lawyer's bold rejoinder.

"A very slight calamity in comparison with his death," returned Lord Dane. "I would give up all my revenues cheerfully, if it would bring him to life again."

So Mr. Apperly had to make out fresh papers and return the ten-pound note, which was something like having a tooth drawn. No chance was there of getting any such douceur from Ravensbird : if that gentleman could not obtain his ends by sturdy independence in a fair field, he would never bribe for them. Mr. Apperly, in his anger, told John Mitchel that the new Lord Dane could not forgive his brother for having " played the idiot " that night : and John Mitchel forthwith rushed off to the coastguardsman, with reproaches loud and deep, which nearly brought another fit on that weak and shrinking man.

Ravensbird paid down the requisite money, and, on the departure of Hawthorne, took possession of the Sailors' Rest. One singular clause Lord Dane caused to be inserted in the lease ; that, by giving Ravensbird six weeks' notice, he could at any time oblige him to leave the house. Ravensbird demurred to this ; he had never heard of such a proviso in any lease in the world, he said, and he should like to know the motive for inserting it. Lord Dane did not give his motive, but he was resolute as to its insertion : and Ravensbird at length signed the lease, objectionable clause and all, and entered into possession.

" Much good Ravensbird would do at it ! or any other man who had no wife ! " was one of the gratuitous comments offered · by the busy neighbourhood. " Who ever heard of an inn prospering without a landlady ? " Ravensbird heard all with the coolest equanimity.

Changes took place at the Hall. Miss Bordillion was moving out of it into Cliff Cottage, taking Edith with her. She had saved a very little money out of her hundred a year, which she expended on furniture, and Mr. Lester desired her to send down any articles she liked from the Hall. Tiffle made a face over the generosity, and bewailed it openly ; though Miss Bordillion chose very few things, and those of the plainest.

On the day following Lord Dane's funeral, Mr. and Lady Adelaide Lester quitted Danesheld for Paris ; an unknown place to Adelaide, which she had long been wild to see, believing it to be neither more nor less than the paradise

of the lower world. Mademoiselle Sophie Deffloe had re-
peatedly assured her that it was nothing else. This gave
Miss Bordillion time for her arrangements : as *they* were
gone, there was no immediate hurry for her quitting the
Hall : but she would leave it before they returned.

Tiffle was playing her cards well. Upon Lady Adelaide's
coming home in the unexpected manner related, Tiffle, though
apparently all smiles and sweetness, was inwardly full of
vengeance, and vowed to leave at the month's end. But during
the very few days that Lady Adelaide and Mr. Lester remained at the Hall, Tiffle began to discern that she might
possibly make it worth her while to remain. Lady Adelaide
was young, careless, inexperienced, and yielding : when
Tiffle went to her for orders, she would say, "Oh, I don't
know anything about it ; do as you like ; ask Miss Bordillion :" and it dawned upon Tiffle's mind that with this
young lady at the head of the household she *could* do as
she liked ; more effectually than she had done even during
the timid sway of that other lady. And so Tiffle gave her
cards a shuffle, and set about ingratiating herself with the
new mistress, making things easy and comfortable for her
on her return.

The weeks went on. Miss Dane still inhabited her former
home, the little ivied house—very much to her own dis-
satisfaction. Dane Castle seemed an enviable place to
live at : it was very strange, she thought, that her brother
could not have her with him, and one day she told
him so. She paid him a visit of many hours almost every
day, and received, as the Castle's mistress, any visitors who
might call. She and her brother were standing together
at the drawing-room window when she spoke, their eyes
following a carriage that was rolling away smoothly down
the road ; a well appointed close carriage, whose inmates,
Mr. and Lady Adelaide Lester, had just been paying their
first visit to the Castle. Miss Dane stood by her brother in
deep mourning, with her drooping curls and pink cheeks.

It was the first time Lord Dane had seen Lady Adelaide
since her marriage. He called at the Hall after their return
—fulfilling punctually the social requirements of life—but

they had gone out for a drive. The sojourn in Paris had lasted two months, and Lady Adelaide, who had plunged into all the gaiety that the season allowed, seemed glad to be at home again.

"How changed she is, Herbert!" exclaimed Miss Dane, as the carriage receded from their sight.

"Shall you ever remember to drop that name of mine, do you think, Cecilia?" was the rejoinder of Lord Dane.

"Geoffry, then, to please you. I do forget; but it does not matter much, does it, dear? Don't you think she's changed somehow?"

"Not particularly, that I see."

"Oh! but she is. She's thin and pale and worn; she looks like one who is wearied to death."

He made no rejoinder. He was leaning against the deep window-frame, his eyes fixed on the distant waves beyond the ruins, his fingers unconsciously playing with his watch-guard. Was he thinking of those happy meetings he used to hold with her, his best and dearest love; with her who was now the wife of another?

"I hope she has not made a mistake," resumed Miss Dane, in her little chirping voice. "It must be very nice to be married, and have a beautiful home, and a husband of your own, especially if he's handsome, and not too old; but, oh dear! if it does not turn out happily afterwards! I should have a bower made of weeping willows, and sit in it with my guitar, and cry all day, if it were my case. That would be a little relief, wouldn't it, Geoffry?"

Geoffry just moved his lips by way of intimating that he heard. But Miss Dane was one of those happy persons who can talk on with unruffled equanimity, answered or unanswered.

"He's very handsome; every one knows that. Sometimes, when I'm looking at him in church, I wonder whether there's another face in the world as beautiful as his. But I never fell in love with him, Geoffry; I never did, indeed; he has had one wife, you know, and very nice she was, though delicate: and his children are half as old as I am. Perhaps Adelaide thinks of that, now that it's too late. Oh dear!"

Lord Dane took up a glass that lay on the table behind him, and gazed attentively at a ship that was passing. The sun's rays played upon his bright hair, upon his pale features, on which there sat a sad, subdued sort of expression, that Miss Dane did not remember to have previously seen.

"Geoffry, *you* look changed," she said, shaking back her smooth ringlets: "and do you know, you *are* changed, now I come to think of it! You are so much more silent than you used to be, and you seem always to be thinking. I'm sure you did not say three words to Adelaide just now, and that was not polite of you; she's a bride, you know, dear."

"I was talking to Mr. Lester."

"Not much. Herbert, I'll tell you what it is—Geoffry, I mean—you are getting moped through living alone in this great place, not a soul to speak to, morning and evening, but the servants. And I'm sure I'm moped at home."

"That vessel has the Prussian flag flying, Cecilia," exclaimed Lord Dane, steadying the glass. "She's a queer build. Wouldn't you like to look at her?"

"I don't care to look at flags and ships. I want something else, Geoffry."

"Well, what do you want?" he asked, looking down kindly on the weak, childish, but ever sweet-tempered face, turned pleadingly to his.

"I never teased you about it, Geoffry, but indeed I wish you'd let me. It's hardly right, now that you are the great Lord Dane."

"What is not right?"

"To leave me in that poor little house all alone, whilst you enjoy this large fine castle," she answered, smoothing down the crêpe trimmings on her gown, as we sometimes see a timid little maiden smoothing down her white pinafore as she stands shyly before us. "You might let me come and live here, Geoffry. It is strange you should not. We always have lived together, and I am your only sister."

"Whenever I settle down at the Castle, Cecilia, you shall come to it."

"But have you not settled down?"

"No. I am going away from it almost immediately. It

has been my intention to travel ever since my uncle died ; but business matters have delayed my departure. I shall soon go away, and perhaps for a long time."

" Oh dear ! " ejaculated Miss Dane.

" I have never had an opportunity of visiting the continental world, beyond one or two brief visits to Paris ; I have been too poor, as you know," resumed Lord Dane. " There's nothing to prevent me now."

" What am I to do ? " she asked, piteously.

" Make yourself happy at home with your birds and your flowers, Cely, as you will be. There's not a woman living who possesses a more cheerful and contented mind than you."

" But, Geoffry, can I stay all alone by myself ? "

" I should not trust you," he answered, with a faint attempt to be gay. " You shall have Mrs. Knox with you, and I'll allow you any amount of income you may ask for."

" I shall like to have Mrs. Knox," returned Miss Dane, who was as easily pleased as a child. " And how long shall you be away, Geoffry—three months ? "

" Three years, more likely."

" Oh, Geoffry ! "

He interrupted the startled scream. In truth, he had spoken in careless haste, not having intended to admit so much.

" I really cannot tell how long I shall remain away, Cecilia. Possessing no definite plans, it is impossible to say what I may do, or where I may go. Of one thing you may rest assured—that I shall come back some time, Heaven permitting me ; and when I do come, you shall make your home here at the Castle, and be its mistress."

" How nice that will be ! " she said, twirling her fingers in and out of her light-brown ringlets. " But, Geoffry, you may be bringing home a wife. You may, you know."

Geoffry Dane shook his head. " I think not," he answered, and his tone was rather peculiarly decisive. " But, Cecilia —about yourself, during my absence. You would like a pony-carriage, would you not ? And you must keep one or two additional servants ; I should prefer it. You will be more comfortable, I know, in the small home, than you would be in this rambling, gloomy old place without me. When I return you shall play the great lady in it."

Cecilia Dane clapped her hands; but even in the very act, some feeling stole over her, which caused her to bend her pink cheeks and droop her eyelids in confusion.

" What is it, Cely ? "

" I may be married myself by that time, Geoffry. Don't you think so ? "

Lord Dane laughed. " Of course you may. But, Cecilia " —and his tone turned to gravity—" you must promise me one thing : that you will not marry any one, that is, that you will not engage yourself to any one, without first writing to consult me. I'll never stand in your way, when it is for your real happiness; but you have money, and will have more, and you don't know what sort of pretenders may be coming after it. Confide in Mrs. Knox, as you did when you were a little girl ; and write constantly to me. You will promise all this ? "

" I promise it faithfully, Geoffry ; for I know I am not wise."

And Lord Dane knew that he might implicitly trust her. As she said, she was not wise, and she was older than he, but she was very easily guided; and she yielded to his judgment always, with the perfect simple faith of a child.

Did you observe the remark made by Miss Dane in the above conversation which related to Lady Adelaide Lester ? She was changed; was thin, and pale, and worn, looking like one who is wearied to death.

As the days and weeks went on, others began to make the same remark : Lady Adelaide seemed to have something the matter with her. She was happy enough with Mr. Lester, so far as the world saw; but there was a listless apathy in her manner which does not generally accompany content-ment. There was one peculiarity that had never been observed in her before : when accosted suddenly, she would start as if in fear, and be some moments recovering her self-possession. Had she made a mistake in marrying George Lester? Had the conviction come to her, now that it was too late ? Lord Dane, her once betrothed lover, had warned her that her days, if she did marry him, would be one long unsatisfied yearning—a yearning for escape from the existence she had imposed on herself. Had he spoken with prevision? That she was a disappointed woman, who had some dark shadow following her, a keen discerner could not doubt.

One, at least, did not see or suspect this; and that was Mr. Lester. That gentleman's fondness for his wife was as a passion, in which all ordinary observation was lost. He only lived to love her, to study her wishes, to obey her as a slave. Her slightest will was made law; her most trifling wish was carried out. That it would render her imperious and exacting was almost certain; but Mr. Lester was too completely absorbed in the present to think of the future. He never suspected that she was not happy. Since her marriage her health had been rather delicate; quite sufficient, in that fond man's judgment, to account for her loss of spirits; and he supposed, as she regained her strength, and the past troubles at the Castle grew more distant, the old gaiety and the saucy repartee would return. She had no ties at the Hall; Wilfred Lester had returned to Rugby, and Maria was at Cliff Cottage, under the charge of Miss Bordillion. In Mr. Lester's doting love for his new wife, the love of his children was fading to a very faint sentiment. He had never been a man to bestow upon them much tenderness, and it is probable that his wife had it in her power to draw him effectually from them, if she chose to do so.

"Shall Maria remain at home with a governess, or shall I place her with Miss Bordillion?" he had asked his wife on their return from Paris.

"Place her with Miss Bordillion," said Lady Adelaide at once; "there will be no responsibility on me, and we shall be better alone. She can come and stay with us at times, you know."

So Mr. Lester made the arrangement with Miss Bordillion, paying her a liberal sum with Maria, and the Hall was free.

One morning Sophie Deffloe came to her mistress. She would give warning, if my lady pleased—she hoped my lady would allow her to leave as soon as it was convenient.

Lady Adelaide, much surprised and annoyed, for anything seemed to have power to surprise or annoy her now,
inquired, with some asperity, what Sophie meant; and
Sophie, with matter-of-fact equanimity, as became one of
her nation, replied that she had made up her mind to marry
Richard Ravensbird.

"Ravensbird has taken the Sailors' Rest!" exclaimed
Lady Adelaide.

"Oh dear yes, my lady, these three months past, and very
well he is doing at it."

"But, Sophie, you would surely never go to live there; to
stand in the bar and draw ale for people!"

"My faith, but I would," said Sophie. "Why not? I
think it is just the sort of life I should like, my lady."

Lady Adelaide made a gesture of contempt: there was no
accounting for taste. "But should you like Ravensbird?"
she asked. "He is very ugly."

"As I tell him every day; but for myself, my lady, I don't
find him so ugly. It has happened before now," added the
bold Sophie, "that wives have been happier with ugly men
than with handsome ones. Any way, I mean to try it, when
your ladyship can suit yourself."

The retort did not altogether please Lady Adelaide, and
she haughtily told Sophie Deffloe that she was at liberty to
leave at once. But Sophie knew better than to take her
lady at her word, for Lady Adelaide could not have got on
without her, until she had some one to replace her. But at
this juncture Tiffle stepped in; Tiffle with her deferent
manner, and her smooth tongue. If my lady pleased, she
would supply Sophie's place for the present; she thoroughly
understood the duties of a lady's-maid, and her housekeeping
office was not so onerous but that it left plenty of time on
her hands.

For Tiffle voluntarily to offer to saddle herself with a
double duty would have astounded her friends, had they
heard her make the offer. But Tiffle knew what she was
about. To get Mademoiselle Sophie Deffloe and her independence out of the house, Tiffle would have worked her
hands to the bone, so that she might acquire greater and

greater sway over her yielding young mistress. There was not much chance of that whilst Sophie was there; so Tiffle made the offer she did. She had been living in a state of chronic rage with Sophie, for Sophie utterly repudiated the authority of the housekeeper, which was exercised with so crafty a hand over the rest of the household.

Lady Adelaide accepted the offer. Anything for a change; and, besides, during the last few months, she had fallen into a habit of shrinking from her maid, instead of reproving her, when the girl on occasion spoke with unwarrantable freedom. In her inmost heart she was perhaps glad to get rid of the French girl; and Sophie found she was really at liberty to depart when she pleased.

So the arrangement was carried out. Sophie Defloe became the wife of Richard Ravensbird, that newly-elevated lady taking up her post in the bar at nine o'clock on the morning after her marriage-day, with all the cool and easy self-possession of a Frenchwoman; and Tiffle entered on her duties as maid to the Lady Adelaide. It was intended by the latter to be only a temporary arrangement, whilst she looked out for some one to replace Sophie; but Tiffle became so delightfully useful, that Lady Adelaide was in no hurry to commence the search. Tiffle made herself quite necessary to her mistress, and beguiled her listless ears with no end of insinuating gossip, touching the household, touching Miss Bordillion, especially touching Master Wilfred Lester. Tiffle meant from the first to prejudice her mistress against that unconscious young gentleman, and Tiffle succeeded.

And thus the months went on. Lord Dane had departed on his continental tour, Bruff and one or two servants being left to take care of the Castle. Miss Dane remained at the little ivied house with her birds and flowers, and her new pony-carriage and her guitar, and Mrs. Knox, a worthy middle-aged lady who had once been her governess. Ravensbird and his wife did well at the Sailors' Rest, and Tiffle wormed herself further and further into the confidence of her mistress.

No little excitement was created one day in Danesheld by

the arrival of a packman in close custody, who had been
arrested at Great Cross. A zealous policeman, noticing
that this man's appearance tallied with the description of
the one supposed now to have been the murderer of Harry
Dane, arrested him forthwith, and took him off to Danesheld.
However, when Drake was sent for, he declared that he was
not the man whom he had seen disputing with Captain
Dane, and Squire Lester confirmed this. Both were tall,
big men, it was true; but the faces were quite dissimilar,
said Mr. Lester: this was rather a pleasant-looking man,
and seemed honest enough; the other was evil-looking.
So the man perforce was set at liberty again, as Ravensbird
had been.

"Shall you ever find the right one, do you think, Bent?"
Mr. Lester stopped to ask the sergeant.

Bent shook his head. "I hardly know what to think, sir.
The fellow has hidden himself effectually, that's certain;
but these things mostly do come out, sooner or later. I
suppose, sir, you never hear your lady make any allusion to
that night's work?"

"Not any. It would not be a pleasant theme for her to
converse upon."

"It was very odd, but I could not divest myself of the
notion at the time, that her ladyship knew more than she
told us," resumed the sergeant.

Mr. Lester turned his face on the speaker, the haughty
expression, which had begun to dawn upon it, giving way to
surprise.

"Lady Adelaide took an oath that she did not, sergeant."

"I know she did," answered the sergeant, biting the end
of a straw.

"Then you need not raise any further question on that
score. Good-day, Bent."

"I'm aware I needn't," said the sergeant to himself, as he
gave his parting salutation to Mr. Lester; "would it be of
any use if I did? But I know one thing—that if any woman
ever puzzled me since I joined, it was that one, oath or no
oath. She's a deep one, I'll swear, is my Lady Adelaide."

Thus matters progressed at Danesheld. And for the next

nine or ten years no particular change occurred that we need pause to notice. A very long period, you will think, nine or ten years. True; but they do not seem so long in passing to the actors on life's stage, neither did these uneventful years appear to linger to the inhabitants of Dancsheld.

CHAPTER XIV.

WILFRED LESTER COMES TO GRIEF.

You would observe the term in the last chapter, "nine or ten years," and possibly think it more vague than it need be. But it was said with a purpose; for, though the narrative will finally and very speedily progress after the end of the tenth, we must first of all notice something that occurred at the end of the ninth.

Danesheld Hall was alive with little feet, and merry voices, six children having been born to Lady Adelaide Lester and her husband. They had not altogether brought peace with them; they might have brought more had they entailed less expense. Mr. Lester was now a man of care and perplexity, scheming how he might best meet the heavy calls upon him. But he believed in his wife still, and loved her as few men, arrived at his age, do love.

And she? Ah, well, I hardly know what to say. Were I to say that she had been a bad wife, it would not be quite true. A strictly faithful wife she was, but a very heartless one.

Women, as well as men, must have some object in life, whether good or bad, unless they would be hopelessly miserable. Lady Adelaide Lester had none. It seemed that she did not care sufficiently for existence to have one. The old listlessness had settled into a state of hopeless ennui, and she passed her frivolous days in escaping from it. From the very first she had run heedlessly into expense, and

carried her husband along with her; the scale of expenditure
that would have been moderate for the head of Dane Castle,
was simply ruinous for the master of Danesheld Hall; but
Lady Adelaide had not the sense to see this.   Her dress
alone cost, Heaven knew how much; ten times more than it
ought to have done.   They had a town house now, and
entered into all the gaieties of the London season, year after
year; they spent the early spring in Paris as a rule, and
Lady Adelaide said she could not exist without it; indeed,
the only time when they were tolerably quiet was the
autumn of the year; and that was spent at Danesheld.
How all this could be supported on Mr. Lester's compara-
tively slender income of three thousand pounds a year, I
will leave you to judge.   It was not quite three thousand
pounds now; he had been obliged to sell out capital, and
so had lessened it, and a large portion of this belonged to
Miss Lester.   The fifteen thousand pounds bequeathed to
Lady Adelaide by the late Lord Dane was as a drop of
water to the ocean, and had been spent long ago.   The
children, coming so quickly, were no hindrance to the restlessness, the extravagance of their mother; there was a
temporary seclusion as each little being appeared, and then
it was turned over to a hired nurse, and the Lady Adelaide
was herself again.   It was not that she did not love her
children; she loved them with a jealous, exacting love;
but she thought that *to be* with children was one of the
cardinal ills of earth, and, except at Danesheld, rarely
had them with her.   She loved them so much as to be
blindly unjust; but she attempted no sort of training.
She liked them to come in to dessert extravagantly
dressed, and she would take them out in the carriage,
decked out like little dolls.   At these times they were
ruinously indulged.   Poor Mr. Lester thought all the care
that had come upon him was only the natural result of a
large family; and he bemoaned his ill fate that the
gods had not been favourable to him in curtailing the
number.

Tiffle was at the Hall still, and Tiffle flourished.   She
retained her post as maid to Lady Adelaide, and she ruled

the servants with the hand of authority, strong, firm, and indisputable. In the first years of the marriage, Tiffle had accompanied Lady Adelaide in her journeys ; but, when the family increased, it was found necessary for Tiffle to remain at the Hall in control, and Lady Adelaide engaged a French maid ; an airy damsel who talked French with the little ones when she was at the Hall, and during these sojourns yielded very much of her place about her lady to Tiffle.

In one matter Tiffle had succeeded to her utmost satisfaction—that of stirring up a bitter feud between Lady Adelaide and Wilfred Lester. There was no open warfare, and Wilfred saw little of Lady Adelaide at any time ; but it is not too strong an expression to say that there was mutual hatred in their hearts. In Lady Adelaide's blind injustice, she regarded Wilfred as an interloper in the house ; as one who would inflict a grievous wrong upon her own children if Mr. Lester should bequeath to him—as it might reasonably be supposed he would—his due share of patrimony. Wilfred's share would have been a large share, since half Mr. Lester's fortune came to him from his first wife. Wilfred, on his side, naturally resented in his heart the second marriage of his father, since it had resulted in virtually breaking up a home for himself and sister. They occasionally went to it, it is true, but as visitors more than children of the house—as interlopers, in fact ; and it was made evident to both that they were so regarded ; and more especially evident was it made to Wilfred. This injustice of course created a very bitter feeling in Wilfred's heart. His father seemed to be weaned from him more and more as the days went on, and Wilfred *knew* that Lady Adelaide made mischief between them.

Wilfred went to college early, and when he had kept a few terms a commission was purchased for him in one of the crack regiments. It will set him up, said Lady Adelaide to her husband ; and, she mentally added to herself, prevent him from being a nuisance here. Set him up ! Every one knows what are the expenses of the officers in an exclusive corps ; not absolutely necessary expenses, but rendered essential by custom and example. The pay of one of these officers is as nothing compared with his expenditure ; and those who do not possess a reserved purse, and a tolerably heavy one too, have no business to join, for they are certain to come to grief. Mr. Lester ought to have weighed these considerations, and remembered how very little he could afford to allow his son.

He did not weigh them ; and Wilfred entered. Careless, good-natured, attractive, and remarkably handsome, he was just the man to be made much of by his brother-officers. Never was there a young fellow more popular in the corps than Cornet Lester ; and—it is of no use to mince the matter—never was there one who ran more heedlessly into extravagance. Example is contagious, and Cornet Lester suffered himself to be swayed by it—swayed and ruined. Had Mr. Lester made him a better allowance—as he ought to have done, or else not have placed him in the regiment— it would still have been swallowed up, though affairs would not have come to a crisis as soon as they did. Wilfred had been in it just four years, when Mr. Lester was summoned to London in haste. Mr. Wilfred had fallen into the hands of the Philistines, and was in durance vile. He confessed his position openly enough to his father, and laid the full statement of affairs before him. Money he must have ; and not a small sum either.

" I can't give it you," said Mr. Lester.

" Then it will not be possible for me to remain in the regiment."

" It is not possible. You will have to sell out, and apply the money to the liquidation of your debts."

The young officer looked blank.

" It is a cruel alternative, sir."

" It is an imperative one," said Mr. Lester. " I have not said a word of reproach to you, Wilfred, as some fathers would have done, for I blame myself as much as I blame you. I did know something of the temptations you would have to incur: but it seems to me that young men—of necessity, as you have just told me—spend three or four times as much as they did in my day. It is a most unfortunate affair, and will be utter ruin to your prospects. I would help you if I could, Wilfred—I would, indeed; but it is not in my power. I am pressed for money myself in a way that I do not care to speak of even to you."

" Thanks to the extravagant career of my lady," thought Wilfred in his heart.

" You must sell out," continued Mr. Lester. " My undertaking—which you will have to make good—will release you from here, I suppose, and things can be managed quietly. If this list comprises all your debts, the proceeds of your commission will be about enough to liquidate them."

" And after that ? "

" After that ? I'm sure I don't know. You should have thought of the future before. I suppose you must come home for a time. Perhaps I may be able to get you some government appointment."

And this alternative was adopted. But having to sell out was a cruel blow to Wilfred Lester. Neither were the funds thus realized found to be wholly sufficient, and Mr. Lester had to screw out the rest in the best way he could. It is possible that he felt his son—his eldest son—had not been dealt with precisely as he ought to have been, and the feeling made him lenient now. Wilfred knew he had not. He saw his prospects cut off—his future hopeless—and when things were finally settled, and he went home to the Hall, like bad money returned, he felt as a blighted man, caring little what became of him. The extravagant rate of home expenditure was kept up on his own mother's money ; but for his father's second wife and the second family, he should not have suffered ; and he regarded himself as a sort of sacrifice at the shrine of everything that was unjust.

Lady Adelaide received him with very little graciousness. Outwardly, she was freezingly polite ; but she dispensed the politeness in her own way, and Wilfred had never felt himself so like an interloper. A tacit antagonism was maintained between them, in which Lady Adelaide, from her position, of course obtained the advantage. Tiffle fanned the flame. Tiffle's prejudices had not lessened with years ; and her passive hatred of the boy had grown into active hatred of the man. Wilfred occupied himself

listlessly with outdoor sports—hunting, shooting, fishing,
according to the seasons—and at length he took to spending
his evenings at Miss Bordillion's.

It was well he did so; at least in one sense of the word,
for soon, very soon, the ennui was dissipated. The dis-
pirited, listless young man, who had been ready to throw
himself into the ponds instead of his fishing-line, and in
truth cared little which of the two did go in, was suddenly
aroused to life, hope, and energy. Far from the present
time hanging about his neck like a millstone, it became to
him as a sunny Eden, full of the sweetest rapture. The indistinct future, so dark and visionless to his depressed view,
suddenly broke from its clouds, and shone out in colours
of the rosiest hue—for he had learnt to love Edith
Bordillion. Not with the unstable, fleeting nature of man's
ordinary love, but with a pure, powerful, absorbing passion,
akin to that felt by woman.

They had not met for four years until he returned to
Danesheld; never once had Wilfred visited it during his
soldier's career. He had seen his father and Lady Adelaide
occasionally in London, and had found that sufficient. So
that he and Edith met almost as strangers. The little fairy,
whom he had regarded as a sister, seemed altogether a
different person now; this elegant young woman, and the
laughing familiar girl of the days gone by, were distinct
beings.

A few months given to dreamy happiness, and then
Wilfred spoke to Mr. Lester. The appeal perplexed Mr.
Lester exceedingly. He could have no objection to Edith;
she was of as good family as his son; it may almost be said
of the same family; and there was no doubt she would
inherit a snug fortune. at the colonel's death, for she was
his only child. Colonel Bordillion had been in India now
for many years, spending little and making money. What
perplexed Mr. Lester was *his* share in the affair. Wilfred,
in his eagerness, protested they could live upon nothing—
or as good as nothing. He did not wish to hamper his
father; let him allow them ever so small an income, and
they would make it suffice. Edith had said so.

" You are both of you a great deal too young to marry," said Mr. Lester.

" I am twenty-three," answered Wilfred. " Edith is only two years younger."

Lady Adelaide at first favoured the project. If Colonel Bordillion would allow them an income, and they could be contented, poor creatures, with love in a cottage, why, let them marry: it would bring forth one great good—the final departure of Wilfred from the Hall. Cunningly she put this to Mr. Lester; not saying that she wished to get rid of Wilfred; she had been always cautious on that point; and brought Mr. Lester round to her way of thinking. He spoke to his son.

" But you will allow me something, surely, sir?" remonstrated the young man. " I cannot be indebted to my wife for everything, even though Colonel Bordillion were willing it should be so."

Mr. Lester fidgeted and grumbled. He was by no means of a mercenary nature, only he was so dreadfully embarrassed. He pointed out to his son how very little he could allow him; he would try and manage a hundred and fifty pounds a year; it was the very utmost he could do. Wilfred had better write and explain to Colonel Bordillion why he, Mr. Lester, could not make it more, and he would see what the colonel said.

Wilfred took the advice, and, whilst the colonel's answer was being waited for, he hired the tiniest and prettiest cottage in the world, and began putting into it a few necessary articles of furniture. It was an exemplification of a young man's prudence, no doubt, but he did it; and meanwhile he and Edith lived on in their golden dreamland. Alas! before the answer could reach them there arrived a letter from the colonel to Miss Bordillion. It hinted at some overwhelming calamity, but did not give any particulars.

The next mail brought them. Colonel Bordillion was ruined. The Indian Bank, in which he had hoarded the savings of years, had failed. He did not know what dividend there would be, or whether there would be any at all: the affairs were in a state of dire confusion. A note

was enclosed to Edith and Wilfred jointly, in which the
colonel said he should have been delighted with the proposed union, and cordially have given them his blessing,—
nay, would give it them still, could it be carried out; but
of assistance he had none to give. If his old friend, Squire
Lester, would make it right for them for a time, he might
be able to do something later on.

Wilfred Lester sat on in gloomy reverie, the letter in one
hand, Edith's fingers imprisoned in the other. She was a
bright-looking girl with golden hair.

"Would you mind risking it on two hundred a year,
Edith?"

Edith's dimpled face broke into smiles. "I will do anything you ask me to do. Papa's sure not to be quite ruined,
and he will help us by-and-by."

"Now, Edith, that's a promise; you will do what I think
best?"

"Yes, I will."

She had such perfect faith in Wilfred that she would
have leaped with him blindfolded into the deepest and
darkest pit. The state of things at the Hall was fully
understood at Miss Bordillion's, and that lady, Edith, and
Maria Lester were in a secret state of indignation against
Lady Adelaide for her treatment of Wilfred.

Wilfred took the train for Scarborough, where Mr. Lester
and his wife were temporarily staying. He placed Colonel
Bordillion's letters in his father's hands, and asked what was
to be done.

"It would be madness to marry now, Wilfred," was the
hasty remark of Mr. Lester.

"I can't give her up, sir. I have been building upon the
marriage these two months, night and day, and I—I must
marry. I have been thinking that if you would increase
.the hundred and fifty you promised to two hundred, we
might manage upon it until something turns up. Edith is
willing. There's plenty of game and plenty of fish, and
house rent's cheap in Danesheld. Dear father! it is not
much that I ask you. Do not refuse me! Remember your
own early days."

He had taken his father's hand in his emotion. Mr. Lester looked up at the pleading face. It was one of delicate beauty, just as his own had been before care and gray hairs came to him. He saw the earnest entreaty of the deep blue eyes, and his own suddenly became dim, and his voice husky.

"It would be so terribly imprudent, Wilfred, I am afraid. Think of Edith."

"I do think of her; I plead for her as well as for myself; Edith has been looking forward to the marriage as much as I have. You have said that you have no objection to her."

"Objection to Edith! Until to-day I have always thought you were lucky to get her. I should like to see you married at once, if means would allow. Two hundred a year would be nothing."

"Not much for a permanency, but something is sure to turn up later. I shall get a post some time; and the colonel, it is to be hoped, will not lose all. Do not deny me, father!"

"Well, Wilfred, I'll see what can be done," at length said Mr. Lester. "It will be terribly hazardous, though that is your own look-out; and how I shall contrive the two hundred a year I hardly know. When do you say you want to go back to Danesheld? to-morrow morning? I'll talk to you again, then, before you start."

Wilfred Lester looked upon it as settled, and felt himself upon a bed of roses. He met with a friend, a former brother-officer who was staying at Scarborough, and the two fraternised, and were altogether happy. But what was Wilfred's consternation the following morning when he was met by Mr. Lester with a freezing look and with still more freezing words.. Upon considering the matter well over, he found the imprudence of such a step so great that he must withdraw all countenance to it.

Wilfred's eyes flashed.

"And you will allow me only the hundred and fifty, sir?"

"I will not allow you anything,". said Mr. Lester, coldly and calmly. "I am sorry to say that in the first flush of the subject yesterday I did not see the great impropriety of the scheme. I cannot give my sanction to anything of the sort; for your sake as well as for Edith's, I cannot and ought not. I am going to write to Lord Irkdale to-day, Wilfred, and ask if he can't interest himself with the Government for you. He has been useful to them of late, and perhaps they will listen to him."

" Then Lord Irkdale may keep the application for himself," flashed the indignant young man, not over dutifully. " I know to whom I am indebted for this change—it is to Lady Adelaide."

Reproach would do him no good; neither would Mr. Lester listen to it; and they parted in coldness. Wilfred went rushing to the hotel and poured out his wrongs to his sympathising friend; the officer, being a young officer and going to be married himself, was full of indignation, and he applauded Wilfred's expressed determination—to " marry Edith Bordillion in spite of it."

" I should do it myself," said the captain—" on my word of honour I should, Lester. And, look here : if a fifty-pound note's of any use to you, I have it with me, and you may borrow it for as long as you like."

No one need question the acceptance of the offer. Wilfred Lester felt himself a rich man, and went back to Daneshold in triumph with a marriage licence in his pocket, and openly claimed Edith's promise.

The step they took was one of the most foolish that could be imagined. Miss Bordillion remonstrated against it, urging them to consider its terrible imprudence, if nothing else ; and to wait at least until fresh news could arrive from Colonel Bordillion. Wilfred would not listen : a secret voice seemed to whisper to him that if he and Edith parted now they would be parted for years, perhaps for life ; besides, as he represented to Edith—as he really thought— when once they were married, his father would relent, and allow him at worst the annual' hundred and fifty pounds. And so the preparations went on ; not for a positively secret marriage, but for one somewhat equivalent to it.

A few days, and the carriage of Mr. and Lady Adelaide Lester, which had been to the station for them, dashed up to

Daneshcld Hall. It was a lovely September evening, and
the rays of the western sun fell on the bright face of the
Lady Adelaide as she descended from it. A bright face still
in colouring—the cheeks delicately blooming, the hair like
silken threads of gold—but worn and weary in expression.

She went up at once to her chamber to dress for dinner,
the French maid, Mademoiselle Celine, hastily throwing off
her own travelling bonnet and shawl, and coming in to
attend upon her in a great bustle and with profuse
apologies. Would my lady vouchsafe to excuse her
déshabillé? A miserable accident had happened—she had
lost the keys of her own boxes, and could not get at one of
them ; would my lady pardon it ?

My lady did not seem to care whether Mademoiselle
Celine was *en déshabillé* or not. She had been impatient to
kiss her children, and was vexed at finding them out with
their nurses, and Lady Adelaide was not of a temper now to
meet trifles calmly.

" Make haste with my hair," she said, snappishly ; and it
was the only answer she returned.

Celine had just finished the hair and put on the dress,
when Tiffle entered. Tiffle had aged more than her lady ;
but those shrivelled, ill-tempered faces do age wonderfully
quickly. She had not lost her old habit of rubbing her
mittened hands one over the other, and she came in, doing
it, with her soft mincing step and her rich black silk gown.

" How could you send the children out when you knew I
was expected, Tiffle ? "

" My lady, that they are out is thanks to somebody else,
not to me," was Tiffle's answer. " I'm of no authority beside
Miss Lester, and she came here this afternoon and told the
nurse it was a shame to keep the children in this lovely
afternoon, and she ordered them out.—There, that will do ;
I'll hand my lady her gloves and fan."

The last sentence, delivered in sharp accents, was
addressed to Celine. Glad to be off, in search probably of
her keys, the waiting-maid disappeared. Tiffle closed the
door upon her and came back to Lady Adelaide, her hands
lifted, and the whites of her eyes turned up.

"Oh, my lady! the iniquity that has come to my knowledge this day! I have been turned inside out with indignation—if I may say as much—to think how you and the squire are being deceived. Those two mean-spirited weasels are going to get married on the sly."

By intuition, as it seemed, Lady Adelaide knew of whom she spoke. Wilfred had been right in his surmise: it was his step-mother who had interfered and caused his father to withdraw all countenance to the marriage. Her motive was one of utter selfishness: she feared the new household would have to be supported by Mr. Lester; she begrudged the hundred or two a year it would take from her children, and from her own extravagances.

"What are you saying, Tiffle?"

"My lady, it's Gospel truth. Mr. Wilfred and Miss Bordillion's fine niece are going to get married underhandled. They are going to church by themselves alone, here in Danesheld; and of all the impident acts I ever saw done, that'll be about the most impident. Here in Danesheld, my lady!"

"Does Miss Bordillion countenance it?" breathlessly asked Lady Adelaide.

"She's capable of it," returned Tiffle, "but I've not heard so far. French leave they are going to take, and fine luck may it bring 'em! I can't come at the precise day, but I know it won't be long first. It may be to-morrow."

"How do you come to know at all?" asked Lady Adelaide. "How do you come at things?"

"I keep my eyes and ears open, my lady," answered Tiffle, her countenance wearing an expression of simple innocence.

"You must listen at doors, Tiffle, and behind hedges."

"My lady, whatever I do, it's done out of regard for your ladyship; that you should not be compressed in by a set of designing serpints. And I tell you for a truth—he is going to convert that young lady into Mrs. Wilfred."

"That can soon be stopped," said Lady Adelaide with composure. "Squire Lester will see to it. The gold bracelets." ·

"Begging your humble pardon, my lady, it can't be so soon stopped. He is his own master, and she's of age. Squire Lester has no more power of them than I have. They determined to do this as soon as the bad news came from Injia, and they will do it."

There was a pause. Tiffle was clasping on the gold bracelets. Her fingers, it must be confessed, were deft enough. Presently she spoke, not looking up from the bracelets, the clasp of one of them appearing to have something wrong with it.

"Were it my case my lady—not that I should presume to give advice, and I'm sure your ladyship knows that—I should just let it go on. If it's interfered with, there's no knowing what Squire Lester may be persuaded into; perhaps giving them an illowance of hundreds a year, to the wronging of your ladyship's self and the dear lambs. But when master comes to find that they have gone and done it themselves, in defiance of him, as may be said, then the fat will be in the fire, my lady, and he won't look at them or give them a farthing, and that will be just what they deserve, and the sweet lambs won't be wronged."

The interview was interrupted by the lambs themselves. Noises were heard outside, and on the chamber door being opened they came trooping in. Lamb the first was a great boy of eight; George, a troublesome lamb, and much indulged; lamb the last was a little one carried in its nurse's arms; and there were four intervening lambs. Lady Adelaide was nearly smothered for a few minutes, and Tiffle withdrew. Tiffle, as a rule, had the greatest possible aversion to lambs; but Tiffle dissembled in favour of these.

It could scarcely be supposed that Lady Adelaide condescended to take the woman's advice; and yet in one sense she did take it, for not a word said she to her husband. The consequences were precisely what Tiffle foretold. Wilfred Lester was allowed to marry in peace, and a very fine thing Mr. Wilfred Lester thought he had achieved. But when the news reached the ears of Squire Lester, which was not until the following day, then consequences began.

Wilfred Lester had carved out a pretty little plan of appearing before his father with his young wife Edith, humbly to confess, and beseech condonation for the offence; but Wilfred found himself forestalled. Again he felt sure that he was indebted to Lady Adelaide, as he had felt at Scarborough; and in both cases he was right. Neither had she failed in this latter instance to stir up Mr. Lester's anger to boiling point.

A furious interview succeeded between father and son. Squire Lester hurled reproaches on the young man's head; Wilfred retorted by sundry reflections, more pointed than polite, on his step-mother. When they parted, Mr. Lester had openly cast him off, and protested that he was glad to do it. He declared that Wilfred should have no further assistance from him whatever, in life or after death.

Down strode Squire Lester to Miss Bordillion's. Cliff Cottage was not situated near the sea, as might be supposed from its appellation, but was at the back of the Hall, beyond the wood. He bounced into the pretty little drawing-room, where sat Miss Bordillion, a faded lady now with silvered hair.

"Did you know of this mad escapade of Wilfred's, Margaret?"

"Yes, I did," she replied. "I said what I could against it, but it was of no avail."

"Said what you could against it!" retorted Mr. Lester, using a tone he had never used before to Miss Bordillion. "Why did you not tell *me?* You knew I had come home the night before, I suppose? I think you must have been an accomplice in the matter."

"I did not know that you had come home. But if——"

"Did Maria go to church with them?" he thundered.

"No. But I was going to say," continued Miss Bordillion, "that, if I had known you were at home, I believe I should not have put myself forward to bring you information. All that argument and persuasion could do I did; beyond that I did not think it was my place to interfere. I do not believe that even you would have succeeded in stopping the marriage, for both were bent upon it. It is lamentably imprudent, of course. Putting that out of the question, I think a great deal may be said on both sides."

"Then, perhaps, as you have not interfered to prevent this when you might have prevented it, you will keep them when it comes to starvation, for that will be the end of it," retorted Mr. Lester, as he went out in a fury.

But for that loan of fifty pounds, Wilfred might never have ventured on the hazardous step. With gold in his hand, things look to a man all couleur-de-rose. Part of the fifty pounds added a few more trifles to the pretty cottage, and the rest, the largest portion of it, set them going in housekeeping. If we could only see into the future as we see into the past!

Squire Lester continued implacable. When he met his son in the street he did not speak to him ; he looked straight out over the head of his daughter-in-law if he saw her coming. He would not forgive Miss Bordillion, and intercourse between the two houses ceased, except what was kept up by Maria. How long Mr. Lester would otherwise have suffered his daughter to stay on with Miss Bordillion must remain a question, but he had her home immediately, and withdrew the income hitherto allowed with her. He forbade her to go near her brother's house, but he had not as yet forbidden her Miss Bordillion's.

In the spring of the next year, May, Mr. Lester and his wife departed for London, taking Maria to make her curtsey to the Queen. She was presented by her stepmother, and tasted for the first time of that whirl, a London season. They returned to Danesheld in August ; but during their sojourn in town they had met an old friend, who had been a stranger to them for ten years.

It was Lord Dane. Greatly to the wonder of Danesheld, somewhat to the discontent of Miss Dane, Lord Dane had never once visited his home since quitting it. It was ten years ago now. Ten years! Where he had spent them he could hardly have told, except that he had sojourned in nearly every unknown town in Europe, avoiding the frequented capitals, and staying in none of them very long. He laughingly said to the Lesters that this London season

was his return to life. He went down to Danesheld before
they did, and was established in the Castle with a retinue of
servants, and his sister for its mistress, and had made his
peace with the neighbourhood for his long absence. The
only household, rich or poor, to which he had not penetrated
in his free, affable way, was Wilfred Lester's. It might
have been thought that the state of Mrs. Lester's health
kept him away, for poor Edith was very ill; a little baby
had been born to her and died, and she could not recover
her strength. Not so. When he and Wilfred first met, and
Wilfred had gone up to him with outstretched hand and a
glow of welcome on his handsome face, Lord Dane's manner
seemed chilling, though it is true he touched the hand with
the tips of his fingers.

"My father and her ladyship again," thought Wilfred:
and again he was right. Mr. Lester and Lady Adelaide had
given Lord Dane a woful account of Wilfred and his ill-
doings, known and suspected.

What had the twelvemonth brought forth for Wilfred?
A great deal; and most of it very sad, very blamable.
Danesheld was beginning to whisper curious tales about
him; to say he was fast becoming one of its black sheep.

As long as the residue of the fifty pounds lasted, Wilfred
Lester was happy as a prince, never repenting the deed
he had done, or believing he ever could repent it. When
the money failed he took to credit; and when that failed—
for there must be a limit to it in these hopeless cases, and
there was to his, although he was Squire Lester's eldest son
—then Wilfred began to taste a few of the annoyances of
life on a reduced scale. It was currently believed that Mr.
Lester had disinherited him; indeed, Mr. Lester himself
had not scrupled to say so, and people do not like to risk
losing their money: where small shopkeepers are concerned,
as was the case here, they cannot afford to lose it. And so
the credit was stopped; and Wilfred, in his resentment
against things in general, was beginning not to care what
he did, or what became of him, or what tales to his prejudice were circulated; which is a dangerous state of mind
to fall into. He had spent the summer chiefly in fishing;

and some talked about unfair snares in the ponds; and, now that shooting had come in, Wilfred could not follow it for two reasons: one being that he had not the money for a licence; the other, that he had months ago pledged his gun.

No help whatever had come from Colonel Bordillion. He was not able to send it. In the last letter they received from him, he told them he was going down to some place with a name that had about twenty letters in it, and that no one could read. It appeared to be a formidable journey; and meanwhile, he said, it would be of no use their writing until his return to Calcutta; of which he would send due notice.

And now I think I have told you as much of the doings of the ten years as you would care to know. Old events were nearly forgotten: Harry Dane and his sad death, and its undiscovered author; the mortality succeeding it in the Dane family, with the unexpected succession of the present peer, had lapsed into history; children had become men and women; men and women had gone on a decade towards the sere leaf of life.

Lord Dane was rising ever in public opinion and in honour. The Lord-Lieutenancy of the county was conferred upon him, the nobleman, who had held it since the death of the late Lord Dane, having just died. It had been held by the Danes for many years, so that it had only returned to the family in the present peer: that runagate who seemed to be winning golden opinions from the world.

CHAPTER XV.

LORD DANE HOME AGAIN.

It was stormy weather. The winds had been high ever since September came in, some ten days ago now; and each day they appeared to be gathering strength. Never had

a wilder or more ominous day been experienced than the
one now passing; never did the trees sway, as now, to the
blast. The sun was setting with a lurid glare, the sea-
gulls flew overhead with their harsh screams, the waves of
the sea were tossing mountains high: all signs seemed to
predict a fearful night.

Maria Lester stood before the glass in her chamber,
dressing for dinner. Rarely did glass give back a sweeter
face. Her features were the Lester features, delicate and
clearly defined, with a soft flush of damask on her cheeks,
soft dark eyes, and silky dark brown hair. She was of
middle height, graceful and elegant, very quiet and unpretending in manner.

People thought that so attractive a girl, if permitted,
could not fail to marry early. Maria was twenty years of
age now, and had received one offer whilst she was in
London. That is, Mr. Lester had received it for her, and
he took upon himself to return a summary refusal. Maria
laughed when she heard of it, and felt much obliged to him.
If permitted! The scandal-talkers of Danesheld opined
that she would not be permitted. Mr. Lester's high rate of
expenditure, and his inadequate income, were matters of
public comment; little likelihood was there of his giving
away his daughter when he must resign nine hundred a year
with her!

A booming sound, more like a great gun going off than a
gust of wind, drew Maria to the window. She could catch
a glimpse of the far sea and its boiling waves as she stood
looking out. She wore a violet silk dress, with some
narrow white lace edging its low body and short sleeves.
Suddenly her white arms and hands were raised in sup-
plication.

"May God help all who are on the sea this night!"

Lady Adelaide was in the drawing-room in a costly and
beautiful evening robe of white brocaded silk, gleaming with
jewels, when Maria entered. The manner in which she
attired herself for a quiet home evening without guests, had
long ceased to appear absurd to the household: they had
grown accustomed to it. Mr. Lester had encouraged this in

their early married days, before embarrassment came upon him; possibly he felt its inconvenience now. Maria sat down unnoticed, feeling as she always felt, *not at home :* very little attention did she ever receive from Lady Adelaide. The eldest lamb, George, was lounging in an easy-chair.

Mr. Lester and the announcement of dinner came together: their hour when at the Hall was early, six o'clock. He gave his wife his arm, and Maria followed. No guests were with them that evening, and the meal was soon over. Lady Adelaide had chosen that George should be at table; she very often did choose it: and the boy, indulged and forward, allowed no one to be heard but himself. With dessert came two more of the lambs, and when the whole were well plied with good things there was a lull in the noise.

Not in the wind. A terrible gust swept past the windows, and Mr. Lester turned his head.

"How they will catch it at sea to-night!"

"I thought once the ponies would have gone over the cliff," said Lady Adelaide, languidly. "Ada, what's the matter? Have you eaten too much? Take her on your lap, Maria."

"Did you venture on the heights to-day?" asked Mr. Lester. "Not quite prudent, that, Adelaide."

"I soon came off again when I found what the wind was," answered Lady Adelaide, with as much of a laugh as she ever cared to indulge in. "I suppose you got no shooting?"

"Impossible, in the face of that whirling blast. Dane came out equipped for it, though; I laughed at him. He said he should look in this evening, Adelaide."

She raised her brow quickly at the words, and a frown passed over it; but soon her voice assumed its usual listless tone.

"I should think the wind would keep him at home. Maria, is that child asleep?"

Maria Lester hastily looked down at the little girl she held; the child was nodding with a piece of cake in her hand.

"It's time she was in bed," said Mr. Lester. "The wind has tired her: I know it has me. Take her upstairs, Maria."

Gently gathering the little thing in her arms, Maria went to the nursery. The head-nurse sat undressing the youngest child; two more were on the carpet, crying and fractious.

"Look at this child, nurse! She fell asleep on my lap."

"Tiresome little monkey!" responded the nurse. "They all want to be undressed together, I think. Please to lay her down in the bassinet, miss."

"But where's Susan, this evening?" asked Maria, as she stooped over the berceaunette.

"Oh, Susan! What's the good of Susan for evening work? I really beg your pardon, Miss Lester, for answering you like that," broke off the woman, as recollection came to her, "but I am so put out with that Susan, and my temper gets so worried, that I forget who I'm speaking to. The minute the children are gone into dessert, Susan thinks her time is her own, and off she goes, and will be away for two mortal hours, leaving me everything to do. I can't quit the nursery to go after her, and I may ring and ring for ever before she'll answer. Celine used to come in and help me, but she has not done so this time."

"Where does Susan go to?"

"She goes off somewhere. I have no more control over her, miss, than I have over the wind."

"But why do you not speak to Lady Adelaide?"

"I have spoken, but it is of no use. Susan makes her own tale good to my lady, and Tiffle upholds her. She's Tiffle's niece, and my belief is that Tiffle sends her out. The fact is, Miss Lester, Tiffle is the real mistress of this house, and I don't care much who hears me say it. You tiresome little thing, don't cry like that! I'm going to take you directly."

Miss Lester went to the bell and rang it. It was not answered: though, in truth, she scarcely gave sufficient time, but rang again, a sharp, imperative peal. Of all the servants, who should appear then but Tiffle. She came in, loudly abusing the nurse, and asking what she wanted that she should ring the house down.

"It was I who rang," curtly interrupted Miss Lester. "I rang for Susan."

Tiffle stood still and held her tongue, somewhat taken aback. Her manner smoothed down to meekness—false as it was subtle.

"For Susan, miss! Does nurse want her? I have just sent her out to do a little errand for me, thinking the young ladies and gentlemen were in the dining-room, and that she couldn't be required in the nursery. I'll send her up the moment she comes in, miss."

"You see that she is wanted, Tiffle," gravely replied Miss Lester. "Here are three children, all requiring to be undressed at once, and it is impossible for one pair of hands to do it. Nurse tells me that Susan makes a point of being away at this hour. I shall speak to Lady Adelaide."

"Begging your pardon, Miss Lester, there's no necessity for that, and it will do no good. My lady has unlimited confidence in me and in Susan."

"That may be true, Tiffle, but it is right she should know that the children are neglected. Send Celine here to assist the nurse until Susan shall return."

The tone was imperative. Maria, gentle though she was, yet possessed that quiet, nameless power of command which few cared to resist. Tiffle stood aside as she left the room, and then followed in her wake, her eyes glancing evil.

Miss Lester passed into her own chamber. She stood at its window, contemplating the weather, listening to the howling wind. The sun had set, but the remains of light lingered in the western sky, and the moon was rising. It could scarcely be called twilight even yet. "I think I may venture to go," soliloquized Maria. "In my long dark cloak I can brave the wind. I *must* see Margaret; I must ask her if she has heard anything of this report, which is turning my heart to sickness. Papa asked me at dinner why I did not eat. How can I eat with this dreadful fear about me? Yes, I will go. I will go, were it only to escape Lord Dane."

She put on a close straw bonnet, wrapped her cloak securely round her, and went softly downstairs. A man-servant was in the hall as she passed through it. It was a small, angular hall, various rooms opening from it. Most of the apartments in the house were old-fashioned, except in the drawing-rooms; they were charming, their side windows opening to the grounds.

"James," said Miss Lester, as the man opened the hall-door for her, "should any inquiries be made for me, say that I have gone to take tea with Miss Bordillion."

When Mr. Lester communicated to his wife the fact that Lord Dane might be expected that evening, the passing frown her brow assumed did not escape his notice, and he spoke of it as soon as the children had left the room, and spoke somewhat abruptly.

"Have you taken a prejudice against Lord Dane, Adelaide?"

"A prejudice against Lord Dane! I?"

"It has seemed to me, once or twice of late, that you have looked annoyed upon finding he was coming here."

"Oh, dear no! Lord Dane's coming or staying away is nothing to me," she answered, subsiding with an effort into her usual languor of indifference, and turning away her still beautiful face, to hide its flush.

"I don't wonder at his being fond of dropping in here," observed Mr. Lester. "The Castle must be very dull for him with no companion but poor, silly Cecilia. As your cousin——"

"He is no cousin of mine," she interrupted.

"Strictly, no; but he may almost be called one. And you know, my dear wife, you are given to be capricious on occasion."

"Capricious! Yes, I think I am. When you married me, George, you married me with all my faults and failings, remember. I don't suppose they have lessened with years."

"Dane has not given you any offence, then?"

"None in the world. How that wind howls and shrieks! We shall have an awful night.'

"The conversation took another turn, and by-and-by Lady Adelaide went into the drawing-room. Only one of the rooms was lighted to-night; but it was a spacious room, furnished with all imaginable elegance, and not crowded with encumbrances—monsters, jars, and other useless ornaments, as some rooms are.

She did not sit down! she walked about restlessly : now lifting a beautiful rose from its slender crystal glass ; now glancing at the title of a new uncut book ; now standing before the pier-glass, which reflected herself.   Not to admire her own charms, but in dreamy thought.

There were times when the life, present and past, of the Lady Adelaide showed itself to her in its true, miserable colours.   Marrying Mr. Lester had been a mistake, as Lord Dane once told her it would be ; and she did her best to escape from it.   She did her best to escape from some other haunting phantom that was ever following her, more or less. Very close indeed did it seem to-night.   A dream, of what might have been, came over her ; now, as she stood there, with her fair and jewelled hand pushing back the flaxen hair from her brow.   Had Fate been kinder, she might have been kinder also ;   might have grown to love her fellow-creatures ; whereas she had steeled her heart to all loving impulses ; she had grown hard and harder, selfish and more selfish, false and very false indeed.

At a slight sound at the door, she turned with a start, glancing over her shoulder with that scared look, at such moments observable in her ; just as if she feared her pursuing phantom was coming in visibly upon her.   But it was only Tiffle who entered ; entered with much softness and smoothing of hands, and penitential deprecation for the intrusion.

" My lady, with a thousand pardons for venturing to interrupt you here, I thought I'd make bold to ask whether you would like a fire in your dressing-chamber.   The wind gets higher and higher."

" A fire!   No, I think not ; it is warm.   I don't care either way."

" Then I shall have one lighted, for I think it will be more comfortable for your ladyship," said Tiffle, with a curtsey as she turned to the door.   But, instead of going out of it, she looked round again.

" There's news abroad to-night that the keeper's dying—if

your ladyship will excuse my waiting to mention it. And, my lady," added the woman, dropping her voice, "the slender one, out with the others, *was* Mr. Wilfred Lester. It mayn't be pleasant for any of the parties, my lady, if Cattley dies."

"Tiffle, I cannot altogether believe that story," said Lady Adelaide, seating herself on a sofa, with her gaze bent on the servant. "He would never run his neck into such a noose as that. Why, it would be transportation, at the least! The more I think of it, the less I can believe it; and for Heaven's sake be cautious in speaking, and don't let it come to the ears of Mr. Lester! You must have found a mare's nest somewhere."

"My lady—craving your pardon—are the nestesses I have already found mare's nestesses?" demanded Tiffle, with just the least acidity in her tones. "When I told you that those two deep ones were going to ignite themselves together in matrimony, did that turn out a mare's nest, my lady? Or did the information I brought you a week ago, that he did go abroad at night with a gun, though it's well known his gun is in the pawnshop? And—not to go to other instances, which perhaps may be called to mind—I must beg leave to say that I know my place too well, and what is due to your ladyship too well, to mention any news which I'm not sure and certain of, or any tales that could devolve into mares' nestesses."

"But, Tiffle, how do you learn these things? You must keep a detective at work."

"The detective is my own eyes and ears, my lady, which is being exercised always in behalf of them sweet cherrybims, the lambs upstairs, now sleeping in their little beds. Leave Mr. Wilfred and Miss Lester to their own dervices, and they'd run rough-shod over 'em. Never, while I have eyes to see and a tongue to tell."

Her mistress slightly bent her head, as a hint that it was sufficient, and Tiffle shuffled out with another curtsey. Lady Adelaide threw herself back in a chair, and fell into a soliloquy.

"What can be the reason for its having come back to me?

Ten years! ten long, weary years; surely it was long enough
to live it down! Is it since I have seen *him* again that the
haunting fear has reasserted itself? No: for I found it not
in London, and there we saw him as much as we do here.
It has come upon me since I returned to Daneshold; it is
upon me to-night worse than it ever has been: a miserable
conviction that the past is going to be raked up again; a
dread fear that my sin——"

"Lord Dane, my lady."

The announcement was Tiffle's. A terrific blast had blown
the outer door open, and his lordship and the wind had
entered together, meeting Tiffle in the hall. He was altered
far more than Lady Adelaide. Could it be that the tall,
stern man of eight-and-thirty, with some grey hairs mingling
with his luxuriant locks, and the lines of care upon his broad
white brow, was the whilom slender stripling of only ten
years ago? But he was a very handsome man now,
handsomer than he had been in those days, with the high
Dane features and the proud carriage of the Dane family.
As to the lines, what brought them on *his* brow? Of
distinguished position, of great wealth—for his coffers had
been accumulating since he went abroad—possessed of all
the extraneous accessories for rendering life happy, one might
indeed wonder how care fell upon Lord Dane—as one
wonders how the flies get into the amber.

She stood up to receive him, in her white dress, her
glittering jewels, her conscious beauty. Very many times
had they met of late; but Lord Dane, as he greeted her
to-night, could not help thinking how little she was changed.
Almost as attractive did she look as she had done in the time
when she was his youthful love. There was no peevishness
on her face now.

"What a terrible night!" she exclaimed, as she reseated
herself, and Lord Dane drew a chair near to her.

"Ay, indeed; and blowing right on to the coast," he
answered. "I trust we shall have no disasters at sea,"

"Did you walk here?"

"Walk? Oh, yes, it is not far."

"I was thinking of the weather,"

"I have become inured to that, whatever it may be. My nine or ten years' travel did that good service for me."

"I used to wonder what kept you abroad so long—what the attraction could be. But you did not remain long in one place."

"I went everywhere; everywhere in Europe; not out of it. Except—yes—except that I explored Turkey in Asia."

"And your attraction, Lord Dane?"

"I had none. The very restlessness would imply the want of that. I wandered hither and thither, believing that I should never again have an object in life; certainly never an attraction."

"A rash belief—at your age, with life almost all before you," she remarked, speaking with an assumption of gaiety.

"Well, yes; since I have lived to find its fallacy. I came back to England, caring very little whether I came or whether I stayed away from it for good. And, very soon after my return, the old dead fibres of my heart, that I thought had withered to the roots, sprang again into vitality. It was here, at home, that I met with an attraction; an object in life that I believe will remain with and influence me for ever."

She lifted her eyes inquiringly towards him, and Lord Dane continued:

"When the consciousness of this first dawned upon me, I strove to combat it by every effort in my power; but, the more I strove, the less would it take its departure, and I had no resource but to yield to it. It has become my master, influencing every action of my life, present with me by night and by day. On my sacred word of honour, I thought it was over for me, this love: that my heart and I had alike grown out of it; that 'the song had left the bird.' I feel half ashamed to confess to it now."

She gave a slight start and sat more upright in her chair, her cheek flushing, her eyes gazing at him in astonishment through their half-closed lashes. Lord Dane drew his chair nearer, and seemed somewhat agitated.

"I have been thinking of speaking to you for two or three

weeks; but, I honestly avow, I have not liked to do so. If for an instant I have been alone with you, and would have rushed on my confession, a nameless feeling that perhaps you will understand, a sudden distaste for the task has intruded and held me back. But, as I walked here to-night, I vowed that I would enter upon it, if opportunity were granted. Forgive me; forgive me what I would ask of you: that your own heart should plead my cause. Adelaide—again forgive me, if I speak to you with the familiarity of former years—if you will be my advocate, my suit cannot fail."

He spoke in the low, tender tones that had once been as the sweetest music to her ear; he took her hand in his pleading earnestness. Will you excuse Lady Adelaide for the error she fell into? With the remembrance of old days so vividly just then upon her, it was perhaps a natural one. She thought he was pleading for *her* favour, not for her influence with another. A powerful emotion ran through her frame—it was succeeded by a sort of deadly coldness.

"Have you forgotten who I am?" she asked in low, proud tones, not so much in resentment, but as though she thought he really had forgotten it. "You forget yourself, Lord Dane: I am the wife of Mr. Lester; the mother of his children."

Lord Dane dropped her hand; and an involuntary laugh broke from him before he could check it. Something in its tone jarred upon her ear.

"When you threw me away to marry George Lester, Lady Adelaide, I fully understood that I was thrown away for ever. Believe me, I accepted the alternative there and then, as irrevocable. I have never presumed to think that I could find favour with you again, under any circumstances or contingency whatever, that the chances of the world might bring about. I beg your pardon a thousand times for having expressed myself badly, as I conclude I must have done. I was but asking for your good offices in my behalf with your step-daughter, Maria Lester."

A suffusion of passionate shame dyed the brow of Lady Adelaide. Never did woman fall into a more humiliating error. She could have struck herself for her vain folly; she

could have struck Lord Dane. When she opened her lips to
speak, no sound came 'from them. He had been honest, at
any rate: he had not given a thought to the possibility of
his words being so misconstrued: his mind was full of Maria
Lester; and Lady Adelaide was no more to him, and never
had been since her marriage, than any other man's wife. He
had then thrust her from his heart for ever, whatever she
might have done by him. A thought crossed her that this
humiliating, this bitter mistake of hers must have three
parts repaid him for all she had made him suffer in the
days gone by.

He was good-natured, and strove to put her at her ease;
telling her, in matter-of-fact tones, that he wished to marry
Miss Lester; and that his chief motive in speaking first to
herself was, that she might use her influence with her
husband.

"People say that it is time I settled," he observed: "and
of course it is time, if I am to settle at all. In addition to
any predilection I may have formed, I have begun to see
that it will be better for me: poor Cecilia is not much of a
companion. But before I found out this, indeed before I
came down to the Castle, or had left London, I had made up
my mind in regard to Miss Lester. I never met any one
whom I so thoroughly esteemed," he added, with an emphasis
on the last word, "and I trust to induce her to become Lady
Dane. Hence I come to you, as one old friend will go to
another, to enlist your interest on my behalf with Miss
Lester."

The past had become clear to her. She *had* wondered
what brought Lord Dane so often to their house: perhaps
had set it down within her own breast to a very different
motive. Her face was burning still; but she strove to throw
off her shame defiantly, and drew up her head with a haughty
gesture.

"Why do you not apply to Mr. Lester instead of to me,
Lord Dane?"

Lord Dane explained in the most delicate manner possible.
In common with all Danesheld, he knew that the prospect of
having to relinquish his daughter's fortune would act as an

almost insuperable barrier to Mr. Lester's giving his consent to any marriage proposed for her. Lord Dane, however, wished for Maria alone, not for her fortune; that could remain with Mr. Lester: the settlement he offered would obviate the necessity for Mr. Lester's relinquishing the other. It was *this* he had wished to tell Lady Adelaide; for Mr. Lester's sensitiveness on pecuniary matters was well known, and he might receive the communication better from his wife than from the suitor.

The thought was a generous one. Lady Adelaide could only feel it so; and some of her frigid manner disappeared. "Legal help can of course be called in to ratify the arrangement," observed Lord Dane. "You will be my advocate with them both, will you not, Lady Adelaide?"

Lady Adelaide made no immediate reply. Some stifling weight seemed to oppress her, and she rose from her seat suddenly, in agitation that she could not wholly hide, drew aside the window-curtains, and stood peering forth into the boisterous night. Lord Dane watched her. Was her manner caused by any lingering regard for him? he mentally questioned; or was she angry with herself for her unfortunate misapprehension, and with him for causing it?

"Maria is too young for you, Lord Dane," presently came her voice from the window; but she did not turn.

"That is a question—I beg your pardon, Lady Adelaide—surely that is a question that may be left with herself and me."

"You are double her age."

"Not quite."

There was a long pause, broken at length by Lady Adelaide:

"I would prefer to remain neutral in this affair, Lord Dane," she said, returning to her seat. "If I do not second your efforts to gain Miss Lester, I will at least not impede them. Apply yourself directly to Mr. Lester; speak to him with the candour that you have now spoken to me, and I am sure he will hear you. It is true that he is sensitive on pecuniary points; circumstances, chiefly those connected with his son, have made him so. He must decide for himself.

Maria is his daughter, not mine; and I will not interfere. Your suit must proceed unbiassed, uninterfered with by me."

"You will not be against me?"

"I have said so. My position in regard to it shall be one of strict neutrality."

Lord Dane bowed. In his inmost heart he had suspected she would have been against him in this—against Maria; and this secret fear no doubt caused him to speak to her first, and endeavour to make sure of her interest. Perhaps she conceded as much as he had expected she would.

"Is Miss Lester at home this evening?"

"Yes; but I don't know where she is," replied Lady Adelaide, ringing the bell. "Ask Miss Lester to come here," she added to the man who answered it.

"Miss Lester is gone out, my lady."

"Out! On this turbulent night!"

"She went out directly after dinner, my lady. She told me to say that she had gone to take tea at Miss Bordillion's."

"Maria does do things that no one else would think of," cried Lady Adelaide, as the servant closed the door. "The idea of her going out such a night as this!"

"Some urgent motive must have taken her," observed Lord Dane, who felt surprised himself.

"The urgent motive of her own whim; or possibly a promise to that antiquated piece of propriety, Miss Bordillion," scornfully returned Lady Adelaide. "I wonder Mr. Lester does not forbid Maria's going there, after the countenance shown by that woman to her niece and Wilfred Lester at the time of their marriage. By the way, an association reminds me to ask after your keeper. I hear he is dying."

"No, he is not dying. I hope he will get better even now. He was going on very well until this morning, when the police called at his house and subjected him to a cross-examination. I wish they would be less eager in interfering, those fellows. Cattley was not in a state for it."

"Has it been fully decided who his assailants were?"

"Not at all. Cattley has a suspicion as to two of them, but he cannot swear to it; and the police may spare their pains. That is how these offenders get off, Lady Adelaide."

"I fancy you are inclined to be very lenient."

Lord Dane laughed; he hardly knew whether he was or not, and really did not care. "Is Mr. Lester in the dining-room?" he asked.

"I suppose so: I left him there. He must have dropped asleep."

With a word of apology, Lord Dane left her, and went in search of Mr. Lester, whom he found. Not in the dining-room, but in a small room at the back of the hall, called the study. He was seated at his desk, a heap of papers before him, his spectacles on—which he had lately had to take to at night—and his face full of anxious care. Lord Dane sat down, and quietly asked him for his daughter, hinting at the arrangement he had mentioned to Lady Adelaide.

But for that one troublesome impediment, Mr. Lester would have jumped at the offer. It was a better one than he had ever expected would fall to the lot of Maria. He sat perplexed in thought, giving no reply. It was impossible for him to resign her fortune on the one hand; on the other, he felt it equally impossible to accept any such arrangement as that proposed by Lord Dane. Mr. Lester had always been a sensitive man in regard to the world's opinion, and it occurred to him to ask what would be said of him if he permitted this.

"Surely you do not object to me, Mr. Lester? I can make the most ample settlements; and I love your daughter as I never thought to—to love any one."

"I thank you for your offer, Lord Dane; it does us honour; but these things require mature deliberation. Will you allow me a week or ten days to consider it?"

"So long as that!"

"You would rather have that than an immediate nega-tive?"

"Yes. But why a negative?"

"Indeed I am not prepared to discuss it now," said Mr. Lester, rising. "You must give me my own time for consideration, and say nothing to Maria. Let us join Lady Adelaide."

He glanced at his scattered papers, extinguished the light by which he had been writing, and locked the door upon his room of care. At the same moment the hall-door was opened and Maria was blown in, her bonnet in her hand.

"Oh, papa, it is such a night!" she exclaimed, half laughing at the breathless state she was in, and the disorder of her dress. "My veil has been carried away, and I was lucky to save my bonnet. Look at my hair! Is that Lord Dane? Oh, pray don't look at me."

Mr. Lester stared, as well he might, and asked what in the world had taken her abroad.

"I did not think it was so bad, papa. I went to Miss Bordillion's. She would not let me remain, and sent me home again between Mary and the old gardener. I *should* like to see how they will get back; the wind grows worse every minute."

Laughing at the reminiscence, throwing her cloak and bonnet on a bench in the hall, Maria smoothed back her hair and went into the drawing-room on the ready arm of Lord Dane.

CHAPTER XVI.

RUMOURS.

Miss Lester had walked forth after dinner in the wild night—leaving the Lady Adelaide to her remarkable interview with Lord Dane—and was speedily blown back again by the wind: but, short as her absence had been, it is not without its incident.

Skirting the Hall to the right, Miss Lester struck into a somewhat lonely road : the pastures belonging to her father's house were on the right, the dark wood on her left. She was on her way to Miss Bordillion's, and two roads would

take her to it : the one she was pursuing, the other through
a portion of the wood. She bore up bravely against the
wind. The wood was soon reached, and she turned into it,
as being the more sheltered. It was not yet dark, or she
would have chosen the open road ; but, to people born and
bred in the country, fear when abroad is almost unknown.

Nevertheless, as she went swiftly along the narrow path,
the gloom did strike upon her unpleasantly. The wind
moaned and shrieked overhead, seeming to shake the trees
to their very roots, and imparting a weird, ghostly loneliness
to the scene. Maria began thinking of a certain story she
had read in German, where a maiden was speeding through
a dense forest, and——

Some object suddenly started out from the trees before
her, and she positively screamed. The next moment, however, she burst into laughter. It was only her brother. A
tall and very slender man of four-and-twenty, with the same
delicately beautiful face he had in boyhood : the dark blue
eyes, the long eyelashes, the dark hair. But the joyous,
impulsive manners of the boy had given place to an indifference that bordered upon apathy : some such a manner as
might be seen in one out of conceit with the world, and who
has nearly given himself over to despair.

"How stupid I am ! " exclaimed Maria, alluding to her
cry. "How you startled me, Wilfred."

" I did not intend to startle you. Who was to think you
would be in the wood to-night ? It's not the thing, Maria."

"It is not night yet. I am going to Margaret's, and
chose this way as being more sheltered. I could not keep
in the road for the wind."

He had turned to walk by her side. Maria seemed under
some timid restraint, and cast a stealthy glance at the gun
in his hand.

" Is that your gun, Wilfred ? " she at length asked.

" It's one I have had lent me," he replied shortly, and a
silence ensued. A hundred doubts and questions arose to
Maria's lips, but she dared not speak them.

" I wonder they let you come out such a night as this," he
presently said. " I never remember one like it."

"I did not ask leave; I came without. How is Edith?"

The question was put in a hesitating voice. Wilfred took it up. His mind was in that state of ultra-sensitiveness that warfare with the world frequently entails.

"What! I suppose it is high treason to inquire after her! Have they forbidden you even her name? Come, Maria, confess; you cannot tell me more than I suspect."

Maria was silent.

"Perhaps they have forbidden your speaking to me if we happen to meet?" he pursued.

"No, Wilfred, they have not done that yet. Tell me how you are getting on. Is Edith better?"

"We are not getting on at all; unless going backwards is getting on. It is backwards with us generally, and backwards with Edith. She will never grow strong whilst things remain as they are. If there is justice in heaven——"

"Hush, Wilfred! It will do no good."

"And no harm. But have it as you like, Maria. The next interdict will be, I suppose, against your speaking to me."

"Should it come, Wilfred, it will be partly your own fault," she answered.

"No doubt of it. I am all in fault, and they are all in the right. But I did not expect to hear *you* say it."

"You are petulant with me without a cause, Wilfred. You know that I care for you more than for any one in the world. I fear I do not care even for papa—though it may be wicked of me, and wrong to say it—as I care for you."

"It would be a wonder if you cared much for him," cried Wilfred. "He has not allowed us to care for him. Occupied as he has been with his lady-wife and her children, showing neither common care nor affection for you and me——"

"I don't think we ought to speak of it," came the gentle interruption.

Wilfred disdained an answer.

"You speak of the possibility of our intercourse being forbidden; I say that, if it is, the fault will be yours, Wilfred," she added, gathering courage for a desperate effort. "What are these tales that are being whispered about you?"

"Tales?"

"That you are taking to evil courses; to poaching for game and fish; to going out at night with loose men. They are——" she stopped with a slight shiver, and then went on rapidly—"talking of the attack on Lord Dane's keeper."

"The country for ten miles round is talking of nothing else," returned Wilfred, carelessly.

"But they say—some say—that you were one of them."

"Oh, they do, do they? It's well my back's rather broad just now. Who says it?"

"I don't know."

"Who said it to you?"

"The rumour has reached the Hall in some way. I fancy through Tiffle. Lady Adelaide said a word or two to me, and it turned me sick and faint. I was too terrified to ask a single question; and, if I had, perhaps she would not have answered it. Oh, Wilfred, come to the Hall and deny it if you can! deny it to papa, and get him to stop the rumours."

"If I can?—what do you mean, Maria? Do you think I go out at night to murder gamekeepers?"

"Then you will come to the Hall and explain," was the eager rejoinder.

"Not if I know it. The Hall has been forbidden to me. Don't trouble yourself, Maria; Lady Adelaide and Tiffle can say what they like; my back is broad enough, I tell you."

"They talk of gins and snares; of entrapping game for sale," she shivered.

"I see; they turn me into a regular poacher. Well, Maria, let my father and his wife enjoy the scandal. Were I to get hung or transported, they would have the satisfaction of knowing that they had driven me on the way."

Maria Lester pressed her hands to her chest as if she would still its pain. She felt herself so very helpless. On the one hand, her harsh stepmother and the husband whom she swayed; on the other, this brother being driven to desperation—the brother she loved so dearly.

"How does my father think I am to live, Maria, when he

does not give me anything to live upon? Put Edith out of
the question—Margaret supplies her—had I not married,
surely he must and would have allowed me something, if
only a hundred a year. Let him, in justice, give me that
now. I believe that they wish me to go wrong. I am sure
Lady Adelaide does."

" You are out to-night with that gun, Wilfred."

" And, if I am, I can't use it in this wind."

" But only the carrying it may be brought against you.
You have no game licence."

" Yes, I have."

For a single moment she thought he was uttering an
untruth, and her countenance fell.

" I have taken one out; Margaret helped me."

To hear this was a weight lifted from her heart, for more
reasons than one. She was about to reply, when a movement amidst the trees attracted her attention, and she halted
in fear.

" What was it?" she whispered, pointing to the place.

" I heard nothing except the wind."

" I did not hear—I saw," answered Maria. " Some face
was peering out at us, and I saw it drawn back. It was
like a boy's face."

Wilfred Lester strode to the spot indicated, pushing
through the trees. Not any creature was in sight, human
or animal: but a narrow path, striking off farther into the
wood, favoured escape.

" I think you must have been mistaken, Maria."

She shook her head, and they soon came to the end of the
wood. Farther on, on the open road, was the residence of
Miss Bordillion; to the left, a by-way led to the cottage
inhabited by Wilfred. It was close by, though a turn in
the road hid it from view. As they stood a moment, Wilfred
telling Maria that she had better return home, and not
venture farther in the howling wind, a very curious-looking
boy came running past them. Slim to a degree, with
restless, wriggling movements, he was not unlike a serpent:
and he had that old, precocious face sometimes seen in the
deformed, and sly, very sly eyes. Not that he was deformed,

but only very stunted for his years, which numbered nearly fifteen. An ordinary spectator might have thought him ten.

"Hallo, Shad! Where are you scampering off to?" cried Mr. Wilfred Lester.

The boy stopped. Rejoicing in the baptismal name of Shadrach, he had never, in the memory of the neighbourhood, been called anything but Shad. His other name no one knew, and it did not clearly appear that he had one. Nearly fifteen years ago he was first seen, a baby, in the hut of old Goody Bean. She said he was her daughter's, who had been many a year away from home ; but Goody Bean was not renowned for veracity, and on the whole did not receive credence for her assertion of the child's parentage. To whomsoever he belonged, there he had been from that time to this.

"Please, sir, I'm going home. I've been getting sticks for granny."

He spoke with childlike simplicity ; but, looking at his sharp face, it might be doubted whether the simplicity was not put on. It was one of two things : either he was a very unsophisticated young gentleman, or one of very unusual cunning.

"Have you been in the wood for those, Shad?" demanded Miss Lester, looking at the few fagots in the boy's hand.

"I've been on'y on t'other side of the hedge, miss ; I don't like the wood when the trees moans and shakes."

"Have you *not* been in the wood?" she returned, looking keenly at him.

"I was there yesterday, miss."

"I spoke of this evening."

"No," he said, shaking his head from side to side, something like the trees. "Granny told me to go into the wood, and bring her a good bundle o' sticks, but I wouldn't when I heard the winds ; and I expec's a wacking for it."

He shambled off. Miss Lester turned to her brother. "Wilfred, it was he who was watching us."

"Very likely. He is even less worthy of credit than his grandmother ; and that's saying a great deal. Why! what does *she* want?"

A decent-looking woman, with a sour face, was turning
the angle of the path with a quick step. Wilfred knew her
for his servant: the moment she saw her master her pace
increased to a run, and she called to him in some alarm.

"What now, Sally?" quoth he. "Is the house on fire?"

"Sir," responded Sally, grimly, "the house is not on fire;
but my mistress is lying in a dead faint, and I ran out to
look for you. I'm not sure but life has at length left her."

A moment's bewildered hesitation and Wilfred started off;
but he had not gone many yards when he arrested his steps
and turned to his sister.

"Will you not come also, in the name of humanity?
Your entering my house to say a word of comfort to Edith—
dying as she may be, as I fear she is, for the want of kindness—will not poison Mr. and Lady Adelaide Lester. Judge
between me and them, Maria."

It might have been the ring of bitter mockery in his tone;
it might have been that her own humanity prevailed;
Maria, at any rate, followed. The cottage was near at
hand; a very unpretending cottage indeed, skirting the
wood, the kitchen facing the road, the sitting-room at the
back. Edith was in the latter, lying as Sally had left her.

It was only a fainting-fit, and she was already reviving
when they entered. Fainting-fits had been rather common
with Edith since her illness, but the usually staid servant
Sally (her baptismal name, though people sometimes called
her Sarah with a vague notion of being polite) had for once
felt frightened. Maria, interdicted from going to her brother's, had not seen his wife for many, many weeks, nay, for
months. She stood over Edith, shocked at the change in
her, and fully believing she could not be long for this
world. Maria burst into tears as she kissed her; they
cried together; and Wilfred whispered to his sister that he
was afraid of the agitation for Edith. So Maria said a
quiet word of farewell and withdrew.

"Sally," she impulsively began to the maid in the kitchen,
"what has reduced your mistress to this shocking state?"

"Famine, more than anything else," was the answer given
in the woman's customary blunt way.

"Famine!" repeated Maria, staring at the speaker in bewilderment, and feeling ready to faint herself. "*Famine?* Things cannot be so bad as that."

"They are not much better, and haven't been for some time, so far as she is concerned," was Sally's answer, motioning towards the parlour door; and, if the woman spoke more familiarly than was consistent with the respect due to Miss Lester, it might be put down partly to her natural manner, partly to the fact that she had formerly been nurse to Maria and Wilfred. She had also more recently lived as housemaid with Miss Bordillion, and waited on Edith and Maria when they were girls. "Me and master, we can eat hard food; but she can't. When folks are delicate and weak in health, they require delicate food. Beef-tea and jellies, and oysters, and chicken, or a nice cut out of a joint of meat, with a glass or two of good wine every day; that's what Miss Edith wants. And she's just going to her grave for the want of it."

The parlour door opened, and Wilfred's voice was heard down the passage. "Sally, is Miss Lester gone? If she will wait an instant, I'll see her safely to Miss Bordillion's."

Maria laid her finger on her lips. "Don't tell him I'm here, Sally," she breathed. "He shall not leave his poor wife to come out with me."

"Miss Lester's all right, sir," was the response, delivered with the usual tartness.

"Then come here, Sally. Your mistress wants you."

Sally obeyed the summons, and Maria took the opportunity to steal away. As she went on to Miss Bordillion's she felt as perhaps she had never before felt in her whole existence. Suffering for want of proper food!—dying for it! Maria Lester had read of such things in fiction and sometimes in the newspapers; but to have them brought palpably before her, and in her own station of life, had certainly not been amongst her experiences. Two convictions gradually forced themselves upon her; one that an awful responsibility lay in some not very definite quarter; the other, that she should be powerless to alter the state of things.

Cliff Cottage was soon reached: a small, pretty, white

house, with green venetian blinds outside the windows. Miss Bordillion was a very gentle lady now, with a close cap and white hair. No trace of the heart-conflict she had done battle with was discernible on her smooth features— only in the hair: that had turned white before its time. She was surprised to see Maria come in; and looked up from her tea. Maria threw off her cloak and bonnet and sat down to the table; and the maid brought in a cup and saucer and some butter.

"Are you taking your tea without butter, Margaret?"

"I prefer dry toast sometimes, my dear."

But Maria remembered that Miss Bordillion had never cared for dry toast; and she now saw her get up, and quietly take the sugar-basin from the sideboard, and place it on the table. A light, and a very uncomfortable one, dawned upon Maria.

"Is it starvation here, Margaret?" she said, with emotion. "I have just heard it is, elsewhere."

An explanation ensued, for Maria was urgent. It was not starvation, but it was very strict economy, an abstinence from everything except absolute necessaries. Since Maria and Edith quitted Miss Bordillion a year ago, she had been thrown upon her own resources; an income of a hundred a year. It might have sufficed for herself and her servant— and she kept only one now—but unfortunately she had also Wilfred and Edith on her hands.

"Are you helping *them*, Margaret?" exclaimed Maria.

"To what little extent I can. There is no one else to do it."

"I had no idea of it," breathed Maria. "Wilfred said a word to-night in allusion to it; but I thought I might have mistaken him, your income is so very small."

"My dear child, how do you suppose they have lived? No household can get along without *some* ready money. For some time after their marriage I would not see them, not choosing to countenance the imprudent step. Their money went—what they had of it; and then their few little personal valuables went; next their credit went; and there they were. One day I met Edith—it was about three months before the baby was born—and she looked so worn and weak that I gave her my arm home, and Sally enlightened me as to the state of things. That girl is worth her weight in gold."

"Who is?"

"Sally."

"Oh, Margaret! she was always the crossest old thing!" cried Maria, going back in thought to her own and Edith's girlhood days, when Sally had tyrannized over them.

"She is iron in manner, gold at heart. She had a little money saved up," continued Miss Bordillion; "not much, for she has kept her mother and that bedridden sister; it was a few pounds only, and she spent them in necessaries for Edith when the child came."

"I'll never call her cross again," said Maria, in a flush of repentance. "But, Margaret, don't you think Wilfred is being very badly used? Surely the tradespeople might give him a little more credit!"

"He is already in their debt."

"To a trifling extent. But he is papa's eldest son. The estate must be his some time."

"Must?"

The word was spoken with significant emphasis, and Maria's face flushed. It had touched a sadly sensitive chord in her secret heart.

"It would be so unjust to leave it away from Wilfred," she said, her voice falling to a whisper, as befitted the subject in her own mind, for it was one she had never dared to allude to. "He *is* the eldest son; he was the only one for years until these others came. A great deal of papa's income came from mamma; surely he will at least not leave *that* away from Wilfred!"

"The tradespeople do not appear to think there's much certainty either way," observed Miss Bordillion, in constrained tones.

"You won't speak of this to me, Margaret!"

"I do not care to say anything that may reflect on Lady Adelaide."

"It is her fault, you think?"

"Yes, it is her fault. She has led Mr. Lester into embarrassment, and she most certainly excites him against his son. Maria, I do not suppose she will *allow* Mr. Lester to assist Wilfred; or to bequeath even his mother's money to him."

"She must be terribly unjust. Has she any conscience, Margaret?"

"Conscience is very elastic material in general," replied Miss Bordillion, with a half-smile. "And now, Maria, that is all I wish to say of Lady Adelaide, and I don't know how I have come to say so much. It is a state of things sufficiently patent to Danesheld; and we cannot expect butchers and bakers to practise benevolence in opposition to their own interests."

"And you have really been going without sugar and butter, Margaret, that you may assist Wilfred and his wife?"

Margaret had been going without many other things; but she answered carelessly.

"A very small matter of self-denial, Maria! Be so kind as to guard the secret carefully out of doors."

"Why should it be a secret? Are you afraid of offending papa?"

"Yes. Though perhaps not exactly in the sense you mean. I should not like to offend him, and I ought not to like it. Remember, I live in this house of his rent-free. I spoke to him about paying rent for it after you left it, but he only laughed at me. My fear is, that were it known that I, or any one else, helped Wilfred, he would be thought of in his father's house with all the greater harshness."

"Margaret, what is to become of them?"

"I cannot say—I am afraid to think. You see, putting pecuniary considerations aside, there is no one to give a helping hand to lift Wilfred out of his present position. A Government appointment was talked of; and he would do his best in it, or in anything else, I am sure: but how is he to get it, now that his father has turned against him? I wish Lord Dane would be his friend!"

"And meanwhile they are starving!"

" With the exception of what little I can give them : and
that is indeed little. With two genteel households to be
kept out of a hundred a year," continued Margaret, with an
attempt at gaiety, " you must not wonder that my sugar and
butter are too costly to be approached lightly. The worst
is "—and her tone went back to the very utmost gravity of
which human.tones are capable—" Wilfred has taken up all
this as barbarous injustice, and in heart is resenting it
accordingly."

The words recalled Maria to a sense of what she had come
out that night to speak about; though indeed it could not be
said to need recall, since it had been making itself heard
throughout, in a sort of underlying miserable current.

" Margaret, I wanted to ask you—have you heard the
rumours that are about touching Wilfred? That he—
that he has been seen abroad at night, on Lord Dane's
lands ? "

" Hush ! " interrupted Miss Bordillion, glancing round
with a movement that seemed born of fear.

" Then you have heard it ! Oh, Margaret, tell me !—do
you think it is true ? "

" I think rumour of all kinds, Maria, just as likely to be
false as true. Our better plan is always to ignore it."

" Margaret, I came out this boisterous night to ask you,"
she piteously said. " I was obliged to come ; I could not
rest. Do you know anything for certain ? "

" I do not," was the calm reply—and it seemed to Maria's
sensitive ears that Margaret had suddenly grown calm and
cold.

" I met him just now with a gun. I don't know what he
was doing with it at this hour. He said it had been lent to
him. Do you know if that is true ? "

" No, I don't know anything about that. I dare say it is
true."

" He told me you had helped him to take out a shooting
licence."

" That is true."

" Should Wilfred do anything wrong, I think it would kill
me," murmured Maria, lifting her pale and pleading face.

"It would kill Edith."

"And you won't put me out of my suspense, Margaret?"

"Maria, understand me. I really know nothing of this, except that I have heard that rumours to Wilfred's discredit are abroad. I do not think that they are true—I hope they are not: and it will be well that you and I should entirely ignore them."

"It is not putting me out of suspense," sighed Maria.

"I will tell you what I am going to put you out of— and that is out of my house," said Miss Bordillion, laughing, "or you will not get home to-night. Hark at that wind."

Maria fell into a most disheartening reverie; revolving all she had heard and seen—all she feared. But Miss Bordillion did not allow her time to indulge in it. She bade her maid call Mr. Lester's gardener, an elderly man who lived close by, and despatched Maria home between them.

And what with the elastic spirits of youth, and what with the pranks the wind played them, which seemed to grow higher as the moon rose, Maria arrived at the Hall in a state of struggling and laughter, her bonnet a close prisoner in her hands, her veil gone off on an aërial voyage, and her hair flowing.

CHAPTER XVII.

THE SHIPWRECK.

RARELY had such a night been known within the memory of the oldest inhabitant of Danesheld. The storm of wind was terrific, sweeping through the air with a rushing, booming sound; shaking old gables and tall chimneys, unhinging shutters, and crashing down outhouses. But for the wind, the night would have been almost as bright as the day, for the clear moon was at the full; but the clouds that swept madly across its face constantly obscured its brightness, and threw a dark shadow upon the earth.

A knot of men were congregated in the tap-room of the
Sailors' Rest. They were sheltered certainly, but the house
was exposed on one side to the sea, and seemed to rock with
the blast. Richard Ravensbird, looking not a day older
than when you saw him last—hard, composed, phlegmatic
as ever—was waiting on his customers, and saying little, as
usual. Ravensbird had done well at the Sailors' Rest. He
and his house were alike irreproachable, and he had earned
—and gained—the respect of Danesheld. If his object had
been to live down the old scandal of suspicion attaching to
his name, he had eminently succeeded; and even that depot
of gossip, the coastguard station, would have suspected any
one in the town or county to be guilty of a great crime,
rather than the landlord of the Sailors' Rest.

Mrs. Ravensbird was in the bar parlour. Her usual
place in the evening was the private sitting-room; but that
happened to look on to the sea, and she had come out of
it stopping her ears. Sophie did look older, in spite of her
smart caps. Frenchwomen, after thirty, age unaccountably,
and Mrs. Ravensbird was no exception to the rule. She had
not changed in manner, but was free of tongue and ready at
repartee, just as she always had been. There was one
child, a boy, to whom they were giving an excellent educa-
tion, and who was almost always away at school. He was
born a twelvemonth after their marriage; and it appeared
likely that he would be the only olive-branch.

"How is Cattley getting on?" inquired one of the
company in the bar, as he began to fill a fresh pipe. It was
the same bar in which we once saw Mr. Hawthorne drop a
brass ladle, when Ravensbird's head rose above the screen,
to the unhappy landlord's consternation. The screen was
there still, but considerably enlarged: it made the sweep
of the room now, shutting out only the entrance as a
sort of passage. A great improvement; and few rooms
wear a more comfortable appearance than did this bar
of Ravensbird's with its well-kept furniture and bright
fire.

Ravensbird, whom the speaker had addressed, took no
notice of the question. He had just given a jug of ale to

another of the company, and was counting the halfpence returned into his hand.

"I say, landlord, have you heard how Cattley is?" repeated the speaker, who was owner of a fishing-boat, and named Marls.

"Cattley may be better or he may be worse," was the short and not very gracious reply of Mr. Ravensbird; and one, skilled in tones, might have suspected that the subject was not palatable to the landlord. "I don't meddle in business that does not concern me."

"That's as much as to say that I do," said Marls, with good humour. "Not that it's much meddling, inquiring after a half-murdered man. When I went out, three days ago, it was thought he was dying."

"A fine trouble your boat had to get in!" interrupted a coastguardsman. I was on duty this afternoon, and watched it alabouring against the gale."

"Trouble!" echoed Marls; "I never was out in such a gale, and the wind blowing us right on shore. It took us all we knew, I can tell you, to make the port and not the beach. Has nobody heard aught of Cattley?"

"Cattley's better," spoke one who was sitting near the fire. "The police must put themselves into it, and nearly do for him though, with their worrying, wanting him to swear to Beecher and Tom Long. But Cattley couldn't swear to them, though he said he'd no moral doubt that they were two of the lot. Old Beecher came forward with all the brass in the world, and swore his son was at home in bed at the time. Nobody would believe old Beecher on his oath, but there was no proof, as Cattley couldn't swear. My lord's savage about it. It's said he is going to be as sharp over his preserves as it was thought he'd be lenient. He told old Beecher that his oaths went for nothing, and regretted the evidence was not more conclusive."

"Have they got the third?" asked another fisherman. "There was a third, wasn't there?"

"Said to be: Cattley speaks of another who was watching at a distance. Keeping guard, no doubt."

"That was Drake, then," spoke Marls. Smuggling or

poaching, it all comes alike to him. I'd lay a crown it was Drake."

"You'd loose it, Marls. The third fellow was a tall, thin man. Drake's short and stumpy. Landlord, there's the missis calling you."

And, indeed, Mrs. Ravensbird's voice was heard in some commotion, calling "Richard, Richard!" Ravensbird went out, leaving a smart maid to do duty for him. Sophie stood just inside the parlour, a candle in her hand.

"Richard, I have been upstairs, and I protest I was afraid to stop there. The house rocks as if it would fall."

"The house is all safe," returned Ravensbird. "It has weathered out gales as bad as this."

"I don't think we have ever had such a gale as this. Hark at it!"

She shivered as she stood. Ravensbird, who was a very good husband on the whole, though sometimes a little crusty, took the candle from her hand, and bade her sit down, drawing a chair near for himself. A short while and the smart maid came in.

"They are calling for more ale in the taproom, sir," she said. "Am I to serve it? It wants but two minutes to eleven."

"Oh, for goodness' sake, Richard, let them stop on as long as they like to-night," interposed Sophie. "Better be in danger in company than alone, and I'm sure I shall not dare to go to bed."

"Not dare to go to bed!" repeated Ravensbird, in surprise. "Why, Sophie, what's the matter with you? Folks sleep best in windy weather."

"It's a worse wind than I've known since I came to the Sailors' Rest," returned Sophie, who invariably had the last word. "For my part, I wish they'd stop on in the tap-room till morning."

Ravensbird returned to the bar, and told the company it was eleven o'clock. They did not, however, seem inclined to move: and, whether it was the wind howling without, which certainly induces to the enjoyment of comfort within, or whether in compliance with his wife's words, Ravensbird

proved less rigid than usual as to closing his house at
eleven, and suffered more ale to be drawn. The servant
was handing it round, when a fresh customer entered. It
was Mitchel, the preventive-man. He took off an oil-skin
cape he wore, and sat down.

"Why, Mitchel! is it the wind that has blown you here?"
were the words Ravensbird greeted him with. "I thought
you were on duty to-night."

"The wind won't let me stop on duty, Mr. Ravensbird,
so it may be said to have blown me here," replied Mitchel.
"I saw you were not closed, through the chinks in the
shutters. It's an awful night."

"Not much danger of a contraband boat-load stealing up
to the beach to-night," laughed one of the company.

"No; the Flying Dutchman himself couldn't bring it
up," said Mitchel. "There's a terrific sea rolling in."

"The men have not been on duty below all day?"

"Couldn't have stood it," answered Mitchel; "the sea
would have washed them away. It's great rubbish to have
men there at all, now they have put us on to the heights.
I'm afraid of one thing," he added, lowering his voice.

"What's that?"

"That there's a ship in distress. My eyesight's uncommon good for a distance, as some of you know, and I
feel sure that I made her out, and even her very lights.
I pointed her out to Baker just now, but he could see
nothing and thought I was mistaken. Not I!"

"And she's in distress?"

"Could a ship be off the coast, in such a storm as this,
and not be in distress?" was Mitchel's answer. "And the
wind blowing dead on shore! Mark me! if that is a ship,
she'll be on the rocks to-night. I——"

The man's voice stopped abruptly, and the assembly
simultaneously started to their feet. A heavy, booming
sound had struck upon their ears. Mrs. Ravensbird rushed
into the room.

"Is that a cannon?" she exclaimed, in alarm.

If it was a cannon, it was firing off quick, sharp strokes,
one after the other, as no cannon ever had been known to

do yet. Some of those startled listeners had heard that sound before; some had not.

"It is the great bell at the Castle!" uttered Mitchel. "I am sure of it. The last time it rang out was for that fire in the stable, before the old lord died. What can be the matter?"

With one accord the company left their seats and went into the road, peering towards the Castle with the thought of fire. Sophie accompanied them, holding on her real lace cap with her hands; the barmaid followed, holding hers. They could not see anything alarming, but they talked and shouted to each other, and might be heard above the howling wind.

"I wish you would be still for an instant," interposed Ravensbird. "Listen: as keenly as the wind and that bell will allow you."

They hushed their clamour and bent their ears in obedience to the injunction. And then they caught what the noise in the taproom had prevented them from hearing before: a minute gun fired at sea.

"It is the ship in distress," eagerly spoke Mitchel; "I knew she would be. She's signalling for help. And the Castle bell is giving notice of it; as it used to do in old times."

At this juncture, one of the Dane retainers was discerned speeding past on the main road. They knew him by his white and purple livery, and the group rushed up the by-way and seized him.

"Don't stop me," he exclaimed. "I'm going in search of Lord Dane. There's a large ship in distress. She looks like an Indiaman, and may be filled with home passengers."

"I said so," observed Mitchel. "How did you make her out?" he asked of the footman.

"Some of us fancied we heard signals of distress from sea, and went up to the turret chamber, and there made out the ship, and saw quite plainly the flash of her minute-guns, though the wind deadened the sound. Mr. Bruff gave orders then for the alarm-bell to be rung, and sent me off to Squire Lester's in search of my lord."

A very short time, and all Danesheld who could trust to their legs found themselves on the beach, called there by the alarm-bell. The ship, drifting gradually in-shore, was nearer now, and her guns were louder. They could plainly discern a noble ship in the intervals of bright moonlight. One old sailor who possessed fine eyesight, keener than even Mitchel's, professed to make out her build, and declared she was an American. Whatever she might be, she was certainly drifting rapidly to her doom.

Her position was a little to the left hand as the people stood, and she would most likely strike just beyond the village, towards Dane Castle. The wind was a hurricane, howling and shrieking, buffeting the spectators, and almost taking away their breath; the waves rose mountains high, with their roar; and the good ship cracked and groaned as she bent to their fury.

And the scene on board! Awful indeed seemed the jarring elements to the spectators; what, then, must they have been to those who were hopelessly in their power! Confusion reigned, distress, unbounded fear. Almost as terrible as that Great Day of the Last Judgment. For them that Last Day was at hand—time was over; eternity was beginning—and some were not prepared to meet it!

Lord Dane and Mr. Lester came up together, arm-in-arm, and the crowd parted to give them place. Mr. Lester carried a night-glass, but the wind rendered it useless.

"Why, she's close in-shore!" exclaimed Lord Dane, in accents of horror.

"Another half-hour, my lord, and she'll be upon the rocks," responded a bystander.

"Heavens! how fast she's drifting!"

"My men," said Mr. Lester, addressing himself to the fishermen and sailors there congregated, "can nothing be done?"

One unanimous, subdued sound was heard in answer: "No!"

"If one of them could leave the ship and swim ashore with a lead line, that's their only chance," observed an old man. "Not that I think he'd succeed; the waves would swallow him long before he got to shore."

" There's the life-boat ! " cried Lord Dane.

The crowd shook their heads with a pitying smile. " No life-boat could put off in such a sea as this ! "

Never, perhaps, had been witnessed a more hopeless spectacle of prolonged agony. Again and again blue lights were burned on board the ship, showing, even more distinctly than the moon had done, the crowd on deck, some of whom were standing with outstretched hands. And yet those on shore could give no help. Men ran from the beach to the heights, and from the heights to the beach, in painful excitement; and they could do nothing.

On, on she came towards the shore. The night wore on; the hurricane raged in its fury; the waves roared and tossed in their terrific might, and the good ship came on to her doom. Singular to say, now death seemed inevitable, the despairing cries had ceased.

In two hours from the time that the Castle bell boomed out, she struck, and the first sea washed many overboard, who began battling with the waves as hopelessly as the ship had battled with them. Cries came over the water then, and were heard by those on shore; some of whom—women —fell on their knees in their nervous excitement, and prayed God to have mercy on the spirits of the drowning.

" She'll go to pieces ! and no earthly aid can save her ! "

As these words were spoken, another person dashed into the throng—one who appeared not yet to have been amongst the spectators. It was Wilfred Lester. He wore his sporting clothes, as he had done when Maria met him earlier in the evening. Pressing through to the front, he leaned his arms on the rails of the little jetty, and contemplated the beating vessel.

" Good heavens ! " he uttered, after a few moments' steadfast gaze; " she must have struck. What is that in the water ? " he continued, after another pause.

" Human beings, drowning. They are being washed off the ship ! "

" Human beings, drowning ! " he repeated, his voice harsh with emotion. " And you are not attempting to rescue them ? Are you mad, all of you ? "

A man by his side pointed to the foaming sea.

"Let that answer you."

"It is no answer," said Wilfred Lester. "Where's the life-boat?"

He turned in his impulsive indignation, and Mr. Lester drew himself away into the midst of the crowd: he had not cared latterly to come into contact with his son. Lord Dane, on the contrary, pressed up and laid his hand upon the young man's arm.

"You are excited, Lester," he quietly observed: "and the sight is sufficient to stir the most stoical. But nothing can be done. You might as well talk of a balloon as a life-boat: the one could no more reach the ship than the other."

"The effort might be made," returned Wilfred, in angry tones, as he dashed his wild hair from his brow.

"And the lives of those making it would be sacrificed," rejoined Lord Dane.

Wilfred Lester disdained further reply, and turned to where a group of fishermen were congregated. He was familiar with them all; and had been from boyhood.

"Gand, where's the life-boat?" he asked of that weather-beaten tar, who looked sixty at the least, to judge by the wrinkles on his face. "Is she ready?"

Gand pointed to a small and snug creek at some little distance: he was not a man of many words. The life-boat was moored in the creek, and could be out at sea in a few minutes.

"Was made ready when the Castle bell tolled out, Master Wilfred," answered he.

"And why have you not put off in her?" demanded Wilfred, in a tone of command.

"Wouldn't dare, sir. And the sea's higher now, if anything, than it was then."

"Wouldn't dare!" scornfully echoed Wilfred Lester. "I never knew a British sailor could be a coward until now; I did not think 'wouldn't dare' was in his vocabulary. I am going out in the life-boat: if there's one or two amongst you who can overcome fear, you had better come with me."

He turned to quit the spot and made for the creek, but

fifty voices assailed him. "It would be sheer madness to attempt." "Did he mean to throw away his life?" "He and the life-boat would be swamped together!"

"Then swamped we will be," retorted Wilfred.

How contagious is example; several "good men and true," influenced by the words, declared themselves ready to man the life-boat; and nearly the whole crowd trooped off in the wake of Wilfred Lester.

He was fleet of foot, and was already busy with the boat when they reached him. A voice called out that if she must go out Mr. Wilfred had best not be one of those to man her; he was no sailor. Wilfred Lester caught the words, and turned his handsome face towards the speaker: very pale looked his features in the moonlight—pale, but resolute.

"Who said that?" he asked.

It was old Bill Gand. And Bill avowed it.

"You are not yourself, Bill Gand, to-night. Should I urge on others a danger I shrink from myself?"

"Venture in that there boat, Master Wilfred, and you wunna reach the ship alive," cried Bill, "let alone come back. Nor the rest, nor the boat neither."

"It is possible; but I think we may hope for a better result," was the answer: and in truth Wilfred Lester seemed lifted out of himself to-night. "We are embarking in a good cause, and God is over us all."

The last words told: for, of all men, a sailor has the most implicit trust in God's mercy—a simple, childlike trust, that many who call themselves more religious might envy. They were contending now who should man her, many being eager to do so; and there appeared some chance of its rising to a quarrel.

"This is my expedition," said Wilfred Lester, and his voice had all that command in it that these moments of danger will sometimes bring forth. "But for me you would not have attempted it; allow me the privilege, therefore, of choosing my men. Bill Gand, will you make one of us or not?"

"Yes," answered the old sailor, "if it's only to take care

of you. My wife's in the churchyard, and my two boys are under the waters: I shall be less missed nor some here."

The others were soon named, and they went into the boat. Wilfred was about to follow them, when some one glided up, and stood before him.

" Will it prove availing if *I* ask you not to peril your life ? "

The speaker was Mr. Lester. Wilfred hesitated a moment before he answered :

" I could not, for any consideration, abandon the expedition : nevertheless, I thank you ; I thank you heartily, if you spoke out of interest for my welfare. Father, this may be our last meeting : shall we shake hands ? If I perish, regret me not ; for, I tell you truly, life has lost its value for me."

Mr. Lester grasped the offered hand in silence, a more bitter pang wringing his heart than many of the bystanders would have believed : but the incident had been almost unnoticed amidst the thronging crowd. Wilfred leaped into the boat, and it put off on its stormy voyage.

What a fine picture the scene would have made, could it have been represented both to the eye and ear—not unlike those old paintings of the Flemish school. The doomed vessel and her unhappy human freight, the life-boat launched on her perilous venture, making some way in spite of the wind, and battling with the furious sea : the anxious faces of the spectators, and their breathless interest, as they watched the progress of the boat, or the dim and dreadful spot farther on ! The bright moon lighted up the whole scene ; cloud after cloud was hurrying along the night sky : the faint sound of a bell might be heard ever and anon from the ship, and the great Castle bell boomed out still at intervals.

Would the boat reach the ship ? Those in the boat, as well as those on shore, were asking the question. Bill Gand, the oldest of them, declared that he had never wrestled with a gale so terrific, with waves so furious. The mystery to Bill then—and it would remain a mystery through all his after-life—was, that they *did* wrestle with them. Minute after minute, as they strove to labour on, and the angry sea beat them back, did he believe would be their last; that the next must see them in eternity: all who were with them believed so, including Wilfred Lester. How was it that they did escape? It appeared nothing less than a miracle; and, when endeavouring to account for it afterwards, they were wont to repeat the words Wilfred Lester had spoken on shore: "It was a good cause, and God was over them all."

But they did not reach the ship. No: too many poor wretches were struggling with the waves, nearer to them; and they picked up as many as they could—picked them up until the boat would hold no more. It was a very small boat at the best, almost an apology for a boat, and was nearly filled by those who manned it. Danesheld had long cried out against it: but it was easier to complain than to get a new one. Shouting a cheering word of hope to the wreck, which the wind probably took to itself and kept, they turned in-shore again.

Going back was less labour, for they had the wind with them: but it was not less dangerous. Some of the men, powerful, hardy sailors that they were, felt their strength drooping; they did not think they could hold out. Wilfred Lester encouraged them, as he had done in going, cheering their spirits, almost renewing their strength. But for him, they would several times have given up the effort in despair, when they were first beating on for the wreck.

"Bear on with a will, my lads," he urged; "don't let fatigue master you. I and Bill Gand are good for another turn yet; but we'll leave you on shore to recruit your strength, and bring others in your stead. You shall join again the third time. On, now, with a will!"

One of the rescued spoke up in answer; apparently the only one yet able to do so. The others were lying, hurt or exhausted, at the bottom of the boat. He was a thin, light, able-bodied seaman, and seemed none the worse for immersion in the water.

"It would take several times, sir; but you'll never have

the chance of going to her a third time, if you do a second. She was parting amidships."

" Parting amidships ! "

" The captain said so. I think she must have struck upon a rock ; she was grinding and cracking awfully."

" Where does she come from ? "

" From New York. A passenger ship. A prosperous voyage we have had all along from starting, and this is the ending ! A fine ship, eleven hundred tons register, her name ' The Wind.' I didn't like her name, for my part, when I joined her."

" Many passengers ? "

" Forty or fifty ; about half-a-dozen of them first class ; the rest, second."

The above conversation had been carried on in snatches, as the howling wind and the struggling boat permitted. Soon it ceased altogether, for every energy had to be devoted to the boat, if they were to get her to the shore.

A low, heartfelt murmur of applause greeted their ears as they reached it ; it might have been louder but for the remembrance of what the brave adventurers had yet to do, and their small chance of success—the very small portion these few formed of those still to be saved. As Wilfred Lester stepped ashore, his face white with exertion, the salt foam dripping from him, it is possible that he looked for a father's hand to welcome him, a father's voice to encourage him. If so, he was mistaken. Mr. Lester was there still, but he did not press to the front ; did not appear to recognize that Wilfred was even known to him. Ah, what a difference does it make in our feelings of regard for our friends—their resuscitation from probable death, compared with their embarking upon it !

Another spectator had been added to the scene : Mr. Lester's wife. Lady Adelaide, braving the wind, had actually come forth in her woman's curiosity, and was now standing on the beach between her husband and Lord Dane. Was her presence the obstacle that prevented Mr. Lester's further notice of his son ?—or was he already repenting his late greeting? Wilfred saw her standing there; but he was too busy to give it more than a passing thought.

He stood, prepared to help the rescued out of the boat, almost jealous, as it seemed, that any one else should touch them. Suddenly he turned his white face full on the spectators, and his voice bore the nameless sound of command it had previously done, when urging the expedition.

" Have any of you thought to provide warm beds and fires? Otherwise these poor rescued creatures might almost as well have been left to the water."

Richard Ravensbird was the first to respond, pressing forward a little beyond the crowd as he did so.

" I can receive two or three; my wife is at home making ready for them. I have not been able to do anything towards saving, but I can towards sheltering. There's a coach here, and Jessop is bringing down his omnibus."

Lord Dane spoke up, offering the Castle and every accommodation it could afford. But the Castle was too far off to be of much use to men half drowned. As they raised one man from the bottom of the boat, he spoke faintly. He had very little clothing on, and seemed to be getting in years, for his wet hair shone white in the moonlight.

" What part of the coast have we been thrown on?" he asked. " What place is this?"

" Danesheld."

" My head," came the feeble rejoinder. " I am cold. A shawl for my head."

One of the bystanders—it happened to be Mitchel—divested himself of a cloak, and it was put over the rescued man. He feebly pulled the cape over his head and face, to guard them from the wind; and another of the rescued, a young man fully dressed, as if he had flung himself into the sea without a moment for preparation, hastened to assist him. It seemed that he was in attendance on him, as friend or servant; or, it might be, only as fellow-passengers. Both were passengers; not sailors.

" I should be glad to have him conveyed to a decent inn," said the young man, " if there is such a thing at hand."

"Mine is an inn, and close by," said Ravensbird. "We will do all we can for him."

The coach was brought up close, and the man lifted into it. The younger was about to follow, when he grasped Wilfrid Lester's hand:

"That we owe our lives this night to you, under God, there is little doubt. I shall hope to thank you better than I can do now."

The voice proclaimed his condition. It was that of a gentleman, its tones remarkably pleasant, its accents refined. A third followed them into the coach; a sailor this, whose head was much cut; and the coach took its departure for the Sailors' Rest, Ravensbird having gone on before to be in readiness for the arrival.

Wilfred Lester began mustering his second crew, Old Bill Gand again making one of them.

"Not you, Dick," cried Wilfred, putting back another man with his arm. "I won't have you."

"And why?" said the man. "I'm strong enough. I've been stronger than ever since that illness in the summer."

Strong? Well, perhaps he was; but it might be that Wilfred Lester was thinking of other reasons. The *man had a wife and seven young children.*

"I will not have you, I say. Stand back, Dick! We have no time to lose."

Scarcely had the words left Wilfred Lester's lips, when a sound, as of a cry from many united voices, came to them, borne on the wind.

"What's that?" asked the crowd.

Ah, what was it? Another cry went up from those questioners when they knew; a cry of sympathy and horror. The rescued sailor's words had been too surely and swiftly verified. The vessel had parted amidships, and was settling down in the water.

Oh, for the life-boat now! One more voyage, and it may yet save a few of those now launched into the sea. Before it could take a third, the rest will have been launched into eternity.

And the life-boat hastened out once more amidst loud

cheering upon its mad career. But it rescued only one. It was blown back and buffeted, and all but lost itself; and when there came a lull, and it still pressed on to its work of mercy, there were no souls left to be saved. The hungry waters had made sure of their prey.

CHAPTER XVIII.

AT THE SAILORS' REST.

A BUSTLING night was that for Mrs. Ravensbird. She had all the tact of a Frenchwoman, and was equal to the occasion. Warm beds were in readiness for the shipwrecked, hot flannels, and other restoratives. The three mentioned in the previous chapter were alone conveyed to the Sailors' Rest, the others found accommodation in the guard-house and elsewhere. Ah, so few in all! for the boat could not make the wreck again.

The middle-aged passenger was placed in the best room: a comfortable apartment on the first floor. As he was assisted from the coach up to it, Madame Sophie cast a keen glance at him, and came to the decision that he was a tall old man. His hair was silvered, and his features looked white. But he had recovered from his exhaustion sufficiently to decline all assistance in his chamber, into which he shut himself, and when he had got into bed between the hot blankets he then rang the bell.

He asked for a basin of hot gruel, with some brandy in it.

When the maid took it to him, she brought with it a message. The young man, his fellow-passenger saved, wished to know if he might come in, or whether he could do anything for him.

No, was the answer returned. And the young man had better lose no time in getting into bed himself. He might come to him in the morning, if he would be so good: and no one else was to disturb him unless he rang for them.

Mrs. Ravensbird, in common with half Danesheld, did not go to bed that night. She had her hands full; and was glad also of the excuse for sitting up. She busied herself attending to the rescued sailor's head, which seemed to have been very much cut about, and in drying the younger passenger's clothes, for he had been fully dressed when rescued.

It appeared that these two were the only passengers saved. The others had all gone down: the officers had perished; for the two or three others saved were ordinary seamen. As Mrs. Ravensbird doctored the head of the one under her charge, she inquired particulars of the two sleeping men above, but the sailor could tell her nothing: they were first-class passssengers, he said, but he did not even know their names.

"Are they gentlemen?" asked the inquisitive landlady, who was learned in social distinctions, the result, possibly, of her residence at Dane Castle; "or merchants, and people of that sort?"

The sailor could not say, but gave it as his opinion that they were most likely merchants, "for lots of trading folk" came and went between England and the States.

"It's odd you handful of folks should have been saved, whilst all the rest, except one, perished," remarked Sophie. "Quite a miracle, as one might think."

"I don't know about miracles," answered the man, rather obtusely. "I think it was because we took to the ship's life-boat, and managed to launch her and get into her; she swamped after a bit, and drowned some of them in her, but it brought the rest of us, you see, nearer to the life-boat that put off from shore."

"What a fight it must have been amongst you, on board ship, who should get into the life-boat?"

"Law bless you!" cried the man. "A fight!—it was rather the other way. We could hardly get enough in her: of the two, the ship seemed the safest. The captain said she couldn't live in such a sea, even if we got her clear of the vessel: and he was right; she didn't live long. Don't cut off more hair than you can help, ma'am."

Soon after eight Mrs. Ravensbird was in the bar-parlour alone, rather angrily giving vent to some grievance in her native language, a custom she had never abandoned, when she suddenly found herself interrupted in French as fluent as her own, and rather purer. Turning round in her surprise, she saw the younger passenger, attired in his dry clothes; by which, in fact, she recognised him, for she had scarcely seen him the previous night. And Madame Sophie, in that first moment, thought she had never seen so pre-possessing a man. He was about four or five-and-twenty, his figure very fine, his features clearly cut, his hair dark, and his countenance and manner singularly attractive.

"Monsieur is French," remarked the gratified Sophie, with a laugh.

"You are, I hear," he replied, laughing also. "And somewhat put out just now."

"Ah, monsieur should have her servants just for a day," was the rejoinder. "That tiresome animal of a barmaid; thinking of her finery, and not a bit of her work!"

"Are you a clever needlewoman?" inquired the gentle-man in English — English as pure and good as his French.

More and more won over by the attractive looks, the courteous manner, the pleasant voice, Mrs. Ravensbird protested that there was not a better needlewoman in the world than herself. She had been externe pupil for seven years in a French convent, she said; and let the sisters alone for making girls expert at their needle! "Did mon-sieur want a button sewn on?"

The gentleman smiled. Had it been only that, he thought he could have managed it himself without troubling her, provided she had supplied him with needle and cotton. "I had those with me," he continued, "but they have gone down with my luggage."

"You have saved nothing, sir?"

"Nothing except a pocket-book and a few papers which I happened to have about me. What I want you to do," he

continued, " is something that requires rather more skill than
sewing on buttons. I want a shade made for the eyes."

Sophie raised her glance to the eyes looking down at
her ; clear, bright eyes they were, of a dark grey ; and she
wondered what they could want with a shade.

" It is for my fellow-passenger," he proceeded to explain.
" I have been to his room, and all his cry is for a shade for
his eyes. He suffered with them during the voyage, I
observed, and the light of the room this morning affects
them much. He wishes it made large, he says, of thin
cardboard, covered with dark blue or green silk, and tape
to tie it on with."

" Tape!" ejaculated Sophie, in reproof. " You mean
ribbon, sir."

" Anything you like. He will not care what the materials
are, provided his eyes are shaded. I asked if I should
order breakfast for him, but he seemed only anxious for the
shade."

Sophie soon had her necessary materials in hand ; a sheet
of cardboard, which she unearthed from somewhere, and
some purple silk, the remnant of a dress ; and set to work.
The gentleman sat himself opposite on the arm of an old
horse-hair sofa, and watched her fingers. His orders were,
he said, laughingly, not to go up again without the shade.

" Who is he?" asked Sophie, as she worked. " He
seemed to me last night quite an old gentleman. Do you
know much of him, sir?"

" I saw a good deal of him on board."

" It's curious how intimate fellow-passengers get on board
ship!" observed Mrs. Ravensbird, whose tongue never
failed her. " Is he a merchant?"

The gentleman laughed. " You must inquire of him,
Mrs. Ravensbird, if you wish to know. I have not been so
inquisitive as to do so."

" I suppose he is an American," she continued, nothing
daunted. " What is his name?"

" That question I have just asked of himself, for I do not
remember to have once heard it mentioned on board," was
the reply. " He tells me it is Home."

"Mr. Home!" complacently continued Sophie, as she gave a turn to the purple shade, now satisfactorily progressing. "And I hope you will give me the gratification of hearing yours, sir. I am sure it's a pleasant one."

"Do you fancy so?" he laughed. "I see nothing much in it myself. Lydney."

"Lydney!" repeated Sophie, after him. "That's not a French name."

"My father was not French. My mother went out to America from her own country; and she married him there."

"Ah," said Sophie, "that accounts for your speaking the two languages equally well. Then you would be called an American, sir, not a Frenchman. What a shame!"

"I suppose I should be," he assented, his bright grey eyes full of merriment.

"And have you come over here on business, sir?"

"In truth, I think I came for pleasure; to look about me—never having had the honour of seeing old England before," he answered, with good humour. "How many more questions would you like to ask me, Mrs. Ravensbird?"

"But it's my French nature, and I must ask you to excuse it," she replied, with ready politeness.

"Suppose I ask you one in return? Is there such a thing as a tailor in—what do you call this place—Danesheld? Look at me!"

The salt water had caused his clothes to shrink, and he certainly did not appear dressed in the height of fashion. Sophie laughed, and rattled on in her own tongue.

But yes, there was a charming tailor, fresh from a London establishment. He had grown ill in the great stifling metropolis, and he came down here, where his wife's friends lived, and opened a shop, next door to Mr. Wild, the surgeon's, and his cut was perfect. My Lord Dane himself had honoured him with an order for a suit last week. The gentleman did not know my Lord Dane?

"Not I," answered Mr. Lydney. "He is your great man here, I presume?"

"The greatest of all for miles round," Sophie answered,

"and he lived at Dane Castle. He was down on the jetty last night when the life-boat brought in Mr. Lydney and the rest. Ah, heaven! what a wreck it was!"

All the pleasure went out of Mr. Lydney's face as she recalled it, to be replaced by true and earnest pain.

"I awoke three times in the night, and each time that I slept I had the whole scene before me," he said in low tones. "I feel that it will haunt my dreams for weeks to come."

"You must be thankful that you are amongst the few saved, sir."

"I am," he answered, very quietly. "When the boat was being launched, the gentleman upstairs touched me on the arm. 'I shall risk it,' he said, 'it may give us a chance;' and I leaped into it with him; not, however, thinking that any chance remained to us, either in the boat or the ship."

"What did he do with his clothes?" asked Sophie.

"He ran up on deck without them, washed out of his berth. A large, warm cloth cloak, that he had flung on, was lost in the water."

"He seemed ill last night, I thought, apart from the shipwreck."

"He has been very ill all through the voyage. Some inward complaint, I believe. Ah, thank you."

Mrs. Ravensbird was holding out the shade completed. He said a few words of gallant admiration for her and her quickness, as he took it from her hand.

"I have not put my best work into it," she observed. "You hurried me too much for that. When would you like breakfast, sir?"

"Presently. Let us see what this sick gentleman wants first. He is older than I am."

Mr. Lydney went upstairs with the shade, and Mrs. Ravensbird began searching her memory for its records of her own country. That she had somewhere seen handsome features to which his bore a resemblance, she felt certain, and had little doubt that in her own young days she must have known his mother in France. "My heart warmed to him from the first," quoth she. "It may even turn out that his mother was a friend."

In the course of the morning, Lord Dane walked into the Sailors' Rest, to make inquiries after the rescued. Richard Ravensbird was not in at the moment, but his wife was quite equal to receiving his lordship. She did not forget the old days when he, the poor and obscure Herbert Dane, was fond of chattering to her, Sophie Deffloe; and her manners towards him retained far more of ease than did those of some of his dependents in Danesheld. She began pouring into his ear all the news she had been able to collect regarding the two passengers, coupled with her own additions; for Mrs. Ravensbird was one of those who form conclusions from their lively imagination, and then assume them to be facts.

"They were coming over from America," she said: "the elder one, a Mr. Home, travelling for his health, especially for a weakness in the eyes; the other, a Mr. Lydney, for pleasure. They had met on board as fellow-passengers, and become friendly, and the younger one seemed inclined to be grateful and attentive to the old one, for it was through him he entered the boat and was saved."

"Both Americans, I presume?" observed Lord Dane.

"Mr. Home, yes, certainly; Mr. Lydney was half American, half French," was Mrs. Ravensbird's answer. "Ah, le malheur! when she had taken him for a pure Frenchman, if ever there was one on earth. Never was such an accent heard out of Paris. And he was the pleasantest man in the world; charming in manners; affable and free as my lord himself used to be in the bygone days." And Madame Sophie cast a half-saucy glance to my lord when she said it.

"Are they gentlemen?" inquired Lord Dane.

"Without doubt; the younger one at least," answered Mrs. Ravensbird warmly, "every inch of him. There is no taking him for anything inferior. And, do you know, his face puts me in mind of some lady I must have known in France in my early days; but for the life of me I can't think who, though I've been ransacking my memory all the morning. Wouldn't it be curious, my lord, if it should turn out that I was acquainted with his mother?"

Lord Dane smiled. "Is he up?" he asked.

"Up!" echoed Sophie; "he was up hours ago; at seven o'clock this morning. He went out after breakfast to put a letter in the post, and to find the new tailor; and I'll be bound he then went down to the wreck, for he is in a great way at his luggage being lost, especially some particular box that was amongst it; and wants to know whether there's any chance of things being got up. Does your lordship think there is."

"A few things may be, perhaps. I cannot tell."

"The other one is not up," ran on Sophie. "I thought I would take his breakfast in myself, and inquire after him, but it wasn't much he would answer. All I could see of him was his gray hair and the purple shade I made him. He was lying buried in his pillow, under the bedclothes, with his face to the wall; and he just told me to put the tray down by his bed and leave it, and he'd help himself."

"Poor man! I daresay he was thoroughly exhausted. Will you convey a message to him for me, Mrs. Ravensbird? Say that I shall be happy to render him any assistance in my power; and if he would like me to pay him a visit, I can do so now."

Mrs. Ravensbird ran up to the invalid's chamber, and came back, shaking her head.

"I'll lay any money he's a cross-grained old bachelor," cried she; "he seems afraid to look at us. And he won't see you, my lord. I call it quite rude of him. 'My service to my Lord Dane,' said he, 'but tell him I am a private individual, seeking nothing but repose, and am not desirous of making acquaintance with any one at present. I'll pay my respects to his lordship when I'm better.' Some of those Americans know nothing of courtesy."

"Oh, very well," returned Lord Dane, not at all gratified at his friendly offers being rejected, "I won't trouble him again; he can call on me when he chooses, if it pleases him so to do."

As Lord Dane turned from the Sailors' Rest toward the town, Mr. Lydney was approaching it from the beach. Lord Dane did not happen to look that way, and consequently did not observe him.

" Who was that gentleman?" inquired Mr. Lydney of
the landlady, who had attended his lordship to the door,
and stood looking after him.

" It's Lord Dane, sir."

" Lord Dane!" came the answer, spoken in surprise.
" How young he looks!"

Sophie felt rather offended on Lord Dane's account.
" Did you think he was old?" she asked. " Why should
you have thought that?"

A short pause, and Mr. Lydney broke into a laugh.

" Now that's the force of association," he cried. " You
had spoken of this Lord Dane being the chief of Danesheld,
and my mind at once pictured a venerable man, with hair
as white as the invalid's upstairs, or whiter. He is a tall,
fine man, and looks quite young."

" All the Danes were that. He came to inquire after
you and the old gentleman, to offer a visit and his services.
I took up the message to Mr. Home, but he would not see
him, and his lordship's gone off in dudgeon."

" Perhaps he'll see him when he's up."

" Perhaps he won't," answered free Sophie. " Lord Dane
said he should not come again; if Mr. Home wanted him
he might go to him. I must say, sir, it is not very polite
of your friend."

" I don't suppose politeness had anything to do with it
one way or the other, Mrs. Ravensbird. Mr. Home may
have felt physically unequal to receiving a visitor; he
certainly seemed so this morning."

" Why doesn't he call in a doctor then?"

" I suggested that to him the first thing to-day, but he declined; saying all he wanted was rest and quiet. I think
he's right; he is not in any way injured."

" And about his dinner?" continued Mrs. Ravensbird,
rather resentfully. " I went in myself, just before my Lord
Dane arrived, asking whether he would like slops, or a nice
little chicken, but he growled out something about wanting
no dinner at all, and would hardly answer me. Perhaps
you'll try, sir."

Mr. Lydney laughed, and ran lightly up the stairs.

It was a most comfortable room, the one in which Mr. Home lay, and Mrs. Ravensbird was in the habit of calling it the state chamber. The apartment occupied by Mr. Lydney was at the opposite side of the passage; a small room scantily furnished. Mrs. Ravensbird secretly wished the respective occupants had been reversed. She hinted at this in her liking for the young man; and he, in his free, good-humoured way, said his chamber was paradise after his berth in the life-boat. At the end of the passage was a sitting-room, looking out over the sea. Mr. Lydney took possession of this, and his meals were served in it.

The invalid lay in bed the whole day. Towards dusk, Richard Ravensbird went in and found the chamber almost in darkness. The heavy curtains were kept drawn before the windows, on account of the invalid's weak eyes; the fire had gone down. Ravensbird stirred it into a blaze, and was quietly sweeping up the hearth, when Mr. Home suddenly addressed him:

"What sort of a neighbourhood is this?"

"Sir?" he cried, turning round.

"What sort of a neighbourhood is this?"

Mr. Ravensbird probably wondered in what light he was to take the question, whether as to its natural, social, or political features. But he did not inquire.

"It is rather a dull neighbourhood," said he, "except when we have an event like the one last night."

"Lord Dane is your great man of the locality, I hear from my fellow-passenger in the next room."

"Yes, sir. The Danes have been the lords of Danesheld from times unheard of. And plenty of state they have kept up. But, to have the Castle closed, or as good as closed, has been like a blight upon the place. The present Lord Dane has not lived at it."

"Why so?"

"He went abroad almost as soon as he came into the title, and has not long returned. Eight or nine years he must have been away. Perhaps more; time flies. It's thought he will remain now, and I dare say he will; he has made changes in the establishment at the Castle."

" He is not married, is he ? "

" No, sir. His sister, Miss Dane, is with him at the Castle at present, acting as its mistress."

" Perhaps you will inform me what you are talking about," cried the invalid, after a pause. " Lord Dane has no sister."

" Yes he has, sir. And she is with him, as I tell you, at the Castle."

" Then I tell you he has not a sister," was the sick man's irritable answer, though his tone was, and had been, remarkably low and subdued throughout. " I met a Mr. Dane once in Paris, I remember ; it was the present peer ; there was no sister then."

It was Richard Ravensbird's custom, when people insisted upon a proposition that he knew to be a mistaken one, to let them hold their own opinion uncontradicted. He did so now. He stretched his neck to get a sight of the invalid's face, feeling sure it was an obstinate one, but did not succeed : the upper part was under the purple shade, the lower part under the bed-clothes.

" Yes, I met the present peer in Paris, and had a sort of acquaintance with him," continued the invalid. " I heard afterwards that he had succeeded to the title, and of the accident to the younger son, Captain Harry Dane. Has he ever been heard of ? "

" Who, sir ? " asked Ravensbird.

" Captain Dane ! " '

Mr. Ravensbird did not answer at once. He was wondering whether the stranger could be cognizant of his having been charged with the murder—a point on which he was still sensitive—and was saying this deliberately to insult him.

" Did you know the particulars of that accident, sir ? " he at length asked.

" Yes, I did. I did not get them from Mr. Dane, though. A nasty pitch over for him. Was he ever heard of ? "

" He was heard of, sir, in so far as that his body was found. He lies buried in the family vault,"

" Where was it found ? "

"At sea. It was picked up by one of our fishing-boats. Not that it had been in the water all the time. But for me, I doubt if they would have recognized it. I knew it by certain marks the moment I put my eyes on it, and I happened to be on the beach when it was brought in."

"Why should you recognize it more than other people?"

"I was Captain Dane's servant, sir; had been with him several years."

"Oh, ay; then I must have heard of you," remarked Mr. Home. "Was there not some quarrel talked of? I'm sure it was reported so."

Richard Ravensbird came to the conclusion that the gentleman had heard the other report, touching him—the accusation—and was leading up to it. He therefore set himself to speak of it calmly and openly, as he always did, to those aware of his arrest; otherwise he preferred to maintain a complete reticence on all points relating to that night.

"Yes, it was a fatal fall, a nasty struggle," Ravensbird observed: "and who the adversary was remains a mystery to this day. Two or three were suspected. I, for one, and was taken up on suspicion: and a packman for another, who was seen in angry contest with the captain on the heights just about the time. In my own mind, I suspected somebody very different."

"Pray whom did you suspect?"

"I should be sorry to tell," answered Ravensbird.

"And what were the grounds for suspecting you?"

"A quarrel I had had with Captain Dane. It occurred in the morning, and he kicked me out of the Castle; the catastrophe took place the same evening, and people's suspicions—naturally enough, I acknowledge—flew to me. But they were wrong. I would have saved my master's life with my own: I would almost bring him back to life now at the sacrifice of my own, were it in my power. I was much attached to him, and I am faithful to his memory."

"In spite of his turning you away?" put in Mr. Home.

"Tush!" returned Ravensbird, nettled. "I beg your

pardon, sir. A dispute of a moment, in which we both lost
our tempers, could not destroy the friendship of years.
Yes, sir, I presume to say it—friendship. He was the
Honourable Captain Dane and I but his servant; and
though he never lost his dignity any more than I forgot my
place, there was a feeling between us that might be called
friendship. No man ever had a more faithful servant than
I was to my master."

A silence ensued. Ravensbird mended the fire, which
was getting low, and the invalid turned in his bed.

"What has become of the cousin, Herbert Dane? I used
to hear of him. He was to have married some young lady
staying at the Castle—at least it was thought there was an
attachment between them."

"Lady Adelaide Errol," said Ravensbird, who had not
clearly heard the first part of the question, through some
noise with the fire-irons. "Yes there was an attachment,
but she would not have him after all, and she married
a gentleman whom we call Squire Lester. Ah, she was
another mystery."

"In what way?"

"Well, I thought so at the time. She has a whole troop
of children now. The young man who was chiefly instru-
mental in saving you last night, sir, was Squire Lester's
eldest son, Mr. Wilfred Lester: his mother was Squire
Lester's first wife. But for him, the life-boat would never
have gone out. He is under a sad cloud, poor fellow?"

"What sort of a cloud, pray?"

"More sorts than one, sir. He is out at pockets and out
at elbows; tales are told that he and his young wife are
starving; and when a gentleman is reduced to that condition, he's apt not to be too particular as to what he puts
his hands to. It's a miserable business altogether, and
Lady Adelaide's at the bottom of it."

"You are speaking in riddles, landlord."

Ravensbird explained. Telling briefly the circumstances
that led to Squire Lester's son being reduced to his present
position, and certainly not sparing Lady Adelaide in the
recital,

"It's a pity," was the comment of Mr. Home, when he had listened. "I did not take much notice of him last night, was not in a condition to do it, but he seemed a fine young fellow. We were speaking of Mr. Herbert Dane. What has become of him? Is he at Daneshold?"

"Yes, sir, he is now at the Castle."

"At the Castle! What for?"

Ravensbird gave his neck another stretch, thinking if he could get a tolerable glimpse of the face under the bed-clothes, he might be able to draw some deduction as to whether its owner was in his right mind. In vain; he could see nothing but the tip of the nose—a thin and handsome nose, it's true, but what of that?

"He has come to the Castle to reside there, sir."

"He! Does Lord Dane tolerate him in it?"

The usually impassive face of Mr. Richard Ravensbird was for once blank with astonishment. Light dawned on it.

"Why, sir, is it possible you do not know that Herbert Dane is the present peer? Lord Dane, that we have been speaking of, he who called to inquire after you to-day, was formerly Herbert Dane. He succeeded the old lord."

Mr. Home raised himself on his elbow, and peered at Ravensbird from under the purple shade.

"Then what on earth has become of the eldest son—Geoffry—he whom I was with in Paris? Where was he, that Herbert Dane should inherit?"

"He died at the same time as his brother," answered Ravensbird, shaking his head. "Before the body of my master was found, the remains of Mr. Dane were brought home for interment in the family vault."

"Where did he die? What did he die of?" reiterated Mr. Home, who appeared unable to overcome his astonishment.

"He died of fever, sir. I can't take upon myself to say precisely where, for I forget; it was near Rome, and I know he was put on board at Civita Vecchia. My lady went almost as quickly; and the old lord did not live above a month or two,"

"I know, I know," cried the stranger, with an impatience that seemed almost feverish; "I saw their deaths announced in the newspapers; and I saw the succession of the new peer, 'Geoffry, Lord Dane.' Not Herbert."

"His name is Herbert Geoffry, sir," explained Ravensbird. "As soon as he became heir, he was no longer called Herbert, but Geoffry. It is a favourite name with the Lords of Dane."

Mr. Home lay down again and covered his face. Ravensbird waited in silence, rather wondering,

"It has been quite a shock to me, look you, landlord. I had thought to renew my former acquaintance with the Geoffry Dane I once knew, never supposing but that he was the present peer. When they brought me word up to-day that Lord Dane had called, I took it to be him; but I did not care that he should see me in my present state. Herbert, Lord Dane! I can't believe it now."

"Indeed he is, sir; and has been for this ten years past."

"Is he liked?"

"Yes, very much. Not that he has given great opportunity to be liked or disliked, stopping away so long," added Ravensbird. "He has made himself popular since he did come back; and he behaved generously in the matter of Lord Dane's will. The will left a large amount in presents and legacies, but my lord died before he signed it, consequently it was null and void. The new peer, however, fulfilled all the bequests to the very letter, as honourably as though he had been legally bound to do it."

"That was well."

"Fifteen thousand pounds were left to Lady Adelaide Errol: a large sum, but it was paid with the rest."

"Why did he not marry her?" rather sharply put in the invalid, as if forgetting his former question on the subject. "He was rich enough and great enough then."

"She turned round, sir, as I tell you, and would not have him. It was a whim, I suppose. My wife was maid to Lady Adelaide at the time, and she heard of the refusal and told me, but we did not talk of it. In fact it was not generally known that there was ever anything between them."

"Perhaps there never was much."

"O yes, there was, sir; when he was plain Herbert Dane," significantly replied Ravensbird. "Ah, he little thought then, or my Lady Adelaide either, to be what he is now— the Lord of Danesheld."

"And he has not married, you say?"

"Not yet; and there's no heir. If he were to die, the title would become extinct. People think he may perhaps marry now, as he has come back to settle down."

Mr. Home made no reply. He turned his face to the wall; 'and nothing more was to be seen of him but his silvered hair, and the purple shade.

CHAPTER XIX.

THE BOX THAT THE SEA CAST UP.

It was a stirring scene; the sun shone down on it in all its brightness, as if in very mockery. One might have thought a fair was being held on the heights of Danesheld, for people elbowed and jostled each other in eager curiosity: rich and poor, old and young, gentle and simple—all had congregated there on the morning after the wreck; and if we did not speak of this scene quite in its proper time and place, it was because other things claimed our attention. Venturesome spirits had come out to the beach by daylight, but the heights were unapproachable then from the violence of the wind. Below was the wreck of the once good ship, partially visible at low tide, lying with her larboard side to the shore. Quantities of chips and pieces of wood were floating about. The masts, the yards, the bowsprit were gone; all in fact had gone that could go, save the old hull which might disappear with the next tide. Mr. Bill Gand, an authority on such matters, gave it as his opinion that "nothing was left inside of her," meaning that stores, cargo, and passengers' luggage had alike been washed away; but that was not altogether certain. Something more than wood or spars floated in occasionally: not near enough, however, to scare away the watchers on the heights, quite half of whom were of the timid sex.

Mr. Lydney was amongst them, very anxious: a box that had been on board contained valuable papers, and he was very eager to recover it.

Standing imprudently near the edge of the heights in their sympathy and sad curiosity, were Miss Bordillion and Maria Lester. A confused story had reached Maria's ears that morning of her brother's heroism; she had hastened with it to Miss Bordillion's, and they came out together.

"Margaret, do you think it is true that papa shook hands with Wilfred, and begged him not to risk his life?" reiterated Maria, as she stood on the brow of the heights.

"My dear, you have asked me that question three times over, and I can only repeat to you that I do not know," calmly replied Miss Bordillion.

"I cannot help being anxious; I do hope it is true. Why, Margaret, it might lead to a reconciliation between them."

"I will tell you what I heard, Maria: that when Wilfred came in with his boat of rescued men, saved as from the grave, and people were pressing round to clasp his hand in congratulation, Mr. Lester and Lady Adelaide held aloof from him."

"It is very unjust," cried Maria, passionately.

She took a step forward as she spoke, and bent over the heights, partly in her petulance, partly to see what some noise might be about that had arisen below; wholly without thought. At that moment a blast of wind, more furious than any experienced for the past hour, swept over them.

"Take care, Maria!" shrieked out Miss Bordillion, in an agony of terror.

Whether Maria *could* have taken care must remain a question. That the wind caught her, and that she might not have been able to recover her balance was certain; when at the very moment of peril a strong arm was thrown

around her, and unceremoniously snatched her back to
safety. A moment's pause, and then Maria turned her
face, white with terror, to her preserver. She had felt her
own danger.

She saw a stranger. A gentleman about the age of her
brother Wilfred, who had nobility stamped on every lineament of his face.

"I thank you very much," she said, greatly agitated.
"I did not know the wind was still so high."

"Let *me* thank you," exclaimed Miss Bordillion, putting
her hand into the stranger's in her gratitude. "I do believe
you have, under God, saved her from destruction."

Poor Maria, rather overcome altogether, burst into tears;
which, of course, she felt very much ashamed of, and
hastened to dash away.

"I was saved from much more certain death last night,"
remarked the stranger to Miss Bordillion. "I was a passenger
in that ill-fated ship, and was one of those rescued by the
life-boat."

"Is it possible!" cried Miss Bordillion. "We heard
that only an old gentleman was saved, besides some of the
crew."

"Yes, I was saved also. But for a gentleman who took
command of the life-boat, and shamed (as I hear) some
sailors into manning her, we should all have perished. He
was only a young landsman. I must find out where he
lives and thank him."

"Shall I tell you who it was?" spoke Maria, looking up
to him in her love for the young landsman he spoke of.
"It was my dear brother, Wilfred Lester."

The stranger smiled as he gazed down at the glowing
damask cheeks, the earnest eyes, and thought he had never
seen a face half so beautiful."

"Lester? Yes, that is the name I heard."

Miss Bordillion interrupted: she was as much taken
with the stranger as she had ever been at first sight with
any one in her life, setting aside his having rescued Maria
from peril.

"I am Miss Bordillion," she said; "the nearest relative

Wilfred Lester and this young lady have, except their father. You will allow us to hear your name?"

"William Lydney."

And continuing to converse, in a few minutes it seemed as though they had known each other for years. There are seasons and events that break the barriers of restraint more effectually than time can do.

The next to appear on the scene was Wilfred himself. The two young men clasped hands, and William Lydney spoke a few low, heartfelt words to the other. "I am thanking you for both of us," he said; "for myself and the other passenger, who is now at the Sailors' Rest."

Again Miss Bordillion interrupted, telling of the danger just incurred by Maria, and of Mr. Lydney's ready hand to save. When Wilfred's first alarm was over, he laughed and said: "If I saved him, you have saved my sister, so the obligation on either side is over." But Mr. Lydney merely shook his head in reply.

The wind seemed to be rising again, and Miss Bordillion and Maria were glad to leave the heights: Margaret giving her address to Mr. Lydney, and with it a cordial invitation to call upon her. He shook hands, and said he should not fail to avail himself of it.

As they turned away, Squire Lester happened to be passing. He was merely lifting his hat to Miss Bordillion, to whom he had been very distant since his son's marriage; but Margaret arrested him, telling of Maria's escape, and that the shipwrecked young man had probably "saved her life." Mr. Lester rather laughed at that; but reprimanded his daughter for being so imprudent. Lord Dane came up as they were speaking, and heard the news.

"Who is the young man, I wonder?" cried Mr. Lester. "I must say a word of thanks to him."

"He is some young American," said Lord Dane, who had then come straight from his interview with Mrs. Ravensbird. "The old man we saw lifted out of the life-boat last night was also a passenger and an American."

"Relatives?"

"Oh no; fellow-passengers only. I expect most of the

people on board were Yankees," continued his lordship.
" But I am glad he happened to be near *you*, Miss Lester,
when you imprudently ran into danger."

" She would not be standing here now, had he not been,"
warmly observed Margaret Bordillion.

The days went on. The wind gradually fell to a calm,
and Danesheld regained much of its usual quietness.

People were busy trying to get up articles from the
wreck. The preventive-men remained on active duty day
and night, keeping guard over anything that might be
saved or washed up, so that no depredations should take
place. The divers' exertions, however, appeared likely to
meet but with very little reward.

One visitor the beach constantly had ; and that was the
young stranger, William Lydney. In fact, it may be said
that he passed three parts of his day there, in anxiety about
that missing box, already mentioned. One day, when
Wilfred Lester had strolled down, he rallied him on his
disquietude.

" One would think all your worldly wealth was entombed
in that chest, Lydney. Does it contain gold ? "

" Neither gold nor bank-notes," was Mr. Lydney's answer.
" But it contains valuable deeds and documents, some of
which could not be replaced to the owner."

" To the owner ! Was the box not your own ? "

" No ; I was only in charge of it. The fact makes me
doubly anxious."

" Suppose it never turns up ! Would the loss be
irremediable ? "

" Upon my word, I cannot say. Some of its papers could
be replaced ; but others—I would rather not dwell on the
possibility," he broke off.

" Well, I don't know ; it seems to me, that the chance of
its recovery is a very faint one," remarked Wilfred. " A
hundred to one against it."

" True ; but I am of a hopeful nature, and something
whispers to me it will turn up yet. A few boxes have been
got up, larger than that one."

" How large is it ? "

"Not large. About two feet square; but it is heavy from its casing, which is impervious to water."

The two young men reached the spot where the divers were at work, and gazed at the relics the sea had cast up. They were of various kinds; things most opposite, as may well be imagined. Part of a beam of wood; a gold Albert chain; a small cask containing salt meat; a sealed case, holding letters; and a few boxes.

With an eager step, when he saw a few fresh things, did William Lydney hasten to inspect them. Owners had been found for none of them; not for one of those articles lying on the beach. Their owners would awaken no more in this world.

"Is it among them, sir?" asked the preventive-man, coming up as Mr. Lydney stood over the boxes; for his anxiety to recover the chest was no secret. "There's one japanned case, you see, sir, but I fear it's larger than you describe yours to be."

William Lydney lifted his head, his face expressing keen disappointment.

"It is not there," was all he said.

He and Wilfred Lester walked away together. They had become very friendly, and in the daytime might sometimes be seen arm-in-arm, as now. But Wilfred had never invited Mr. Lydney inside his house; his wife's ill-health was the ostensible excuse; but in reality, it was a home of privation, that might not be laid bare to strangers. The only house to which Mr. Lydney had been welcomed was Cliff Cottage. He had hastened to respond to Miss Bordillion's invitation, and soon became intimate there, almost going in and out at will. Thus he frequently saw Maria Lester—had more than once escorted her home in the evening, when there was no one else to do it. The time was to come when Miss Bordillion took terrible remorse to herself for so imprudently admitting a stranger, of whom she knew positively nothing, to intimacy. The imprudence did not strike her now. She must have been blind, she was wont afterwards to say when Danesheld nearly drove her mad with its reproaches. That Mr. Lydney was a thoroughly well-read man, an accomplished gentleman, was indisputable; that there was a peculiar attraction in himself, and in his manners, was also true; Miss Bordillion had, unthinkingly, assumed all this to be an earnest of his worth, his truth, his honour—and that was the best that could be said of it. Unfortunately, it happened that another was also assuming it, and was, unconsciously, becoming fascinated—one to whom it could bring more danger than to Miss Bordillion.

"How long shall you remain in Danesheld?" questioned Wilfred Lester, as they left the beach and came in view of the Sailors' Rest.

"How long will it be before the box turns up?" retorted Mr. Lydney. "I can't go without it."

Wilfred just suppressed a shrug of the shoulders. In that case, his private opinion was that his new acquaintance would remain on for ever and a day.

"Does that old American get better?" he suddenly asked, as they halted at the door of the inn.

"Mr. Home? He is better, but not well. I think he fluctuates. Some chronic complaint, I believe. He has not left his room."

"Good-day," said Wilfred. "Better luck to you."

He walked away, and Sophie, in her gossiping propensities, came out to the door. She, at any rate, had as yet found no fault in Mr. Lydney, for her manner to him was decidedly more respectful than at first.

"Is there any news yet, sir?" she asked in French.

"No," replied the young man, knowing that she alluded to the box. "I don't lose heart, though."

"Mr. Home has been asking twice, sir, whether you've come in."

Mr. Lydney went straight to the invalid's room, to whom he was exceedingly attentive. He continued very unwell indeed, and he was making the young man's trouble about the box his own. It tended to excite him, and that was not good for the malady under which he laboured.

William Lydney's hopefulness did not fail him. On the day following this, when he went as usual down to the

beach, he found the divers in the act of bringing up
another relic. Mitchel, the preventive-man, now standing
there on duty, was looking on.

"Is that it, sir?"

But the man, glancing at Mr. Lydney, need not have
asked the question. Intense joy was lighting up his face,
proving the box to be in truth the one so coveted. In the
moment's excitement he took it, single-handed, from the
grasp of those who bore it. William Lydney was a strong
man, but scarcely strong enough to lift that heavy case in
ordinary moments.

"It's him you've been looking for, master?" came a
diver's question, as it fell on to the beach.

"Yes it is. You shall be well rewarded, my men."

It was a japanned box, about two feet square, just as
Mr. Lydney had described it. The initials, V. V. V.,
surmounted by a Maltese cross, were studded on it in gilt
nails. Mitchel was almost as pleased as Mr. Lydney, of
whom he had seen a great deal upon the beach. His liking
for Mr. Lydney had begun when that gentleman brought him
a handsome gratuity from his elderly fellow-passenger for
the loan of the cloak the night of the wreck; and it had
increased for Mr. Lydney's own sake.

"Those are not your initials, sir," remarked Mitchel.

"I never said they were," returned Mr. Lydney, with a
laugh.

"But the box is yours, sir."

"No, it is not. I am only in charge of it. Just as I now
leave you in charge of it, Mitchel," he added, "whilst I go
and get Ravensbird to send some men down with a truck or
barrow. Take you care of it, for it's very precious."

"I'll take good care of it, sir," answered Mitchel, with a
smile. "It's all in my duty and my day's work. Where you
leave it there you'll find it."

But Mr. Preventive Mitchel had reckoned without his
host.

Hardly had Mr. Lydney sprung away—with a light step
and a lighter heart—when Lord Dane appeared upon the
scene. He was in a black velvet coat and dark leggings, his

usual sporting attire, and many in Daneshold thought his fine figure never appeared to better advantage than when this was donned. His keeper had gone to the preserves with the guns and dogs, and Lord Dane was on his way there also, but turned off for a moment to the beach, and came up to Mitchel. Mitchel stood over the things in pursuance of his duty, and over the box especially, as he promised Mr. Lydney.

"Is this all?" exclaimed Lord Dane, in an accent of surprise. "I thought they must have got up half the shipful. That young boy you call Shad came grinning up at me, saying the beach was covered."

"A light-fingered young rascal," apostrophised Mitchel; "I have just driven him off the beach. It would take a man with a dozen eyes to watch him. No, my lord, they have not got up much, as you see, and I don't suppose they will. That box has turned up at last, that the gentleman has been in such a worry over. He said all along he was sure it would!"

"What gentleman?—what box?" inquired Lord Dane, who lived in too exalted a sphere to become readily cognizant of the interest of temporary sojourners at the Sailors' Rest.

"That fine young man who was saved in the life-boat, and is staying at Ravensbird's, my lord. I should say nobody was ever so anxious over a lost box before: as if it was full of thousand-pound bank notes: and this morning it has turned up. That's it behind your lordship."

Lord Dane turned at the words, and stood gazing at the box. That something in it particularly attracted his attention, was apparent to Mitchel, for he remained as one transfixed. When he lifted his head it was to walk round it, and attempt to lift it; in short, he looked at it just as a curious child looks at a new toy, and as if he would very much enjoy pulling it to pieces to see what was inside it.

"To whom do you say this belongs, Mitchel?"

"To that young American, my lord, who was brought ashore in the life-boat. Your lordship must have seen him about the place. A fine, handsome man, he is; pleasant to speak to. I mean Mr. Lydney."

"Lydney—Lydney? Oh yes; I remember the man now," observed his lordship. "Lydney!" he repeated to himself. "The name does not at all strike upon my memory, as one I have known. And he claims this box, does he, Mitchel?"

"Yes, my lord. It's the one he has been in such a fever over. The letters don't stand for his own name," continued Mitchel, observing the peer's keen glance at the initials, and fancying he discerned the drift of his thoughts. "I remarked to him at once that they didn't, and he answered me that he had not said they did. He is gone to send a barrow to remove it to the Sailors' Rest."

Lord Dane examined the rest of the things, suffering his keen glance to linger on each one individually. The scrutiny ended, he turned to Mitchel.

"Does any of this belong to him?"

"No, my lord; nothing but that japanned box. He says he had a good bit of luggage on board, but he has not seemed in the least to care for any part of it except this box."

Lord Dane walked away very quickly, and Mitchel remained on guard. Presently, to the coastguardsman's surprise, he saw Lord Dane coming back again, followed by an empty cart and two men. The cart belonged to a miller on the Dane estate, and had been on its way to fetch wheat to be ground. Lord Dane encountered it as he turned off the beach into the road, and pressed it into his own service, for what purpose you will see.

Down came the cart, its two attendants, and his lordship; halting close to Mitchel and the recovered débris. Lord Dane pointed to the things, and spoke curtly to the miller's men.

"Hoist them in."

The men did so, to the astonishment of Mitchel, and made short work of the process. None of the articles were heavy, except the japanned box. That went in with the rest. Then the cart and its contents proceeded to move away again, and Mitchel found his tongue.

" My lord," cried he, in a perfect ecstasy of consternation, " they must not take off the things; especially that tin chest. I am left here to see. that nobody does so."

" I have ordered them to the Castle for safety," said Lord Dane.

" But that tin case, my lord—its owner is coming down for it directly. And I passed my word that he should find it here safe and untouched. If he complains to the supervisor I may lose my place, your lordship."

" Lose your place for yielding to my authority!" returned Lord Dane, in a good-humoured tone. " We don't know yet to whom these things may belong, and they will be in safety at the Castle."

" But—I hope your lordship will pardon me for speaking —this tin box has its owner," persisted Mitchel. " When the gentleman returns for it, what am I to say to him?"

" Mitchel," replied his lordship, quietly, " you must understand one thing, which you do not yet appear to be aware of. As lord of the manor, I possess a right to claim all and everything fished up from that wreck, whether the owners be alive or not. I do not wish to exert this privilege: I should not think of doing so; but I do choose that these things shall, for the present, be placed in the Castle, that they may be in safety. You may say that to Mr. Lydney."

The cart was half-way off the beach by this time, and Lord Dane strode after it, leaving Mitchel mute and motionless. The procedure did not meet with his approbation at all, either on his own account or Mr. Lydney's. In defiance of the lord of the manor's assurance, he did not feel clear that no trouble would arise to him in consequence, and he was sure it would make Mr. Lydney angry. There he stood; and there he remained staring and wondering.

CHAPTER XX.

VANISHED!

DOWN came Mr. Lydney almost directly, Ravensbird with him and a man with a truck. The former cast his eyes around.

"Why, where are the things—where's the box?" he exclaimed, turning about. "Mitchel, what have you done with the box?"

"I don't know," replied Mitchel, "speaking as helplessly as he looked. "I have not done anything with it. Lord Dane came down, and sent it away; and the other things also."

"Sent it where?" asked Mr. Lydney.

"Up to the Castle, sir. He was lord of the manor, and possessed a right to claim what was got up from the wreck, he said. Not that he should think of claiming them, but they must be put in the Castle for safety till the owners turned up—which, of course, they are never likely to do. But perhaps he meant their friends."

"The owners of that japanned box had turned up," cried Mr. Lydney. "His lordship had no business to interfere, so much as to put his finger upon it. How could you think of allowing it, Mitchel? You are to blame for this."

"If you were not a stranger here, sir, you would never think of asking that question," was the reply. "Lord Dane is master of everything—Danesheld, and the people in it. I had no more power to keep your box back, when Lord Dane said it was to go, than I have to stop that sea from flowing."

"Nonsense," said Mr. Lydney, who appeared much provoked. "Lord Dane cannot be allowed to play the martinet over all the world."

"Well, sir, I assure you it was no fault of mine," answered the aggrieved Mitchel. "He happened to come on the beach and see the things, and he went and brought

down a miller's empty cart, that I suppose he met, and sent
the things away in it. He seemed quite struck with your
box, sir; I suppose he thought the cross on it looked odd."

"Mitchel, I tell you, you should not have allowed even
Lord Dane to touch my box," said Mr. Lydney quietly.
"I left it with you in trust; in trust, do you understand?"

"I'm more sorry than you can be, sir; and I wish Lord
Dane had chanced to walk any other way than on this
beach," was poor Mitchel's answer. "But, of course, he'll
give it up, sir, as soon as you apply for it."

"Not so sure of that," put in Ravensbird, who had
listened in silence.

"Why?" asked Mitchel.

"Well—when my Lord Dane gets crotchety on the score
of his own 'rights,' he's rather difficult to deal with," was
the reply. "I don't think you'll get it readily, sir," turning
to Mr. Lydney. "You'll have to go to work cautiously."

With a curl of the lip, and an angry toss of the head,
but without saying another word, William Lydney strode
off in the direction of the Castle. The man and the truck
followed him, in obedience to orders. Ravensbird turned
away to his own home.

Ringing a peal at the gate, it was opened in the same
minute by the butler, Bruff, who was still in the service,
and happened to be coming forth.

"I wish to see Lord Dane."

"His lordship is out, sir."

"I was informed he had just returned here, in charge of
some property got up from the wreck. Let me in, if you
please."

Bruff looked at the speaker, who was thus presuming to
speak in those scornful tones of Lord Dane and his doings;
and Bruff came to the conclusion that no man had ever
come to that Castle yet, possessing in an equal degree the
bearing of a master. Bruff bowed low, and threw wide the
gate.

"My lord did return here, sir, with the men who brought
the things, but he went out again directly, as soon as they
were put away."

"Amongst those things was a box, which I claim," proceeded Mr. Lydney. "I must request you to deliver it to me."

"It is not in my power, sir. I dare not meddle with the things against the orders of Lord Dane."

"I say that I claim the box," quietly returned Mr. Lydney. "I must have it given up to me."

"I am sure, sir, when you remember that I am Lord Dane's servant, you will see how impossible it is that I can meddle with anything contrary to his lordship's orders."

"The things are in the Castle?"

"Certainly they are, sir. His lordship had them put in the death room that they might be in safety. He gave me the key, and charged me not to let them be touched."

"The death room!" echoed Mr. Lydney.

' I beg your pardon, sir, the strong room, I ought to have said—as it is called now. We used to call it the death room, and the name comes naturally to me."

"Do you know that you may do me an irreparable injury by refusing to deliver up that property?" pursued Mr. Lydney.

"I am sorry to hear you say so, sir; but my lord charged me not to allow anyone access to the room, on any pretence whatever."

Mr. Lydney felt nonplussed. He saw how useless it would be to argue the point further with the retainer.

"Is there anyone who holds authority at the Castle, to whom I can apply?" he inquired.

"Miss Dane is at the Castle, sir, my lord's sister : but as to authority—you can see her if you please, sir."

The visitor motioned with his hand in reply, and Bruff ushered him indoors, and led the way up to the drawing-room.

"What name, sir?" he asked, pausing with his hand on the door.

"Mr. Lydney."

Miss Dane was there, playing with a canary bird, and turned at his entrance. She had not aged very much since

we last saw her; the lines of the face were deeper, and the
hair was perhaps a little thinner, but luxuriant still. She
was in her forty-second year, but would have gone into a fit
of hysterics, had she supposed Danesheld remembered it.
She assumed still the dress and manner of a girl of twenty.
Her cheeks were pink, though perhaps less pink than of
old; her features were small and pretty; her brown glossy
ringlets fell low on her neck, and her blue eyes had a habit
of shyly shrinking from the gaze of other eyes, especially
of gentlemen. Putting her vanity and her affectation aside,
Miss Dane's real simplicity had something pleasing in it.
She was attired in a light-blue silk gown and jacket to
match, set off with silver buttons. At the first moment,
William Lydney really thought she was a young girl.

"I have the honour of speaking to Miss Dane?"

Miss Dane shut the canary bird into its cage, and curtsied
and simpered. She retained her old propensity for admiring
attractive strangers, and had never seen one more attractive
than this before her. "What a noble-looking man!" quoth
she to herself, and fell in love with him forthwith, hoping
he was returning the compliment.

Mr. Lydney, however, was too much engrossed by his tin
box and its appropriation to admit softer impressions just
then, even though he had been as susceptible as the lady.
He gave her a concise history of the affair, and inquired
whether she would not issue orders that his box should be
restored to him.

"I never heard of such a procedure," cried she, in her
pretty little weak voice, as she shook her ringlets affectedly.
"Geoffry—my brother—went down to the beach, and
ordered the recovered things up here, you say? Why did
he do that? What did he want with them?"

"That is precisely what I should be glad to know, Miss
Dane."

"I don't think they can have come here; I fancy there
must be some error. I will ring for Bruff."

She tripped to the bell before Mr. Lydney could forestall
her; and Bruff appeared in answer to the summons.

"Bruff," asked Miss Dane, "have any boxes and things

been brought here this morning belonging to that wrecked ship?"

"Yes, miss," answered Bruff, for Miss Dane, though living at the Castle as its mistress, never would submit to be addressed as "madam." It might have made her look old.

"Is this gentleman's box here?"

"I suppose it is, miss, if it was in the cart with the rest of the things. They were all put in the strong-room."

"It is of the very utmost consequence that I should have this box, Miss Dane," struck in the claimant. "Lord Dane would surely not object to its being returned to me were he at home?"

"Of course not, sir," warmly acquiesced Miss Dane. "Bruff, you cannot do wrong in giving up to this gentleman his own property."

"My lord's orders were that the things should not be touched under any pretence whatever, miss," remonstrated Bruff.

"Yes, I can understand that. When there were no claimants for them, he naturally would wish them to remain in security. But this gentleman claims his box and requires it. You must give it to him, Bruff."

"Not upon my own responsibility, miss," returned the butler. "If you order me to do so, that of course alters the case."

"Dear me, Bruff, how tiresome and precise you are!" ejaculated Miss Dane, with her childish simper. "It stands to reason that his lordship, in taking possession of the property, could only have had regard to the interests of the owners; therefore we cannot do wrong in delivering up to this gentleman what belongs to him."

Mr. Lydney turned to Bruff. "It is a japanned box, with initials and a cross on the lid in gilt; you cannot mistake it. But I may as well go with you and point it out."

But Mr. Bruff scarcely saw his way clear, even now. The man was willing enough to give up the box: he knew it ought to be given up; but he did not care to risk his master's almost certain displeasure. He stood looking almost as helpless as Mitchel had done.

"Miss Dane," he said at length, with much deprecation, "you know what my lord is, when disobeyed. Now, I really dare not deliver up this box myself; if you will do it, that's a different thing."

"But I am doing it, Bruff. I am ordering you to do it."

"Yes, miss, I know. Perhaps you'd not mind coming to the strong-room and taking the matter into your own hands. If you give up the box there to the gentleman, my lord can't well blame me."

Miss Dane did not mind it at all; she rather liked the expedition, especially when the handsome young stranger gallantly offered his arm as an escort. Down the broad staircase they went, leaving the fine hall to the right, and straight on through the passages to the strong-room, Miss Dane mincing and chattering as she walked. Bruff produced the key and unlocked the door.

The cold, gray room was just what it used to be; the floor of stone, the windows high; no furniture whatever was in it, but the things from the wreck lay indiscriminately on the flags as they had been hastily thrown down. Releasing Miss Dane with a bow, Mr. Lydney turned to the heap, his eyes rapidly scanning the articles one by one. A look of stern anger arose to his face.

"My box is not here!" he exclaimed.

It was a contretemps that neither Miss Dane nor Bruff had expected—and it may be that the latter felt rather relieved by it than otherwise. Certainly no japanned chest was amongst the articles lying there. Mr. Lydney turned to the butler.

"Where has it been carried to?" he demanded, and his voice, though perfectly quiet, bore an unmistakable sound of command to the man's ear.

"If it is not here, sir, it was not brought to the Castle," was the prompt reply. "The things were carried from the cart straight to this room, and I can be upon my word that nobody has been near them since."

"It was brought to the Castle safe enough," returned Mr. Lydney. "If you saw the things taken out of the cart, you must remember it."

"A small japanned box you say, sir," cogitated Bruff, casting his thoughts back. "I don't remember to have seen it. The fact is, I took no particular notice of the things, though I can attest that they were all placed in this room."

"Then it has been removed since," was the rejoinder of Mr. Lydney.

Bruff shook his head. "Indeed, sir, I can equally attest that that could not be. The key has never been out of my own possession."

Mr. Lydney said no more. He felt sure the box *had* been removed, and he began casting his eyes around in search of hiding-places. They fell upon the door of a closet, and he pulled it open by the key which was in the lock. Excepting a pair of trestles that leaned against the wall, it was empty. There were no signs of the box.

"It is like magic," observed Miss Dane. "If the box was positively brought up in the cart, as you affirm, dear sir, the cart must have taken it away again; that's the only solution I can come to. My brother, hearing it was yours, may have sent it to your lodgings."

But this hypothesis was destroyed by Bruff, who declared that when the cart drove away from the gate it was perfectly empty.

Mr. Lydney appeared to consider, and then inquired at what hour he could see Lord Dane. Bruff, and Miss Dane also, said there was no certainty of his being in much before dinner. They were going to dine early that day— at six o'clock.

Wishing Miss Dane good morning—to her great reluctance—Mr. Lydney was shown out by Bruff, and went in search of the cart and the miller's men, Bruff having readily told him where he was likely to find them. He found them without difficulty, but the fact did not serve him. They were a couple of dull, stupid clodhoppers, of that species of rustic whom we are apt to marvel at, and almost question whether they can be human beings; possessing just sufficient brains to get through their day's work at the miller's.

"A tin box, japanned, wi' gilt marks outside on't? They
didn't know: my lord telled 'em to pick up the things what
laid on the shingle and take 'em to the Castle, and they
did so. There couldn't be no box missing out of 'em,
'twarn't likely,"

"But I tell you that it is missing," said Mr. Lydney.
"As to your not recollecting it, if you lifted it into the
cart, and then removed it from the cart to Lord Dane's
strong-room, you must have observed it. It was a peculiar-
looking box, very heavy."

The men could not remember. They moved the things
for sartin theirselves, but they didn't mark one thing more
nor another. By token, my lord hisself had watched the
cart safe up.

"And you left *all* the things at the Castle?" questioned
Mr. Lydney.

They left 'em all, and come away with the empty cart to
fetch their sacks o' wheat.

And nothing more definite than this could William
Lydney draw from them: it was all they knew. And he
went home to the Sailors' Rest in anything but a satisfactory state of mind.

Mr. Bruff entertained an idea that there was no policy equal
to that of "taking the bull by the horns." Accordingly he
quitted the Castle, after the visitor's departure, and contrived
to cross that portion of the Dane preserves where he deemed
it most likely he should find Lord Dane. Upon seeing him
(as if by accident), he went boldly up and related the oc-
currences of the morning, dwelling upon the fact that the
room had been opened by Miss Dane's orders, against his
own remonstrance.

Lord Dane was sitting on the stump of a tree, solacing
himself with a sandwich and something from a flask. Bruff
stood humbly before him, expecting little less than that his
head would be snapped off. Few people visited disobedience
more sharply than Lord Dane.

"As a general rule, Bruff, you know that what I say
is law, and may not be violated with impunity," cried his
lordship. "In this instance the matter was not momentous;

but I shall speak to Miss Dane, who appears to have been more in fault than you. Did you give the young man his box?"

"The box was not there, my lord; at least the one he said he was looking for," replied the amazed and relieved Bruff. "A tin box, japanned, with gilt initials, he described it. There was nothing answering to the description, your lordship."

"Then what brought the fellow intruding at the Castle?" cried his lordship, testily. "That's just what I expected it would be,—that every man, woman, and child, who might have ever so remote an interest in the ship, would be coming up to look at the relics; and it was for that reason I ordered you to keep the room closed."

"The young gentleman says the box was found and brought to the Castle, my lord," returned Bruff, believing Lord Dane was mistaking the facts. "But, as I told him, if the box came with the other things, there it would now be, with them."

"And of course it is with them," carelessly returned Lord Dane. "It could not sink through the floor. You must have overlooked it, Bruff."

"If I could overlook it, my lord, the gentleman wouldn't: he was too eager about it," was Bruff's rejoinder. "He said he should call at the Castle and see your lordship about it."

"He is welcome to do so," replied Lord Dane, rising to resume his sport.

Bruff went home again. A little before six, Mr. Lydney again made his appearance at the Castle, and was shown into the great hall—or, as they more often termed it now, the audience chamber. Lord Dane sent word he would be down immediately. His lordship had but just returned home from shooting, Bruff said, and was dressing. He soon appeared and received the stranger with frank politeness. As they stood together, that young applicant and the lord of the Castle, one might have almost fancied a likeness between them; both were tall, fine, upright men, *noble* men, as they have already been called, and both had features cast in a noble form : Lord Dane was the better-looking, according to the lines that are supposed to constitute beauty, but in the other countenance there was a good sense, a keenness of intellect, a nameless power, that might have adorned a face older than that of William Lydney.

"My butler has been telling me some rigmarole about a box vanishing out of the strong room," began his lordship, in free cordial tones. "But the thing is impossible. If the box was placed in the strong-room, it must be there still."

"The box was certainly put into the cart to be brought to the Castle—to that Mitchel can testify," returned Mr. Lydney, in a tone as independent as his lordship's, though somewhat more haughty. And Lord Dane wondered who the young fellow could be, presuming to address him on an equality. "The question is, where was it placed after it reached the Castle?"

"Did Mitchel take notice of the box?"

"Yes," emphatically replied Mr. Lydney. "And Mitchel says that your lordship also took notice of it; something passed about the initials not being my own."

"Is that the missing box?—the one with three V's upon it?" exclaimed Lord Dane. "Oh, that was certainly placed in the cart; I saw the men put it in."

"May I inquire why your lordship should have meddled with the box at all?"

"I had the things brought up for security," replied Lord Dane.

"But I had claimed that particular box, had left it in Mitchel's care, whilst I went for means to remove it; and this was represented to you," said Mr. Lydney. "It appears to me that it could not be any concern of your lordship's. As to safety—Mitchel, I say, was in charge of it."

"Were you accustomed to see much of wrecks, which I do not imagine you are, you would know how next to impossible it is for any preventive-man to stop the pilferers that infest the coast. It was my duty, as lord of the manor, to take care that the things recovered remained intact," continued Lord Dane, loftily, for the benefit of the American; who could not be supposed to know much about the rights of lords of the manor, or of lords either, for that matter.

" I want my property," said Mr. Lydney.

" And you are at liberty to take it," was the candid answer, spoken in a kindly tone. " Bruff might have given it to you, under the circumstances, without waiting for my permission."

" But where is it ? " questioned Mr. Lydney. " It is not with the rest of the things brought up from the beach."

" Sir, to reiterate such an assertion makes me quite angry," tartly rejoined Lord Dane. " A box locked up safely in a strong-room could not vanish from it : it must be there still. I told Bruff so."

" It was not there to-day, when I was introduced into the room."

Lord Dane would not contend further. He opened the inner door of the hall and conducted his visitor to the passage, calling to Bruff to bring the key of the strong-room. The butler did so, and the two gentlemen entered it together.

" Your lordship must perceive that the box is *not* here," said Mr. Lydney, pointing to the things as they lay on the floor.

Lord Dane glanced at them with a keen and curious eye. When he found beyond doubt that the box was really missing, he looked confounded and appeared on the point of losing his temper. Striding to the door, he shouted for Bruff, and the man came back in haste.

" Whom have you dared to admit to this room ? " demanded Lord Dane. " This gentleman's box must have been removed from it."

" I declare, my lord, that not a soul has entered it except the gentleman himself and Miss Dane ! " exclaimed the unhappy Bruff, confused at the tables being turned on him in this unexpected manner. " The key was never out of my pocket. The box could not have been brought to the room."

" To which other room was it taken ? " asked Mr. Lydney quietly of Lord Dane.

" I assure you, on my word of honour, that every individual thing taken out of the cart was brought to this room and to no other," was the peer's emphatic answer; and even Mr. Lydney, prejudiced though he was, could only acknowledge that it sounded like a true one. " The men had no opportunity of entering any other, and did not enter one."

" I can bear my lord out in that, sir," interposed Bruff, turning his honest face upon the stranger. " The things were brought straight to this room through the outer passage, not the inner; had the men wished to enter another room, they could not have done it. Besides, I was with them all the time, and my lord also was looking on."

" I surmise how it is, " said Lord Dane : " the men must have omitted to remove the box from the cart."

" No," said Mr. Lydney. " I have questioned the men, and am satisfied that it was brought into the Castle."

" My lord," put in the butler, " I watched the cart go away from the gates, and it was quite empty."

" Well, I cannot understand it," returned Lord Dane, half testily, as if he would give up the affair as hopeless. " I can certainly affirm that the box was put into the cart; I saw the men lift it in, and thought how heavy it seemed ; and I can also affirm, if necessary, on my oath, that everything in the cart was brought direct to this strong-room. The men must have lost it on the road."

" Did your lordship notice the box after the cart reached here ? " asked Mr. Lydney.

" No, I did not; I paid no particular attention to the things then. The truth is, I was impatient to be gone, for my keeper had been waiting for me some time. Were its contents of value ? You appear to set great store by it."

" Its contents were of great value : they consisted of documents which cannot be replaced."

" Was it your own box ? "

" It was not mine; but I was in charge of it, and am responsible to the owner, who entrusted it to me in America."

"Who is the owner?" asked Lord Dane, some curiosity in his tone.

"That question is superfluous to the present matter," was the reserved and haughty answer.

Lord Dane smiled.

"I allow for your vexation, sir, and all I can say is, that I hope the box will soon be found. Lost it cannot be."

"It shall be found if there be law or justice in England," warmly spoke the young man.

"A moment, sir. You appear to throw blame on me; surely that is not just."

"It is in my nature to be candid, even where unpleasant suspicions are concerned, and therefore I avow my opinion that your lordship has possession of the box," was young Lydney's bold rejoinder, and Mr. Bruff stared to hear it. "Had it been lying on the beach unclaimed, as the other things were, when you ordered it to the Castle, I could have understood it; but that you should do so in the face of Mitchel's assurance that it was mine, and that I was then bringing assistance to remove it, does appear to me to be a procedure fraught with suspicion. I can only believe that your motive was to obtain possession of the box, and that you have yourself removed it from the room."

"Why! what do you suppose I wanted with the box?" exclaimed Lord Dane.

"I am unable to say."

"You are smarting under this loss, sir, which I confess is vexatious, and therefore I excuse your language," returned his lordship with equanimity. "Perhaps you have not reflected how void of foundation your suspicion must of necessity be. That the things were all brought to this room I have testified to you; my servant has done the same, and you say you have questioned the miller's men. Now this room is not near the other rooms in the Castle: it is some distance from any one of them; and I ask you how it would be possible for me to carry a heavy box, which most likely I could not even lift, through the passages. You may be capable of deeming that my servants helped me, or

carried it by my orders; but I give you hearty leave to
question them. No, Mr. Lydney, I saw the things put into
this room, and I locked the door upon them, and gave the
key to Bruff. Since then their safety lies with him."

Bruff looked up deprecatingly, but did not again defend
himself. He thought it very unreasonable of the gentleman
to cast suspicion on his master, but excused it on the score
of his youth and inexperience.

There was nothing to be gained by lingering in the
strong-room, and Mr. Lydney quitted it, Lord Dane following and Bruff remaining to lock the door. Mr. Lydney
was sorely perplexed, and it may be that the good sense of
Lord Dane's defence was making its way within him. Only
—where could the box be?

He had to return to the hall, for he had left one of his
gloves there. Standing just inside it, close to the dining-
room door, was Miss Dane, apparently having run in after a
little pet dog, in reality watching for the handsome stranger.
Her ringlets were now interspersed with blue ribbons, and
her white muslin dinner dress, sweeping the beautiful
mosaic pavement, was made in a girlish fashion, and also
decorated with blue. She came forward with a little start
of surprise, dropping her hands and eyes like a timid
child.

"Oh dear, sir! is it you again? Oh, I do hope you have
found your box!"

"It cannot be found," was the answer. "It appears to
have vanished in some unaccountable manner from Lord
Dane's strong-room."

"Vanished as the ghosts do," she said with a pretty
simper.

"Exactly. Only that the days of ghosts are over, Miss
Dane."

She put out her hand when he was bowing his adieu, and
he frankly met it, and gave it a hearty shake. Lord Dane
drew down the corners of his lips at the young man's
presumption. If his sister was absurd, he had no right to
take advantage of it; and would not, had he been a
gentleman, was the peer's thought. He condescendingly

bowed him out of the hall on his own score, and into the charge of Bruff.

"Is his box quite gone, Geoffry?" sighed Miss Dane, gently shaking back her curls and her blue ribbons.

"Gone! It can't be gone. It seems to have disappeared in some inexplicable manner."

"What a pity! Geoffry, did you ever see anyone so good-looking before?"

"H——m," returned Lord Dane, laughing at his sister. "Not a bad figure though."

"Of whom does he put you in mind, Geoffry?"

"I can't think. He does put me in mind of some one; there's no doubt of it."

"It's his face," she cried. "It is like Lady Dane's, Geoffry."

"What Lady Dane's?" exclaimed Geoffry in surprise.

"I never knew but one, Geoffry. Old Lady Dane, my aunt and yours."

"Nonsense, Cecilia!"

"But, Geoffry, dear, it isn't nonsense. I've rarely seen such a likeness in my life. It struck me when he first came in."

Poor Cely! As Lord Dane took her kindly on his arm to lead her into the dining-room, he thought how very many foolish things had struck her in the course of her simple life.

"I wish you had asked him to stay to dinner, Geoffry!"

"Ask *him* to stay!" echoed Lord Dane. "My dear Cecilia!"

"Wouldn't it do, Geoffry?"

"No, indeed, it would not do," said Lord Dane. "A doubt is dawning on my mind, Cecilia—and I have cause for it—whether this young American, this Lydney, is not an adventurer."

"Oh, Geoffry! But he is so good-looking! He is just like a prince in a fairy-tale."

"That's just it. I fancy he means to trade on his good looks."

Miss Dane gave a little cry of mortification. It was

genuine; not affected, as her cries were in general. She knew how clear-sighted her brother was; how generally right in his judgment; how charitably-judging as a rule; and therefore she accepted the opinion as a fiat. But, apart from it, she had never seen any stranger in whom she could have put so much trust as in William Lydney.

CHAPTER XXI.

SEARCHING DANE CASTLE.

BRUFF, meanwhile, was showing out the said adventurer, or gentleman, or whatever he might be. The butler felt a little uncomfortable at this singular disappearance, and could not allow Mr. Lydney to leave without attempting an excuse.

"I hope, sir, you do not attribute this loss to any fault or carelessness of mine?"

"I do not," was the ready answer. "But you must admit that the disappearance of the box is strange in the extreme."

"I can't make it out in any way, sir. Turn it about as I will, I cannot possibly see where the box has gone to."

"Lord Dane delivered the key to you immediately after the things were put into the room?"

"He did, sir," was Bruff's hearty answer. "After the men had put the things in, I followed them to the gate, and saw them drive away with the empty cart. I then turned back along the passage to the room, and there stood my lord, outside the door, waiting for me. He locked the door just in my sight, gave me the key, and charged me to allow no person to enter. He went out as he spoke, and returned but now: and as for the key, it has not been out of my pocket, except when I opened the door for you and Miss Dane. Now, sir, even allowing that my lord had an inclination to remove that box elsewhere, as you seem to suspect, he could not by any possibility have had the time, either to do it himself, or to get it done: and my own moral persuasion is, that the box never did come into the Castle. I should not say so much, sir, but for your thinking my lord must be in fault."

"At any rate, I do not think you are in fault," was the rejoinder, given with a pleasant smile, and Mr. Lydney slipped a heavy gold piece into the man's hands.

"Oh, sir, indeed you are too good. I——Holloa, you young eavesdropper! What do you do here?"

The interruption was addressed to a boy, lingering in close proximity to the Castle gate. It was Shad. Mr. Lydney turned hastily, and thought he had never seen so queer a specimen of young humanity. The butler pointed his finger of authority, and the boy shuffled off.

"Had the box been light, I might have thought that young reptile had pilfered it from the cart," observed Bruff. "He must have stolen up after the cart when it came here from the beach, for I saw him hovering close by as the men were taking the things from it. A box of that weight of course he could not take."

Mr. Lydney strode away, overtook Shad, and laid his hand upon his shoulder. "What is your name?" asked he.

"Please, sir, it's Shad."

"Shad—what? What's your other name?"

"Please, sir, I never had none."

"The divers recovered some things this morning from the wreck, and a cart took them up to Dane Castle. You followed it, I believe. Did you see the cart unloaded?"

"I didn't finger nothing," was the response of the boy.

"That is not what I asked you. *Can* you speak truth?" proceeded Mr. Lydney, a doubt crossing his mind whether one possessing such a countenance as that he was gazing on could do so.

Shad made no reply, except that his wide mouth parted with a grin.

Mr. Lydney took a sixpence from his pocket, and held it

up. "You see this, Shad? I am going to ask you a question or two; answer me with strict truth, and it shall be yours. Equivocate only a word, and instead of the sixpence, you shall get something of a different character."

"I know what you'd ask me," burst forth the boy, forgetting his usual *rôle* of "simpleton" in the fascination of the sixpence. "It's about your lost box, that a row's being made over, her with the three brass letters on it, and t'other thing a-top of 'em. I see it took into the castle."

"You did?"

"I see it with these two eyes o' mine," avowed Shad, lifting his sly orbs, sparkling now, to the face of Mr. Lydney. "It was a'most the last thing left in the cart; the two millers carried of it in, and Mr. Bruff went a'ter 'em up the passage."

"Where was Lord Dane, then?"

"I didn't see him. I think he was a-gone into the Castle afore."

"What made you follow the cart to the Castle?"

"'Cause Mitchel had druv me off the beach, and I'd got nothing to do. I didn't follow it for no harm. I see 'em unload it, and I see it go away empty."

"You are sure it was empty?"

"I'se certain; there warn't a thing left in her," replied the boy, earnestly. "I've told ye the truth, sir, and now, please, for the sixpence."

"Should I find later on that you have not told the truth, it shall go hard with you," said Mr. Lydney, dropping the sixpence into his hand. "But if you could only learn, Shad, how much better it is to speak the truth than the contrary, what a great amount of trouble it saves, you would never say another false word again."

Shad's only reply was to shamble off, his arms flung about in wild delight at possession of the sixpence: and Mr. Lydney went down to the Sailors' Rest. There he at once sought an interview with his elder fellow-traveller, and asked his advice on the state of affairs. Ravensbird was called into the room, and certain questions were put to him, chiefly touching on the disposition and habits of Lord Dane.

Mr. Home's opinion—sitting with his purple shade on whilst he gave it—was that Lord Dane had taken possession of the box, and concealed it somewhere. A doubt certainly crossed him, whether it might not have been abstracted, whilst the cart was on its way to the Castle, by some light-fingered gentry, plenty of whom, Ravensbird said, prowled about Danesheld; and this doubt also arose to Mr. Lydney.

"It was a conspicuous box, you see," the latter observed to Mr. Home; "the cross and initials rendering it so. I am, therefore, surprised—if the box really did go to the Castle—that the butler, Bruff, should not have noticed it. Lord Dane also says he did not observe the box amongst the things when they arrived at the Castle."

"If Lord Dane is concealing the box for any purpose of his own, he, of course, would not confess to having seen it there," remarked Mr. Home. "What do you think, Ravensbird?"

"I think it amounts to this, sir : has Lord Dane a motive for possessing the box, or not? If he has why then no doubt he has secured it; if he has not, I should be inclined to fancy it was taken from the cart on its way to the Castle."

"There's a suspicious phase in the affair, and it's one I can't get over," said William Lydney, warmly, to Mr. Home; "and that is, ordering the box to the Castle at all. Mitchel told Lord Dane the box was claimed by me, that I had gone for assistance to move it away; nevertheless, he conveyed it at once to the Castle, and that in the teeth of a remonstrance Mitchel ventured to speak. I'd lay any money he has the box."

But, even allowing this hypothesis to be correct, what was to be done? Mr. Lydney felt himself in the position of a bird with its wings clipped. Lord Dane was a man not to be approached lightly, or accused without due reason : and he really appeared to know nothing of the box. William Lydney walked about the invalid's room in a fever of un-certainty, and the commotion could not have been altogether agreeable to the elder man.

"What would you advise, sir?" he suddenly asked.

"If you will sit down quietly, I will tell you," answered Mr. Home. "I incline to the belief that my Lord Dane has the box; and in that case——I can't talk unless you sit down."

Lydney closed the door, and sat down, controlling his impatience. They were alone then, for the landlord had been called away; and Mr. Home quietly discussed the matter, and tendered his opinion and advice. And as he talked, the younger man became more fully impressed with the conviction that the box was in Dane Castle, in the secret keeping of its lord. He did not ask himself how this could be, in the face of the improbabilities mentioned by Bruff; he only succeeded in persuading his own mind that it was so.

Later in the afternoon he took his way to Danesheld Hall, on a mission to Squire Lester, and met that gentleman coming out of it with Lady Adelaide. The carriage waited at the door, and they were apparently in a hurry.

"I fear I have come at an unseasonable hour," remarked Lydney. "I wished to speak to you, Mr. Lester, on a matter of business."

It happened that Lady Adelaide had not met the young stranger before. She had seen him in the street, and thought him a very attractive man. Attractive men had charms for Lady Adelaide still, and she was gracious to Mr. Lydney now.

"I hope your business can wait," she said. "Mr. Lester is going out with me, and we are already late. Will this evening not do for it."

"Certainly, it shall do," replied Mr. Lydney.

"Step in this evening, then," added Squire Lester. "Any time; eight o'clock or nine; when you like. Lady Adelaide will give you a cup of tea."

Mr. Lester's feeling towards young Lydney was a kindly one. He had thanked him for the service rendered to Maria, and a speaking acquaintance had sprung up between them. Mr. Lester supposed him to be a gentleman; otherwise, he would never have dreamt of giving the invitation just proffered.

And between eight and nine William Lydney duly arrived. But as the servant was showing him to the drawing-room, he arrested the man's steps, saying that he would first of all see his master in private. So he was taken to Mr. Lester's study, and that gentleman came to him.

"It is not a very seasonable hour for business, and I must ask you to excuse my entering on it," observed young Lydney, as they shook hands, and sat down. "You are, I believe, in the commission of peace for the county?"

Mr. Lester nodded.

"Then I have to proffer a request, which—which will, perhaps, surprise you; nevertheless, I hope you will accede to it. I want you to grant me a warrant to search Dane Castle."

Had Mr. Lester been asked for a warrant to search his own house, he could not have evinced more intense surprise. For a few moments he only stared at the applicant.

"Search Dane Castle!" he echoed at last.

Young Lydney entered on the explanation. The unaccountable loss of the box was already known to Mr. Lester, as it was to all Danesheld, for the place had lost none of its propensity for tale-bearing.

"Rely upon it, Mr. Lester, that box is in Dane Castle, purposely concealed there."

If anything could have added to Mr. Lester's surprise, it was that assertion. But he resented the insinuation.

"What grounds can you possibly have for such an opinion?" he questioned in tones of remonstrance.

"I draw my deductions from facts," was the reply. "What right had Lord Dane to interfere with that box at all? Mitchel told him it was mine; that I was most anxious about the box; that I had gone for people to take it up to the inn where I was staying. In the face of that, he took possession of it, and sent it to his Castle. I ask what his motive could have been?"

"I do not myself see the necessity for his doing so," reflectively replied Mr. Lester. "As to his motive, it must have been zeal—over-zeal that no harm should happen to the things—your box amongst them. He can have no reason for detaining or concealing your box. If it were in his hands he would be only too glad to restore it to you as the claimant."

"One would think so," was the reply, tinctured with sarcasm.

"Were I to hazard a conjecture, I should say the box fell from the cart unseen, on its way to the Castle."

"I think that would scarcely be your conjecture if you knew how heavy the box is, Mr. Lester. It could not fall unseen or unheard; and one of the men walked behind the cart. Lord Dane, as I hear, was also behind, keeping the cart in view. This supposition may be wholly put aside, for the box was seen carried into the Castle.

Mr. Lester pricked up his ears. The last bit of information was new to him.

"Seen! By whom?"

"A somewhat noted young gentleman of your vicinity, Shad, saw it taken in there."

Squire Lester interrupted with a laugh. "Pardon me, Mr. Lydney, but the remark proves what a stranger you are. Shad! Why, he's the falsest boy you can conceive; he tells more lies in an hour than anyone else would in a life-time. I doubt if he ever spoke a word of truth yet, knowing it to be truth."

"I agree with you in all that," replied Mr. Lydney, who had sat perfectly composed until the laugh was over. "My landlord has told me what he is; and from my own limited observation of the boy, I should judge him to be an exceedingly bad boy, an habitual and systematic deceiver. Nevertheless, I avow my belief that in this instance he has told me truth. He says the two men carried the box into the Castle, that it was nearly the last thing taken out of the cart, and that Lord Dane's butler followed them in."

"But I thought you convinced yourself that the box was not in the Castle."

"I convinced myself that it was not with the rest of the things. That it was taken into the Castle, I feel certain."

"Then what can have become of it? You surely don't suspect any of the servants of having taken it?" hastily added Mr. Lester. "Bruff is as honest as the day; a most respectable man: was butler to the late lord."

"I do not suspect the servants. From what I can gather, none of them, except Bruff, went near the things."

It was an unlucky admission, destroying all semblance of a plea for granting the warrant; at least in the opinion of the magistrate before him.

"Then whom do you suspect?" rejoined Mr. Lester, fixing his eyes on the young man. "Surely not Lord Dane?"

"It is a nice question, Mr. Lester; one that I am not entirely prepared to answer. I do believe the box to be in Dane Castle, either inadvertently concealed there, or purposely concealed, and therefore I am asking you to grant me a warrant to search for it."

"I cannot grant it you," replied Mr. Lester. "I am sorry to refuse it; but—putting other considerations aside—I really believe neither law nor circumstances would justify it. All the evidence you have, that the box went into the Castle, is from Shad; scarcely one upon whose word we could venture to thrust the insult of a search-warrant upon Lord Dane. Besides, I am not sure but that he would have power as the lord-lieutenant, to draw his pen through it. You will never get it from me or from any other magistrate. And now let us go and have some tea."

Lord Dane was in the drawing-room with Lady Adelaide and Miss Lester. He had come to spend the evening, and learnt that Squire Lester was just then engaged with Mr. Lydney.

"With Mr. Lydney!" echoed his lordship. "Oh, ay; the young American lodging at the Sailors' Rest;" and there was a patronizing tone in his comment that somehow caused Maria's cheeks to burn. "What is his business with Mr. Lester?"

"I know nothing about it," said Lady Adelaide. "We asked him to come to us for an hour this evening."

"Here? Lydney!" was the surprised question.

"Yes."

Lord Dane drew down the corners of his lips, and mentally wondered in what sort of guise the American would present himself, to the evening society of English gentlewomen.

His doubts on the point were speedily solved. Mr. Lester came in, and his guest with him, in evening attire as orthodox and simple as my Lord Dane's.

Again, let it be remarked, they did not look unlike each other, allowing for the difference in age. Of the same height; the same noble cast of feature; wearing the same sort of quiet evening dress. Maria Lester's heart fluttered when Mr. Lydney shook hands with her as it had never fluttered for Lord Dane.

It may as well be stated that Lord Dane had not as yet spoken formally to Miss Lester, or personally urged his own claims. That she knew he wished to prefer them, he was aware; but her manner gave him no encouragement, and he deemed it well to wait a little.

She was a fair prize. None could feel that more deeply than Lord Dane felt it as she stood before him to-night, in her evening dress of light-blue silk, with a necklace and bracelets of crystals set in gold, and a single white rose in her hair. Far more lovely in Lord Dane's eyes than even Lady Adelaide had been in those bygone days. Adelaide Errol had never possessed the sweet countenance, the gentle spirit, that characterized Maria Lester.

One thing gave displeasure to Lord Dane, and that was the manner of Mr. Lydney. Far from appearing to feel his inferiority of position, he held his own just as though he were an equal. Had he been ennobled as my Lord Dane himself, his manner could not have been easier or more self-possessed. He seemed accomplished, too, at least in music; played with a soft skilful touch, sang with the quietest and sweetest melody.

Lady Adelaide suddenly asked if he could sing a certain duet; he said yes, if Miss Lester would sing it with him and play the accompaniment. Maria sat down to the piano.

"A trifle quicker than you played it last night," said Mr. Lydney to Maria, as he bent over her to look at the music.

" Quicker ? "

" I think it would be better."

Lord Dane, standing by, caught the colloquy, and rather opened his eyes. " Were you singing this with Mr. Lydney last night ?—here ? " he inquired of Maria.

" Not here ; at Miss Bordillion's," said Mr. Lydney, answering for her.

And the answer by no means pleased Lord Dane. It was not at all the thing for Miss Lester, whether as the daughter of Mr. Lester of Danesheld Hall, or as his future wife, to be subjected to the chance companionship of unknown young Americans, cast up by the sea ; especially of those who assumed the manners of gentlemen.

" What do you know of him ? " abruptly asked Lord Dane of Mr. Lester when the evening came to an end, and Mr. Lydney had departed.

" Know of him ? Nothing. The young fellow called here about his lost box, and I asked him to come in to tea."

" Is it wise of you to admit a stranger indiscriminately ? "

" Oh, I don't know," indifferently answered Mr. Lester, who hated music and was feeling tired to death. " It's only once in a way. I dare say he'll never be inside the house again. But I think he is a gentleman."

The morning came. And Mr. Lydney, bearing in mind a remark of Squire Lester's, that he would not get a magistrate to grant a search-warrant for Dane Castle, went direct to the police-station and asked to see the chief officer. It was a roomy station, newly built, containing cells for refractory prisoners, and a large front room, in which was a railed-off compartment with two chairs and a desk, and taking in one of the windows ; the windows looking out on the street and the opposite shop of Minn the tailor.

Mr. Bent was at Danesheld still : formerly sergeant, now inspector. He had grown portly, and rather bald. Bent, however, was not in when Mr. Lydney called, and one of the subordinates invited him to a chair inside the rails, and listened to what he had to say. The purport of the application was the lost box ; and a demand that Dane Castle should be searched for it.

The policeman shook his head with a faint smile. He could not take the responsibility of answering such an application himself, he observed, but would report it to his superior, and the gentleman had better call again.

Little was William Lydney acquainted with the usages of the neighbourhood, and with Lord Dane's sway in it, if he supposed the police could receive such an application and not make his lordship acquainted with it. The inspector himself carried it to the Castle in the course of the day, and Lord Dane accorded him a private interview.

"Search the Castle, forsooth!" ironically cried Lord Dane. "Search it for what? For that lost box of his? Does the American suspect my servants?"

Mr. Bent presumed that the American did.

"It were more to the purpose that he permitted himself to be searched, for who he is, and for what he is," cried his lordship angrily. "Look at the facts of the case, Bent. Here's a Yankee saved from a wreck with what he stands upright in; he is sheltered in a public-house and remains there; dresses up in new clothes like a gentleman, and worms himself into the best houses in the neighbourhood. All very well this, provided he *is* a gentleman; but who is to prove it? He is silent as to his antecedents; has been asked of them, to my knowledge, but does not answer; and I say it is altogether fraught with suspicion. How do we know that he is not an adventurer? For my own part, I believe him to be one; I have my reasons for thinking so. He spent last evening at Squire Lester's."

Mr. Bent, who had gained experience and was moreover a tolerably shrewd man, was struck with the argument. Coming, as it did, from Lord Dane, it made all the more impression on him.

"He has become positively intimate at Miss Bordillion's —intimate," went on the peer impressively, "and possibly so at other houses. He came up here, to the Castle, and got admitted to my sister, just as boldly as though he carried his credentials in his hand."

"Why, there's no knowing what it may end in, your

lordship, if the man is really an adventurer!" exclaimed the dismayed inspector.

"It will end in the neighbourhood's having cause to repent its credulity; at least, that is my opinion," said Lord Dane. "Stay, don't go yet, Bent; we have not finished about this box that he claims: a box which he acknowledged to me was not his own. Between ourselves, it is just as likely to have belonged to some other passenger, who has gone where he can't claim it."

Summoning Bruff, Lord Dane went with Bent to the strong-room. The butler unlocked it, and Lord Dane pointed to the floor.

"Here the things are, Bent, lying just as they were thrown down yesterday. Does it stand to reason that if the box had been put here, it could have vanished?—and Bruff will testify to you that no one could have come in to remove it; he has not suffered the key to go out of his own possession. Why, it was not, as I hear, five minutes after the articles had been brought in, that this Lydney came up, and saw for himself that the box was not amongst them. Who is to know that he did not contrive to get it from the cart himself, and is making this fuss to throw the police off the scent? No end of unpleasant suspicions are suggesting themselves to my mind."

As they were to Mr. Bent's. "A pretty fellow, my lord, to talk of getting a search-warrant for the Castle!"

"I'd see him hanging from the yard arm of the tallest ship in the harbour before he should execute it," haughtily spoke his lordship.

And Mr. Bent nodded approvingly.

"But," resumed Lord Dane, "I am far from wishing to impose the same restriction on the police. If you, Bent, would like, for your own satisfaction, to go through every room and examine every nook and corner of the Castle, you are at liberty to do so. Bruff will guide you, or you may go alone, just as you please. Here's the trestle-closet," he added, throwing open the door. "Begin with that."

"Certainly not, my lord; I should not think of doing so. Unless it would be for your lordship's satisfaction," added

Bent, a thought striking him. "Your lordship does not
cast a doubt on any of the servants?" he added in a low
tone. "The men, down at the station, thought that must
be what the American was aiming at."

"No, I do not cast suspicion on my servants," coldly
returned Lord Dane. "But there, you had better go
through the Castle," he concluded; it will set the matter at
rest."

And accordingly Inspector Bent did go through the Castle,
searching it thoroughly, without finding any trace of the
lost box. Lord Dane's manner had changed to one of chilling
hauteur when the officer rejoined him.

"Look you, Bent. When this man—Lydney, or whatever
his name may be—shall presume to speak to you again of a
search-warrant for Dane Castle, inquire a little as to whom
he may be himself, and what he is doing here."

"I will, your lordship."

"Understand me," said his lordship, thawing a little, "you
have my private orders to do this. I wish to know who and
what the fellow is."

And as Mr. Bent walked back to Danesheld, he turned
the affair over in his own mind, and came to the conclusion
that Lord Dane's view, of there being much to doubt in the
conduct of this young Lydney, was a correct one.

CHAPTER XXII.

APPLYING TO INSPECTOR BENT.

THE shades of evening were gathering in the wood at
Danesheld as Maria Lester walked quickly through it with
her brother. Once more she had transgressed home
mandates, and gone to see Wilfred's wife; and the visit had
been productive of a pain she scarcely cared to conceal.
Things seemed to be growing worse in their cottage home :
Wilfred's reputation was not growing better.

" Is there nothing that you can do ? " she suddenly asked, in an access of despair that rendered silence intolerable. " Try and get a situation of some sort—no matter what; anything that will enable you to earn a little. Throw pride to the winds."

" Pride ! " he repeated, as if he and pride had no longer much to do with each other. " What situation would you suggest ? " he added, with sarcasm. " I have thought of several, but nothing comes of it. I cannot open a general shop, for want of funds ; I cannot engage myself as keeper to Lord Dane—he hasn't a vacancy ; I don't suppose I should be hired if I offered myself as footman to my father, to replace the one I hear is leaving."

" How can you turn what I say into ridicule ? " rejoined Maria. " I did not mean places of that sort."

" You meant, no doubt, something more suited to a gentleman ? " he rejoined. " I am not eligible for it—possessing no clothes ! "

" Oh, Wilfred ! No clothes ! "

" Except this velveteen suit, everything else is put away ; and I may have to put this away, if they'll take it, and go about scandalizing Danesheld in shirt-sleeves."

Her cheeks were crimson, tears rested in her eyes. She had suspected all this, and more ; but it was not pleasant to have it put pointedly before her. And his mocking tone troubled her worse than all.

" A little bird whispered to me, Maria, that you were likely to marry Lord Dane," he resumed, his tone changing to one kindly and serious. " Is it true ? "

Her face flushed. " Little birds are a great deal more busy than they need be."

" I have no right to interfere, I suppose. But, Maria, I would have you think twice ere you unite yourself to Lord Dane. He is nearly double your age. Do you care for him ? "

" No, I don't care for him, Wilfred—not in that way. I like Lord Dane very much as an acquaintance, but I should not like to be his wife. Neither has he asked me yet."

They came to the end of the road, and Maria said good-evening, and hastened onwards, for the dinner hour was at hand. The emotion she would not give way to before her brother had its own course now, and for a moment the tears rained from her eyes. An unlucky moment. At the turning near the Hall, she met a foot-passenger face to face, and it was William Lydney. Maria brushed away the tears, and spoke cheerfully, carrying off matters in the best way she could.

"Have you found your box yet, Mr. Lydney?"

"No," he replied, turning to walk by her side. "I have been dancing attendance at that police-station all day, and have not yet managed to see its head—Bent, I think they call him. They have now told me he will be visible in half-an-hour, and I am walking my impatience off until the half-hour shall expire."

"I wish you could hear of it. It seems a strange thing altogether—unless it was lost on its way to the Castle. Were the contents of so very much consequence to you?"

"They were of the very utmost consequence to the owner. Strictly speaking, neither box nor contents belonged to me, but I would rather give every shilling I possess in the world than not recover them."

"Then I sincerely hope you will recover them," she said, as Mr. Lydney rang the Hall bell; and she held out her hand to say adieu. "Indeed, you have my best wishes."

"Thank you. Yes—I feel sure I have. What was grieving you just now?" he resumed, as he held the hand in his, and looked straight into her eyes.

The flush came into her cheeks again, but she made no answer.

"Is it anything I may share—or alleviate?"

"No, no; don't ask me," she hurriedly answered, as the door opened. "It was not my own trouble; it is nothing I can speak of. Thank you very much, Mr. Lydney."

He knew just as well as she did that it concerned Wilfred, for the gossip of Danesheld had reached his ears. Maria entered. She saw her father in his study at the back of the hall, and went straight to the room.

"Papa," she said, closing the door, and untying her

bonnet-strings, partly in haste at the approach of dinner,
partly from inward commotion, "there was an embargo laid
on me, more implied than expressed, that I should not go to
Wilfred's house."

"Of course there was," replied Mr. Lester.

"I have come to tell you that I have transgressed it twice,
papa."

Mr. Lester surveyed his daughter for a minute in silence.
"And pray what took you there ?"

"I went to see Edith. Papa, I fear she is dying."

The glasses across Mr. Lester's nose—for he had been
reading a letter when interrupted by Maria—went down.
He made no answer.

"And she is dying of hunger—of famine," continued
Maria with emotion. "Dying of famine, papa."

"Don't talk absurdly," came the angry reproof.

"It is so, papa. Edith cannot eat ordinary food, and she
is sinking for the want of better nourishment. Sally tells
me she is slowly dying of starvation and neglect. Slowly
dying. Oh, papa! will you not help them? Let me take
her something from our superfluities."

It may be that a question crossed Mr. Lester whether he
might venture (having his wife before his mind) to accede
to the prayer, for he hesitated. But only for a moment.

"No, Maria. Wilfred and his wife have deliberately
brought this state of things on themselves, defying me ;
and they must abide by it."

The tears came streaming from Maria's eyes. "If you
would only give me a little ready money for them,
papa——"

"Be silent," testily interrupted Mr. Lester. Ready
money had become a scarce commodity with him ; and his
daughter was making him feel disagreeably uncomfortable.
As to "famine," he put that down to a flight of imagination.

"It is no affair of yours, Maria ; they have brought it on
themselves, I say. I desire that you do not go near
Wilfred's place again."

"Please do not impose that command upon me," she

interrupted.   "I am not sure—dear papa, pardon my
saying so—but I am not sure I could strictly obey it.   He
is my brother; he is deserted of all; and I fear it may be
my duty to stand by him a little—even though you bade
me not do so.   Do not bar all intercourse between us.   I
will promise to go but rarely—never unless occasion should
seem to need it; and if you like, I will always tell you
when I have been.   Our mother is dead; you have other
ties: but I and Wilfred stand alone."

Not a word spoke Mr. Lester.   He was taken by surprise, possibly.   Never had he seen his daughter display
similar agitation.   After a moment's pause, Maria turned
slowly to the door, and had opened it, when he addressed
her.

" If you are determined to take your own course in this
matter, why did you speak to me ? "

" I could not be disobedient without telling you, papa."

He said nothing more, and Maria left the room.   Ah !
but she had not told him all she had hoped to do.   She had
wished to hint at the unpleasant rumours touching Wilfred's
doings, as an additional reason why he should be helped ;
but her courage had failed her.

The dinner-bell was heard, and as Maria went upstairs,
she met Lady Adelaide in dinner dress, a fan and bouquet
in her hand.

" Don't you intend to appear at table to-day, Miss
Lester ? " she coldly asked.

" Oh, thank you, Lady Adelaide; never mind me to-day,"
was the answer returned, as if the speaker were agitated.
" I have a headache."

My lady swept on down the stairs, and poor Maria went
up.   Tiffle came out of a nook near the study, and cast a
stealthy glance after Maria.

" Shouldn't I like to have the shaking of that young
woman ! I'd make her remember her interference—with
her Wilfreds and her famishings !   My lady must be
warned of this plot; Guy Faux's was nothing to it."

By which it may be inferred that Tiffle had mysteriously
heard what passed inside the study of Mr. Lester.

Meanwhile Mr. Lydney went again to the police-station, and found Inspector Bent waiting for him. As before, he was accommodated with a chair within the railings of the front room, under the gas-burner, but was not taken to any more private place. They had lighted up early at the station to-night. The inspector stood in the shade, leaning against the desk in a careless fashion, listening carelessly (as it seemed) to what the applicant said. In reality, he was at work most attentively and cautiously, endeavouring to learn what he could of Mr. Lydney and his belongings.

"Am I to understand that you accuse Lord Dane of stealing the box?" asked the inspector.

"I do not accuse him, not having sufficient proof at hand," was the bold answer. "That Lord Dane had the box taken away in the cart is indisputable; that it must have reached the Castle is almost equally indisputable; and also, in my opinion, that it entered it. Where, then, is the box? Lord Dane does not give it up; he either cannot, or he will not—one of the two; and the only course left to me, by which I may obtain redress, is to have the Castle searched by the police."

"But only think what an insult that would be to my Lord Dane," said Mr. Bent, fencing with the question. "You must remember who he is—a peer, lord-lieutenant of the county, lord of the manor, a man of high charac-ter——"

"High character!" interrupted the young gentleman.

"Why, yes—high character, and very high," answered Mr. Bent, staring at the applicant. "Have you anything to urge against him?"

"That I have, if he has taken my box."

"Enough!" said the inspector, tartly. "Before we can listen to any such charge—if you were thinking of making it—we must know who it is that would bring it."

"What difference does that make?"

"It makes all the difference," was the significant answer. "Were any unknown worthless fellow to come to us with some trumped-up complaint against Lord Dane, we should show him the door for his temerity; but were any such

complaint preferred by a gentleman of character and position, it might carry weight with it.   Now do you see the
distinction ? "

Such distinction of course Mr. Lydney could not fail to
see.

"I am a gentleman, if you require that assurance," he
observed.   "I am entitled to position and consideration."

"Can you prove it ? "

"You have my word for it."

The inspector smiled in a way that annoyed Mr. Lydney.
But he continued quietly :

"It is a word that has never yet been doubted."

"Maybe, sir ; but words don't go for much in law, unless
backed by proofs.   You are an American, we have been
given to understand ? "

"In so far as that I was born on the soil—no further.
My father was an Englishman, my mother French.   My
father's family are of repute in England, and know how to
hold their own."

The inspector's ears were opened an inch wider, and his
answer was ready.

"Where do they live?   In what part of England?
Lydney?   Lydney?   The name is not familiar to me as
borne by any family of note."

"I cannot give you further information.   It is as I have
told you, and you must trust to my word."

"But where can be the objection to speak out ? " urged
the officer.

"That is my business," was the cool reply.

"Very well, sir ; you have said just as much as I expected you to say, and no more," returned the police-
officer.   "You assert that you are somebody, and when
I ask you for proof you decline to give it.   Now, *do* you
think that any charge from you against my Lord Dane
would be listened to ? "

Lydney regarded him in silence.   He was thinking.

"Will you tell me what your business may be in this
neighbourhood?—and how long you intend to stop in it ? "

"My business in the neighbourhood!" echoed Mr.

Lydney. "Why, did not the sea cast me upon it? As to my remaining, if I choose to remain in it for good, I believe there is no law to prevent me. I can promise you one thing: I don't quit it until the box is found."

"Our conference is at an end, sir," said the inspector. "My time is valuable."

"Am I to understand that the police refuse to assist me in my efforts to recover the box?"

"Not at all," more cordially replied Mr. Bent; "we should be very glad to find it for our own satisfaction. What we decline to do, is to act in any offensive manner towards Lord Dane. Especially," he pointedly added, "when a stranger, and one who won't declare anything about himself, urges it. But now, sir, I am not ill-natured, and if it will ease your mind at all to know it, I can testify that the box is not in the Castle."

"You cannot know that it is not."

"I never testify to a thing that I don't know," returned Mr. Bent. "I searched the Castle myself for it to-day."

"You!"

"I did. I searched it effectively and thoroughly. There was not a space the size of that," holding up his hand, "that I did not go into. When you went the length of applying for a search-warrant this morning, we thought it time to acquaint my Lord Dane, and I stepped up to the Castle towards middle day. My lord was indignant, which was to be expected, and said he'd see you far enough before you should search his house. But he cooled down in a few minutes, and said if I liked to go through it for my own satisfaction, I might. I availed myself of the offer, and can swear that the box is not in the Castle. Every place that it was possible to put a box into was thrown open to me by the butler, who seemed as anxious to find the box as you can be. It is not in Dane Castle, and, I feel persuaded, never was in it."

The information took Mr. Lydney by surprise.

"Then where can it be? What can have become of it?" he exclaimed aloud.

"I can't say; to my mind, it's a queer business altogether," acknowledged Mr. Bent. "I don't much like the fact of that Granny Bean's Shad having been near the cart when it was unloading. That imp would lay his hands on anything he could; a japanned box, got up from a wreck, would be the very treasure he would like to finger. Still, that idea does not go for much with me. That he did not carry it off himself is certain—first, because he could not, from its weight; next, because I have evidence that when the cart went away empty, he shambled off, empty-handed, after it."

"You have been collecting evidence upon this loss, I perceive."

"Undoubtedly. When losses take place, especially mysterious ones, it is our business to do so. We were yesterday in possession of all the facts—so far as they go."

"And what are your deductions?" asked Mr. Lydney. "Can you give a guess as to how or where the abstraction took place?"

"Not the faintest. It's about as uncertain a case as ever I had to do with. It is your own box, I think you said?" the inspector carelessly added, with a keen rapid glance of the eye.

"I did not say so. It was in my charge, and I have authority to claim it as such; but neither the box nor its contents belonged to me."

"May I inquire whose it was?"

"When the box shall be found," was Mr. Lydney's rejoinder; and his caution did not tell well for him with the man in authority. "I may rely, then, upon your efforts to help me in finding the property?"

"Yes—in a legitimate way. We'll do our best."

Mr. Lydney went out, the inspector standing at the door and looking after him, as he disappeared in the darkness of the evening. In acknowledging that it was a "queer" business, Mr. Bent spoke exactly as he thought; and now that he had seen and conversed with the claimant, he put away that idea first suggested by Lord Dane, of any nefarious acting on Lydney's part. The young man's bearing and speech were those of an honest man and a gentleman; and Mr. Bent had found himself a great deal less short with him than he had previously intended to be.

"I'll be hanged if there isn't something about him that puts me in mind of the old Lord Dane!" said the inspector, arousing himself from his train of thought. "He has just the same commanding way. As to the box——Halloa, sir! is it you back again?"

"It has occurred to me that it might be of use to offer a reward for the recovery of the box," said Mr. Lydney. "What do you think?"

"Well, yes, it might," answered the inspector. "I have been turning the matter over in my mind this last minute or two, and think the box must have been stolen from the cart on its way to the Castle. I can't see any other way out of the difficulty. We have two or three loose characters in Danesheld, I can tell you, sir—older and stronger than Shad. If any of them were hanging about, why, that's how the job was done; and in that case, a reward would be almost sure to get the box back."

"Then be so good as to take the necessary steps to announce it. Spare no trouble, no time, no expense; you shall be well repaid."

"Very good, sir. What reward shall we say? Five pounds—ten pounds?"

"Offer a thousand pounds."

"*Sir!*" cried the inspector, backing a step or two in his astonishment.

"A thousand pounds; to be paid to any one who shall restore the box intact," continued Mr. Lydney, as quietly as though he had said a thousand pence.

"A thousand pounds!" echoed the inspector, startled at the munificence of the amount. "The box must be valuable, sir, and you rich, to offer that."

"The box, to its owner, is valuable. As to the money, it would be paid from his pocket, not from mine."

"A tithe of the money would fetch back a score of such boxes, whatever their contents, from the minor sort of base characters we have about here, whose business chiefly consists of poaching and smuggling."

" And," pursued Mr. Lydney, " as you have remarked upon my being unknown, I may as well mention that vouchers for the money can be deposited with you whenever you please, as a guarantee for the good faith of my offer."

He turned with the last word, and departed, Mr. Inspector Bent gazing after him, and unable just yet to recover from his amazement.

" I said it looked queer all along," was his mental comment. " A thousand pounds! What on earth can his box have got inside it ? "

CHAPTER XXIII.

A BATTLE ROYAL.

Mr. Lydney walked away with a slow step, his brain working. The assurance of the police that his box was not in Dane Castle upset his previous conclusions. He began to think he had misjudged Lord Dane, and to fall into the theory of the inspector, as the only feasible conclusion—that the box had been stolen on its way to the Castle. If so, there was one person who must undoubtedly have witnessed the theft —and that was Shad.

Somewhat impulsive in what he did, and very anxious, William Lydney determined to seek Shad on the instant, and question him again. Mr. Shad was perhaps keeping the secret, but a glance too cunning, or a word too sharp, might betray the fact. He was not quite sure which road would best conduct him to the hut inhabited by Granny Bean ; he had a general impression that it lay on the outer border of the wood, and concluded that it must be down somewhere by Wilfred Lester's. So he marched along, swiftly now, in the starlight of the summer evening, until he came to Wilfred's cottage.

" I believe now I ought to have gone on by Miss Bordillion's, and taken the further turning," he soliloquized, halting in his course. " Suppose I ask Lester ? "

Opening the gate, he stepped into the little porch, where something occurred that considerably startled him. The door unclosed stealthily, and he was pounced upon by a tall female, and pulled into the dark passage. It was no other than Sally, and she spoke in a whisper.

" Thanks be to goodness you've not gone yet ! Now it's of no use your being angry and struggling to get off ! I have had you in my arms when you were a baby, Mr. Wilfred, and I know what's right and what's wrong. I've heard a whisper that the keepers are going on the watch to-night, and there'll be bloodshed again, as sure as death, if the poachers show themselves. You shan't go, sir ! You are killing your wife outright, for she's beginning to suspect something. I've just been vowing you are in the kitchen, smoking your pipe by the fire. Come in, sir, and let me bar the door ; come in."

" My good woman," he exclaimed, when he found himself able to speak, " for whom do you take me ? I am Mr. Lydney. Is your master at home ? "

Sally fell against the wall without a word. Mr. Lydney repeated his question.

" I'm just a fool and nothing else," cried she, turning the matter off with a laugh. " I've been expecting a friend to-night, and I thought it was him. You must please to forgive me, sir. The master ? No, sir, I think he must have gone out. I've been up in my mistress's sick-room, and can't find him in the house."

" Never mind. I merely called to ask some of you to direct me to Goody Bean's. Am I going right for it ? "

" Yes, sir ; straight on. You'll have to keep to the left of that three-cornered field that divides the wood, and you will come to the place in a few minutes—a little low cottage hid in the trees, standing by itself. Sir," she added, " I beg your pardon for my mistake, and I hope you'll not think about it, or talk of it."

" Not I," answered Mr. Lydney, with a laugh. " Make my compliments to your master."

The laugh was a pleasant one, the tone gay, purposely made so ; nevertheless, the woman's unintentional disclosure had struck a chill on William Lydney's heart. It seemed a confirmation of the damaging rumours that were being whispered.

A few minutes brought him to a low dwelling, half cottage, half hut, on the borders of the wood, which he had no doubt was Goody Bean's domicile. It was closely shut up, and he might have imagined its inmates, Granny and Shad, had retired to rest, but for a commotion that was taking place within. Now an old woman's voice rose in shrill shrieks of rage ; now Shad's in shriller whines. Mr. Lydney knocked first at the door, then on the shutters ; but little chance was there of his being heard whilst the noise lasted.

"You wicked young imp !" he heard her say, with a profuse sprinkling of language, which the reader would not care to have transcribed ; "to go and rob your granny of her hard-earned savings ! You'll come to the gallows, you will."

"It's not yourn," returned Shad, his denial interspersed with similar embellishments. "The new gen'alman gave it me yesterday for telling him about the box, and I'll take my oath to it. Come ; hand it over."

"You vile story-teller ! As if any gen'alman would go and give *you* a whole silver sixpence ! Now, will you be off ? You ought to have been on the watch a good half-hour ago."

Mr. Shad apparently turned restive. "I won't go on the watch," said he. "I won't stir till I gets my sixpence. I've kep' it in my pocket till I gets twopence more, to buy that there gray rabbit off Ned Long."

A fresh contest, sounds of blows, and a final shout of triumph from Shad, which seemed to proclaim him the victor. Mr. Lydney gave a loud knock on the shutters.

Total silence supervened : the summons had been heard, and evidently startled the disputants. Stealthy movements inside ensued, and Mr. Lydney thought he heard a door shut. He knocked again.

It brought forth the head of the woman at a window-casement on the right. The cottage had two rooms, both on the ground-floor, a window in each. She opened the shutters, and thrust her face through the aperture, reconnoitring—a red and wrinkled face, surmounted by a cap in tatters, the result probably of the recent conflict; the head shaking as if she were suffering from palsy.

"Have you been committing murder here?" demanded Mr. Lydney.

"I was a-saying of my prayers out loud, if that's murder," returned the dame. "What now? what do you mean?"

The bold assertion deprived him of speech for a moment. Of what use bandying words with such a woman? "I want Shad," he resumed.

"Shad! I can't go for to disturb him from his rest to-night. Shad's a-bed and asleep."

"Why, you audacious old creature!" he could not help exclaiming, "I wonder you dare tell so deliberate a falsehood! You and Shad have just been at it, tooth and nail, fighting after a sixpence. Let me tell you the sixpence is his, for I gave it him."

"Now, did you indeed, sir?" was the bland whining answer, the surly tone changing as if by magic. "What a dear, good, generous gentleman you must be! You haven't got another about you, to bestow in charity upon a poor, lone, wretched, half-starved widder, have you? I'd remember you in my prayers ever after, I would."

"If I had fifty, I would not give you one; and I don't imagine your prayers will do yourself much good, let alone anyone else. I want Shad, I say."

"Shad's a-bed and asleep, which I'll swear to, and I darden't break into his night's rest," was the impudent retort. "A delicate child as he is, and the stay and staff o' my life—if I was to lose him, I should die of grief. Come any time in the morning, sir, when his night's rest's over, and you're welcome. I tucked him up, the darling, an hour ago, in his little bed, and a sweet sleep he dropped off into."

"Of all extraordinary characters I think you must be the worst!" exclaimed Mr. Lydney. "Shad's no more in bed than I am. I heard your conflict, I tell you. These false assertions sound perfectly awful from a woman at your time of life."

"Strange noises is heard outside this hut at times; folks have said so afore," said the old woman with a sniff. "It's the witches a-playing in the air, I fancy; and it's them you must have heard—unless it was me at my prayers."

"Will you send out Shad?"

"I'm sure I'd obleege you in any ways but that, such a nice gentlemen as you seem to be; but I wouldn't wake up my poor sickly gran'child for anything—no, not if you offered me fifty sixpences."

Giving a good-night to Granny Bean more emphatic than polite, Mr. Lydney strode away. He must put off seeing Shad until the morning. He struck round to the back of the hut, where he believed he should find a path that led direct through the wood, which would cut off a portion of the way homeward. Curiosity induced him to turn and look at the cottage, and there he saw a door; so Master Shad and his reputable granny had entrance and exit by the back way as well as the front.

Pursuing the path which was narrower than he had expected, Mr. Lydney sped on with a quick step, buried in thought. It was a light night in the open ground, but dark and gloomy in the wood. He was half-way through it, when a sound as of one pushing through the brambles caught his ear. Knowing that certain suspicious characters were said to haunt the place, Mr. Lydney drew just within the trees, and looked out to see who might be approaching.

It was Wilfred Lester. Panting, eager, excited, he came tearing along, at right angles with Lydney, where there seemed to be no pathway. He crossed the open path at a bound, penetrated the trees on its opposite side, and went pushing on, as though making straight for home.

Mr. Lydney remained immovable, wondering what the movement could mean, and what Wilfred was about. That he was excessively agitated was apparent, and the words spoken by the servant, when she had so unceremoniously made him a prisoner, rose with apprehension to his mind.

He was, as the saying runs, "putting this and that together," and by no means liking the look of things, when something else attracted his attention.

Stealing out on to the path in the trail of Wilfred Lester, came Mr. Shad like a young hound scenting its prey. Once in the path he made a dead stoppage, unconscious that any eye or ear was near him.

"He's tored home to his house," soliloquized he aloud, looking at the direction in which Wilfred Lester had disappeared. "No good to track him further to-night. I'll go and tell her."

Mr. Lydney had stretched out his hand to lay it on the boy, but a second impulse prompted him to hesitate. Far better follow this erratic gentleman, and discover, if possible, what treason was being hatched. That some plot was on foot against Wilfred Lester, that he was being watched to his own possible destruction, Mr. Lydney felt convinced. He also felt very nearly convinced of another thing—that Wilfred was hatching enough mischief of his own accord against himself.

Shad fled down the path in a direction opposite to Granny Bean's, and at the end of the wood, near to Squire Lester's, entered the trees again to the right. Mr. Lydney followed. Agile and slender, he could penetrate the trees as well as Shad; and when Shad stopped, he stopped.

Shad was in his favourite attitude; twined just like a snake round the thin stem of a tree skirting the road. Mr. Lydney halted sufficiently near to see and hear. He wondered who the "her" was to whom Shad was bound. Having had experience by this time of the insatiable nature of Madame Ravensbird's curiosity, and of her great amount of information on all subjects, a half suspicion crossed his mind that it might be to her that Shad was hastening. Not so, however.

In answer to a soft whistle of Shad's, a female emerged from a low gate on the opposite side of the road, a gate that led to the back entrance of Squire Lester's house. She crossed the road with a stealthy shambling gait, not unlike Shad's own, entered the trees, and stood with Shad in a

small clear space. Mr. Lydney recognized in her the upper
servant at the Hall—Tiffle.

" Well ? " began she, rather sharply.

" He's gone right off home," said Shad in answer. " When
I got up to 'em, they was having hot words—him, and
Beecher, and Drake, and another, which I think were Bill
Nicholson. Lester was a-blowing of 'em up for wanting to
go right off where the keepers would be, which might cause
blood to be spilt, he said; and they got in a passion one
and t'other, and Lester he swore he'd have nothing to do
with 'em, and went off back again. I say, Mrs. Tiffle,
where'll be the pull o' my dodging him, if he takes to
shirking ? "

" How did they ferret out where the keepers would be ? "
asked Tiffle, who had listened in silence.

" Can't tell," answered Shad. " I only got up at the tail
o' their conflab. I didn't hear nothing of what they'd been
saying afore."

" Then you were late, and a wicked, inattentive, good-for-
nothing little villain."

" Yes, I were late, and it were granny's fault," boldly
announced Shad. " She set on me and a'most killed me.
You should be hid in the oven some day, and see her in her
tantrums; you'd not believe it was anything but Old Nick's
mother let loose. Look here ! here's where she bited me,
and here's where she kicked at me, and here's where she
scratted me, and clutches of my hair she tored out by
han'fuls."

Shad exhibited various damaged spots about his face and
arms, and let fall a shower of tears. Tiffle became remarkably demonstrative in her sympathy, clasping Shad
to her with tenderness, and kissing the places with her own
lips. It caused Mr. Lydney's eyes to open—in more senses
than one.

" My poor boy! Granny's a regular hyenia when she's
put up. I'll be even with her. What did she do it for ? "

" She have the nastiest, slyest ways," returned Shad, who
appeared not to relish the embrace in an equal degree with
Tiffle, and wriggled himself from it as soon as he possibly

could. "She dives into my pockets, she do, and to-night she found a sixpence in 'em, and she set on and swored it were hern, and said I'd robbed her on't, and she grabbed it from me, and—my! wasn't there a shindy! and such a row came to the shutters amid it. I got it again, though," concluded Shad, with glee, as he took out the bright sixpence and exhibited it to Tiffle. "Why, she haven't a sixpence to grab!"

Tiffle did not look at it with equanimity. She came to the conclusion that someone had been robbed of it, if not Granny Bean, and her affectionate mood changed into wrath.

"You little divil, you! If you begin to grab money now, you'll end your days a-working in gangs and irons. Now you just tell me where you stole that."

"If ever I see the like! You're as bad as granny," whined the boy. "I might as well be a mad dog, and roped up at once! That there sixpence was gave me by a gen'alman; gived out and out."

"Gave for what?" sharply responded Tiffle.

"For telling about his box. It's that tall spark what's stopping at the Sailors' Rest. He asked me did I see the things took up to the Castle gates, and I said I see 'em; and then he said if I'd tell him the truth, and no lie, whether the box went into the Castle or not, I should get a sixpence; and I did tell him, and he give it me."

"Did you see the box taken in?" quickly asked Tiffle.

"What should ail me?" responded Shad. "I were stood there watching,"

"And it was taken right in?"

"It was took right in," answered Shad, his eyes glistening: "as right in as ever anything was took into that Castle yet. Them two miller's chaps carried of it, like they did t'other lots; and that big Mr. Bruff might have see'd 'em if he'd looked, only he was talking to a lady what passed."

"That young fellow's name's Lydney, Shad; and——"

"*I* know," interrupted Shad, with a careless emphasis that seemed to carry with it an assurance there were few things he did not know.

"Well, I want you to keep your eyes on that Lydney,"

proceeded Tiffle. "Look after him just as keen as you are looking after Will Lester. He looks like a gentleman, but he might be one of them gentlemen that come to places after watches, and chains, and rings; and I heard my Lord Dane drop a doubt of him. You find out what you can. I've got my reasons. And just you note down in your head whenever you see him with Miss Lester."

Mr. Lydney, from his hiding-place, felt infinitely indebted to her.

"I've see'd him often with her," returned Shad. "I see'd him with her this evening. They went right up to the Hall together. He have took to come to the wood, too, he have, that Lydney! And, I say, Mrs. Tiffle, Miss Lester went to her brother's place this evening."

"Yes, she did," said Tiffle, sharply. "But now there's no more to be done to-night, Shad, and you cut home as quick as you can, and get to bed."

"And if granny sets on me again?" whined Shad.

"Leave granny to me; I'll see to her."

Shad turned into the wood; Tiffle looked cautiously out on either side, and then hurried across the road. She had barely gained the gate leading to Mr. Lester's premises, when my Lord Dane appeared from the direction of Miss Bordillion's. He was probably coming from the railway station. The line of rail had now been extended to Dancesheld, its station being beyond Miss Bordillion's, and this was the nearest way to it from the Castle. Tiffle waited at the gate when she saw who it was.

"Is it you, Tiffle?" cried his lordship, gaily. "Enjoying a ramble by starlight?"

"Oh, my lord, you are pleased to joke," simpered Tiffle. "My days for starlighted rambles are over. I leave 'em for the young now, my lord; I've had my turn. This evening that over was, I see Miss Lester walking cosy in the starlight—leastway, the evening star was out—and I thought how romintic it was; putting me in mind of my own sentimintal days, my lord. That gentleman was with her that the wreck cast up."

Had it been daylight instead of starlight, Tiffle would

scarcely have presumed to fix her eyes so keenly upon my
Lord Dane. Amongst all cunning women, she wore the palm,
and she knew she was throwing out a shaft that would tell.

"Wrecks cast up rogues as well as gentlemen," observed
his lordship, in a tone of stern displeasure. "An American,
whom nobody knows, is scarcely one to be walking by
starlight with Miss Lester. Good-night, Tifflo."

Every word could be heard by William Lydney in his
retreat, from which he had not yet been able to get away.
The road was very narrow; in fact, it was more of a lane
than a road; and the tones came over it with perfect dis-
tinctness in the still night air.

Lord Dane walked on, and Tifflo disappeared from view.
But Mr. Lydney felt by no means sure she was not on the
watch still, and therefore he did not choose to step out into
the road and show himself. He penetrated further into the
wood to gain a path that would bring him out at the back
of the town. His rambles with Wilfred Lester, who seemed
to prefer the wood for exercise to the open country, had
rendered him tolerably familiar with it.

This night appeared prolific for Mr. Lydney in adventures
and encounters. As he was pursuing his way, he came suddenly into contact with a man dragging himself covertly
and noiselessly through the trees — a youngish man, as
far as could be distinguished, who appeared alarmingly
startled at the encounter, and levelled his gun.

"Halloa, my man! what's that for?" demanded Mr.
Lydney, speaking with equanimity, and showing neither
fear nor hurry. "Have the goodness to drop that."

"If you don't say who you are, and what you are doing
here, I'll shoot you," was the reply.

"I feel infinitely obliged to you. Have you any more
right to be in the wood than I have? I should be glad to
know."

Mr. Lydney spoke with courtesy; and the man could not
fail to remark that his voice was that of a gentleman. He
had no doubt feared a keeper.

"You were posted there to watch me!" he exclaimed.

"Nay," said Mr. Lydney; "I may with equal reason

reverse the accusation, and say you were watching me. I
don't know who you are; I never saw you in my life that I
know of. Why should I watch you? You must have
escaped from a lunatic asylum."

The man let fall his gun. He had been peering at Mr.
Lydney as well as the obscurity allowed him, and made out
that he was not a foe.

"I ask your pardon for my haste," he said; "I thought
you were somebody else. The fact is, none but suspicious
characters are ever prowling in the wood so late as this,
unless it's those confounded keepers who are ready to swear
an innocent man's life away."

Mr. Lydney laughed — a kindly laugh. He had no
objection to a spice of adventure—was just of the age and
temperament to relish it.

"Are you aware of the self-accusation those words imply?
Nobody but suspicious characters? Meaning, I conclude,
poachers."

"And keepers too," growled the man.

"Very good. I am neither the one nor the other. If
you choose to beat about this wood from January to Decem-
ber, a gun in one hand and snare-nets in the other, you are
welcome, for all the business it is of mine. Were they my
preserves, it would be a different matter."

"You won't go and say to-morrow that you dropped upon
me here with a gun?"

"I should be clever to say it, seeing I know you neither
by sight nor by name. But if you prefer a specific promise,
you may take it. Life is short enough, my man; better
pass it in kindliness than in doing gratuitous injuries."

The poacher liked the tones and the words; and that
rather hardened part within him which did duty for a
heart, went out at once to the speaker in a manner he would
have been puzzled to account for.

"I think, sir, you are the gentleman stopping at the
Sailors' Rest, whose box is missing? I nearly got into
trouble over that box yesterday."

"How was that?" inquired Mr. Lydney, his interest
suddenly awakened.

" I happened to be passing the Castle on my way home as the cart was unloading, and I halted a few minutes and looked on. Those keen police got to know of it, and I'll be hanged if they didn't have me up to the station ? Whether they thought I had walked the box off, or had seen anybody else walk it off, I don't know. I laughed at them. Young Shad and two or three more urchins could testify that I didn't go near enough to touch anything on the cart."

" You must have heard the box described. Did you see it ? "

" I did not see it, sir, to my recollection. But if, as I hear, it was underneath the rest of the things, I was not likely to see it. I stopped but a few minutes, and they had only then begun to unload."

" You cannot guess where it is gone, or who took it, I suppose ? " resumed Mr. Lydney.

" No, I can't ; I have not thought much about it. That Shad's as ready-fingered as a magpie, but they say it was too heavy for him to lift."

" I would give a good reward if it were restored to me untampered with."

" Would you, though ? " quickly rejoined the poacher, as if the sound were music to his ears.

" Fifty guineas."

" Fifty guineas ! " uttered the man, as much astonished as the inspector had been that evening at mention of a thousand pounds.

" Fifty guineas, and no questions asked, provided it be restored to me before to-morrow night. After that, a different offer may be made, *and* questions asked—pretty sharp ones."

" By jingo ! that's worth looking after," exclaimed the man. " I know two or three fellows who *have* done a little in the fingering line, sir, and I'll—I'll be on to them. If I can hear of the box you shall have it on those terms. Honour bright, though ? "

" Honour bright, on the word of a gentleman. The fifty guineas shall be paid, and no inquiries made. I fancy you may perhaps hear of it amongst your friends."

Little cared Mr. Ben Beecher, junior—for it was no

other—for the last delicate insinuation. A golden vision had been opened to him, and in that he was absorbed.

But the two, so strangely met, were not to part without being observed. Ben Beecher offered to show Mr. Lydney a short-cut out of the wood that would bring him nearer the Sailors' Rest than the exit he had been making for. The outlet gained, Ben Beecher was stealing into the wood again, when Mr. Lydney stopped him for a parting word.

" You will not fail me ? "

" I'll not fail, if the box is to be had. But look here, sir," added the man after a minute's thought, " couldn't you meet me here in the wood? I shouldn't care to be seen going after you to the Sailors' Rest."

Now it happened at this critical juncture that no less an individual should be passing than my Lord Dane. Cattley's cottage lay in this direction—the gamekeeper who had been injured—he was progressing slowly, and Lord Dane, in his affability, had turned out of his way on leaving Tiffle to make a personal inquiry after the man. He stayed a few minutes with him, and was walking back, on his way home, when the sound of voices caught his ear.

Recognizing the one for Mr. Ben Beecher's, Lord Dane's thoughts naturally flew to the poachers, who were giving him at the time a great deal of trouble. In the moment's impulse, he stepped aside into the trees as noiselessly as Mr. Beecher himself could have done, and gazed through at the speakers. Yes, sure enough, there was Mr. Ben Beecher, gun in hand; the other Lord Dane could not see, but felt convinced it was either Drake or Bill Nicholson—the latter he thought, by the height. He hushed his breath, for this one was beginning to speak.

" Why so ? " was the short question asked of Beecher. And Lord Dane seemed to have a confused remembrance of the voice ; and it was not Nicholson's.

" Well, for reasons," answered Beecher. " I'd rather you were not seen openly working with me in this, sir, if you can understand me."

" I daresay you wouldn't, Mr. Beecher ! " mentally apostrophised my Lord Dane from his hiding-place.

"I will be at the fairy circle in the wood—the spot we passed two or three minutes ago—at eight o'clock to-morrow night, if that will do," continued Beecher

"Very well," replied the voice that was puzzling Lord Dane. "I'll meet you there at that hour."

"All right—all right," mentally repeated Lord Dane. "I'll be down upon you, my gentlemen, to-morrow night. Whose *is* that voice? I've heard it somewhere."

Stretching his neck, he prepared to take a good view, for he to whom the voice belonged was coming forth. And the view nearly drove Lord Dane backwards.

Lydney!

His lordship rubbed his eyes to make sure he was awake. That this interview and the one appointed for to-morrow night could have reference to anything but poaching purposes never entered his imagination. He was very excessively astonished, and came to the conclusion that Mr. William Lydney was even a lower and more disreputable character than he had supposed him to be.

"I'll lay any money he stole the box originally!" cried his lordship. "Perhaps ran away with it from America."

Mr. Lydney was already out of sight, making the best of his way to the Sailors' Rest. He went straight into Sophie's private parlour, as he frequently did. Madame Sophie was just finishing her supper of bread and cheese and salad, with some thin claret wine. She wore a coquettish cap of lace and scarlet ribbons, and a black silk perfectly-fitting gown, with narrow bands of Irish linen, by way of collar and cuffs.

Mr. Lydney sat down and began gossiping—or it may be more correct to say, that he said a word or two to set her off, and she gossiped. Insensibly he continued to lead her on to the subject of the Beechers—in particular to young Mr. Ben. Mrs. Ravensbird tossed her head.

"A nice lot, those Beechers! The old father was nothing but a smuggler: and the son's a poacher. A very nice lot they are, sir!"

"He's quite a young man, is he not, the son?"

" Not much over twenty.   Old Beecher did not marry till
he was getting in years."

"Rather superior for what he is, I fancy, that young
Beecher?"

"He might have been," returned Sophie, with a considerable amount of scorn, meant for Mr. Beecher, junior.
" His mother was a very respectable woman indeed, sir, with
a life income; old Beecher married her at a distance, and
it's thought he deceived her as to his position and means.
As long as she lived, the boy was well taken care of—sent
to boarding school, and all that; but he has gone all wrong
since she died, and idles his time away shamefully."

Ah! this explanation accounted for what had rather
surprised William Lydney—the superiority in Ben Beecher's
accent and manner as compared with his condition in life.

CHAPTER XXIV.

A DISCLOSURE TO WILFRED LESTER.

PERCHED on the arm of the sofa in his little sitting-room, the
sun shining brightly on him and his employment—that of
making artificial flies for fishing—was Wilfred Lester.   It
was the morning following the night mentioned in the last
chapter, and Mr. Wilfred was giving his thoughts to sundry
events of that night much more than he was to his flies.

Had he been more observant, he might have seen that
something was troubling his wife in an unusual degree.
She sat on the sofa, reclining her head on the opposite arm
to where Wilfred was sitting.   A fair, fragile girl she looked
—her features painfully delicate, her blue eyes unnaturally
bright, her light hair taking a tinge of gold in the sunlight.
She wore a white wrapper, or dressing-gown, which made
her appear still more of an invalid.   Glancing at her husband

once or twice, as though she wished to say something and
could not, she at length burst forth with a courage born of
desperation, her voice timid and trembling.

" Where did you go last night, Willy ? "

Mr. Wilfred Lester took a momentary and rapid glance at
the speaker. Something in the tone of the voice rather
startled his conscience.

" Where did I go last night ? Nowhere in particular,
that I remember. Bother the catgut ! I was out and about
talking to one and another."

" So you always say, Wilfred," and the girl's tone dropped
to one of dread, and she seemed to shiver as she spoke. " You
had that gun out with you."

" Ay. It's lock has a trick of catching, and I meant
to show it to the smith ; but the shop was shut," replied
Mr. Wilfred, beginning to whistle the bars of a popular
song.

Perhaps the greatest misfortune that had as yet fallen upon
Edith Lester, was having been an involuntary hearer of a
certain conversation a few days back. Sally, ironing before
the open kitchen window, had been accosted by some passer-
by, and Edith had listened to words (or, rather, to questions)
regarding her husband that turned her sick and faint.
" Was it true that he had joined the poachers ? that he had
been in the recent attack what had nearly killed Cattley ?
that he went regularly out at night ? If so, he'd get taken
up and transported, as sure as apples was apples ! "

Words which were bad enough in themselves for a poor
young wife's ears, but which were rendered all the more
forcible by the servant's vehement denial. Over-zeal tends
to destroy itself; and Sally entered on a defence that was
untruthful. She protested, in the most unblushing manner,
that her master never was abroad after sunset—how could
he be when he sat reading to his poor sick lady till bed-time,
and then retired to rest with her ? Granny Bean could not
have done it more audaciously.

The assertion, suspicious enough in itself—for it was
after sunset that Wilfred usually went out, and sometimes
remained out for hours—was rendered more ominous by the

suppressed fear in Sally's tones, all too apparent to Edith Lester. An awful dread took possession of her; and though, when she ventured to ask a timid question of Sally, that worthy domestic denied the conversation in toto, and declared her mistress must have heard it in a dream, the misery had been sown.

"Why do you choose the night for going out, Willy?"

"Oh, just to stretch my legs," he answered, breaking off his song to do so, and resuming it again.

Far better, perhaps, that he had treated it differently : this assumption of unconcern defeated its aim. Edith Lester had sound sense, but she also possessed one of those vivid imaginations that are peculiarly subject to be acted upon by terror. She rose from the sofa with a cry, and caught hold of her husband. Wilfred dropped his whistling and his flies together.

"Why, Edith, what has come to you?"

"Oh, Willy, tell me the truth! Were you with the poachers when they attacked Cattley?"

"Most certainly *not*," was the emphatic answer; and he seemed in earnest enough now. "You silly girl! What next will you be fancying? I would no more join in attacking a keeper than I would attack you."

"Do—you—ever—join in taking the game wholesale?" she asked, scarcely able to bring out the words between weakness and agitation.

He burst into a laugh.

"Serve Lord Dane right if I did. He has sent me to Coventry ever since he came here. Serve my father right if I took his and left not a single bird for his table and Lady Adelaide's. My darling, you just reassure that poor little fluttering heart. I'll take care of myself and of you."

"Willy, if anything happened to you, I should die! *Is* it true?"

"No, it is not true," he said very hastily. "For goodness sake get rid of these fancies, Edith, or you'll be worse than you are. But for you, I should like to get into some desperate escapade; it might shame my father to reason. As it is, I shall keep straight for your sake,"

The emotion had exhausted her feeble strength, and she lay down on the sofa, white, sad, and only half-convinced.

" The very fact of my continuing so hard-up, and unable to get you proper necessaries, Edith, might prove that I don't make a fortune at poaching."

" I have all I want," she eagerly said, lifting her wan face pleadingly to his. " Oh, Willy, don't think of me ! I shall grow strong soon. It is hard for both of us just now, but if we can only be patient, it will grow better—I am sure it will. Only let us endure ! Only let us put faith in God ! People say we could not expect anything better, and are suffering for our disobedience. It may be so, but a happy ending will come to it all, Willy."

That an end must come, and not very long first, he knew only too well; whether it would be a happy one, was not so certain. He went on with his fly-making, his manner gay, his heart aching for his wife's sake, his spirit terribly rebellious against his father and Lady Adelaide. Presently, in the midst of a light song, he put down his working materials, and went into the kitchen for something he wanted. The servant sat at the table, shelling broad beans.

" Where's the gum-bottle, Sally ? "

" Up there," answered Sally, rather unceremoniously, indicating a shelf of the dresser. " But it's empty, sir."

He took down the bottle, saw with a rueful look that it was as she said, and put it back again. Sally pointed to the beans.

" I don't know what's to be done for my mistress to-day. She can't eat these."

" There's a partridge in the house," answered Wilfred.

" Well, sir, the truth is, she can't eat partridge any longer. She has managed to swallow a bit lately, but she's one of them, and I'm another, whose tastes turn at game. When folks are sick, too, they take likes and dislikes ; and you know, sir, that for the last month there has been nothing but game in the house. I have tried the partridges every way to tempt her ; I've roasted 'em, boiled 'em, fricasseed 'em, fried 'em, and one day I chopped 'em up, and made 'em into balls ; but it didn't do. It *was* partridge, and that was enough. She has made a show of eating before you; but she can't pretend any longer."

Wilfred Lester stood near the table, gloomy and perplexed. He knew no way whatever of procuring anything else for Edith; all credit was gone. If a mutton chop would have saved her life, he must pay the butcher for it before it was sent in.

"Can't you do up some eggs for to-day?" he asked.

"I could if I had 'em. Eggs are no more to be had than anything else, without money. And there's another thing, sir, staring us in the face: the coals are almost out."

Can you imagine how bitter were his feelings as he stood there, knowing that he was powerless to answer these appeals? He turned back into the parlour again, and took up his flies, glancing at Edith. Her eyes were closed now, as if she would sleep, and the lashes lay on her wan cheek.

Suddenly commotion arose in the kitchen. Wilfred had left the doors unclosed, and the sounds penetrated to the quiet parlour as clearly as though uttered within it. Sally's voice was heard in angry dispute. Wilfred turned his head, and Edith's ears and eyes opened.

"Then I say he's not in, and he won't be in to-day—that's more. So just you walk out, please."

"I say he is in," responded a man's gruff voice. "I see him with my own eyes through that there kitchen winder, and here I shall stop till I can speak to him. I've a private message, which I can't give to you."

Wilfred Lester did not recognize the voice, but the intimation "private message" struck on his ear. Private messages, not expedient to be intrusted to other people, especially to Sally, came to him once in a way. Never a thought of treachery entering his head, he threw down his flies, and went into the kitchen. There stood Sally, armed with the tongs, which she presented at the stranger in a menacing manner to bar his farther progress. The man quietly put a paper into Mr. Lester's hand, and went out with a laugh. Sally flung the tongs back on the hearth in a passion.

"Now, why couldn't you keep out of sight?" she ex-

claimed, in wrath. "Where's the use of me telling a
hundred lies in a day for you—and I hope Heaven will
forgive me—if you are to upset 'em in this way? I know
what it is. As long as he didn't serve it, you were safe."

"He'd have served it to-morrow if he hadn't to-day,"
answered Wilfred, opening the document. "Don't make
a fuss about it."

"No, he needn't," retorted Sally. "You might have
dodged——My goodness, ma'am! what's the matter?"

Edith had come into the kitchen, shaking like a leaf, the
image of terror. She clung to her husband in an excess of
hysterical emotion.

"What is it all? What paper is it? Show it me. Oh,
Wilfred, show it me!"

"My dear, don't agitate yourself for nothing," he mis-
takenly answered, as he crumpled the paper in his hand.
"It's nothing but a bill."

Sally gave a snatch at the paper; Wilfred would not
release it, and there was actually a tussle for its possession,
in which the paper was torn, and Sally conquered. She was
rather in the habit of domineering over the two in her
superior age and wisdom.

"There, ma'am; now you can see that it's nothing but a
demand for money," cried Sally, laying it open before her
mistress. "Couldn't you just read that she feared something worse, sir," she added, in an undertone of reproach to
her master.

And the woman was right; she had keen perceptive
faculties and strong sense. Edith Lester was connecting the
visitor with the wild rumours afloat of the night-work;
terrific visions arose of handcuffs, a prison, a criminal trial,
perhaps death.

But what with one thing and another, Sally grew alarmed,
and she went out that day, and laid all her trouble and fear
before her late mistress, Miss Bordillion. Wilfred Lester,
in his pity for his poor young wife, and his resentment against
the world, was growing more reckless, and unless substantial
help came for Edith, Sally's opinion was that he would be
caught at something desperate.

" I can't take the responsibility of concealing these things any longer, ma'am," she said · " and it isn't right that I should."

" But what is to be done, Sally ? " was Miss Bordillion's piteous answer.

" Well, ma'am, it seems to me that if Squire Lester won't give some help, he should be made do it."

" Made ! " echoed Miss Bordillion, as Sally left her.

She sat on, after the woman's departure, in sad deliberation, endeavouring to find out where her duty lay.

She was aware of a fact which, if disclosed, might bring great help to Wilfred ; but in disclosing it, she would be acting directly against Mr. Lester, and also be guilty of an interference that under most circumstances would be unjustifiable. But now Miss Bordillion not only weighed the whole matter according to her own poor judgment, but prayed to be directed to the right. In an hour's time, she despatched a note asking Wilfred to come to her.

" I have surprised you, no doubt, by sending for you to my house, Wilfred," she said, when he entered it, for the first time since his marriage, and she drew a chair for him near to herself; " but not more than I shall surprise you by what I am about to say. You know how very much I esteem Mr. Lester," she proceeded, the delicate pink rising to her cheeks. " How unwilling I have been throughout this business to say a word that could reflect on his judgment or on Lady Adelaide's——"

" Margaret, excuse me, but I would rather not discuss Lady Adelaide. I might lose my temper," interposed Wilfred. " It was a dark day for me and Maria when my father married her."

Margaret thought within herself that it had not been a particularly bright day for someone else. She resumed. " Did you ever know that there was a sum of money given you by Mrs. Hesketh, to be paid to you when you came of age."

" No; I think not."

" I am not speaking of a trifle that was left to you in her will, and which only devolves to you on the demise of

Mr. Lester; I speak of a sum of twelve hundred pounds.
Mrs. Hesketh was your godmother, as you know; and the
day you were christened, she brought with her a deed, which
she flung—I remember it well—into Katherine's lap—I
should have said your mother's lap, Wilfred. It was a deed
of gift of twelve hundred pounds. The money was at once
paid over to Mr. Lester, and he holds it still. The deed
stated that it was to be paid to you absolutely the day you
were of age, your mother receiving the interest towards your
maintenance."

Wilfred's dark blue eyes lighted up with a fire not recently
seen there. "And where is the deed! Where's the
money? Who has it?" he reiterated.

"Mr. Lester has the deed. I spoke to him about the
money a short time ago, when things were getting bad with
you and Edith. His answer to me was, that the money had
been paid to you in the shape of an allowance; that finding
himself unable to furnish you with funds from his own
resources, he had used this money of yours for that purpose.
Now, I think Mr. Lester could not do this. So far as I
believe, he was bound to pay that sum over to you when you
came of age, with proper legal formality. If so, it is due to
you still; and you might, I think, claim it without further
delay."

Wilfred rose up. "What a shame!" he uttered.

"Listen, Wilfred. Mr. Lester *may* have been legally
justified in paying it to you, as he says. In any case, I feel
sure he could no more pay you the whole sum than I could
pay it. My advice to you would be to go to him in a
friendly spirit, and ask what he will or can do. If he
gave you a hundred pounds to begin with, it would be
something."

A hundred pounds! A hundred pounds would be as a
gold mine to poor reduced Wilfred. In his glad impulse,
he was darting away, but Margaret laid her calm hand on
his and made him sit down again until he should more fully
understand the case, and had discussed with her his precise
line of conduct. Above all, she begged him not to quarrel
with his father.

That same afternoon, Wilfred went to Danesheld Hall, and presented himself before his father in the study. Civilly and respectfully he requested a few minutes' audience, and Mr. Lester was surprised into making no resistance to the petition. Wilfred sat down and entered on his business, temperately stating what had come to his knowledge: that there was a sum of money, twelve hundred pounds, belonging to him, now lying in his father's hands, but not stating whence he had derived the information.

Mr. Lester was taken aback, but he did not show it. He was perfectly cool, answering, with matter-of-fact equanimity, that Wilfred had received the money.

"I think not, sir," said Wilfred. "This money requires to be paid over to me formally, and you know that nothing of the sort has been done. You have never as much as mentioned to me that you held it."

"Miss Bordillion has been giving you this information, I see," observed Mr. Lester. "The money was paid to you in the shape of a yearly allowance, and you spent it, which of course was your own affair."

"But the money could not be so paid to me," persisted Wilfred. "The deed of gift, as I understand, was so worded that it could not be paid in that way."

"You are mistaken, Wilfred."

"Have you the deed?"

"I have. It is there."

Mr. Lester pointed to a small iron safe, which had stood in the corner of his study as long as Wilfred could remember.

"Will you allow me to read it, sir?"

"Certainly not. To what end? You can believe my word. After I had paid over the money to you as an allowance, a doubt arose to myself whether what I had done was legal, or whether I was not still responsible for the sum. Upon that I submitted the deed to counsel."

"Well?" cried Wilfred, for Mr. Lester had stopped.

"Well, the opinion returned to me was, that the deed was not so clearly worded as it ought to have been, and therefore the interpretation I had put upon it (that of

paying over the money in a somewhat different manner
from what on the whole it appeared to enjoin) would hold
good."

There was a pause.

" You must let me see the deed, sir."

" I shall not let you see it," said Mr. Lester.   " To what
end, I ask ? "

" That I may be myself convinced that there is nothing
coming to me."

" You may allow my word to convince you of it, for it is
the truth."

And Wilfred Lester knew by the hard, set countenance,
the firm tone, that further pressure on this point would be
hopeless.   Never, with his father's consent, would he obtain
sight of the deed.   And the colloquy went on to hasty words :
but Wilfred calmed down.

" I did not come wishing to inconvenience you, sir.   I
should not think of asking for the whole sum at once," he
resumed, really wishing to be friendly and conciliate his
father.   " If you would only let me have a hundred pounds
of it now, I should be satisfied."

Mr. Lester quite laughed, and Wilfred, with some agitation,
entered on his troubles, and craved some help as a favour,
if not as a right.   He showed his father the writ ; he spoke
of his wife's absolute necessities.

" You must be aware that you have brought all this upon
yourselves.   What else could you expect would come of
such a marriage as yours ? "

" You make a pretence of punishing me for my marriage,
but I don't suppose you blame me so much in your heart,"
said Wilfred boldly.   " Father, from my soul I believe you
would have done the same under similar circumstances.   I
believe you would have sanctioned it yourself but for Lady
Adelaide.   She has always been my enemy ; she has stood
between us ever since she entered the house."

" That's enough," said Mr. Lester.

Wilfred rose.   His lips were quivering, his dark-blue
eyes went out with a strange yearning to his father's.

" Give me only a little help, father ! This poor ten pounds

for which I am about to be sued. I ask it for Edith's
sake."

There was—or Wilfred fancied it—a shade of pity in
Mr. Lester's countenance. He might possibly have yielded
—possibly; but at that moment Lady Adelaide entered the
room, her air and countenance imperious. She drew aside
her gown with a scornful gesture as she passed Wilfred to
confront her husband.

"They told me your son was here, but I did not at first
believe it. Can you allow his presence, Mr. Lester? and
thus make light of filial rebellion in the sight of my
children?"

"He is not here by my wish, Adelaide. I had already
dismissed him. There's the door, sir. Why don't you
go?" he sharply added, turning from his wife, for whom he
was drawing forward a chair.

Wilfred crushed the writ into his pocket, and swung
away with an ugly word, to tell Margaret of his defeated
mission. By the time he reached her house, he was in a
comfortable fury, and could no more have helped giving
vent to it than—— But he did not try to do so. Mr. Lydney
was there; Maria was there; but it was all one to the
angry man.

"He means to keep me out of the money altogether, Margaret. He wholly refuses me a sight of the deed, though it
was in the very room at his elbow. I told him my wife was
dying of want; I told him I was going to the dogs, or
something worse. Look here" (dashing the writ out of his
pocket), "I showed him this, and begged him like any men-
dicant to help me over *this* stile, and save me from prison.
But no——"

"Oh, Wilfred! what's the matter?" came the interruption, wrung from Maria in her terror. "What is that
paper?"

"Pshaw!" returned Wilfred, crushing it into his pocket
again. "Margaret, I do think he would have helped me a
little; but Lady Adelaide came in and stopped it. If there's
justice in heaven—— Maria, what's the matter? Don't pull
at me like that."

" I think you want a strait-waistcoat, Wilfred," put in Miss Bordillion. " You will frighten me presently, as well as Maria."

" He as good as taunted me with my wings being clipped, when I said something about going to law with him," continued Wilfred, in his passion. " I'll get at that deed if I have to break into the house whilst he's sleeping; I will. The money's mine, and he's afraid of my reading it."

" I will not hear this, Wilfred," interposed Miss Bordillion, with stern authority.

" Very well. I see you are all against me. I may go to the dogs my own way."

Snatching up his hat, he went forth from the house in the same passion that he had entered it. Margaret Bordillion, regardless of the fact that she wore neither bonnet nor shawl, went into the road after him.

Of course the scene had told Mr. Lydney a great deal. Maria, ashamed, puzzled, and terrified, began some apology for its having taken place in his presence—the presence of a stranger.

" A stranger ! " he replied, standing before her. " I was in great hopes that you no longer considered me in that light, Miss Lester."

" It is true," she murmured, " we do not. And yet, when I look back and remember how very short a period, counting by time, it is that we have known you, I can only wonder at the fact. We seem to be like old friends ; but I fear it is very bold of me to say so."

His lips parted with a smile, and somehow it brought the colour back to Maria's face. " I wish to be a friend," he said, his voice assuming a low tone of earnest confidence. " I think your brother wants one, Miss Lester. May I speak to you on this subject without reserve ? "

Indeed, she needed some one to do it, for her heart felt sick and faint within her for her brother's sake. She looked at Mr. Lydney by way of answer—a piteous, beseeching look, and half her terror went out of her. It may have appeared to her that there was help, protection, in that strong form ; it had long appeared to her that there was perfect truth in the good, earnest, handsome face.

"I dread—I scarcely know what I do dread," she murmured.

"You dread that, smarting under privation and unmerited wrong, Wilfred may be drawn into escapades not altogether honourable to the son and heir of Squire Lester ? "

The son and heir! Was the word spoken in mockery? The burning tears rushed into Maria's eyes.

"Have faith in me," he impressively said, bending a little as if to give an earnest to his words, and taking both her hands in his. "All that one man can do for another, I will do for your brother. He saved my life; I will try and save him from trouble."

"I have so loved Wilfred," she said, in apology for her fast falling tears; "I have until now so looked up to him; he is four years older than I am. Mamma died; papa grew estranged from us; we had only each other to care for."

"Trust to me, Miss Lester."

But she could not get her hands free, and felt rather confused in consequence, her words and manner being confused likewise.

"He is so impetuous, you see; he thinks he is being wronged; and he is painfully anxious about his wife. Oh, Mr. Lydney, if you *could* help him! I should not know how to thank you; I could never repay you."

A very peculiar smile arose to his lips, a warm light illumined his eyes, and a sudden glow thrilled through Maria Lester's heart. Mr. Lydney released the hands, for Miss Bordillion was coming in.

CHAPTER XXV.

THE RENDEZVOUS IN THE WOOD.

MR. LYDNEY and Wilfred Lester stood together against the railings of the cottage. The former, hastening to overtake the latter, had found him leaning, in a woo-begone fashion, on the said railings. In truth the disappointment resulting from the interview with Squire Lester was great, as well as the reaction from the anger into which Mr. Wilfred had subsequently put himself. Lydney laid his hand upon his shoulder.

"Shake off dull care and send it packing, Lester. What's the matter?"

"The matter! You were present just now at Miss Bordillion's."

"There's no need for you to be out of heart."

"When a fellow's out at elbows and out of credit, out of help and out of friends, there's enough need. I'm hard-up in all ways; and by Jove! I don't care who knows it: the shame lies with others, not with me."

"If I am cognisant of your troubles, you may thank yourself for speaking of them before me. Pardon me if I——"

"I don't care who knows of them, I say," said Wilfred, impatiently interrupting the implied apology. "I'd mount a public rostrum with pleasure, and proclaim them to the world. Still, I don't see any good in your recurring to the subject."

"No good at all, unless I could help you out of them; which I dare say I can do, if you will only behave like a reasonable being. Lester," he continued earnestly, a genuine emotion checking his free utterance, "I owe my life to you; but for your brave exertions that awful night, I should not now be here. At the risk of your own life, you saved mine. It is a debt that I can never repay, but you may lessen my sense of the obligation by allowing me to be your friend, by treating me as a brother."

"Risking my life!" said Wilfred, with a mocking laugh.
"As to that, it's not so valuable to me that I need care to
prolong it."

"It may be valuable to your wife, at any rate. Suffer me
to be to you what a brother would be, if you had one. You
are wrongfully kept out of money: I have more than I
know what to do with. Let me be your banker."

The red colour flushed into the face of Wilfred Lester.
He did not speak, and Mr. Lydney resumed:

"Borrow of me as one friend would of another—as I dare
say you have been borrowed from in your day—as I may
have borrowed. You can repay me, you know, when things
come round again."

"When things come round again!" echoed Wilfred
Lester in derision. "They will never come round. That
twelve hundred pounds—but I swear I'll not relinquish that
without a fight for it."

"Never mind thinking of it now. How much shall I
lend you?"

"Are you serious in making this offer?" asked Wilfred
Lester.

"Serious!" returned Lydney; "what do you mean? Is
it anything so very great, that you should doubt or
hesitate?"

"Then you are a good fellow, Lydney, and it's more than
anyone else has done for me. I'll take ten pounds, to get
rid of this cursed writ."

"Nonsense about ten pounds! You must——"

"No more—no more," interrupted Wilfred, the sensitive
colour dyeing his face again. "Save me from prison, and
I'll thank you; but I want none for myself."

Mr. Lydney looked him full in the face, and spoke in low
tones.

"There may be others who want it, if you do not."

"Not a fraction more," said Wilfred, passionately. "I
would not take this, but that it's necessary I should keep out
of prison."

"Oh, Lester! why won't you treat me as a friend?"

"I am treating you as a friend in taking so much; and I

thank you truly, Lydney, and will repay you when I can. As to other assistance—no." And the emphatic denial closed the matter.

Wilfred Lester paid a visit to Mr. Apperly, the solicitor. He was formerly the man of business of Squire Lester, but a rupture took place between them, and the master of Danesheld Hall went over to an opposition house, which Mr. Apperly had never forgiven.

"Tell you about the deed of gift!" exclaimed the lawyer, in answer to Wilfred. "What is there to tell? I believe the fact to be just this: that when Mr. Lester made you the yearly allowance before you came of age, he had not the least intention that it should come out of your own money. But he had become so embarrassed in his circumstances when the time arrived for paying the twelve hundred pounds, that he seized upon the pretext of having paid it in that yearly allowance. That, I fancy, was the case: and I shouldn't care if he heard me say it."

"What he says is, that he paid it me after I came of age; that it was, in fact, the allowance he made me when I was in the Guards."

"Oh, that's what he says, is it? I misunderstood you. Well, it amounts to almost the same thing."

"Could he do it—legally?"

"That depends upon how the deed is worded."

"Did you never read it?" asked Wilfred.

"Yes, I read it at the time the gift was made, when you were a baby. Too long ago for me to remember its provisions now. My impression is that he could not do it."

"In which case I could now compel him to pay me the twelve hundred pounds?"

"Clearly. And with interest for the years that have elapsed since you were twenty-one. Of course I only give this opinion conditionally," continued Mr. Apperly. "It would depend entirely on the wording of the deed."

"Would you take up the affair for me?" inquired Wilfred, his eyes lighting with eagerness.

Mr. Apperly paused. He did not by any means approve of Mr. Wilfred Lester's recent escapades, from his marriage

down to his poverty; men, as a rule, had no more business
to be poor than they had to contract a marriage with nothing
to live on. On the other hand, he liked justice in the
abstract, and he would very much like to administer a
wholesome pill to Squire Lester.

"I could not answer your question one way or the other
without first seeing the deed."

"But he won't let me have the deed."

The lawyer raised his eyebrows. "Then I cannot help
you."

Wilfred sat, gloomily twirling his shabby felt hat, believing—as he had long believed—that all the world was
against him.

"Would you mind doing this much, Mr. Apperly—write
to my father, and request him to allow you to look over the
deed? To look over it on my part as my solicitor?"

"I don't mind doing that. And if he lets me see it, I
will then tell you whether I think you can stir in the affair
or not."

And there it was left. Wilfred took his departure, and
Mr. Apperly wrote to Mr. Lester, and awaited his answer.

The facts were very much as the lawyer surmised.
Squire Lester, in his increasing embarrassments, had made
no move to pay the money over when his son came of age.
Wilfred was unconscious of the bequest, and there was no
one to come forward and compel Mr. Lester to pay it.
Later, when conscience told him that he might be liable to
be called upon for it at any moment, he hit on the expedient
of pleading that it had been paid in the yearly allowance,
should he ever be questioned. To give Mr. Lester his due,
he was not sure whether the law would or would not uphold him in this: and once, when a gentleman was temporarily staying with him, a young man just called to the
bar, he opened the matter, showed him the deed, and asked
whether the law would not justify his view of the case.
Whatever this young barrister's opinion might have been, he
clearly saw what his host wished it to be: perhaps he had
no very certain opinion himself either way. It seemed to
him to be a nice question, he answered—one he could not

speak positively upon ; but Squire Lester had probably the
law with him.

Squire Lester put the parchment back in his iron safe,
reassured, and had thought no more about it from that day
to this.

It was a clear night, as bright as stars could make it,
when Mr. Lydney walked forth to his rendezvous with Ben
Beecher the poacher. The place appointed—a circle, or
ring, in the wood where the trees grew not, and the moss
was soft underfoot, which had probably given rise to its
appellation in Daneshold of the "Fairy Circle"—was as
obscure a spot as Mr. Beecher could have chosen.

Nevertheless, Mr. Lydney and his friend were not alone.
One was assisting at the interview whom they little suspected—my Lord Dane. To give that nobleman his due, he
was above playing the eavesdropper in general ; but his
suspicions in regard to Lydney had been unpleasantly
awakened, and he felt it to be a duty to society to confirm
them by any means in his power. Good-natured also, and
easy though he was in general, those troublesome poachers
were carrying things beyond a joke. To imprison the
whole lot for two years, Lydney included, would have
greatly solaced the heart of Lord Dane.

" It has been of no go, sir," was Ben Beecher's salutation,
as he came stealing up through the trees to Mr. Lydney,
who was at the spot first. " The box has not been lifted."

" No ! " exclaimed Mr. Lydney, in an accent that betrayed
his keen disappointment.

Lord Dane's ears were strained to catch the tones. But
now, see how unkind was fate ! Instead of taking up their
position on this side of the circle where my lord was, the
two conspirators took it up on the other. His lordship,
ensconced where the trees were densest, did not dare to
move an inch either way, lest the rustling of the leaves
should attract their attention. It is true, Mr. Lydney and
Mr. Beecher paced about occasionally whilst they talked,
by which means Lord Dane's ears came in for a few chance
words. That they were conspiring against every head of
game upon his lands he fully believed.

"I have seen the right men, sir, and I can assure you they know nothing whatever of the box," continued Mr. Beecher. "They think you must look for it in the Castle."

"What reason have they for thinking so?"

"Well, I don't know that they have much reason, but it's their opinion. Sharp cards they are too, and their opinion's worth having, sir. For one thing, they say that if the box had been stolen they should know of it. Young Shad asserts that it was carried into the Castle."

"But Shad's word is not to be depended on."

"He would not deceive these men," returned Beecher, in significant tones. "At any rate, sir, if the box is not in the Castle, they have no notion where it can be."

The words bore an accent of truth, but Mr. Lydney was aware that these men might deceive as well as Shad.

"Would a higher reward bring forth the box?" he asked.

"Not if you offered a bank-full—not if you offered a thousand pounds," answered Beecher, unconsciously naming the very sum he announced on the morrow. "What they haven't got they can't give up; and they think you must look for it in the Castle."

"But Lord Dane says it is not in the Castle. More than that, the police say so, and they have searched it."

"Has Lord Dane any interest in hiding or detaining the box?" asked Beecher; and Lord Dane heard the audacious words, for they had halted near to him.

"Why do you ask that?"

"Because it's said that there are places in the Castle where things could be put away; and the police would never suspect them—no, not if they went about with magnifying-glasses. I was talking to my old father about this matter. Says he: 'If my Lord Dane wanted to keep that box in hiding, he could do it fast enough.' Tales go, sir, that in years gone by, smugglers used to stow their booty in the Castle, and that Lord Dane (he was grandfather to the late lord) was in league with them."

How did my Lord Dane's ears like being regaled with that? Mr. Lydney was surprised; he put little faith in the information.

"Does your father know where these hiding-places are?"

"Not a bit of it. He's not sure there are any; it's only a sort of tradition. No one would brave Lord Dane's anger by saying such a thing openly."

"A martinet, when crossed, I suppose?"

"All the Danes are something of that sort," was Beecher's answer; "even the captain was, and he was the most liked of all. He was killed, poor fellow!"

"Ay, I have heard him spoken of since I came here. My landlord was his servant. A hot-tempered man, he says, but generous."

"Why, sir, Ravensbird was arrested for the murder," cried Beecher, "but he was soon released again. After that they suspected a packman, but they could never find him."

"Was the present Lord Dane—Mr. Herbert he was called then, according to Ravensbird—ever suspected?" asked Mr. Lydney, carelessly.

"Heart alive, no!" returned the poacher in astonishment. "Whatever made you think that, sir?"

"My good man, don't run away with a wrong notion. I merely asked the question. Gentlemen quarrel and wrestle, sometimes, and Captain Dane's fall might have been accidental."

Beecher shook his head, and Lord Dane from his hiding-place distinctly saw him do it, for they were near him still.

"There was not a breath of suspicion against him, sir, no grounds for it. That puts me in mind, though. At the time it happened there was a chap declared he saw Mr. Herbert Dane run off the heights; but he was three sheets in the wind, and couldn't see straight. We made him hush his tongue."

"What chap was it?"

"Well, it was a sort of half-brother of mine. He's dead now."

Beecher's words were interrupted by a shot. He turned his head, listening, and then crossed quickly to the other side of the circle, peering through the trees. Mr. Lydney followed him, and this took them beyond the hearing of Lord Dane.

"If it was later, I should have said that shot's a ruse to deceive the keepers," remarked Beecher. "They have grown sharp, now Lord Dane's at home. We had a rare time of it whilst he was away. It was within an ace of being hot work last night."

"What pleasure can you find in this lawless life?" asked Mr. Lydney in tones of remonstrance. "It is full of danger."

"A man must live, sir."

"But a man might live honestly."

"Not when he has gone in for this sort of thing, and made it his trade. Who'd trust him, or help him to honest work again?"

"I would for one. If a man turned back to the straight path after straying from it, I would give him countenance and help."

"Ah, well, sir, it's easy to talk. I wish I could have found your box: that fifty guineas might have helped some of us."

"Keep a look-out still; it is possible you may hear of it. Meanwhile, that will repay you for the trouble you have already taken."

Ben Beecher looked twice at the sovereign before he believed it was real.

"I tell you what it is, sir," he cried, in a burst of gratitude; "if we had such people as you to deal with in this Dancsheld, we might turn back into straight paths yet. Thank you, sir; and a hearty good-night to you."

When the coast was clear Lord Dane emerged from his place of concealment, wiping his brow like a man in utter consternation.

"A pretty devil's plot these fellows are hatching!" quoth he. "Secret places in the Castle, forsooth! If ever a man deserved hanging, it's that traitor Lydney. The whole set of poachers are gentlemen compared with him."

And in fact, Lord Dane, having heard only snatches of the conversation, and those snatches happening to affect himself, did believe he had cause to take up a very bad opinion of Lydney. The incidental question put by that gentleman: "Was Mr. Herbert suspected of having been the adversary of Captain Dane in the night struggle?" was enough to anger him from its very insolence. He went home deliberating in his own mind how to rid the neighbourhood of so doubtful a character.

On the following morning a handbill appeared outside the police-station. It contained a description of the lost box, and offered a reward of a thousand pounds for its recovery intact. The notice took Danesheld by storm, and the crowds that collected to stare at it and make their comments, sensibly impeded the traffic.

It happened that Lord Dane was in the town rather early, and came right upon the commotion at the police-station.

When he saw its cause—the handbill—he stood still with astonishment, feeling inclined to rub his eyes, and make sure that he was not dreaming. Striding through the crowd, he went into the station.

"What's the meaning of that notice, Bent?" inquired he of the inspector, who was standing writing within the railings.

"Ah, a fine mob it's collecting, isn't it, my lord?" returned Mr. Bent, respectfully coming forward to receive his noble visitor. "Stupid people! It's a pity but they had something better to do."

"The reward, I alluded to. What's the meaning of it?"

"It's being offered, my lord. We had the bills ready yesterday afternoon; but Mr. Lydney stopped their issue until this morning. We are having them put up on the walls, and in the shop-windows. The box must be valuable, my lord, to call forth the offer of a thousand pounds reward."

"But who does offer it?" asked Lord Dane in his astonishment. "Where's your authority?"

"We have it from Mr. Lydney."

Lord Dane's lip curled.

"Take care what you are about, Bent. It is very easy to *offer* a large sum. I might offer a million, without being able to find it. This Lydney could no more find a thousand pounds than he could find fifty."

" My lord, he said freely that the box was none of his, and that the reward would come from the pocket of the owner, not from his own. He offered to deposit vouchers for the money."

" Had you taken him at his word, you might have found what the offer was worth. Do you remember the charge I gave you, Bent—to try and discover who this man is, and what he wants here ? "

" Yes," said Bent; " and I put a few questions to him, but I got nothing satisfactory in reply. He said he was of English descent, and of good family, and that's about all he would say. When I asked what his business was in the place, he said the sea had cast him up upon it, and here he should stay till he had found the box. He seems to be a gentleman, my lord."

" A gentleman ! " scornfully echoed Lord Dane. " Whilst you have been questioning, Bent, I have been working, and I have discovered a great deal more of this Mr. Lydney and his doings than he would like to have known. Accident gave me a clue, and I followed it up."

Lord Dane's manner was peculiar : his voice had dropped to a low tone. Mr. Bent drew nearer to him.

" He is in league with the poachers—a poacher himself. I traced him last night into the wood; he was there with that Ben Beecher, the two conspiring together. They were there the previous night also, to my positive knowledge ; in fact, they are together every night, beyond doubt. That's your gentleman of family ! "

" Is it possible ! " uttered the inspector. " Perhaps I had better take down the notices."

" You can use your own discretion in regard to that," was the answer, delivered loftily, as if the point, one way or the other, were quite beneath the noble speaker. " But I must request you to understand one thing, Bent : that I have told you this in confidence, for yourself only. Keep things quiet, and you may get at something. My only object is to banish the fellow from the neighbourhood ; to put him on his guard will not aid me in this. He can neither be driven from the place, nor yet put into prison, unless he breaks the law. The wood is my property, but its paths are open to the public, and the man cannot be taken up for frequenting them, however evil his intentions may be. Wait and watch, and we shall have him. You take me, Bent?"

"Quite so, your lordship."

Lord Dane went out, and Mr. Bent fell into thought. To doubt the information did not occur to him, though he could not have believed it of a young man who seemed so entirely a gentleman. Something of this latter feeling caused the inspector to hesitate as he was about to tear down the bill posted outside. It might be as well, perhaps, that he first of all spoke to Lydney, for the young man *had* offered to give vouchers for the money, and there was no ignoring that. So he sent a message to the Sailors' Rest, desiring Mr. Lydney to come up at once and speak to him.

And the result was, that before the day closed, Mr. Lydney's landlord, Richard Ravensbird, became security for the thousand pounds reward to the police authorities.

This fact exceedingly astonished Lord Dane when he heard of it. He deemed it his duty to give a hint to Ravensbird, although he was no particular favourite of his —the man's manner was too independent to allow of his being much of a favourite with anyone, and especially independent it had been towards Lord Dane. Taking an opportunity to walk down to the Sailors' Rest, he was received by Mr. Ravensbird himself in Sophie's parlour.

"I called to speak to you on a little matter, Ravensbird, in your own interest," began Lord Dane, accepting the chair presented to him, whilst the ex-servant of the family stood. "You have been answering, I hear, for the thousand pounds offered by this lodger of yours, Lydney. Is it true?"

"It is, my lord," replied Ravensbird.

"But if the box is found, you may be called upon to pay it!"

"He would pay it himself," returned Ravensbird. "The police thought it well to be on the safe side, and my answering for the money was a matter-of-form, just to satisfy them."

"But you may be called upon to find the money, I say!" reiterated Lord Dane.

"No, my lord, I've no fear of that. This young Mr. Lydney has shown me documents and papers to convince me that he is sufficiently responsible."

"What documents?" came the quiet question.

"Bonds for invested money and railway shares," replied Ravensbird. "At first Mr. Lydney thought of depositing these with the police, but he concluded it would be a shorter way if he showed them to me, and I answered for him. Of course Bent knows I am good for a thousand pounds," added Ravensbird, with a slight laugh.

"Well, now, Ravensbird," returned Lord Dane, and his tone invited confidence, for he really wished to do a friendly action, "I came here for the purpose of giving you a quiet hint of the state of affairs, and you had better withdraw your word whilst there's time. It was exceedingly rash of you to promise such a thing for a stranger.

"But he showed me these bonds and vouchers, my lord," repeated Ravensbird, speaking as if the fact were an unanswerable argument.

"They were false, Ravensbird. False, or forged, or something of the sort: I could take upon myself to answer for it. In short—but I say this only to your private ear—I have discovered that this fellow, Lydney, is a bad character. He consorts with poachers, is no doubt one himself: an adventurer who schemes to live. Withdraw your word to Bent without loss of time; and the next thing turn the fellow out of your house."

"Surely I can't do that, my lord, as long as he pleases to stay in it."

"Not do it! Does he pay his bill?"

"Yes; he does. He settled up with me this very morning."

"Ravensbird, you will oblige *me* by getting rid of him," rather peremptorily spoke Lord Dane. "I never show quarter to that sort of characters, or approve of its being shown. If the man is not in your debt, which I am surprised to hear, turn him out on some other plea."

"But, my lord," debated Ravensbird, "I cannot put forth a

gentleman in that fashion. So long as he conducts himself
properly in my house, and pays his way in it———"

"A gentleman of course you could not; but an impostor
you can," interrupted Lord Dane. "The man has wormed
himself into some of the best families here, and—and—
knowing what I do know of him, I feel myself in a degree
answerable for any unpleasant consequences that may
ensue. Is that a man to countenance in your house,
Ravensbird?"

Ravensbird shook his head: not a more obstinate spirit
existed than his, when he took up an opinion.

"What Mr. Lydney may do out-of-doors, or where he
may visit, I know nothing of, my lord, and it's not my place
to enquire into it. I see nothing wrong in him myself,
neither have I heard it of him. In this house he conducts
himself as a quiet, well-behaved, honest gentleman; and
that is all I have to regard. My wife is uncommonly taken
with him.

"I particularly wish this done, Ravensbird. You are my
tenant, and must oblige me."

"My lord, I am your tenant, but I pay you rent for your
house, and am master of it. In taking the Sailors' Rest, I
did not part with my freedom of action. I should be happy
to oblige your lordship in any other way, but to turn out a
harmless gentleman (as far as I see) is what I can't do."

"Say you won't, Ravensbird?"

"Well, my lord, I'll say I won't if you prefer it,"
answered the man, though with every token of civility and
respect. "If this young Mr. Lydney behaved himself ill
under my notice, it would be a different thing."

The sturdy independence of his tenant, compatible
though it was with the character of Ravensbird, angered
Lord Dane not a little.

"Have you forgotten that I could thrust you from this
house at six weeks' notice, Ravensbird?"

"Well, no, my lord, I am not likely to forget it; and I
have never known why you inserted the clause in my
lease."

"You stand a chance, I think, of its being acted upon."

"As your lordship pleases, of course," was the equable answer: and Mr. Ravensbird never stood his ground more independently than now, as he gazed into the face of the peer. "I should be sorry to leave my house, for it suits me; still, there are other tenements to be had in Danesheld."

Lord Dane moved to the door, putting on his hat. "It seems that I have met with little satisfaction in coming here," he observed. "Considering that you were once our servant, Ravensbird, I think it is your duty to behave differently."

For once, a tinge of red flashed into the man's sallow face.

"I beg your pardon, my lord; I was servant to the Honourable Harry Dane, I was not servant to Mr. Herbert."

It needed not that to complete his insolence. Lord Dane strode haughtily away, Ravensbird attending him with due respect. At the outer door, a doctor's boy was giving in a bottle of medicine.

"For Mr. Home," said the lad.

It reminded Lord Dane of the other passenger who had been saved from the wreck. He wheeled round on Ravensbird.

"Has Mr. Home not gone away yet?"

"He has not found himself well enough to go, my lord; we have had to call in Dr. Green. He is waiting, too, for remittances, he says."

Lord Dane threw back his head as he walked away. The answer seemed to imply that Richard Ravensbird stood a chance of losing by this other traveller. "And serve him right, too!" thought my lord.

CHAPTER XXVI.

A DOSE FOR TIFFLE.

A LAPSE of time occurred, and it was now October. The thousand pounds reward still stared Danesheld in the face at conspicuous halting points, but nothing came of it; the japanned box had not turned up, and at times Mr. Bent felt inclined to indorse Lord Dane's opinion, that Lydney himself had possession of the lost property.

Depredations on Lord Dane's preserves went on audaciously. Whole dozens of game were bagged, the poachers seemed to enjoy their full swing, and the keepers were set at defiance night after night. People given to irony said the keepers kept out of the way instead of showing fight— that their easy reign during their lord's ten years' absence had made them timid. Lord Dane heard this, and went into a fit of wrath, subsequently to be visited on his keepers. He was losing patience, and felt inclined to offer a thousand pounds himself to catch the poachers. Heartily would he have given it had Lydney been entrapped with them; but nothing tangible could as yet be brought against him. That he was sometimes in the woods at night, making himself at home with the poachers, Lord Dane knew for a fact; and at these times he was generally side by side with Wilfred Lester.

For Wilfred Lester appeared to be going in for lawless doings quite as openly as the poachers. A very bitter feeling, born of despair and of a sense of injustice, had taken possession of this young man. Squire Lester had promptly answered Mr. Apperly's note, and declined to allow the deed to be read; the money had been paid over to his son, he wrote, therefore, to read the deed would answer no purpose whatever. Before Wilfred had ceased his explosions at this answer, the lawyer left Danesheld for France, on business for a client. His stay there was destined to be protracted; and Wilfred Lester was not the only client incommoded by it. Mr. Lydney, who had tardily

made up his mind to consult the lawyer as to future proceedings touching the lost box, called at Mr. Apperly's office
for that purpose the very day after that gentleman's departure, and was now waiting his return with impatience.

Meanwhile, things seemed to be going on more smoothly
at Wilfred Lester's in regard to domestic affairs. Sally
applied to some relative of hers at a distance, that she called
her " step-uncle," and it brought forth a little ready money.
She also contrived, by dint of large promises, to obtain
further credit from different tradespeople. Mrs. Lester
secretly would sigh, and wonder, with fear and trembling,
when the supplies would be paid for. Her husband evinced
that utter indifference to consequences which is akin to
despair ; and, had Sally pledged his credit for hundreds, it
was all the same to him. All Wilfred Lester's wrath just
now was directed against his father for refusing him permission to read the deed ; he took up a notion that the deed
would prove the money was still due to him, and that Mr.
Lester's refusal arose from that fact. At first he was very
loud and noisy over it, threatening revenge, vowing he
would obtain possession of the deed by some desperate
means ; but this subsided into sullen silence, and he spoke
of his wrongs no more.

A coolness was arising in Daneshold towards Mr. Lydney.
And this not from any private disclosure of Lord Dane's,
but from a doubt springing naturally out of the state of
things. The heads of families who had learned to welcome
him, began to notice that he said no more of who he was,
and what he was, as intimacy increased ; on the contrary,
he observed a marked reticence on the point, and quietly
parried cunning hints as well as direct questions. It was
so very strange, people began to say, that a young man
should be thus thrown amongst them and never breathe a
syllable of his circumstances. When anything of this was
talked of in the presence of Lord Dane, his head would be
thrown back with a haughty gesture, and his lips curl in
scorn ; and this, coupled with Lord Dane's marked avoidance
of Mr. Lydney, was enough to damage him of itself. Mr.
Lydney was conscious of the doubtful feeling, and tacitly

bowed to it, withdrawing himself gradually from the houses where he had been welcomed; he still chatted with the families when they met abroad, but that was all. The only house where he was yet a frequent visitor was Miss Bordillion's, and he went now occasionally to Wilfred Lester's; at rare intervals, also, he called at Danesheld Hall. Lord Dane said little openly against him—he was waiting for proof.

Another week or two, and Danesheld awoke one clear, bright morning to be shaken to its centre. There had been a night encounter at last between the poachers and the keepers, and Lord Dane was enraged. The miserable keepers were worsted—one of them rather seriously hurt by a blow—and the poachers had got off triumphantly, scot-free. Lord Dane bestirred himself with a vengeance, and it was thought the men would be in custody before night.

Poor Maria Lester! She heard a whisper of evil, dropped by Tiffle, and an awful fear smote her for her brother. Sick, faint, trembling, she sat until sitting became unbearable, and then framed some excuse for going into Danesheld, thinking she might gather either confirmation or contradiction. She chose the path through the wood—a narrow public path much frequented in the day—and went along, quite unconscious that she had a follower. Tiffle happened to have devised an errand for herself into Danesheld at this hour, and took the opportunity to keep Miss Lester in view.

Maria was about half-way through the wood, and very near to the fairy circle, when she met Mr. Lydney, who was coming along with a smart step. Hastening towards him in her glad impulse, he caught her hands in his, and saw that she was unable to speak from agitation.

That the mutual attachment, which perhaps had taken root the first day they met on the heights, had grown into an impassioned, fervent love, was tacitly known to both of them. Not with love, however, was Maria trembling now, but with fear, as she murmured a question as to whether he had heard the news.

" I heard of it the first thing this morning," he said with a smile, retaining the hands he had taken in greeting.

" Do you know "—she could scarcely get out the words in her terrible agitation—"what men were in it? Have you heard of any in particular ? "

" No. I think the lawless fellows had their usual luck, and escaped recognition. I saw one man sneak out of the wood myself at one in the morning ; but it's no business of mine. I was returning from your brother's, where I spent the evening."

Maria's countenance changed ; her lips parting with suspense as she listened.

" And what Mrs. Lester will say to me for sitting there with her husband to that unconscionable hour, I know not," he resumed, appearing not to see the varying cheek. " I am going there now with this ; I promised it to Wilfred."

He touched a small pocket-book that lay in his breast-pocket. But Maria could keep up the play no longer ; and her very lips turned white.

" Oh, is it true ? You are not saying this to content me ? Are you sure you were with him all the evening ? "

" I never tell you anything but truth," he said, pressing her hands warmly. " It is all right indeed, Maria. I got into a discussion with Wilfred, and kept him up until one o'clock : the time slipped by unwarily."

The encounter with the keepers had taken place before half-past twelve, as Maria knew.

" How kind you are ! " she exclaimed, in the sudden revulsion of feeling.

" In what way ? " he asked, with a laugh. " Kind for telling you this, or for keeping Wilfred up shamefully, and running the risk of Mrs. Lester's displeasure ? "

" Kind in every way, I think," she answered, her face radiant. " But for you——"

Mr. Lydney raised his hand with a warning gesture, and Maria looked round in surprise. Clearing some spaces with a bound, he sprang upon young Mr. Shad, who was entwined round a tree in his favourite attitude, and listening with all his ears. He drew him forth, partly by the hair, partly by the arm, Shad yelling unmercifully. Maria said good-morning to Mr. Lydney, and went her way, leaving the capturer and the captured. Shad kicked, struggled, writhed, roared, but Mr. Lydney held him fast. In the midst of the disturbance, up came Tiffle.

"Well, if ever I heard such a noise!" cried she, innocently; "I thought it must be some young panthier got loose. Who is it? It's something like Granny Bean's Shad."

"He's going to kill me! he's wanting to whack me! he'd like to pull my hair up by the roots!" shrieked Shad. "Make him let me go."

"Let him go, please, sir," said Tiffle. "I'm sure you're too much a gentleman to strike a poor little weak boy."

"I'm sorry I have not my cane with me," said Mr. Lydney to his howling captive. "You should have tasted it well. But now listen, Mr. Shad: if ever I catch you dodging my steps or Miss Lester's again, I'll do my best to get you a month at the treadmill. You came up opportunely, Mrs. Tiffle," he added, releasing the boy.

"To prevent the beating?" cried Tiffle, peering round with her sly eyes.

"No; to hear my promise. The next time he attempts anything of this sort he shall surely suffer for it, although he is only your cat's-paw. Therefore you had better think twice before again giving him orders to track people."

"Oh!" screamed Tiffle, with a great show of indignation, "what treasonous words are these? *I* give him orders to track people! What have I to do with him? Am I a perlice officer?"

"You have more to do with him than the world suspects, and in more ways than one, unless I am mistaken," was Mr. Lydney's significant whispered retort. "Now, my good woman, set him to watch me again!"

The rush of scarlet on Tiffle's face was succeeded by a livid pallor. She shook her fist after him in impotent rage as he went on his way further into the wood.

"I vow I'll be revenged on him!" she breathed softly.

"I know what," cried Shad, "I saw him last night just after the row. I think he'd been in it!"

"Where did you see him?" returned Tiffle, eagerly.

"A-coming out o' Wilfred Lester's. I see him with my two eyes. The clocks was striking one. Maybe they'd just got home there from the fight."

"Did you see Will Lester, Shad? Was he out with them?"

"I didna see Lester, but I dare say he was in it," was the boy's reply. "I couldna see all that was there. Maybe Lester got wounded, and this one took him home. Any way, I'll swear he was coming out o' there as the clocks struck one: and Lester, he have never come abroad yet this morning." ・

Tiffle, giving a few directions to Shad, continued her way to Danesheld in a state of mind not to be envied. In turning out of a shop, during the execution of her commissions, she saw Lord Dane on the opposite side of the way, crossed over, and presumed to stop him. Tiffle had had plenty of time to cool down: but to cool down from an evil spirit was not in her nature.

"Well, Tiffle, and how are you?" cried Lord Dane, in his usual affable manner, albeit he rather wondered at the woman's putting herself in his way.

"I'm none the better, my lord—craving your lordship's pardon for answering so—for the dreadful tales told by every shop you go into. Is it true, my lord, that one of the poor keepers was cut in half?"

"Not quite," replied Lord Dane, checking a momentary inclination to laugh. "He is hurt rather badly in the head. I wish I could lay my finger on the villain that did it."

"My lord," said Tiffle in a low tone, as she glanced round to make sure there were no eaves-droppers passing at the moment, "one that's sure and safe, but that I should decline to name, saw him at one o'clock in the morning at Mr. Wilfred Lester's door. The opinion is," continued Tiffle, raising her sly eyes, "that Mr. Wilfred Lester was out too, and got wounded, and this other had been taking him home. If your lordship could get that Lydney transported, it would do good service to some in Danesheld, which is including of Miss Lester."

"Why do you bring in Miss Lester's name in particular?" returned Lord Dane, rather haughtily.

"Because there's cause to do it," answered Tiffle. "She's getting enthrilled by him; she is, my lord. I saw 'em meet just now in the wood. Miss Lester happened to be before me, and I was following on respectful, thinking of nothing, when he came swinging along—and a regular swing in the walk he has that Lydney, which is like his insolence, for I never saw anybody with it in these parts except the Danes. He squozed her two hands into his as if he had been her lovier."

Lord Dane's face grew black as night. Tiffle left her shaft to tell, and recurred to the other subject, before passing on.

"They do say that Mr. Wilfred has not been seen this morning, which, if he's wounded, my lord, is accounted for."

Lord Dane strode away. The woman's communication had not pleased him; at least that portion of it that related to Miss Lester. He did not fear with Tiffle that she was "getting enthrilled," but it vexed him very much that she should be even on speaking terms with that doubtful man, Lydney. Truth to say, Lord Dane, absorbed by these other unpleasant interests, had a little neglected his wooing; he had received Mr. Lester's permission to address Maria, but had not yet done so.

But that did not impose the necessity for his entering on it in this desperate haste. After quitting Tifflo, he went in search of Maria, and overtook her as she was returning home. Raising his hat, a pleasant smile on his handsome face, he shook hands with her, and walked on by her side. And there, in that hasty manner—in that perhaps not very appropriate place—he asked her to be his wife.

Her answer was in the negative; a gentle, hesitating sort of answer: for Maria really liked Lord Dane very much as an acquaintance, and was sorry to pain him. Of course he pressed his suit, and then she spoke more positively.

"Tell me why you reject me," he said, in his mortification.

"Indeed there is no particular reason, except—that I—do

not—do not care for you sufficiently to become your wife," she answered, blushing painfully.

"Ah, I see; I have spoken prematurely," he murmured, partly to himself. "Well Maria, we will let the question remain in abeyance for a time. Have you seen your brother this morning? Do you know how he is?"

"I met Sally, their servant, in the town just now, and she said her master and mistress were well," replied Maria, speaking absently, her thoughts elsewhere.

"Then there is no truth in the report that he is wounded?"

She turned her startled face on Lord Dane. He saw how incautious he had been.

"*Wounded?*"

"I heard it. I make no doubt it was an idle report."

"I am sure it must be," she said, trying to bring some colour into her lips again. "Mr. Lydney told me he was at the cottage last evening with Wilfred, and stayed there until one o'clock this morning. The time slipped on unwarily, he said."

The allusion angered Lord Dane; his face blazed with scorn.

"I do not doubt it," he rejoined; "I think it exceedingly likely they were together until that hour. Birds of a feather —but I should be very sorry to class Wilfred Lester, with all his faults and follies, with a man of Lydney's stamp."

"Mr. Lydney is a gentleman," she observed, in a low voice.

"Allow me to ask what proof you have of that, beyond his own assertion?"

Not being able to give any conclusive answer to this, Miss Lester walked on in silence, her face rather raised, its expression somewhat hard, and her heart beating with resentment for Lydney's sake. Lord Dane continued his hints against Lydney, but Maria was as one who heard not. She could have doubted the whole world rather than him.

"Mr. Lydney told me one day," she said, "that his search after his lost box had brought him into contact with some odd characters. He laughed as he said it."

" Ay, anything for a plausible excuse," was Lord Dane's
sarcastic answer. And it was on the tip of his tongue to
open the full budget of Lydney's misdoings—of his being
under the surveillance of the police. But he restrained
himself. At that moment Wilfred Lester came into view,
walking as well as he ever walked in his life, with no sign
or symptom of a wound about him. As if not wishing to
meet them, he leaped a fence and struck into the wood.
Maria looked at Lord Dane.

"Yes, I see that rumour at least was false. I wonder
whether I could not get him some Government appointment," mused Lord Dane aloud. "There are places to be
had where the work's easy enough and the pay good; four,
six, eight hundred a year. It would be very desirable to
get him out of Danesheld."

Desirable! Desirable for Wilfred to exchange his present
life of poverty, ill-repute, danger, the fear of which was
turning Maria's heart to sickness day and night, for respect-
ability and comfort and hundreds a year! She turned her
lovely face, crimson now with excitement, on Lord Dane.

"Oh, will you not interest yourself to get him one?"

"Willingly! Upon condition that you interest yourself
with yourself for me."

He spoke entirely in the moment's impulse, never intending to be dishonourable : for he really was above it.
Her fading colour recalled him to his words and the con-
struction that might be put upon them.

" I spoke in jest, Maria," he murmured. "As to Wilfred,
I will get him something if I can. The worst is, one has
to wait so long for any appointment that's worth having."

Lady Adelaide was in the drawing-room alone. Lord
Dane went in, but Maria ran upstairs, considerably shaken.
It is not possible for a thoughtful girl to receive an offer of
marriage unmoved. In Maria's case, she had been expecting
it, fearing it, and she had all along done what she could in
a quiet way to discourage its being made. It had come,
however, and had shown her, as if in a mirror suddenly
presented to view, the cause of her secret repugnance to it
—that her whole heart and love were given to William

Lydney. There was not so much as a corner in it for my
Lord Dane, or for any one else in the world.

And the conviction half terrified Maria, for Lydney was
a stranger, an alien, unknown to all; and trusted, as it
seemed, by none.

Lady Adelaide Lester was leaning back on the sofa, her
eyes closed in listlessness of spirit. The appearance of
utter ennui could not be mistaken: and her start at being
interrupted was one almost of terror. She wore a morning
robe of delicate hue, a sort of pale primrose; her golden
hair was shaded by a charming cap of lace, and her checks
flushed as she rose to greet Lord Dane.

"Yes, I was feeling very dull," she said in reply to a
remark of Lord Dane's. "I think I must have been asleep
since Mr. Lydney left."

Lord Dane's pulses stood still. "Has *he* been here? I
understood—I fancied he was not admitted here now."

"He came on some business, I think," carelessly returned
Lady Adelaide. "I know he spoke of an American document that required a magistrate's signature. No, we scarcely
ever see him now."

"Which perhaps may be no loss," was the slighting
answer. "A stranger, without introductions, is not always
to be received on trust, Lady Adelaide."

"That is true. I think what made me rather take to him
was his likeness to the Danes."

"His likeness to the Danes!" echoed his lordship, all the
Dane blood within him rising up in resentment.

"There is certainly a general resemblance. Did it never
strike you? He puts me in mind of both my aunt and
uncle; and, a little, of—Harry Dane."

She paused before the last name, as if not caring to
speak it. Lord Dane turned to the window and looked out
from it.

CHAPTER XXVII.

LORD DANE IN THE CHAPEL RUINS.

A few days, and time and events went on again. One gloomy evening close upon November, when it was very dark in the wood, and growing dark outside it, three men were together in close conversation. They thought themselves alone : but, lying flat on the ground, was Shad, the little serpent, listening, not for plans of another battue on the pheasants, but to as nefarious a scheme of house-breaking as was ever concocted. Shad had not yet assisted at great crimes, and his hair rose up on end as he cowered there. What with his personal fear (for Shad fully believed that if any untoward accident betrayed his proximity he should be riddled through with bullets), and what with the low tones the men conversed in, Shad obtained but a partial insight to the plot. Some mansion was about to be broken into, and the plate "bagged." Shad at length made out that it was Dane Castle, but that the night had yet to be fixed.

Waiting until the men dispersed—for he did not dare to move before—Shad rose up and tore along at his full speed to the spot where he was in the habit of meeting Tiffle. She was not there to-night, and Shad, with all his cunning, was at fault. He scarcely dared approach Mr. Lester's, which was strictly forbidden by Tiffle, but he was burning to be delivered of his secret. At length he crept, in his stealthy fashion, to the servants' entrance, and humbly asked to speak to Mrs. Tiffle.

The message was carried to Tiffle, and it brought forth an explosion of virtuous indignation. Granny Bean's Shad want her? Her! It must be a mistake! Tiffle, however, flounced out, and there, sure enough, stood the boy. Her first impulse was to treat him to a shaking.

"Don't you begin upon me, then, till you know why I come," whined Shad, cleverly dodging out of her reach. "I've been hearing murder."

" Hearing murder ! " repeated Tiffle.

" They are going to break into the Castle, murder Lord Dane, and lift the plate," whispered the boy. " It were them three, Drake, and Ben Beecher, and Nicholson. I've been with my nose to the ground ever since dark, listening to 'em, afraid to draw breath. I say, I wonder they go in for murder."

Tiffle wondered also. In point of fact, she was more intent on working petty ills and aggravations to her species than on great crimes. Murder bore as much horror to her ear as it does to most people's, and Tiffle received the communication with considerable doubt. Mr. Shad, however, was both positive and earnest, and he did not want either for brains or cunning.

" It's the murder that they're going for, more nor the plate," persisted the boy. " They said one to another, that while the business was being done they'd get a minute to stow in the plate-chest, and nobody be none the wiser. They said it twice over. I says to myself, as I listened, What *is* the business if it's not the plate-chest ? It must be to murder Lord Dane."

" Good boy ! " apostrophised Tiffle, proud of the excellent sense displayed. " Is Lydney to be in, Shad ? "

" That he is. They named his name only once, and then the rest said hush ! and after that they called him ' L.,' but I was up to it. It was him set them upon it; I heard 'em say so. Why, they said that while ' L.' went forward and ' did the business' they'd secure the plate. I say, shouldn't Lord Dane be told ? Look here ; one on 'em dropped this as they moved away."

" What ! is it you, Mrs. Tiffle ? You'll catch cold. And young Shad, as I'm alive ! "

The speaker was one of the Hall footmen, who had been out on some errand of his own. Mr. Lester and Lady Adelaide had gone that day to Great Cross, and the servants were in a degree at liberty.

" Come to beg a drop of my linerment for Granny Bean's rheumatics," responded Tiffle, shuffling into her pocket the paper Shad had produced. " Her back's a'most double with it to-night, he says. Have you brought a bottle, young Shad ? "

" A-groaning awful ! " returned Shad, on the verge of sympathising tears for the suffering Mrs. Bean. " And please, ma'am, I fell down coming along, and the bottle broke."

" What a careless boy you must be ! " reprimanded Tiffle. " I suppose I must find one. Wait there."

Tiffle sent out the stuff, or something that did for it, and then put her things on, casually remarking in the hearing of the servants that she had an errand to do for her lady in Danesheld. Not into Danesheld, however, did she bend her steps, but to Dane Castle.

Now, it may as well be stated that Mrs. Eliza Tiffle had her dreams of ambition. To become the housekeeper of a fine establishment like Dane Castle, with a master who, being a bachelor, could not be expected to look too clearly into things, was very dazzling to her aspiring vision. The housekeeper at the Castle was old, nearly useless, and Tiffle meant to be promoted to the place. Of course, should the thread of Lord Dane's life be severed by any such summary process as the one hinted at by Shad, Tiffle's rise into society must fade into air. She went to the Castle, and sent in a message by Bruff.

Lord Dane was alone in his dining-room—the large handsome room opening from the great hall. Solitary enough he looked in its depths. The rays of the chandelier fell on the dining table, with its snow-white cloth and rich appointments. A tempting table : but its master had turned his back on it to face the fire, where he sat musing.

" Tiffle ? What can she want with me ? " he wondered aloud to Bruff. " Send her in."

" Oh, my lord, the most wicked plot ! " began Tiffle, when admitted, throwing her bonnet back in her flurry, and putting up her hands. " The Castle's going to be rifled, and your lordship murdered promiskeous in your bed."

Lord Dane had never felt a greater inclination to laugh. The first doubt that crossed him was, whether the woman had not been making free with her master's wine.

" You can sit down, Tiffle. You seem a little excited."

" My lord, it may sound absurd to you; no doubt at the first going off it does," returned Tiffle, who was not without a sense of probabilities and the fitness of things; " but it's gospial truth ! "

" What is ? " asked Lord Dane.

Tiffle sat deprecatingly on the edge of the chair, calmed down, and told her tale. It comprised all she had heard, and a trifle that she had not heard, for Tiffle's news unconsciously increased in telling, which happens to many of us. Lydney was breaking into the Castle to murder his lordship; and Ben Beecher, Drake, and Bill Nicholson were intending to steal the plate on their own account. Tiffle went over the story twice before Lord Dane could make head or tail of it. She particularly dwelt upon the point that the expedition was Lydney's.

" Was it you who heard this fine plot ? " he asked.

" Me, my lord ! As if I should be trailing about the wood at night, hazarding of my repitation ! " .

Lord Dane looked at the wizened old face before him, and coughed to keep down a smile.

" Who did hear it, then ? "

" I could not impart that point to your lordship."

" Then you had better not have imparted the tale," was the rejoinder, delivered carelessly. " We don't fight with shadows."

" But, my lord, you'll have the catastrify occur for certain," cried the alarmed Tiffle. " Something must be done."

" Just so; and you must put me in communication with this person, whoever it may be. Otherwise I shall cause the matter to be investigated to-morrow before Squire Lester."

This would not have suited Tiffle at all; and yet she did not care to mention Shad. But there was no help for it; and Lord Dane, sitting there with the resolute Dane face, was not to be trifled with.

" My lord, it's not that I have any particular motive for denying who it was—and your lordship might see him, of

course—only I could not have it known. He's useful to me
in many ways. I give him a penny in charity now and
then, or a pair of old shoes, which he's attached to me
through, and keeps his eyes open, and brings me news unsuspected; so I hope your lordship wouldn't publish him
abroad."

"Agreed," said Lord Dane, divining Tiffle's meaning
through her vague words.

"It's that unfortunate boy, my lord, that nobody knows
who he is, or whence he is, or whether he didn't grow out of
the earth—Granny Bean's Shad."

"Granny Bean's Shad!" was the surprised echo. "Why,
every second word that boy speaks is a barefaced lie."

Tiffle bent her face a little towards Lord Dane, and the
light of the chandelier fell upon it. Something in its
earnestness—an expression he had never seen before—
arrested his attention.

"That Shad will tell you the truth in this, my lord, I'll
answer for with my own life. He has less faults and more
sense than Danesheld thinks for."

"I'll see him," said Lord Dane. "When do you say
these gentlemen purpose making the attack?"

"My lord, they didn't know themselves. Not for some
nights yet. They are waiting for something, but Shad
could not hear what: perhaps it's for the moon to go."

"Very well; send Shad to me. Take care you don't
speak of this: to do so might defeat the ends of justice."

Tiffle gave an emphatic nod. To defeat the ends of
justice where Mr. Lydney was concerned, was certainly not
her wish. As she rose to leave the room, she put a scrap of
torn paper into Lord Dane's hand, having kept her best
card as a bonne bouche until the last.

"One of the conspirators dropped this right ag'in Shad's
head, my lord."

It proved to be part of a note, the latter portion only remaining. Lord Dane read the following words:

"———*impossible to join you to-night, but to-morrow you
may expect me without fail.—W. L.*"

"It's Lydney's," said Tiffle. "I have seen his writing

upon pieces of music at our house, and I saw a note of his to Miss Lester. 'Twas only a line or two about a book, but it was that very self-same handwriting, and I'll swear to it, my lord, with the same autigriff at the end of it, ' W. L.,' which is the short for William Lydney."

Lord Dane put the scrap into his pocket-book, and Tiffle withdrew, remarking that the matter was in his lordship's hands now, and out of hers. His lordship, to tell the truth, was a little puzzled what to do with it, now that his hands had it; for he scarcely knew whether or not to believe the tale. He felt altogether unable to fathom the motive for any such attack. Loose in character as the three men mentioned had been, running raids on game and smuggling petty flasks of brandy, they had never been capable of this sort of dangerous crime. As to Lydney—he did not seem the kind of man to attempt murder and housebreaking.

The more Lord Dane thought of it, the less he understood it. Calling to Bruff that Miss Dane was not to wait tea for him, he took his hat and strolled out; a dim purpose of speaking to Bent confidentially looming hazily in his mind. The night had changed. The wind, veering round to the east, had chased away the gloomy clouds of the day; in the clear air there was a suspicion of frost; the moon was high in the sky, and unusually bright.

As Lord Dane stood at the gateway in deliberation, he became conscious that something was approaching him with exceedingly cautious and hesitating movements; and he recognised Shad. Tiffle had sent him at once, the gentleman having been on the watch for her when she left the Castle. Lord Dane conveyed his visitor across the road to the opposite heights, where there was no chance of his being overheard, and bade him speak out.

Shad told his tale, speaking a little more earnestly than usual, and forgetting for once his ordinary *rôle* of semi-childishness. And Lord Dane, in the midst of his surprise at Mr. Shad's change of character, felt a certain conviction that the story was not to be despised.

Dismissing the boy with a caution to be silent, Lord Dane crossed the road again in perplexed thought. He could not understand Lydney. Was the man an out-and-out villain? Lord Dane had scarcely believed him to be that : rather one of those cool and plausible swindlers who, whilst they live by their wits, manage to keep their heads above water. What could be his motive for originating this attack? Could he want to share in the booty of the plate-chest? If his object was to murder him—but on this point Lord Dane remained entirely sceptical—better take a high-wayman's shot at him from some convenient corner ; it might be safer. To say the truth, it was this one point, the absence of motive on Lydney's part for so damning a scheme, that in Lord Dane's mind threw doubt on the tale.

Pacing gently to and fro before the Castle-gate, his best discernment directed to the puzzle, Lord Dane balanced the question whether or not to take Mr. Bent into confidence. The police had not pleased him of late. He had suggested that the notice of the thousand pounds reward should be withdrawn, unless Lydney satisfied them of his own personal ability to meet it, and they had not done it: it was taking an unfair advantage of Ravensbird, to allow him to peril his word and his property ; besides this, Bent——

All at once, a thought darted into his brain with the quickness of a revelation—Lydney's motive. Lord Dane actually stopped still and laughed. Laughed to think how obvious it was, and how obtuse he had been not to see it before. *He was breaking into the Castle in search of the box !* Where had his, Lord Dane's, wits been?

All was explained now. That which had appeared so in-comprehensible, was made clear as the sun at noonday. There was no murder in contemplation for himself—unless, perchance, he offered resistance, and it came to a personal conflict—but the Castle was to be stealthily ransacked for this miserable box, and the plate-chest visited as a little profitable interlude between the acts. Lord Dane had not forgotten overhearing the poacher, Ben Beecher, inform Lydney that tradition said there were secret hiding-places in the Castle.

"The villain!" exclaimed Lord Dane, his angry eye flashing. "He deserves hanging for seducing those poor poachers into it. And this man has been admitted to people's drawing-rooms here as an equal; has forced himself into the companionship of Maria Lester!"

Sudden remorse, or something very like it, seized on Lord Dane. He had been keeping silence whilst he watched this man, giving him his tether, as it were, hoping to find him out; but he now asked himself whether he had not done very wrong, and whether society would not have just cause to blame him. Another idea came into his head; and it seemed to him most extraordinary that he should never have thought of it before: was Lydney hoping to delude Miss Lester into a marriage, for the sake of her fortune? Every moment the conviction grew upon him that it was so, and a hot flush dyed his face as he remembered his reprehensible silence to Mr. Lester. Ere the flush had cooled, he was striding along to Danesheld Hall.

Mr. Lester and Lady Adelaide had just come in from Great Cross, and Maria was alone in the drawing-room. She came up to him smiling, her hand held out; he thought how charming she looked in her pretty white muslin dress, with the rose-blush on her cheeks. Lord Dane asked for Mr. Lester.

"They will be down directly," said Maria.

Maria sat down, quiet and conscious; very conscious had she felt in his presence since the offer. Lord Dane, as he looked at her, could have bitten his supine tongue with anger—that it should have kept silence before Mr. Lester, and so have perhaps given further opportunities for that adventurer, Lydney, to meet the lovely, inexperienced, and, in some degree, unprotected girl before him. None knew better than Lord Dane how she was neglected and suffered to go her own way by her stepmother.

"Had I known you were at home alone to-day, I would have brought Cecilia to pay you a long visit."

"I was all the afternoon at Miss Bordillion's. We were trying a new game she has had given her—table steeple-chase. Did you ever play at it?"

"No," said Lord Dane. "How many does it take?"

"Oh, I think any number. We were four."

" Yourself and Miss Bordillion, and———"

It needed not his steady gaze to call up the rush of red to her face, as he waited for, the reply, which she could not avoid giving.

" And young Mrs. James, who had called in, and Mr. Lydney."

Remembering what had passed between her and Lord Dane in regard to the latter, she could not have helped the hesitation at his name; remembering, knowing, what her own feelings were, she could as little help the confusion she betrayed. She grew scarlet, her eyelids fell, her fingers nervously trembled. Lord Dane approached, speaking very gently as he stood and looked down upon her.

" I would not say a word to pain you, Maria; I would give the whole world rather than do it; but I did think you would have listened to my warning and avoided that man. A worse man never lived."

" Oh, Lord Dane! you should not say it! "

He bent down and laid his hand upon her shoulder in his earnestness. " I am telling you the simple truth, Maria. And that it is truth will in a very few days be known to yourself, as to all. I do not wish to say more to you just at present; only, take care of yourself."

Mr. Lester appeared. Lord Dane went with him to his study, and there entered on his word of warning against Lydney. The squire, all unconscious, received it with an indifference that provoked Lord Dane. He then bade Mr. Lester take care, for, unless he was greatly mistaken, the man was secretly looking after Maria and her fortune, and was scheming to entrap her into some engagement. Mr. Lester was thunderstruck. The possibility presented itself to him for the first time; and he saw it at once with an inexplicable fear. Looking after his daughter and her fortune! that fourteen thousand pounds that it would just ruin him to give up?

Lord Dane said not a word that could reflect on Maria; he did not even mention the game at steeple-chase. Neither did he breathe a hint of the proposed raid on the Castle. But he enlarged on the gentleman's poaching propensities, his doubtful antecedents : and when he took his departure Mr. Lester felt convinced that so audacious a villain had never gone unhung.

Mr. Lester repaired to his heavy tea in the dining-room, where his wife and Maria were waiting for him. Scarcely had she sat down to it, when the ring of a visitor sounded, and Lydney's voice was heard in the hall. Out rushed Mr. Lester in a storm of anger, and with many unnecessary words of insult, ordered the young man away again. Lady Adelaide stood in consternation, Maria was terrified, the servants came peeping forth.

"What has occurred? What have I done?" were the amazed questions put by Mr. Lydney. But the squire would descend to no explanation. He stormed, and was as insulting as a man in fierce rage can be. Mr. Lydney stood his ground, impassive, unruffled, entirely calm.

"An explanation!—to you!" foamed the squire. "How dare you ask it? There's the door, sir, and if you don't go out of it without further parley, my servants shall put you forth. Never presume to approach this threshold again."

Lydney stood yet a minute, his head raised with a half smile, every lineament of his face, every turn of his bearing, showing proud command, as if he was altogether superior to the insult. Then, making a movement of courtesy to Lady Adelaide, and another to Miss Lester, who was ready to fall, he turned and went out through the door, which the footman was holding open. And Mr. Lester stared after his guest in some bewilderment, for it had suddenly struck him how very much, just then, he was looking like that other guest who had preceded him.

The other, Lord Dane, was striding home, deep in thought, deliberating on the course he should take in regard to this threatened night attack. The evening's work had agitated him, and he crossed to the heights for a little sea air before entering the Castle. He stood on the brow of the cliff in the clear atmosphere, enjoying the rising breeze, and looking out on the broad expanse of sea. All in a minute, it occurred to him that he stood on the exact spot from whence his cousin, Harry Dane, had fallen, and he wheeled round, in sudden discomfort, to walk back again. Right in his path, unless he turned aside, lay the decaying chapel. The moon, never brighter, flickered her light on the picturesque ruins as she had done in the old days, on the broken walls, the tangled green ivy, the worn apertures. Lord Dane had never been inside those ruins since that long-time past, when he was making love to the Lady Adelaide in his heart's fresh romance.

As he stepped into the ruins, the past days came forcibly back to him, as it was natural that they should. The place looked just as it then looked; there were the faint remains of altars, the grave-stones cold and gray, the damp moss, the ghostly-looking open windows; Lord Dane remembered every spot; nothing had changed; but in himself—ah, how much!

Insensibly as he lingered within the ruins, he lost himself in the past. Vanished scenes came back to him, passing before his mind's eye, not as a fleeting phantasmagoria, but as if actually present, a living reality. His love for Adelaide, and her sudden and mysterious rejection of him; their mutual deceit towards Harry Dane, and the awful death of the latter. When he had wandered as far back as this, the reminiscences grew slightly unpleasant, especially in that lonely place, so peopled, according to popular belief, with ghostly tenants and ghostly fancies.

It is just possible that Lord Dane, though as little given to superstition as most practical men, might have acknowledged to some such feeling. At any rate, he was moving to pass out, when a form rose up outside the aperture of a window close by, and stood there in the moonlight looking in; looking as it seemed, at him, Lord Dane.

And if ever my Lord Dane's noble mind could have brought itself to believe in ghosts, it was surely then. He stood still and stared; stared at the face in the aperture. As its lineaments grew upon him, the perspiration oozed from every pore of the skin, and a half-smothered cry escaped his lips: for that face was the face of the dead—of Harry Dane.

They were almost close to each other; that face and his

own. The once familiar features stood out quite distinctly in the moonlight, far too clearly for Lord Dane to mistake them for any other man's. Would he be ashamed, in after-life, to remember that an awful feeling of dread superstition shook him to the centre, and that he glanced round as if seeking some protection from it? It was only for a moment that his eyes were turned away, for when he looked back the figure had disappeared.

An instant given to recalling his senses, and he sprang through the nearest doorway. Nothing was to be seen. He ran round the ruins in search. If it was not a ghost, it must have been a man: one thing Lord Dane was ready to swear to, if necessary, that it was not imagination. No person whatever was to be seen; no thing, animate or in-animate, was within that view: that any one could have escaped across the heights in any direction, was an impossibility, and Lord Dane came to the conclusion that he had seen his cousin's spirit. He was a middle-aged, sensible Englishman, of practical mind, and yet he believed it.

He shook himself to see whether he was awake: he took off his hat and rubbed his damp brow, and stared up at the sky, and into the moon's face, to make sure he was not dreaming. He knew he was thinking of his cousin at the time it occurred, and he knew that imagination is prone to play curious tricks. All in vain. He could neither shake off the belief in the apparition nor the fear it left behind it; so he turned round, and walked across to his home with marked quickness.

At the gateway stood Bruff, airing himself; the butler had always been given to the custom, and it grew with his years. As he drew aside for Lord Dane to pass, he naturally looked at him; and the man quite started. In the pinched, livid features, on which the Castle lamp shone, in the terrified eyes, Bruff could scarcely recognise his master.

"If he don't look as if he had seen a ghost!" cried the unconscious Bruff. And perhaps it was as well, all things considered, that Lord Dane did not hear the words.

CHAPTER XXVIII.

THE LONDON BANKER.

A TELEGRAPHIC despatch went up to Scotland Yard from Lord Dane. It was answered by a chief detective officer in person, who reached Dane Castle early the following morning. He gave in his name as Blair; and Lord Dane, who was only then dressing, hastened to him. He found a gentlemanly sort of man in plain attire, educated, pleasant, well-informed, with nothing remarkable about him, except that he was given to silence and had a habit of partly closing his eyes when he looked at people. Miss Dane, who was curious on the subject of the strange gentleman with whom her brother was going to breakfast in private, peeped out at him as he was being conducted to a dressing-room, and saw a good-looking man of forty, or thereabouts. She waylaid her brother.

"Oh, Geoffry, dear, do tell me who he is!"

He muttered something indistinct about his "man of business."

An appellation which Miss Dane's ideas immediately connected with money. "Do you mean your London banker, Geoffry?"

"That's near enough," carelessly answered Lord Dane, laughing to himself, for he had not the slightest intention of allowing it to transpire who the stranger was. Upon which Miss Dane, confidentially chattering to the household, communicated the fact that it was his lordship's London banker come down on a visit. And the news travelled forthwith to Danesheld. But never in all Miss Dane's experience had she imagined anyone could be so long a time at breakfast as this same London banker.

The meal perhaps was not taking very long, but the conversation was. In Lord Dane's own pleasant morning-room, overlooking Danesheld with a side view of the sparkling sea, he told his tale. Of Lydney's being saved from the wreck; of his claiming the japanned box, and its disappearance;

of his having wormed himself into the best houses in the place; of his discovered secret connection with the poachers and other bad characters; and of his suspected designs on the fortune of Miss Lester, the daughter of Danesheld Hall. The final communication came last—Lydney's projected attack on the Castle.

Mr. Blair listened to the whole in silence. It may be that he did not yet see the absolute necessity for the services of a detective in the matter; but he did not say so.

"The name of the inspector here is Young, I think?" he observed.

"No; Bent," said Lord Dane. "Young was moved to Great Cross a short time ago, and Bent took his place. Bent was always an opinionated sort of man; and, I may be wrong in the notion, but it seems to me that he upholds Lydney, and so I sent for you."

"If I gather your lordship's wishes rightly, you would prefer the attack on the Castle not to be stopped; but that the light-fingered gentry may be caught in the act?"

"Precisely so. The neighbourhood shall have its eyes opened as to the nefarious doings of this Lydney; therefore the attack must be allowed to take place. I am sorry for the other men, and would have spared them if I could; but there's no help for it, and they must share the penalty. They have been too fond of helping themselves to hares and pheasants; of setting my keepers at defiance; of doing a little private business in the smuggling line: but they would no more have ventured to plan such a feat as this than I should. Lydney has drawn them into it."

"I scarcely follow your lordship," said Mr. Blair. "You think Lydney's object in breaking into the Castle is *not* plunder?"

"Not his primary object. He will no doubt take his share of the plunder: but his chief object, as I believe, is to search for the box."

"This boy you speak of, Shad, hinted at an assault upon yourself."

"He took up a wrong idea," was Lord Dane's confident answer. "Rely upon it, they would be too glad that I should sleep, undisturbed, through the proceedings, and only wake up to find them and the plate-chest safely off again."

Mr. Blair seemed to be following out things on his fingers.

"This man, Lydney, as good as accused you of detaining his box?"

"He has insolently accused me of it from the first; both before my face and behind my back. My own opinion is, that the box never belonged to him, never was in his charge; that he put in a claim to it when it was lying on the beach, thinking he could do so with impunity."

"He has offered a thousand pounds reward for its recovery," quietly remarked the detective.

Lord Dane drew down the corners of his lips. "Yes, and got his credulous landlord to be answerable for the money. Bent shirked the subject when I was last with him, simply telling me to my face that they were satisfied."

"Did I understand your lordship correctly, that Bent searched the Castle himself for the box?"

"Yes, immediately after the stir arose respecting it. I allowed it, for he seemed rather to doubt whether any of my servants could have secreted the box. Which, however, was an impossibility."

"And why did Bent not tell this to Lydney?"

"Bent did tell him—told him at once."

"Then, excuse me, Lord Dane, but I do not see very clear probabilities just here. If Lydney has been assured by the police that the box is not in the Castle, how can you suppose that he is breaking in to search for it?"

Lord Dane paused. He did not wish to repeat the scandal he had heard whispered by Ben Beecher, touching possible secret hiding-places in the Castle and former smuggling, even to Mr. Blair. That Lydney was breaking in, in consequence of that communication, to search for secret places, he had not the faintest doubt; but he felt it not altogether convenient to say as much to this detective.

"Rely upon it that Lydney's object is to search for the box," was the impressive rejoinder of Lord Dane. "I don't say but the plate may contribute its attraction."

Mr. Blair mused. "Have you any reason to think this American entertains an ill-feeling towards you?" he presently asked.

"No; except what may arise from his ridiculous suspicion that I detained the box. He is aware, no doubt, that I have found him out to be a bad character: perhaps has heard that I warned his landlord, Ravensbird, against him. I have also warned Squire Lester."

Mr. Blair's fingers were quiet now, but he was evidently thinking. "Where is your police-station?" he inquired.

"In the heart of Danesheld. I will walk with you to it."

"I understand that your lordship gives the entire charge of this business into my hands?" observed the detective.

"Undoubtedly."

"Then you must allow me to go to work my own way. I would prefer to visit the station alone. All your lordship has to do is to keep still."

"And what are your plans?"

"I have formed none at present. There will be no difficulty, of course, in entrapping these gentry when they make the attack: but to find out who this American is, and his antecedents, may not be so easy. And I presume it is on this point you chiefly require my services."

"It is. The attack on the Castle could have been dealt with by the police here; but they are not capable of tracking out the past of this Lydney."

Mr. Blair rose.

"Your lordship of course understands that it must not be known who I am, and what I have come about?"

Lord Dane laughed: "You are a friend on a visit to me, Mr. Blair."

Mr. Blair walked into the town and found the police-station. On its door, conspicuous enough, though greatly soiled, was the notice still, offering the thousand pounds reward for the recovery of the japanned box. He read it rapidly as he entered, not seeming to stop, and thought the description of it somewhat curious: three V's on the lid, surmounted by a Maltese cross.

Perched upon a stool, within the railings already mentioned, was Mr. Bent. Scotland Yard had had communications from Mr. Bent, and judged him to be a shrewd officer, in spite of sundry errors in spelling and composition. The stranger, in a summary sort of way, began asking questions of Danesheld and its inhabitants, of its police-station, and other things. It aroused the ire of the inspector, who was a great man in his own estimation, and objected to be interfered with, except by the local magistrates or by my Lord Dane.

"I should be glad to know who you are—coming in and examining into my business!" cried he, resentfully.

"Should you?" was the quiet answer. "I am Mr. Blair."

"Mr. Blair?" repeated Bent, wondering where he had heard the name, for it seemed familiar to him.

"Of Scotland Yard. I have come down on a matter of business."

It was explained now, and the inspector jumped off his stool in inward tremor.

"I beg your pardon, sir! I had no idea—please to step into the inner room. I'm sure I hope nothing in our office has fallen under displeasure up there?"

"Not that I have heard of," said Mr. Blair, as he followed to the inner room, from which a policeman, quietly reading the newspaper was unceremoniously expelled.

He sat down, and entered into easy conversation with Bent, about nothing in particular, his shrewd perceptions at work all the while as to the man before him: and he saw that he might be trusted and could be discreet.

"Now then, Mr. Bent, I want a little information from you. Who is this American, stopping in the place, named Lydney?"

"Well, I don't know who he is," confidentially rejoined Mr. Bent, who stood whilst he talked, and appeared to prefer it. "We can't make him out, sir. He seems every inch a gentleman: in speech, in manners—in short, you'd not take him for anything less than a nobleman. Perhaps, though, what has led us to the thought is, that there's such a likeness to the Danes about him."

Mr. Blair lifted his head. "To Lord Dane?"

"Well, yes, to Lord Dane: a sort of general resemblance—and particularly to some of the Danes who are gone. The fact has, I think, given us a good impression of him. On the other hand, he mixes himself up with poachers and disreputable people, goes into the woods with them at night, lodges at a public-house, and—in short, we are puzzled. He is an exceedingly pleasant young fellow."

"Was it his own box that was lost?"

"He says not. He has been in a fever over it all along, and has offered a thousand pounds reward."

"When he is probably not worth a hundred pence. Had that box been produced, and the reward claimed, you might have found yourselves in a dilemma. You countrymen are so incautious."

"We have not been incautious in this, though we are countrymen," returned Mr. Bent, with a cough. "I hold the money."

"The thousand pounds!" exclaimed Mr. Blair.

"Yes, sir, in bank-notes. Lord Dane and others seemed to cast reflections upon me for accepting the guarantee of the landlord, Ravensbird, so I spoke to Mr. Lydney, and he brought the notes and deposited them with me."

"Good ones, I suppose?" carelessly remarked the inspector.

Mr. Bent gave a significant nod. "Of course I handed him an acknowledgment, and he can claim them whenever he chooses to withdraw the offer of reward."

"Lord Dane does not know of this."

"Nobody knows of it, sir, but myself: the young man exacted a promise of absolute secrecy. Lord Dane's opinion is, that Lydney himself has possession of the box; but——"

"No, it is not," interrupted Mr. Blair.

"I can assure you that it is," said the inspector.

"I can assure you that it is *not*," authoritatively corrected Mr. Blair. "If his lordship has told you so, he must have had his own reasons for the assertion."

The inspector did not like to contradict again. He looked at his superior, and waited. The latter lowered his voice.

" Have you heard that there's a plot afloat to break into Dane Castle ? "

" No ! " cried Mr. Bent in surprise. " Who's getting it up ? "

So much as he deemed necessary for the furtherance of his own purposes, Mr. Blair told. He said that Lydney's primary object appeared to be to search for the box, his second, the plate-chest. " It is," he concluded, " the business that I have been summoned down upon."

" I never was more perplexed in my life," cried Bent, when he had somewhat gathered his senses. " Lydney break into the Castle after plate ! It seems impossible. I can't understand this at all, sir."

" Neither can I, now that you have told me you hold the thousand pounds," acknowledged Mr. Blair. " It was tolerably clear before. A man capable of offering a thousand pounds reward for the recovery of a small box, and depositing the money, would scarcely break into a house to steal plate. What was in the box ? "

" Documents, he says. He has always expressed a conviction that the box is in the Castle. Surely he'd never break in after it ! "

" But it was never seen to enter the Castle," debated the detective.

" Only by a disreputable boy, named Shad, who is the deuce's own cousin for telling lies when it suits his purpose. He says it did go in, the reptile ; and I don't know in this case why he should say so if it didn't. *I* can't tell ! " concluded the man, as if the matter were wholly beyond him. . " It's the oddest thing in the world where the box can be."

Mr. Blair began to think so too. " Where can I get at this Shad ? " he asked. " I should like to meet him— accidentally, you understand."

The inspector directed him to the wood, where Shad was always prowling about, giving at the same time a description of the gentleman's person, not likely to be mistaken ; and Mr. Blair went out.

And now it is necessary to mention that the first use

Squire Lester made of Lord Dane's communication regarding Lydney, was to carry it to Miss Bordillion, and caution her to drop all intercourse with him.

That lady was not altogether unprepared for the warning. She had for some little time been aware that her own house was nearly the only one whose doors were cordially opened to Mr. Lydney; she began to have doubts herself, and she acquiesced with a sigh in Mr. Lester's recommendation that those doors should be closed in future.

There had been no opportunity for acting upon it, for Mr. Lydney had not called: but on this morning, whilst Mr. Blair was making his visit to the police-station, it happened that he presented himself.

"Not at home, sir," answered the servant, Mary, turning very red with the untruth.

But at that identical moment, who should come to the window—which in the small house was near the door—but Miss Bordillion herself. Mr. Lydney looked at her and then at the servant, a smile crossing his face. The girl felt vexed and confused; and she attempted a justification.

" It is not my fault, sir, that I can't admit you : I am only obeying orders."

" Miss Bordillion has desired you not to admit me when I call ? "

" Well yes, sir, she has. I'm sure I'm very sorry to be rude."

He tore a leaf from his pocket-book, wrote on it some words, and sent it in.

" *Allow me to see you for a few minutes. I ask it as a favour.*"

Miss Bordillion thought one more interview could not signify. With that noble face of his there before her, she seemed to lose all her doubts about him. Rarely had she seen any one, but for those doubts, in whom she could have placed confidence so implicit : and she liked him very much for his own sake.

" I thank you for admitting me," he began, as he entered and held out his hand, which she took as usual. " That I am not in favour with Danesheld, the last week or two has made me painfully aware; but I did hope the prejudice would not extend to you. You have regarded me as a friend, Miss Bordillion, and I now come purposely to ask you to treat me as one. Tell me, if you can, what the rumours against me are, and what form they take."

Miss Bordillion hesitated in perplexity, a flush called up by the unpleasantness of the position in her delicate face.

"You have probably heard that Mr. Lester has turned me from his door," he continued, finding she did not speak; and Miss Bordillion bowed in answer. "I inquired his grounds for that gratuitous insult, but he wholly refused to state them. Yesterday I was passed in the street by Captain Duff and his wife; upon meeting the captain later, I demanded what the cause was, and he civilly evaded the question. It appears to me that I have a right to be told what all this is, and so I come to you, Miss Bordillion. A man cannot meet a charge unless he knows its nature."

"That there are tales, vague rumours, abroad to your prejudice, it would be folly for me to pretend to ignore," she at length answered. "But I think the removing of them rests in a great measure with yourself."

"In what way?"

"It appears to me that you should declare who you are. You have said you are of good family, a family of some note in England. I am sure I received the assertion with perfect reliance on its truth, as I make no doubt others did. But you see a long time has gone on, and you do not give more particulars."

An expression of amusement crossed his face; and it rather vexed Miss Bordillion.

"I suppose people have been searching the Peerage and Baronetage, and all your other red books, to find the name of Lydney," said he.

"Something very like it, I believe," she answered. "You must perceive how it is, Mr. Lydney: had you said nothing about your father having been of good English family, the question would not have arisen. American birth no one thinks of inquiring into."

"Who first originated these doubts?"

Lady Adelaide.   24

"I do not know."

"Lord Dane, in all probability. Miss Bordillion, I did not think *you* would have closed your doors against me."

"I cannot do otherwise," she said, quite distressed at the turn the conversation was taking, yet considering it better to speak pretty freely. "It is impossible that I can fly in the face of society: for one thing the circumstances do not justify it; for another, I should greatly anger my connections at the Hall, the Lesters."

"Ah!" returned he, significantly. "I am accused, I hear, amidst other heinous sins, of entertaining designs on the fortune of Miss Lester."

"Where did you hear that?" she exclaimed in her surprise.

"I am supposed to be doing my best to delude Miss Lester into a runaway marriage for the sake of grasping her fourteen thousand pounds," he continued, passing by the question. "Allow me to assure you, Miss Bordillion, and I do so on my honour, that whenever I do marry, it will be of no moment to me whether my wife shall possess fourteen thousand pounds or not as many pence."

"I wish you would not mention these things," she cried; "they only pain me to hear them. For myself I cannot help feeling confidence in you; there is something about you that I have trusted from the first, and trust still. But if you reflect for a moment, you will see how impossible it is that I can run against the stream of popular opinion by continuing to receive you here. Were you only more open as to yourself, the case would be different. If I were you, Mr. Lydney," she suddenly said, rising and holding out her hand as a signal of departure, "I would not remain any longer at Daneshold."

"That proves how much you share the general prejudice," he rejoined, as he shook her hand heartily. "I do not blame you, Miss Bordillion: and of course I cannot intrude longer: but you must allow me to express a hope that the time will come when you may welcome me again."

The air seemed lighter to Miss Bordillion as he went out. In her confusion of mind, she actually slipped the bolt of the room door. One thought above all others was making itself prominent—that he had not said a single word to clear up the slander. Neither did he betray any shame, but on the contrary had never in his life looked more independent, or carried a lighter air with him.

As he went out, he found Miss Lester talking to the servant. The girl, in fact, still waiting at the front door, was giving her the history of the contretemps. He accosted the young lady, requesting a few moments' conversation with her, and, without waiting for yes or no, drew her rather peremptorily into a small room where she and Edith used to do their lessons in the old days. Trophies in the shape of slates and maps, adorned the walls still. Closing the door, he stood before her: if Miss Bordillion, bolted in her parlour still, had only known it!

"Maria," he began, calling her, as he had rarely done before, by her Christian name, "I am about to put your friendship, your confidence in me to the test. Dark tales are abroad to my prejudice; insinuations that I am not what I appear to be, a gentleman, but, on the contrary, a suspicious character, altogether an adventurer. Do you believe them?"

"No," she quietly answered, lifting her eyes, full of trust, to his.

"Thank you. If I owe refutation of them to any one, above all others it is to you. And yet I cannot do it; the time has not yet come. Will you wait on a little while, never doubting me?"

She looked at him again, her face full of faith and hope; and he took both hands and held them in his.

"It is brought against me, I find, amidst other charges, that I am striving to gain the affections of Miss Lester, for the sake of securing her fortune. Into the state of Miss Lester's affections I may not enter, but I honestly avow that she has gained mine. I can say no more now, except that when I present myself before Mr. Lester to ask his daughter's hand in marriage, he will find that in fortune and condition I am at least his equal. I—I am not offending you, in saying so much?" he broke off, for she was struggling to free her hands.

No, he was not offending her: far from it; her heart only beat more responsively to the avowal; but she was in truth terribly agitated. Here he was—this adventurer, as every one was calling him—making her an offer of marriage, and she was only too conscious that she loved him, whatever he might be.

"Until then, you will trust me," he whispered in a tone of the deepest tenderness.

Again she only glanced at him in answer, but it was quite enough. As he held her hands to him, the temptation to bend his head and kiss the blushing face was very great; but William Lydney was a man of honour, in spite of what they said of him, and he resisted it.

"God bless you, Maria. The cloud will soon pass."

Mary, discreetly waiting at the front door, and giving no warning to her mistress, as of course she might have done, offered a word of excuse to Mr. Lydney as he passed her. "Indeed, sir, I was obliged to do it," she said, looking inclined to cry.

"Of course you were; it was not your fault," he cordially answered, slipping some silver into her hand. "Who's that?"

The "who's that" applied to a stranger who was passing: a gentleman who turned round and looked keenly at him; very keenly, Mr. Lydney thought. It was not, however, an offensive stare; but the eyes that gave it appeared to have a peculiar power of their own for taking in all points of any object on which they rested.

"I hope he will know me again," said Mr. Lydney, good-humouredly. "I wonder who he is."

"It's my Lord Dane's banker, sir," was the girl's answer. "One of the Castle footmen went by just now with a carpet-bag he had been fetching from the station; he told me it belonged to my lord's London banker, who has come down on a visit; and just then the gentleman came in sight and he said that was him. Thank you very much, sir. Good-morning, Mr. Lydney, sir."

The last words, spoken loudly, for Mr. Lydney was already nearly out of sight, reached the ears of the "banker." He turned and accosted the servant.

"Did I hear you call that gentleman Lydney?"

"Yes, sir. That's Mr. Lydney."

Mr. Blair gazed after him until he was out of sight. It might be that Lydney did not answer to the picture he had mentally formed of him.

"He does look like a gentleman," were the words that escaped him; it seemed involuntarily.

"He is a gentleman, if ever there was one," cried the young woman warmly.

"Ah," soliloquized Mr. Blair, "just the fellow to drop down in a country place and take it by storm, whether the good looks are false or whether they're genuine. Bent's right: there's a cut of Lord Dane about him; I wonder——"

What Mr. Blair wondered, was never spoken, even to himself. For he dismissed his thoughts, as not being likely to hold water.

CHAPTER XXIX.

THE NIGHT ATTACK.

LORD DANE'S London banker remained on his visit, and made himself popular. There was scarcely a place to which he did not penetrate, even to Granny Bean's hospitable dwelling, where he won that estimable old crone's heart by a huge present of tobacco, and took a pipe with her. Granny gave him her version of a great many people, and particularly of Lydney and Wilfred Lester. She called them "limbs," and sundry other names.

Mr. Blair became intimate with Ravensbird and his wife, amidst others. The Sailors' Rest was a convenient halting-place in going to and from the Castle, and Mr. Blair took a fancy to some French liqueur kept there, and was continually turning in for a petit verre. Sometimes he would talk to Ravensbird whilst he drank it, sometimes to madame, and he grew curious, in a social friendly way, as to their guest, young Lydney. But with all Mr. Blair's craft, he really elicited nothing that was of service to him, either for or against that young man. Lord Dane had wanted Lydney turned out, Ravensbird said confidentially one day; but he didn't see his way clear to doing it: so long as the American paid for what he had, and conducted himself well, why should he part with a profitable customer? Altogether Mr. Blair obtained no reliable information from any quarter, and so there was nothing for it but to wait until Lydney cut off his own head.

If visits to Lawyer Apperly's office could accomplish that decapitation, it was being done quickly. Never a day passed but Mr. Lydney was there, without any result, demanding whether there was news of that man of law, and when he *would* be at home.

On the Saturday morning, however, the Saturday of the week that had witnessed the arrival of Mr. Blair at Danesheld, news came, and no one was more glad of it than the clerk, young Crofts, for he had grown, as he avowed to his friends, "sick and tired of seeing that bothering Lydney."

"He'll be home to-night or to-morrow," said the clerk. "Any way, in time for business on Monday morning."

"You are sure?" cried Mr. Lydney, eagerly. "Have you heard from Mr. Apperly himself?"

"How could I tell you if we hadn't heard?" retorted young Crofts, resentfully. "Perhaps," he continued, with sarcasm, "Mr. James might let you see the letter if you ask him."

Away went Mr. Lydney with the information to Wilfred Lester. Wilfred received it with indifference. Eager as he had once been for the lawyer's return, latterly he had cooled down about it. What good could Apperly be to him, or any other lawyer, while his father refused to show the deed? For this week past it had struck Lydney that Wilfred Lester avoided him, and the young American asked himself whether *he* also could be influenced by the tales that were abroad to his prejudice. It made no difference to him ; he never lost sight of his promise to Maria, and three parts of his time, night and day, were spent in quietly looking after the movements of Wilfred. But the poachers seemed unusually quiet, and nothing was stirring. Nothing had come of the projected attack on the Castle. Night after night when the household had retired, Bruff, the only one to whom the secret was disclosed, let in a small band of policemen in plain clothes, and let them out again with morning light. Mr. Blair wondered whether his visit was to turn out a superfluous one, and Lord Dane grew fidgety.

On the Sunday evening they were sitting in the dining-room, lingering over their wine, when a faint tap was heard at one of the windows. Lord Dane rose, pulled aside the white blind, and found Mr. Shad's face on the other side of the glass. He had climbed the iron railings and was standing on the spikes, leaning forward and holding on by the window frame.

"You young imp!" exclaimed Lord Dane, throwing up the window, "what brings you here?"

Shad, active as a cat, was in the room in a trice, and stood, out of breath between running and excitement.

"They are coming on this very night, my lard. They—they be there a-planning it."

Mr. Blair advanced, seated Shad upon a chair, and got him to tell his news calmly. The substance of it was that he had seen the conspirators in the wood, and heard enough to convince him the attack was about to be made this night. When he left, they were tying black crape to their hats.

"How many did you see?" asked Mr. Blair.

"I see four: two tall and two short," answered Shad. "The three was them I telled my lard on before; the t'other, which was tallest of all, was like—I didn't see his face, though," broke off Shad. "He was sitted down on the stump all the time, with the black afore his nose."

"Who is he like? Speak out."

"Well, I never heerd him speak, and I never see him get up, but he was like Will Lester."

"Nonsense!" interposed Lord Dane. "As if Wilfred Lester would turn housebreaker! The boy's a fool, Blair, and has always been deemed one. You must mean Lydney," he sharply added to Shad.

Now the boy was not a fool: he had a great deal too much cunning to be a fool; and that cunning he was incessantly calling into requisition. It did not in the least matter to Shad whether the silent gentleman in the crape might be Mr. Lydney or Mr. Wilfred Lester: his opinion was that it was the latter; but as the suggestion appeared to give offence to Lord Dane, who would evidently be better pleased to hear that it was Lydney, Shad's cunning prompted him to veer round.

"Well, I dunno," said he, with admirable simplicity. "Lydney's tall, too, he is: and the man was broad, here," touching his chest, "and so's Lydney. Yes, my lord, 'twas more like Lydney. 'Twas the leggin's made me think o' Will Lester; but I see Lydney with a pair on one day."

"Safe to be Lydney," said Lord Dane to Mr. Blair. And the latter nodded.

"What more did you hear?" he asked of Shad.

"I didn't hear no more, sir. They warn't talking, except a' odd word about the veils; and I crept off to tell his lardship."

Mr. Blair turned to Lord Dane, and they spoke together for a few moments in an undertone. Mr. Shad was then gently lifted on to the spikes again, and told to jump down. This accomplished, Lord Dane gave him a parting word of admonition.

"You go home at once, Shad, and get to bed. If you lingered near the Castle, there might be a danger of your getting shot in mistake for one of the thieves. Should these men be dropped upon through your information, you shall have such a reward as you have never dreamed of in your life. Make the best of your way home."

Away tore Shad, but the moment he was at a safe distance from the Castle, he darted within shade of the friendly hedges of a by-lane, to give vent unseen to his superfluous jollity, quite unconscious that he nearly darted into the embrace of a gentleman. Shad threw up his arms, capered with his feet, performed, in short, all sorts of antics, and muttered:

"Go home to bed, my lard says. Not I; I'd like to see the fun. And as if I didn't know Will Lester, though he have got the black crape over his face! He——"

Shad found himself pinioned. The gentleman was Mr. Lydney, who had strolled out from the Sailors' Rest to smoke a cigar.

"What is that about Will Lester and black crape, Shad?"

Shad began to howl. He was a-going home to his granny's to bed, he was.

"You little hypocrite!" exclaimed Mr. Lydney, "do you suppose I want to hurt you? Look here, Shad; you cannot play the simpleton with me, so just put off that idiotic folly. I ask you what you meant, when you alluded to Wilfred Lester's having black crape over his face, and I ask *to know*. If you don't choose to tell me, I will take you off to the police-station now, and you shall tell it there."

"I daredn't tell nobody," rejoined Shad.

"Yes, you dare: you can tell me. What 'fun' is it that's going on to-night? I mean to know."

A little more skirmishing, and then Mr. Lydney suddenly exclaimed: "Did you ever see a sovereign, Shad?"

"I have see'd 'em," returned Shad, with a stress upon the "see'd."

"Would you like to possess one?"

"Oh!" aspirated Shad in trembling delight, his mouth beginning to water.

"I said I would give you a sixpence if you told me the truth about the box. Tell the truth now of what is doing to-night, and I will give you a golden sovereign."

For that tempting bait, Shad would have sold Danesheld and everyone in it, himself included. A sovereign, twenty whole shillings, really seemed to the boy interminable riches, sufficient to buy up all the tame rabbits within the circuit of his knowledge. But Shad was feeling puzzled. If this was the night of the grand expedition, and Mr. Lydney was strolling about enjoying idleness and a cigar, he could

not be in it, as had been surmised. Shad, with his cunning,
came to the rapid conclusion that he was *not* in it, and that
they had been under a mistake in supposing so. Still he
hesitated, uncertain whether the disclosure might not bring
him inconveniently under the enemy's displeasure. But
Mr. Lydney's sovereign was irresistible to the poor covetous
eyes, and Shad made a clean breast of the secret, putting
him into possession of as much as he knew himself. " The
Castle was about to be broke into that night, and the plate-
chest stoled, and my lord murdered," was the substance.

" I see 'em ; they be a-tying the black crape over their
faces at this very time," was Shad's eager rejoinder.
" There's Drake, and Nicholson, and Ben Beecher ; and
Will Lester was sitting down, ready. My lord broke out
upon me sharp, a-saying it warn't him ; he said it was you."

" Lord Dane said it was I ! " repeated Mr. Lydney.

" Leastways," cried Shad, retracting, lest he might be
getting himself into hot water, " he said, ' Was it Mr.
Lydney, or was it Will Lester ? ' 'cause both was tall. So
I said as I couldn't swear to neither of 'em for certain,
when I see it angered him. As if I didn't know Will
Lester ! "

After some further colloquy, Shad was dismissed, and Mr.
Lydney remained in a state of great perplexity and discom-
posure. That Wilfred Lester had joined in certain night
expeditions of the poachers, he was only too sure of; but
that he would rush madly into crime, he did not believe.

How could he, Lydney, prevent its taking place ? at any
rate prevent Lester's joining in it ? It was indispensable
that he should be prevented, not only for his own sake, but
for his family's ; and a deep flush rose to Mr. Lydney's
brow, as he thought of the terrible disgrace it would reflect
on Maria, of the misery to the poor young wife. As he
thus mused, he became conscious that some men were
passing in the direction of the Castle ; not together, but
singly and quietly ; they were in plain clothes, but he
recognized the faces of two of them, and knew them to be
the police going up to their night-watch in the Castle, as
described to him by Shad, who had tracked their steps

night after night. All Mr. Lydney could do was to follow them; to search the wood for Wilfred Lester then, would be hopeless; and he took up his position so as to command a view of the approach to the Castle back and front; and there he remained on watch.

Meanwhile, the inhabitants of the Castle retired to rest as usual, in blissful unconsciousness that any attack was contemplated, or that Mr. Bruff remained up to admit night-guardians. Mr. Blair privately told the men that the attack might be expected; the lights were put out, and all was in readiness.

They waited, and waited: the men in their appointed places, Mr. Blair and Lord Dane conversing in whispers and listening with all their ears. They waited and waited on. The clock struck one.

"It's odd they don't come," muttered Mr. Blair.

Suddenly shots were heard in the distant wood. The police came out of their hiding-places; Lord Dane and Bruff, unused to this sort of thing, made a silent rush to the hall.

"Back, every one of you," was the stern whisper of Mr. Blair. "It is coming on now."

"They have met with some obstacle and are fighting in the wood," said Lord Dane.

"Back all of you, to your places," reiterated the detective. "Those shots are a ruse to draw the attention of the keepers from the Castle, should any be near it. I expected something of the sort. They'll be here directly now. Whatever you may hear or see, let none stir forth until I give the signal."

Back they went, and the Castle was once more silent. And still they waited and waited on.

Mr. Lydney was also waiting at his post outside, thinking the night and the housebreakers very long. He heard the town-clock strike one; and he heard the shots in the wood. It did not occur to him to take the view of them that the detective had done, and they disturbed him much: but he could not quit his present post. It was a muggy, disagreeable night; the early part of it had been clear, but the weather was changing—anything but a pleasant night to remain on the watch in the open air.

Suddenly, a sound broke on his ear: not, however, as of the covert approach of housebreakers, but of a boy's feet scampering over the ground with all possible haste. Mr. Lydney looked out and encountered Shad.

" So you are here! instead of having gone home to bed ! "

" Don't lay hold on me then, please, sir," panted Shad, who was out of breath. " I'm a-going to the Castle to tell Lord Dane. I know he's up a-waiting."

" To tell him what ? "

" 'Taint the Castle they be on to. It's the Hall."

" What ? " cried Lydney.

" They've a-broke into it: they be in it now. I've been a-dodging on to 'em all the night, and they be gone right into the Hall, instead o' coming here. They've took a pane out at one o' the winders."

All that had been dark grew clear to Lydney. Wilfred Lester was after the DEED—the deed relating to his property which his father persisted in withholding from his perusal. The conviction came upon Lydney with the light of a revelation.

Poor, mistaken, reckless Wilfred Lester deemed he was doing quite a justifiable thing in breaking into the Hall at night to seize upon his own property. Had Mr. Apperly been at home to advise him, it might never have occurred; but Mr. Apperly was away, and had curtly declined to have anything further to do with the business. So Wilfred organized the attack, and persuaded the three men mentioned to join in it. He supplied himself with keys, but they might fail; and in that case the leaden safe would have to be carried away: hence the numerous company. And it perhaps scarcely need be added, that Wilfred was ignorant of the men's intention to do a little work on their own account and to make off with the plate and anything else of value they might chance to lay hands upon ; this was a little private arrangement of their own. They had never gone so far in crime yet, but the opportunity seemed too good to be missed,

With a cry of dismay, Lydney turned towards the Hall; but, ere he had gone a yard, he stopped and grasped Shad.

"You must not go to the Castle, Shad: there's no need to acquaint Lord Dane with this. I will not have you go there."

Shad lifted his cunning and covetous eyes. "They be on the watch, up there, they be; and if I goes and tells his lordship that the lot hain't coming, maybe he'll pay me for it."

"And a pretty thing you'd do!" returned Mr. Lydney, meeting cunning with cunning. "You would put them off their guard at the Castle: and how do you know that the lot, as you call them, may not take a turn up there, after they have done with the Hall? Would Lord Dane reward you for that?"

Shad opened his eyes. The idea had not struck him.

"You be quiet, Shad, that is all you have to do. Be silent as to the doings of this night, and especially as to Wilfred Lester. If I find that you are so, I will do something better for you than even the sovereign."

Lydney sped towards the Hall, and Shad, the prospect of seeing the "fun" being irresistible, shambled off in his wake.

Lydney seemed to reach the Hall in no time. All was silent as the grave. Nothing was to be seen, nothing heard; the blinds were drawn before the windows; the inmates, as far as could be observed to the contrary, were sleeping in peace. Had that iniquitous Shad deceived him, he was beginning to wonder, when he was startled by the report of a pistol within the house. At the same moment, some figure, who or what he could not see in the obscurity, ran out at the front door, and darted into the clustering shrubs on the right. As quickly, and perhaps incautiously, Lydney darted into the Hall, confused thoughts of succouring the inmates and of screening Wilfred, passing through his brain.

Mr. Shad had not been deceitful. The pane was cut out of a back window: and Drake entering, undid its fastenings and admitted the rest. When fairly in, the four stopped to strike a light, to listen and take breath.

"This way," whispered Wilfred Lester, who of course knew the turnings and the windings of the old house, while they did not.

He took them into the front hall, at the back of which, as you may remember, was his father's study. The key was in the door, and they entered it without trouble, and began operations. Wilfred Lester tried his keys on the safe, Ben Beecher held the light, Drake kept the door against surprise, and Nicholson did nothing. The safe yielded to one of the keys.

Strange objects they looked there, with the black crape on their faces. Wilfred Lester could not get at the deed readily; the safe seemed full of papers, and he grew confused in his haste. Some were tied with red tape, some were sealed, others were unfastened. They were disposed in tolerable order; but looking over them took time. He came to one, superscribed "Will of George Lester, Esquire;" and the temptation to open it, and read of his disinheritance, crossed him; his disinheritance in favour of the second children. But he would not be dishonourable: if you can understand the remark of one who was visiting his father's private safe. At length he came to the deed; he knew it by the indorsement, and a suppressed cry of exultation broke from him as he clutched the parchment.

"All right, boys! I have it at last."

The men had doubtless thought the search a long one, and there was a murmur of satisfaction. Whilst he was putting the papers in order again within the safe, Drake and Nicholson attempted to steal out of the room.

"Where are you going?" said Wilfred. "Stay where you are."

"Why, you'd never begrudge us a snack of bread and cheese, sir!" cried Drake. "We shall find it in the pantry, while you are putting straight here: it won't be missed."

Wilfred turned on the man in suppressed anger.

"Drake, you know the bargain. Nothing must be touched in the house; no, not a crust of bread. They shall not have it to say that we came in, like thieves, for plunder."

"I'll take a stroll through the place, any way," answered

Drake, with his natural hardihood. "And as to not taking a mouthful if I see it——"

"I'll shoot the first man who lays his finger on anything in my father's house, no matter what it be," was the stern interruption of young Lester, as he took a pistol from his pocket. "Drake! Nicholson! do you see this? You know the agreement, I say. I have promised you a reward for aiding me; having secured the deed, I shall be well able to pay you; but the contents of the house must remain intact."

The pistol was no doubt a surprise to the men: and it was probable that Wilfred Lester had brought it in anticipation of some such contingency. But the fellows were bold and callous; they had entered on the expedition with an end to their own views and it was not easy to relinquish them. A whispered conversation took place between Drake and Nicholson, whilst Lester arranged the papers in order, so as to leave no trace of the safe's having been visited.

"Now then," said he, as he closed and locked the safe, "to get out as cleverly as we came in!"

This was easy enough to say, not so easily done. Closing the study-door, and leaving the key in the lock as he found it, he pointed to the front door, just before them.

"We'll go out that way," he whispered to his companions. "It is handier, and I know the fastenings."

Stealing over the oil-cloth, he gained the door, undid the bolts, drew it cautiously open about an inch, and looked round for his friends. The men stood as he had left them, not one following him: Beecher was putting the candle on a bracket that rested against the wall.

And now Drake, the hardiest and boldest of the three, threw off the mask of hypocrisy, finding that there were no other means of obtaining his ends, and avowed he would not go away empty-handed.

"We have helped you to your ends, Master Lester; if you don't like to help us to ours, you must wink at them. We came into the house with a resolve to pay ourselves, and you need make no bones over it. You've accomplished your little game, and we'll try and accomplish ours. I take my oath I won't go away without something, if it's only a silver spoon."

Wilfred Lester's reply was to raise his pistol and cock it: not to fire upon them, but hoping to coerce them into withdrawing, under fear that he would do so. Ben Beecher the best of the group, believing life was in danger, stepped close and threw up Lester's arm. The pistol went off; the bullet shattering a glass-door at the back of the Hall, and making a tremendous noise.

"Fools!" bitterly exclaimed Wilfred Lester. "Save yourselves, and be quick over it. Fools! fools!"

He sped through the hall-door, leaving it open for them to follow, and darted into the shrubs on his right-hand, whence he could readily gain the road by scaling the iron rails. It was at this moment that William Lydney had come up and was watching. Beecher and Nicholson ran to escape, but Drake seized upon them.

"Don't show yourselves cowards!" he cried in a hoarse whisper. "We may get the plate yet. If the folks was sleeping sound, the shot mayn't have roused 'em. Wait and see; plenty of time to get off then."

Even as he spoke, an interruption took place that they did not bargain for. The hall-door was opened wider, and in rushed a tall man. At first they thought it was young Lester come back again. But as the light of the candle fell upon him, they recognized Mr. Lydney.

"You misguided, miserable men!" he uttered in agitation. "Where's Wilfred Lester?"

Before they could frame an answer—whether it would have been one of civility, repulsion, or attack—Nicholson's eye caught sight of someone on the staircase in white drapery, whose face was peeping at them through the balustrades. The figure was in a crouching position, and might have been there some time. The sound of the pistol had also done its work: doors were being opened and closed in consternation.

"It's all over!" stamped Drake. "A race for it now, boys."

"Wilfred Lester?" questioned Lydney, in emotion. "Is he in the house, or not?"

"Not; I swear it," said Beecher, speaking up. "I wouldn't deceive you, Mr. Lydney; he escaped as you entered."

Scarcely waiting to realize the assurance, Lydney rushed out again in search of Wilfred Lester. The rest were rushing also, pell-mell; Beecher was last; he waited to blow out the light. He closed the door behind him with a bang; and Tiffle's voice might be distinguished on the stairs as she shrieked out " thieves " and " murder,"

CHAPTER XXX.

MADE PRISONER.

EXCEEDINGLY surprised was the great London detective, Mr. Blair, and in the same surprise must be included his noble host, to find that this night passed off as the others had done —without attack. There was perhaps a little feeling of discomfiture added to it. But when they came to hear that it was the Hall which had been broken into and not the Castle, no words could express their astonishment. Lydney had been in it, and was recognized, rumour ran; and my Lord Dane openly wondered whether he suspected the japanned box had been conveyed there for safety, and so broke in to steal it: he could scarcely be suspected of breaking in to steal Miss Lester.

Mr. Lester was puzzled. Alarmed by the report of the pistol, he came out of his room to find Tiffle shrieking on the stairs. Tiffle began stating what she had seen: " four assassinors in the house, three of them with blackened faces, and the other one not blacked, which was Lydney." Mr. Lester and his aroused men-servants went over the house in consternation. Nothing whatever appeared to have been taken: nothing was disturbed except the pane of glass, which had been cut out: and Mr. Lester thought that plunder could not have been the object of the entrance. But of course the outrage would have to be investigated.

Lord Dane could not understand it at all. He went in the morning to Mr. Lester's, and heard the account given by that gentleman. Lord Dane said nothing of Lydney, or of the expected attack on the Castle: and it must be remembered that Mr. Lester had never heard of it, therefore the whole affair was to him a mystery. Mr. Blair had rather a long interview with Bent: in which Bent shook his head, and declined to believe that Lydney was in it for harmful purposes. He had seen and spoken with him that morning. Mr. Blair said little on his own score: truth to say, that estimable detective was puzzled. At the earnest request of Lord Dane, the expected attack on the Castle was for the present buried in silence—and certainly that could not have had anything to do with the attack upon the Hall. Lord Dane forbade the three men to be apprehended: he spoke with authority, and was listened to accordingly. Perhaps this was not of much consequence one way or the other: for the police, looking after the men on their own private account, found all three had disappeared. Lord Dane would have spared these, and metaphorically speaking, hung Lydney.

Lawyer Apperly had not kept faith. Here was Monday, and no sign of him. Mr. Lydney was "in a way over it," as young Crofts expressed it, "in and out of the office like a dog in a fair."

Early in the afternoon there was a gathering at Danesheld Hall, partly impromptu. Mr. James, the *locum tenens* of Lawyer Apperly, and acting as clerk to the magistrates since his departure, had come by appointment to hear what Tiffle had to say on the matter. Lord Dane, who had happened to call in with his friend the London banker, determined to remain and hear it also, and Mr. Bent received a hint from Squire Lester that he might be present if he liked. The inspector was the last to make his appearance, and he was accompanied by William Lydney. Mr. Lester's face turned red and angry.

"1 thought he ought to come, and so I brought him, sir," whispered Bent. "It's only right that a suspected man should hear the charge against him; besides, I had another reason."

Lydney looked as little like a housebreaker as it was possible to conceive: my Lord Dane himself was not more calmly self-possessed; if the one was dignified, self-contained, and apparently unconscious of evil, so was the other: and Mr. Blair, who saw everything in his silent way and seemed to see nothing, could not help thinking so.

Lady Adelaide was present. Intensely curious on the subject of the midnight outrage, she saw no reason why she should not hear what was to be heard as well as other people. Mr. Lester suggested she had better perhaps retire; her ladyship replied that she should remain. Maria sat in the background, quite overlooked by Lady Adelaide and her father, who were not in the habit of giving superfluous attention to her. She bent over some light embroidery, her trembling fingers almost refusing to control the needle, for she had her theory as to the business, one that brought with it an awful fear, and was turning her heart to sickness. Lady Adelaide did nothing, except hold a screen between the fire and her delicate face, and exchange a languid word or two with Lord Dane. Mr. James, who, by-the-way, was a nephew of the incumbent of Danesheld, sat at the table and dotted down with a pen and ink any point that struck his attention.

Tiffle came in, ambling and curtseying, and smoothing her hands whilst she made her statement.

"I retired to rest last night, sir," she began, addressing particularly her master, "and was unable to get to sleep; the more I tried to shut my eyes and lose myself, the more pertineshously I kept awake. Soon after the clock struck one, I thought I heard a noise downstairs; I heard it twice; and I sat up in bed and listened for some time, and concluded I was mistaken. I'm sure it must have been twenty minutes after that that I was startled again, and if ever I heard supprissed voices talking, I heard 'em then. The flurry it put me in is indiscriptable; I thought the servants

were up to some pranks, for it's a tight hand I have to keep
over 'em, sir, and they'd like to delude me; and I jumped
out of bed and crept down the stairs till I could see into the
front hall. I thought I should have dropped; my heart
was in my mouth——"

"Never mind your heart," interrupted Mr. James.
"What did you see?"

"Gentlemen, I saw this. Three horrid men in the hall,
with black faces; and, close on that, a pistol went off,
blinding me with smoke and fright. The next thing I saw
was a fourth man whisking out at the front door; leastways
I saw his coat-tails. If ever anybody was near fainting, it
was me, gentlemen; but I wouldn't faint; I had the family
to protect, and that gave me courage. I looked down still,
and I saw the man whisk in again, and I'm sorry to say"—
Tiffle coughed and dropped her voice—"that it was Mr.
Lydney."

There was a pause.

"What next?" asked Lord Dane, some eagerness in his
tone.

"My lord, nothing. Except that Mr. Lydney stood a
moment talking with the other three, and then they all four
tore off together, one trying to get off faster than another,
and amidst 'em, they blew out the light, and left the place
in darkness. It all passed in less than a minute."

Mr. Lydney glanced at Maria. The work had dropped
on her lap, and her white face was uplifted. He smiled at
her: it did not look like the smile of a guilty man.

"You hear!" exclaimed Squire Lester to him impatiently.

"I do hear," was the reply.

"Can you offer any explanation?"

"I swear it was him," broke forth Tiffle with animus,
before he could speak. "If he denies it, he'll perjury himself. I saw him as plain as I see him now. I didn't know
the others, because their faces were disguised, but his was
not."

"I did enter your house last night, Mr. Lester, but only
once," said Lydney with marked calmness. "If a man went

out of it before I came in, as your servant testifies, it was not myself."

There was a general feeling of astonishment at his admitting so much. Mr. James looked derisive.

"I happened to be close to the Hall at the moment," continued Lydney. "I heard the report of the pistol; I saw the front door open; and I rushed in, in the moment's impulse, and met the men coming out. My chief thought was of giving help should it be needed."

"If that's your best explanation, it's a lame one," spoke Mr. Lester, harshly. "Can you not justify yourself better than that?"

"Allow me five minutes' conversation with you in private, and I will enter on my justification," was the young man's answer. "You may deem it a satisfactory one, Mr. Lester."

Mr. Lester repulsed the request indignantly. He was not accustomed to grant private interviews to midnight intruders. Had Lydney anything to say, he must speak out. "We don't want half explanations," he added. "If you do not choose to avow publicly why you were near my house at that hour, and why, being in it, you did not arouse me, I shall know what to think. Tell it all out fully before my Lord Dane and these gentlemen, or not at all."

"Then—I think—I have no resource but to be silent," returned Mr. Lydney, hesitating whilst he reflected. "Nevertheless I am innocent of any offence. Yes; for the present, I can only be silent."

Lord Dane took a step forward. "You have called yourself a gentleman?" he remarked, the mockery in his tone remarkable. It seemed to arouse young Lydney's spirit, and he went up and confronted him.

"I am at least as much of a gentleman as your lordship —in all respects," was the firm answer. "Did we come to examine into rank and rights, I might possibly take precedence of you."

The extreme coolness of this assertion set Lord Dane laughing. The room stared at Lydney for making it, and came to the conclusion that he was a very bad man indeed.

Meanwhile, Mr. James, at the dictation of Squire Lester, was making out the warrant for William Lydney's committal on a charge of suspicion of breaking into Dancsheld Hall.

"I am sorry to do it if you are not guilty," said Mr. Lester to him, and the tone of his voice was one of undisguised sarcasm. "There will be an official inquiry to-morrow morning before my brother magistrates: until then you must remain in custody."

"In custody—where?" exclaimed Mr. Lydney, wheeling round. The Squire answered, with much politeness—

"Mr. Bent will take care of you. There's accommodation for guests in the station-house."

"But, Mr. Lester, this is beyond a joke," remonstrated Lydney. "You cannot seriously suppose I broke into your house?"

"At any rate, it will now have to be proved," was the retort. "Bent, the prisoner is in your charge."

"But, Mr. Lester——"

"Silence, sir!" cried the Squire. "I refuse to hear more."

And Mr. Lydney remained silent, not particularly in obedience to the mandate, but in self-communing. It was undoubtedly an awkward predicament to be placed in; and he did not see how he could extricate himself from it without betraying Wilfred Lester.

"You will at least take bail?" he observed.

"No," said Mr. Lester, very quietly. "There's nothing more, Bent."

This was a hint for Mr. Bent to take himself and his prisoner away. He, the prisoner, however, suddenly advanced to Lady Adelaide and Miss Lester.

"Appearances seem against me now: but I beseech you to believe that I have a good motive for not speaking just yet to clear myself. A little while, and what is dark shall be made light. Only trust me."

He addressed them collectively, but it was evidently for Maria that the last words were meant. She raised her eyes to him in answer, full of trust; and there was a whole world of sincerity and truth in his lingering smile as he turned from her.

"I am ready, Mr. Bent. I will accompany you without any trouble."

They went out together—leaving a curiously uncomfortable feeling in the room. Lady Adelaide looked up, as if from a reverie.

"I declare he frightens me. When he came out to the middle of the carpet, meeting you, and drew up his head with that calm proud look, he was so like the Danes that I started back—you saw me, perhaps. It is the very way Lord Dane had with him: and Harry Dane also, though in a less degree."

"He has impudence enough for all the Danes put together," observed Lord Dane. "The insolence of his addressing you and Miss Lester! I declare that I could have knocked him down."

The assembly broke up. When Mr. James got back to the office, he was greeted by the sight of its truant chief. The lawyer had arrived about an hour ago, and the news was spreading in Danesheld. Mr. James, amidst other information, gave him a concise history of Lydney's past doings, and his present apprehension.

The interview was rudely broken in upon by Madame Ravensbird. With her natural independence, she had completely ignored the remonstrance of young Mr. Crofts, that his two chiefs were on no account to be disturbed, and went in at once with her dripping umbrella. The gentlemen happened to be laughing.

"I thought so! only talking and laughing together! Va! Monsieur Apperly, you will put on your hat, please, and come with me."

"I dare say," returned the lawyer, who was rather fond of gossiping with Madame Ravensbird at fitting times and seasons. "I am too busy."

"But I have come for you," cried Sophie, stamping her pretty foot. "There's not one minute to lose. That gentleman at our house has been waiting for you ever since you went away, and he won't wait another minute, now he knows you have come home. He is very ill. He is choleric, too, and he may have an attack."

"What does he want with me?—to make his will? I can't go down to him in the rain," said Mr. Apperly, half-laughing.

"You will come with me in the rain or in the hail, monsieur," cried Sophie, so authoritatively as to surprise Mr. Apperly. "It is of more consequence than you suppose, and you must not dare to refuse or to linger. It is one hour by the clock since he first heard you were come home; it is two hours since he sent out young Mr. Lydney to ask if you were come."

"Sent young Lydney, did he?" rejoined the lawyer, in a slighting tone. "Ah! he has had some business of his own on hand this afternoon: Mr. Bent has him in safe custody at the station-house."

"Mr. Bent has Mr. Lydney, in—what you say?" shrieked Sophie.

"Safe enough, Mrs. Ravensbird. That young Lydney was one of those that broke into Squire Lester's house last night! the only one of the lot as yet recognised; and he is in custody for it."

With a succession of ejaculations Mrs. Ravensbird turned without ceremony, and ran down the street in the rain towards the Sailors' Rest, leaving her umbrella behind her. The lawyer caught it up, took another for himself, and followed.

Some one else was out in the rain that afternoon, and that was Maria Lester. Instinct whispered that her reckless brother Wilfred had been in the trouble of the past night, and that William Lydney, true to his promise to herself, was only screening him. Why Wilfred should have done such a thing she could not tell; her fears were vague, undefined, but almost unbearable.

She stole out towards dusk, when no one was likely to miss her, and hastened to her brother's. The weather seemed to clear up rather suddenly before she arrived there; the rain ceased, and a broad streak of gold illumined the western sky.

Edith was alone in the sitting-room, the light from a blazing fire playing on her face, which was beginning to look so much better than it had of late. Maria cast an anxious glance round the room.

" Where's Wilfred ? " she asked.

" Gone over to Great Cross ! " replied Edith.

" Gone to Great Cross ! " repeated Maria, with a rush of disappointment. " I—I wanted just to say a word to him."

"He will be back soon," said Edith carelessly. " Why don't you sit down, Maria ? " And Maria sat down with a suppressed sigh.

" What a great fire you have, Edith ! " she remarked mechanically, her thoughts far away.

" How Sally manages the coals I can't think," said Edith, turning to her confidentially. " She comes in and throws on half a scuttlefull as if expense were of no moment whatever. It is of no use saying anything : you know Sally. I can't imagine how she gets half the things that she does, unless—it has crossed me at times to think it—Aunt Margaret supplies her with money. Only I don't see where Aunt Margaret can get it from herself."

" What has Wilfred gone to Great Cross for ? " asked Maria, paying no attention to all this.

" To see some lawyer, he said. He was talking rather strangely before he went out, declaring that we should soon be rich now. I don't think he can be well."

" How has he been ? " inquired Maria, her heart beating a shade quicker.

" So very restless—I should say, nervous, if I were talking of a woman," replied the poor unconscious wife. " When people have knocked at the door, he has peeped out to see who they were : twice he bolted the room door, and stood with his back against it. I asked him what he feared, why he was so agitated, but could get nothing out of him. He has seemed frightened at his own shadow."

Terrible confirmation ! Maria's heart went on beating. One thing she did wonder at : that Mrs. Lester did not allude to the occurrence at the Hall.

" Sally has seemed fidgety too, to-day. She would

scarcely open the door to people, but answered them from the window. I heard her talking so crossly to Wilfred this morning. I'm sure if he's ill, poor fellow, she need not be cross to him."

" Perhaps Wilfred has not had a good night's rest; if so, that might make him restless to-day," stammered poor Maria. "Did he go to bed early?"

" Well, now, Maria, that's what I am unable to tell you. I went up at nine o'clock, fell asleep directly, and never woke until morning. Sally says it is good for me, that my weakness is sleeping itself off."

Maria rose to depart; and for all she had learnt she might as well not have come. She had stolen up almost like a criminal, hoping to gain some tidings, some little word of certainty, whether for good or for ill. Have you ever been on the rack of some awful suspense, my reader? Then you will understand Maria Lester's feeling. It is far worse to bear than the worst reality.

Saying good-bye to Edith, she turned into the kitchen as she passed it. Sally was laying her mistress's modest tea-tray, and kept her back turned to Miss Lester with a great want of politeness, but that was nothing extraordinary for Sally.

"Mrs. Lester seems a little better, Sally," observed Maria, absently fingering the corner of a cloth on which Sally was cutting some bread and butter.

" Ugh!" growled Sally. " She might be better if folks would let her."

" Where has my brother gone to?" asked Maria, for she had not known whether or not to believe in the journey to Great Cross.

Sally noted the sound of fear in the tone. Down went the knife and the loaf with a dash.

" If something's not done with him, we shall all be ruined together. He's just going mad; that's what he is: and unless he is got out of Danesheld, why—"

The woman's pause was more ominous than any words could have been. Maria's answer was a low wail of entreaty.

"Oh, Sally, tell me! Indeed I cannot bear suspense. Was he out last night?"

"Yes, he was out, Miss Lester; and I wouldn't tell you, but that it's necessary somebody should be told and something done. I winked, so to say, at the poaching; that is, I kept my tongue still about *him*; and I opened my mind to Miss Bordillion: but it did no good, and now things have come to a climax. He went out last night whilst I was up undressing my mistress, for she's weak yet, poor child. When I came down he was gone: that was about nine. I waited here in the cold, for I had let my kitchen fire out, till going on for two in the morning, and then he came in with Mr. Lydney. I saw his hat this morning, Miss Lester, and of course it told me what he had been at—hearing what took place in the night."

"Saw his hat!" faltered Maria.

"That old felt thing that he wears—indeed he has got no other. There had been black crape pinned on the inside of it," continued the woman. "It had been torn out: but one pin and a bit of the edge was left."

Maria raised her trembling hand to her brow, which was beating wildly. The disclosure was little more than her fears had suggested, but it turned her sick and faint. Visions of a felon's bar, and Wilfred standing at it, rose before her eyes; Wilfred for whom she would willingly sacrifice herself.

"I took the pin out, and I burnt the edge," added Sally. "And I'm sure every knock at the door to-day has brought my heart into my mouth, thinking it might be the officers of justice. If he should be taken upon this, Miss Lester, it will just kill his wife: she'd be in the churchyard in a week. She has heard nothing yet of the matter."

"Has he really gone to Great Cross?"

"Yes, I think he has. He wouldn't dare to be about in Danesheld, I fancy; a rare fright he has been in all day indoors! I haven't said a word to him; it's got too serious for me now."

"What should have brought Mr. Lydney with him?" cried Maria, with hesitation.

Sally threw back her head with a short laugh. "And they've taken him up, I hear, for breaking into the Hall? The fools! not to see that Mr. Lydney is different to that. I could tell them a tale, if I chose to open my mouth. Why, he has just been the salvation of my master till now; looking after him night and day to keep him straight! Mr. Lydney was here for an hour with him after he brought him home, never going away till near three o'clock: he was on the watch for him last night; I heard so much; but couldn't find what he was up to till the mischief was done. Yes, Mr. Lydney did go into the Hall," added Sally, fiercely addressing an imaginary audience straight before her, "but it was to get my master out of it."

"He told me he would try and take care of him," said Maria, very softly.

"And he has taken care of him; in a manner, if all was known, that few men would take care of another," cried Sally, who had worked herself into a passion. "And where's been the good of it, with such an ending as this?"

Maria stood shivering.

"Whatever will be done, Sally? Mr. Lydney can't *suffer* for him, you know."

"It's beyond me to tell what will be done," retorted Sally, crustily. "I have been half mad since I heard he was took up: old Gand told me when he was bringing the shrimps for missis's tea. I think—I do think he'd be generous enough to go to prison, rather than tell on Mr. Wilfred; but your brother, he's generous in his way too, Miss Lester: and what I'm fearing is, that the moment he gets home from Great Cross, and hears what has happened, he'll go right off and tell the truth to the police, so that Mr. Lydney may be released. Hasn't my foolishness come home to me!"

"Your foolishness?" returned Maria, surprised at the avowal.

"Well, yes, Miss Lester. I was soft enough to encourage them in their plan of getting married, telling them I'd serve them, and do the work of two servants. Truth was, I took their part against the cruelty of Squire Lester and his fine wife, and I've loved Mr. Wilfred as a boy of my own ever since I nursed him. It serves me right. But I never thought he'd turn out like this."

"Sally, do you know why he—my brother—did it? what his object was?"

"Not I," crossly responded the woman. "I suppose they were all going shares in the plate, and anything else they could carry away. When a gentleman begins to go from bad to worse, he doesn't stop at much."

There seemed no comfort anywhere, and Maria departed with her dread. The evening was drawing on. In every tree she feared an enemy: in every turn of the road an ambush : even now the officers of justice might be searching for her brother. Some hours had gone on since William Lydney was taken, and he had perhaps declared the truth.

When she reached home, she found a servant holding the door open for her father to come forth. Mr. Lester appeared to be in some commotion. Never, except when he had expelled Lydney, had Maria seen him so angry.

"Set at liberty a prisoner committed by me for an outrage on my house!" he exclaimed. "How could Bent dare to do it? I'll have him taken back again."

He passed Maria in a fury, never noticing her. "What is it?" she asked of the servant.

"Well, miss, there's a report that Mr. Lydney is set at liberty," was the man's reply. "My master is gone to see about it. He and my Lord Dane told Bent to-day they wouldn't hear of bail."

With a beating heart, and a confused idea, Maria ran after her father. Mr. Lester heard the steps, and turned.

"Papa, papa!" she exclaimed, hardly knowing what she said or what she ought to say, "hear me for a moment. Don't pursue this matter further. If they have released Mr. Lydney, or if they are thinking of releasing him, let it be so. We have lost nothing from the Hall; don't pursue it."

"Release Lydney! not pursue the matter!" reiterated Mr. Lester, staring at her. "What do you mean?"

"He is not guilty, papa ; he is not what you think him."

"Your reasons for saying this, young lady?" was the sarcastic rejoinder of Mr. Lester, suppressing his anger.

"I—I have none that I can give," she answered, her countenance terribly distressed. "Except—except the conviction of my own heart."

"The conviction of your folly," exclaimed Mr. Lester. "You ought to feel shame, even to mention the name of this man. I will pursue him to—to the death," added Mr. Lester, using a strong word in the moment's heat.

"Oh, papa, don't, don't!" she exclaimed, and bursting into tears. "Let well alone; let it die away. You don't know what you may do or what dreadful secrets it might bring to light. Has it never struck you that some one else may have been concerned in this, instead of Mr. Lydney?"

"Why, what do you mean?" he asked in consternation, not so much at the words as at her very strange manner. "Are you going mad?"

"I dare not say what I mean,—I dare not say it. But, papa, if you have any regard for your own honour and happiness, you will not press for an investigation into the affair of last night."

She retreated towards the house as she spoke. Mr. Lester looked after her in angry perplexity.

A miserable suspicion that she had become attached to this adventurer, Lydney, was stealing over him. But the eyes of Mr. Lester's mind were blinded, and he never cast a thought to the possibility that she was afraid for any one else, or that his own son Wilfred could have taken any part in the previous night's work.

CHAPTER XXXI.

·THE DEAD IN LIFE.

IN the invalid's room at the Sailors' Rest—for so they had taken to calling the chamber tenanted so long by the sick

stranger—sat Mr. Home in a fever of expectation. He was
not a man accustomed to be crossed or contradicted, or to
wait for the fulfilment of his mandates: he had waited in
ill-disguised impatience for the return of Mr. Apperly to
Danesheld, and now that he had returned, Mr. Home had
peremptorily demanded him.

The lawyer came bustling in at last, marshalled by Mrs.
Ravensbird. He—carrying his own umbrella and hers—
had overtaken her as she was turning into the Sailors' Rest.
Not a word spoke she as she showed him into the room and
shut the door upon him. Ravensbird was standing near the
sofa occupied by the sick man, their backs to the door.
The lawyer, summoned in such peremptory haste, was full
of nothing but some will that was to be made. He stepped
round to the front of the sofa, speaking as he went.

"I am sorry to hear you are seriously ill, sir," he began.
"Mr. Home, I believe."

The invalid raised his head and threw his eyes upon him.
His high features, somewhat attenuated now by suffering,
his keen eyes, and his silver hair, formed a fine picture.
Mr. Apperly gazed at him, and then backed a few paces,
astonishment mingled with terror on his countenance.

"Good heavens!" he uttered, as he wiped his brow. "It
—it—can it be? It *is* Captain Dane! come to life again."

"No, sir," rejoined the invalid, very sharply for one so
ill. "It is not Captain Dane. I am Lord Dane. And so
I have been ever since my father's death."

The lawyer was utterly bewildered, as well he might be.
He turned from the invalid to Ravensbird, from Ravensbird
to the invalid.

"Is it a dream?" he gasped.

"It is not a dream," said Ravensbird. "It is my old
master, sure enough; my lord now. I have been proud to
know it ever since the day after the shipwreck."

Have you been prepared for it, too, reader? It was
indeed, Harry Dane. The fall had not killed him, and you
will hear presently how he escaped; but there is matter on
hand to relate first that will not tarry. He had been living
ever since in the New World, chiefly travelling from place

to place; and completely unconscious that the Lord Dane reigning at the old house was not his brother Geoffry.

"Why you—you—are supposed to be lying in the Danesheld vaults, sir—my lord!" exclaimed Mr. Apperly. "Goodness me!" he broke off in his former hot fashion. "If you are in truth Lord Dane, who is he—the other Lord Dane—at the castle?"

"If I am in truth Lord Dane!" retorted the invalid. "What do you mean, Apperly? I am my father's son."

"Yes, yes, of course; but these sudden changes confuse me," cried the perplexed lawyer. "Who is he at the castle, I say? I can't collect my senses. Were you really not killed, my lord?"

"If I was killed I came to life again," said Lord Dane, intending the words as a joke. "He at the castle is plain Herbert Dane, and has, in actual right, never been anything else. I'm afraid he won't like being deposed after enjoying his honours so long. But now——"

"And how were you saved?" interrupted the lawyer, unable to realize the position yet.

"I was saved by Colonel Moncton, and conveyed on board his yacht to America. And I had not the remotest suspicion, until I was shipwrecked on this coast a few weeks ago, that I had any right to the honours of my ancestors, or that my brother Geoffry was dead. That's sufficient explanation for you for the present, Apperly; and now to business, for there are matters on hand that are very pressing. First of all— Do you enlist on my side, or on that of Herbert Dane, should there be litigation between us?"

"There cannot be litigation, if you mean as to your rights," returned the lawyer impulsively. "Lord Dane—I mean Mr. Herbert—could not hold out against you for an hour."

"But I don't mean as to my rights," was the rejoinder, given with quiet equanimity. "Just answer my question, will you, Apperly—and bear in mind that every moment of time is precious—will you act as my legal adviser, or as his whom you call Lord Dane?"

"As if there could be a question, my lord! As yours, of course; it is my natural right. With Lord—with Mr.

Herbert I have not been very cordial ; or rather, he has not with me ; and he now chiefly employs Mr. Lester's solicitor."

" Good. Had you decided the other way, things for me might have been difficult yet to set straight. About that lost box, Apperly ? I must have it found."

" Young Lydney's," remarked the lawyer in reply. " And a fine row he has been making over it, I hear."

" Ah ! But it's not his ; it is mine."

" Yours, my lord ! " cried Mr. Apperly, after a pause. " Then that explains the mystery of the thousand pounds reward. That a fellow such as Lydney should offer it, astonished Danesheld not a little."

" How do you mean," ' a fellow such as Lydney ? ' " cried Lord Dane, sharply taking up the words.

" Well, of course it has been suspected what sort of a character he is—although he did happen to be your lordship's fellow-passenger, and was saved with you from the wreck. However his career's cut short now, and he is in safe custody. Bent has walked him off to the station-house."

" Walked Mr. Lydney off to the station-house ! " exclaimed Ravensbird, while Lord Dane's eyes assumed an ominous expression, as they looked at the lawyer for explanation.

" Reports have been abroad some time, I find, connecting him with the poachers," said Mr. Apperly ; " but he has now got himself into real trouble. He and three more, with blackened faces, broke into Squire Lester's last night, after the plate : but they were fortunately disturbed before they could carry it off. Lydney was the only one recognised, and he is given into custody."

" How dare you so traduce him, and in my presence ? " cried Lord Dane, his countenance flashing with wrath. " You don't know what you are saying, Mr. Apperly. Are you aware who he is ? "

" Not I, my lord. I know nothing about him, except that his name's Lydney—as he says. Danesheld looks upon him as an adventurer."

" He will be Danesheld's chief, sir ; I can tell you that," returned his lordship, with emotion. " Ah, you may stare, but he will. He is my own lawful son, and will be my Lord Dane before very long, for I fear that my days are numbered."

"Why, it is mystery upon mystery!" exclaimed Mr. Apperly, who certainly did stare, in no measured degree, and grew hotter every minute. "He goes by the name of William Lydney."

"He is my own son, I tell you—the Honourable Geoffry William Lydney Dane. Geoffry is his first name, but we have always called him William: my wife, a lady of French extraction, used to say her lips would not pronounce the Geoffry. And you assert that he is in custody! Ah, well! that will be soon set to rights," concluded Lord Dane, leaning back on the sofa, and calming down from his excitement.

"He certainly was in Mr. Lester's house with the others; he does not deny it," debated the lawyer, hopelessly puzzled.

"Then, sir, he was there for some good and legitimate purpose," cried Lord Dane, with dignity. "I know nothing of the matter; he has not confided it to me; but I can take upon myself to answer for so much. Pshaw, sir! talk of housebreaking in connection with William Dane, one of the best and most honourable of men. Once more let me beg of you to listen to me," resumed the invalid. "That box, about which so much commotion has been made, was originally my mother's, Lady Dane's. The initials stood for her maiden name, Verena Vincent Verner; she was a niece, as you may remember, of General Vincent's, and his name was given to her. There's not the least doubt that Herbert Dane recognized the box as it stood on the beach; he had seen it many times, and he knew that my mother's brother, young Verner, had caused the Maltese cross to be added to it in a freak. This box, as it happened, I had left in Canada when I came over to England on that last visit. Herbert Dane, when he recognized it on the beach, must have been attacked with some vague fears, which caused him to convey the box to the Castle. He may have thought his victim was coming to life again to accuse him."

" His victim ! " cried Mr. Apperly.

" Yes, his victim. It was he who threw me over the cliff; Mr. Herbert Dane. Not intentionally; I admit that; but he suffered my faithful friend and servant here," touching Ravensbird, " to be suspected and accused of it. I know not what he may have feared, and it does not matter what ; he took the box, and is keeping it. And now, Apperly, to my chief business with you. Are there, to your knowledge, any secret places in the Castle, where such a thing might be hidden away ? "

" Yes, there are," was the prompt reply. " Old Lord Dane —your father—once showed them to me. In the trestle-closet in the strong-room—the death-room as we used to call it—there's a secret spring; touch it, and it moves a sliding panel, leading to several small hiding-places."

" Then that's where my box is !" cried Lord Dane. " Young Beecher told William he had heard the castle contained such hiding-places, but I doubted it. And that's why I have been waiting for you. I thought you'd be sure to know. It's strange my father never told me of them."

" I don't think he much cared to allude to them : there was an old tale that one of the lords of Dane had been in league with smugglers," replied Mr. Apperly. " It was partly through accident that he informed me. I showed the place to the present Lord after he came into the title."

" Very well. How can we best get at that box, Apperly ? "

" He may have destroyed it," was the answer.

" I think not. He could not open it without the key, which is a sure one. William had it in his pocket-book when he was saved. And to break it open might cause more noise and trouble than would be convenient to give, in a household, to stolen property."

" And what was in the box ? " asked Mr. Apperly.

" Instead of asking particulars, which may be left till later, suppose you apply yourself exclusively to the matter in hand," suggested Lord Dane, with a touch of the Dane peremptoriness. " How is this box to be got out of the Castle ? "

"I see only one way, my lord : your declaring yourself.
Once you show yourself at the Castle, you are its master."

"Ah ! but I would rather get the box first, if there's a
possibility of doing it," remarked Lord Dane, "I wish I
had a clever detective here ! They find their way to everything."

"There's one in Danesheld at this moment," said Mr.
Apperly. "What his business here may be, I don't know,
but I saw him pass my office this afternoon, and recognised
him : he did some business for me once."

The lawyer spoke in all unconsciousness of recent events,
or that the detective had been for nearly a week at the
Castle ; Ravensbird listened, equally ignorant that Mr.
Blair, the great London banker, could be the gentleman
alluded to.

"Couldn't you bring him to me ?" said Lord Dane.

"I might try," replied Mr. Apperly. "He may have left
again, for all I can tell ; if not I don't know where to look
for him."

"Go out and try," urged Lord Dane. "I must have that
box ; and there's my son in custody for felony : things are
coming to a pretty pass. Go at once, sir," he added, with
authority ; "and don't open the budget to the man yourself ;
leave that for me to do."

The lawyer had no choice but to obey. No end of
curiosity was racking his brain, and the temptation to look
into Mrs. Ravensbird's parlour and have "just a word with
her" was irresistible. The motive was not either great or
good, but it was destined to be rewarded. Standing there,
talking to Mrs. Ravensbird, was Mr. Blair. The lawyer
seemed to come in for nothing but surprises.

"It's my Lord Dane's banker, Mr. Blair," said Sophie,
glancing significantly at Mr. Apperly as she mentioned the
title. "He has been visiting his lordship at the Castle."

Mr. Apperly had heard my lord's banker was visiting
him ; but—*this* the banker ? He looked at the detective :
and the latter, seeing he was recognised, quietly made a sign
to him and placed his finger on his lips.

Mr. Blair's business in Danesheld was over. As Lydney,

through the precipitancy of Squire Lester, was in custody, Bent must deal with the affairs of that adventurer now. Mr. Blair could not altogether fathom things; he and Lord Dane entertained adverse opinions on trifling points, and they had parted coolly. Mr. Blair, on his way to the station, had called in to say a word of adieu at the Sailors' Rest and to sip a final petit verre. The lawyer took him aside: said that a client of his, staying at present in that very inn, had need of the services of a detective, and inquired of Mr. Blair if he would then see him.

"I must promise that you will have to act against Lord Dane, though in what manner I do not precisely understand myself," observed the lawyer. "Will your private feelings allow you to do so?"

"An officer must have no private feelings," was Mr. Blair's reply. "Lord Dane demanded a detective from town, and I was sent down. My business with him is concluded; and if I am required by another party, I have neither wish nor plea for refusing, whether my services may be put in requisition against Lord Dane, or against any other lord. I am at your service."

They went upstairs at once. Lord Dane was then standing by the fire, talking to Ravensbird; who, by the way, might have been surprised at the banker's developing into a detective, had it been in his nature to be surprised at anything. Mr. Apperly remarked that he had soon found his man, and introduced him as Mr. Blair.

"Sir," said the peer, turning upon him his fine face and form, "I have need of advice and assistance against Herbert Dane—Lord Dane as he is called. Can you aid me?"

"I do not know," was Mr. Blair's reply. "I can inform you whether anything can be done, if you will put me in possession of the circumstances. Mr. Home, I believe?"

"No, sir. When I was in want of a temporary name, I called myself Home; but it may be dropped now. I am Lord Dane."

The detective gave a slight cough; impressed with the belief that the gentleman before him was labouring under a mania, and required a keeper rather than a police officer. His eye glanced at Mr. Apperly.

"His lordship says rightly," observed the latter. "He is the true Lord Dane."

"The true veritable William Henry Lord Dane, only surviving son of the old Lord Dane, of whom you may have heard," continued the peer. "You look astonished, Mr. Blair: I thought police officers were surprised at nothing. You may probably have learnt, Mr. Detective, that Captain the Honourable William Henry Dane went over the cliff one moonlight night, by accident or by treachery, and lost his life ; that his body, turned up by the sea some weeks afterwards, was buried in the family vault ! "

" I have heard this," replied Mr. Blair.

" Well, sir—but have the goodness to take a seat whilst you listen," interrupted the peer. " I, William Henry Lord Dane, did not die in that fall : I was saved, and carried to America in a friend's yacht; and I have lived there ever since, always believing that the peer who succeeded my father, and reigned here at Dane Castle, was my elder brother, Geoffry Dane. Sir, he who threw me over the cliff was Herbert Dane, at present called Lord Dane."

The detective raised his eyes a little, but did not otherwise interrupt.

" I saw English journals occasionally," continued Lord Dane. " I knew that my mother was dead, that my father was dead, and that ' Geoffry, Lord Dane,' as the papers called it, succeeded him and reigned : and it never occurred to me to suspect it was not my brother Geoffry. Had I known it was Herbert, and that I myself was the true Lord Dane, the first and fleetest steamer would have brought me over. I had not been friendly with my brother Geoffry ; nevertheless I wrote to him after his (supposed) succession ; I received no reply to that letter, and I resented it in my heart with a haughty resentment, and would not write again. Ah ! we are prone to indulge such feelings, but punishment is sure to overtake us sooner or later. After the lapse of years, when I found my health failing, I deemed it right to return home at once. I had never heard of Lord Dane's marriage, and my son, after me, was the direct heir. We took our passage in the Wind; my poor servant was drowned in her, but I and my son were saved from the wreck, as you may have heard—"

"Your son?" Mr. Blair interrupted, speaking for the first time.

"Yes, sir, my son," returned the narrator, his choler rising. "The gentleman who had been ordered into custody to-day by George Lester, on a charge of midnight plundering is my son."

"By Jove!" exclaimed Mr. Blair, astonished for once in his life.

"William happened to have his pocket-book about him when we were saved. In it were letters of credit and other papers; so that we have been at no inconvenience of that nature. And now you are naturally wondering why I did not at once declare myself. I will tell you. For many hours I was so ill and shaken that I could only remain quiet and avoid excitement. Before that was over, I learned, to my unbounded astonishment and vexation, that it was Herbert Dane who had succeeded instead of my brother. I thought it necessary to be cautious; I continued very ill, fearing excitement, which is so pernicious to my complaint, and I was hoping the box would come up from the sea. My early marriage, sir, had been a private one. I married in Canada, when I first went out, the daughter of a French merchant who had settled there. She was wedded to me in secret, unknown to her father, whose hatred to the English was so great that any attempt to obtain his consent would have been hopeless. My wife lived on unsuspected at her father's house, making plausible absences from it occasionally. During one of these William was born, and was christened Geoffry William Lydney. Her father died, leaving her a very large fortune, and close upon it she died, and the money became my son's. I am giving you only the heads, Mr. Detective," broke off Lord Dane; "there is no time for the details. I had no particular motive for concealing my marriage. from my own family, except that I knew there would be great reproach in store for me on the score of my wife's being a merchant's daughter. When I was last at home I disclosed the fact of my being a widower to Lady Adelaide Errol, whom I was then wishing to marry. I did not tell her of the boy: but I should have declared all openly both to her and my family before the preliminaries of my marriage with her were agreed upon—in fact, the settlements would have necessitated it. Well, I was pitched over the cliff: that is, I and Herbert Dane were scuffling together, and an unlucky blow of his—not an intentional one, I am sure—sent me over. I was found by my friend Colonel Moncton, carried on board his yacht, and thence on to America. All that is of the past: it need not be enlarged upon: but I come now to the point. That box, cast up from the wreck, is, I know, in Dane Castle: how can I get it out of it?"

Mr. Blair drew his chair a few inches nearer to Lord Dane: his part was beginning now.

"Herbert Dane must have recognised the box. My mother gave it me when I first went out with my regiment to Canada, and the very day I was putting my papers and best treasures into it, Herbert Dane, then a young boy of ten or so, stood by and helped me. I remember that the cross on the box surmounting the three V.'s particularly drew his attention; and my mother told him how she had once lent the box to a brother of hers, and it came back to her thus decorated. Why, sir, that box is valuable as a family relic, if for nothing else: but its present contents are to me priceless, for my son's sake."

"Permit me," said Mr. Blair, interposing. "Will your lordship inform me what its contents were when you had it on board?"

"They were varied, sir. Papers and documents relating to my property in America, and to that of my son. My will was also in it. All these can be replaced; but it might be less easy to replace the testamentary papers of my marriage and my son's birth. And, sir, if that birth were questioned, if it could not be proved, Mr. Herbert Dane would be my legal heir, and succeed to the position he has so long unjustly enjoyed. That box has been the cause of my remaining on in this house in secrecy and seclusion," continued Lord Dane. " I never intended, you may be sure, to return home otherwise than openly, as my own proper self; but the moment the life-boat had saved us—for which we may thank young Lester—came the knowledge that we were thrown on this coast—Danesheld. I gave William a hint to be quiet; I was feeling so ill; and afterwards, as I have told you, the news burst upon me that he who reigned as baron was Herbert Dane: and next came his theft of the box."

" He could not possibly have known the contents of the box then," observed Mr. Blair, musingly. " What was his motive for taking it, I wonder ? "

" I don't know. My theory is this : that the sight of the box frightened him ; that some vague fear attacked him of the past being about to be brought to light—I mean as to his share in my supposed death. I don't know what else it can have been: a man with a secret remorse on his conscience is always in fear, more or less; and the sight of the box must have recalled me forcibly to his remembrance. Perhaps Lady Adelaide Lester disclosed my early marriage to him, and he may have feared an heir would turn up to depose him."

" Your lordship speaks of a letter you wrote to your brother; do you think Mr. Herbert Dane received that, and knows you are in existence ? "

" I cannot tell. Will you, now that you are in possession of my story so far—and these witnesses," pointing to Ravensbird and Mr. Apperly, " will corroborate it—help me with your advice as to regaining possession of the box ? "

" Certainly I will."

" Good. Will you also get my son released from custody ? "

" Yes, I think I can do that. Upon condition that he will, to myself privately, account for his presence last night with those men in Mr. Lester's house."

Lord Dane raised his head. " I know nothing about it," he said, " but I do know that William is of the kindest and most honourable nature. All his spare time is spent in looking after that ill-used son of Mr. Lester's—in trying to keep him straight, poor fellow; and I dare say he was after him last night. I'll give you a pencilled line to him, telling him to confide in you. He *may* do it?" questioned Lord Dane: "I mean as to this unhappy young Lester?"

"In all security. I'll listen as a friend, not as a detective. Perhaps I had better go there at once, whilst I think about the other matter, upon which I will give your lordship my advice when I return."

Meanwhile William Lydney—if we may still call him so —sat waiting in the station-house, in the prisoners' room. Not caring to disturb his father with the news of his incarceration, he had done nothing but despatch messengers for Mr. Apperly. The sudden opening of the door gave him hopes that the lawyer had at length arrived; but it proved to be only Lord Dane's banker, Mr. Blair.

"I bring you a line from Lord Dane," began Mr. Blair, putting the folded paper in his hand.

William looked at it, and then at his visitor.

"From whom did you say?"

"From the true Lord Dane," was the answer, given in a low tone, "and I believe I have now the honour of speaking to the future lord. Your father, in that note, bids you confide in me—he has done so. Perhaps it may be in my power to order your release."

"But what can you possibly have to do with it?" exclaimed the prisoner. "You are a friend of—of him at the castle—his town banker."

"You have been flourishing in Danesheld under false colours, Mr. Dane; so have I. I am not Lord Dane's banker—the title will slip out—and how the report got wind is more than I can say. I am one of the chief detective officers of the police force. Your father has called in my aid to assist him, and I am ready to assist you. First of all: What took you to Mr. Lester's with those companions last night?"

"I cannot explain; I cannot tell you anything about it," was the quick response.

"You were not with them?—joining with them?"

" I ! " returned William Dane, as haughtily as any Dane had ever spoken. " You intimated just now your cognizance of my rank! I do not forget it, I assure you, neither am I likely to disgrace it."

"Will you give me your reasons for not confiding in me ? "

" I don't object to doing that. It is because I could not declare the truth without compromising other people."

" Just so : you allude to young Lester, Mr. Dane. But now, I give you my promise that anything you may say shall not harm him. I have not been in Danesheld without acquiring an insight into its gossip ; it lies in my business to do so ; and I know and suspect nearly as much about that misguided young gentleman as you can tell me. I fancy he was the chief actor in that affair last night, not you. Though how he could so far forget himself as to go stealing his father's plate does surprise me."

William Dane saw that the best plan would be to confide the whole truth to the experienced man before him. And he did so. Poor ill-judging Wilfred Lester — though more hardly judged by others than he deserved, emphatically pronounced his friend — had not broken in after the silver, but after his own deed ; it was in defending the silver from attack that the discovery took place : he told all.

" These facts ought to be confided to Squire Lester," observed Mr. Blair. " For his son's sake he cannot pursue this."

" I am not sure but Squire Lester would deem it all the more reason for pursuing it," was the reply. " He is bitterly set against his son. No, I would rather stay where I am than betray Wilfred Lester. He saved my life and my father's."

" You seem wonderfully easy under your captivity," remarked Mr. Blair, gazing at the calm good-looking face.

" A man with his conscience at peace is generally easy under most circumstances. As to the accusation against me, I have only to point to the Sailors' Rest, and say there's the true Lord Dane, returned to assume his rights, and you may know me for his son. Danesheld would soon scatter the charge to the winds."

" I think I can scatter it myself, so far as your detention goes," returned Mr. Blair. " Come with me."

He led the way into the front room, where Bent sat writing. The latter rose sharply at seeing his prisoner come out. That he secretly favoured young Lydney was true ; but not to the length of showing him outward favour, now he was committed.

" I am about to relieve you of your prisoner, Bent," quietly observed Mr. Blair. " This gentleman has satisfied me of his innocence, and he must be set at liberty."

" Where's the authority for it ? " asked Bent, after a pause of blank consternation.

" *Your* authority is that you are bound to obey my orders," was the conclusive reply.

" But how I am to answer for it to my Lord Dane and to Squire Lester ? " cried the unhappy inspector, believing himself to be an excessively ill-used man. " They'll be on to me with all sorts of pains and penalties."

" Refer them to me," said Mr. Blair. " Pass out, sir."

He held the door open as he spoke, and bowed to the ex-prisoner to precede him. There was a suspicion of deference in the bow that caught the attention of the inspector. Had he possessed ten eyes he could not have stared away his perplexity. Mr. Lydney looked back, laughing.

" It's all right, Bent. The time may come when you will find it so."

CHAPTER XXXII.

IN THE TRESTLE-CLOSET.

As a matter of course, news of the arrest of Mr. Lydney had spread all over Danesheld. Therefore, to see him at liberty, walking side by side with my Lord Dane's banker, created no small surprise ; and the popular opinion arrived at was that the wealthy financier must have become bail for him. Quite a *queue* followed them along the street; and one kindly officious man flew off at the top of his speed to tell the news to Squire Lester.

But, as Mr. Blair and his companion were on the point of turning down to the Sailors' Rest, who should come swinging along the middle of the road but my Lord Dane. To describe his amazement when he saw Lydney at large would be altogether beyond the power of pen. Taking a full minute to make sure his vision was not deceiving him, he made a sign to Mr. Blair, whom he was nearly as much surprised to see. Lord Dane was not in the best of humours; for the absence of result in the detective's visit to Danesheld rested on his mind as an unsatisfactory failure; neither had his parting with that functionary been as cordial as their meeting.

"What is the meaning of this?" he haughtily demanded. "Who has dared to liberate that man?"

Mr. Blair turned off the pathway. Lydney, slightly raising his hat—and Lord Dane took the action, meant in courtesy, to be one of mockery—strolled gently on.

"Circumstances have come to my knowledge, Lord Dane, since the proceedings at Squire Lester's which render it inexpedient that Mr. Lydney should be kept in custody. I have deemed it my duty to release him."

"What do you mean?" returned Lord Dane. "Circumstances?"

"They have, indeed: Mr. Lydney is not guilty."

"I think you must be out of your mind," slowly ejaculated Lord Dane. "Not guilty! Why there never were plainer proofs of guilt! Do you know that in thus releasing him you are setting us all at defiance?—myself, Mr. Lester, the police, the—the law itself?"

"I am sorry to have had to do it. When the circumstances I speak of shall be explained——"

"Circumstances explained!" interrupted Lord Dane, too angry to listen further. "What circumstances can excuse the evasion of justice—the releasing from custody of a guilty man? How dared Bent connive at it?"

"Bent had no choice," said Mr. Blair. "When I issue orders he has not the power to disobey."

"I will see whether he has the power to disobey me," foamed Lord Dane. "I shall at once order him to retake this felon, under pain of dismissal from the force."

"I must submit—with all due respect to your lordship—that it will be waste of time for you to do so. So long as I am here, I am chief of the police force, and Bent is my servant."

Lord Dane felt beaten on all sides. Never, since he became Lord Dane, had he been so bearded. He actually stood at bay.

"What do you do in Danesheld still?" he presently demanded. "You left my house for the station an hour ago."

"True. But on my way to the station I fell in with a solicitor of this place, named Apperly, who put some business into my hands. Lord Dane, believe me, I have not ordered the release of this young man to annoy you—why should I?—but because I have learnt that the grounds on which he was given into custody were mistaken ones; and some of us might eventually have got into trouble had he been detained. But I must wish your lordship good-evening, for I have pressing business awaiting me."

He turned away with a salute, leaving Lord Dane standing helplessly. Set *him* at defiance, the lord and the chief of the county! His lordship privately believed that all the social institutions of life must be coming to an end.

He strode on to the station and met Bent coming out of it. The best excuse that ill-used inspector could offer was, that he was nobody whilst Mr. Blair was at Danesheld.

A political dinner, long looked forward to, was held that night in Danesheld, presided over by one of the county members; he was supported on either side by Lord Dane and Squire Lester. Neither of the two supporters were in a genial frame of mind. The release of the prisoner Lydney was an indisputable fact; and as yet Mr. Lester at least was utterly at sea in regard to it, for he had not been able to see Bent,

Whilst they were safely seated at table, Mr. Apperly might have been seen walking at a sharp pace towards Dane Castle. His object was to make a call on Mr. Bruff; and, as if fate wished to facilitate the courtesy, the lawyer found Mr. Bruff standing at the gateway, taking the air there in his usual fashion, and without his hat.

"Good-evening, sir; I heard you had returned," said he cheerily, for the advent of any acquaintance at these moments rejoiced the butler's heart. "You've not come up to see my lord, I hope Mr. Apperly? He has gone to the dinner."

"I come to see you, Bruff," was the response. "I want you to take a walk with me."

"A walk?" repeated Bruff.

"At the request of Lord Dane. Get your hat, and I'll tell you about it as we go down. Say nothing in-doors."

"Bruff came bustling out with his hat, and the lawyer set off at a very sharp pace again, back to Danesheld. The portly butler could scarcely keep up with him.

"My lord's not ill surely!" he cried, thinking it must be either that, or that Mr. Apperly was walking for a wager. "What can he want with me?"

"He is very ill," gravely responded Mr. Apperly. "I— I fear, Bruff, that he will never be well again."

Bruff stopped; an idea had occurred to him.

"For heaven's sake tell me the worst, Mr. Apperly! He is not dead, is he?"

"No, no, no; come along: he is as much alive as you or I. Why, he sent me for you, Bruff; there's no time to lose. I said ill, not dead."

"It was thinking of the other night made me fear it," returned Bruff, putting his best foot forward. "My lord had been for a walk on the heights—a lovely moonlight night it was, about a week ago—and I caught a glimpse of his face as he came in. Mr. Apperly, if ever you saw a corpse you might have thought he was one then! his face was livid and so scared and strange I did not like to accost him. He looked like a man who——"

"Had seen a ghost," interrupted the lawyer.

"A ghost!" returned Bruff, disdainfully. "Like a man who is attacked by some mortal illness, I was going to say. Perhaps it's the same thing to-night. Pray goodness he gets over it."

"I fancied you did not own to any ultra fondness for his lordship."

"Not as I did for the past family," spoke Bruff, with something like emotion; "especially for the old lord, and for Mr. Harry. I never did greatly like Mr. Herbert. But the rest are dead and gone, and he is Lord Dane. He is a good master."

"Could the old family—any one of them—rise from their graves to life, should you deem yourself bound to serve them or the present lord?"

"Why, the present lord would not be Lord Dane in that case," debated Bruff, after a minute given to consideration. "Where's the use of bringing up impossibilities, Mr. Apperly? As if I should serve any one in the world but the old family were they living!"

Mr. Apperly bore on with his quiet step and turned down to the Sailors' Rest. Bruff looked his displeasure.

"Is my lord so ill that they've brought him *here!* It would not have been so much farther to his own house, if they must have moved him."

"Come on and don't grumble," cried the lawyer.

He marshalled Bruff up the stairs and into the invalid's chamber. Bruff cast an impatient glance around. He saw young Lydney, Ravensbird, Mr. Blair, and some one on the sofa whom he took only a passing look at. That he had supposed the one gentleman to be in custody for house-breaking, and the other in the train half-way to London, did not much trouble him at the moment

"Where is my lord?" he cried, anxiously.

"There," said Mr. Apperly.

Lord Dane came from the sofa and stood before Bruff with a smile. Bruff's face grew long as he gazed, and he backed against the wall. Any one believing in ghosts had excited Mr. Bruff's pitying contempt all his life: he could not have asserted that he did not believe in one now.

"Don't you know me, Bruff? I am real flesh and blood."

"It—it's the living image of what Mr. Harry once was, saving the hair!" ejaculated Bruff, staring from one to another in hopeless perplexity and some fear. "But it can't be!"

"Yes, it can, Bruff. Mr. Harry was not killed by his fall over the cliff, and Mr. Harry is living still. I thought you would have known me better."

Ah! the voice came home to his ear. Could he have mistaken other signs, he could not mistake that. The water rushed into the man's eyes, and his very hands trembled with emotion, as he knelt before Lord Dane.

"My lord! my true and veritable lord! I do know you!" he uttered, the tears streaming from his eyes.

Lord Dane took his hand and bade him rise. "I shall not reign there long, Bruff; a short time will see me where I am supposed to be—in the family crypt. But," added Lord Dane, motioning his son towards him, and laying his hand upon his shoulder, "I hope you will serve another as truly and loyally as you would have served me. This will be the Castle's lord in the future."

"He is——?"

"Another Geoffry, Bruff; the Honourable Geoffry William Lydney Dane; he is my only son. Be faithful to him, for his father and grandfather's sake."

"I said he was a chieftain," answered Bruff, his delighted eyes glistening; "the first time he ever came to the Castle I saw he was born to be a chieftain. Miss Dane declared he was like my lady—she did, indeed!"

"Like my mother? Yes, the resemblance has struck me; but he has the Dane features. Bruff, I require a service at your hands. Will you execute it?"

"Ay, my lord; anything for you and yours—though it should be to the laying down of my life."

"Understand first of all, Bruff, it will involve some treachery to him at the Castle, your present master."

"I can't help it if it does," was the old retainer's answer. "And as to his being my master—I hope you'll never let

Lady Adelaide. **27**

me know another master than you, my lord, while you are spared."

"Good.   I don't like treachery myself, but perhaps it's excusable in some cases to meet treachery with treachery. He has exercised it long enough.   You don't ask who it was that sent me over the cliff."

Bruff did not ask even now. A dim suspicion was stealing over him.

"It was Herbert Dane. But not in treachery. The treachery touching that, lies in his having duped every one afterwards by passing himself off as innocent and unconscious.   That is done and over; but something else remains.   Where's that box, Bruff?"

"The missing box!" said Bruff, shaking his head. "My lord, I don't know; I have never known."

"It was my box, Bruff, and my mother's before me. I have reason to believe that Herbert Dane has that box secreted in the Castle.   Mr. Blair—this gentleman—thinks you may perhaps get it out to-night, whilst your master is away at dinner.   His opinion is worth listening to, Bruff, for he is a detective officer."

Poor Bruff's face grew hot.   The affable London banker, who had made quite a friend of him and encouraged him to talk, a detective!   What might he not have said in his incaution?   And as to the box—Bruff could have taken an affirmation, there and then, that it was not in the Castle.

Mr. Apperly set about enlightening him, telling of the secret places in the Castle, opening from the trestle-closet. Bruff wiped his face over and over again as he listened, and thought he should never recover from his surprise.

He entered into the plot, however, with all his heart and spirit, and there was no time to be wasted.   He and Mr. Apperly set out for the Castle, Ravensbird following them at a distance with a truck.   It was better not to call any stranger into the service at this stage of the affair.

He, Bruff, procured the keys, and took Mr. Apperly through the unused passage at the back of the Castle to the death-room.   No one saw their entrance, or suspected it: and Ravensbird, sitting on his truck, quietly waited in an obscure corner outside. The spring in the closet, as once shown to Mr. Apperly by the late Lord Dane, was found without difficulty, and the panel went sliding slowly back.

A small room, seven feet square, lay disclosed to view. It was empty except for one object in the middle—the missing box. " Ah!" cried Mr. Apperly.

Bruff, when he had done gazing at the box—for he had remained somewhat sceptical as to the possibilities—was protesting to himself that he should never feel certain of anything again.

" I'll tell you what," he said to the lawyer: " he must have lugged this in here himself at the moment of his arrival, while I was seeing the miller's men out. Though how he should have had strength to move it I can't conceive."

" I wonder where that leads to?" cried the lawyer, pointing to a little obscure doorway in a corner. " To the vaults, I suppose, below the Castle."

Hovering near Ravensbird and the truck, in case of any surprise from the police which might render his authority desirable, was Mr. Blair. Nothing, however, occurred. The box was deposited in the truck, jealously covered up from the view of chance passers-by, and safely wheeled away by Ravensbird, Mr. Blair and the lawyer keeping the truck in sight. Bruff remained at the Castle: not quite yet was his service to its ostensible lord over.

And when the box, arrived at the Sailors' Rest, was carried up the stairs, still jealously covered, and into the presence of its owner, the real lord, and he saw it was still intact and inviolate, he looked at his son, thanksgiving filling his heart. The true heir of Dane from henceforth, and to be known as such! All need for concealment was over.

" But understand, William, that you do not proclaim yourself; I choose to do it for you, and to take my own time about it," said Lord Dane. " For to-night at least you are William Lydney."

" Very well," was the laughing answer. " Take a week if you like: I rather enjoy the fun."

The young man took up his hat as he spoke, to search for Wilfred Lester. He had not seen him all day, and was unable to get rid of an undefined feeling of uneasiness with regard to him.

He chose the road by Danesheld Hall. Not for convenience; it was the longest way; but there was no other so charming to William Lydney. As he came to the wood-path, he heard voices in something like dispute, and recognised Wilfred and his sister. He had returned from Great Cross, and Maria, in her uneasiness, had gone out again to meet him. She offered him a little money, all she could get together; she begged him to leave the place until the danger should blow over. Wilfred stood in sullen anger. He was fond of Maria, and felt terribly vexed that she should suspect anything. Her entreaties were met with angry denials: one word led to another, and at length Maria burst into tears, and whispered that he would be kinder if he knew that she might have to sacrifice herself for his sake and marry Lord Dane.

"Oh, indeed!" said Wilfred, and just at that moment Mr. Lydney came up. Wilfred had not heard of his late capture; Maria supposed he was out on bail. She felt very much ashamed to be caught crying, and Mr. Lydney was silent from surprise.

"Yes, you may well stare!" said Wilfred, in his reckless spirit. "They have ordered her now to marry my Lord Dane; by which arrangement the Hall will be rid of both of us."

"Oh, Wilfred!" she interposed, her cheeks flaming.

"I was going to your house, Lester," interposed Mr. Lydney, hoping to put them at their ease. "I want to speak to you."

"All right; you can walk back with me," he readily answered, rejoiced at the prospect of getting rid of Maria and her suspicions. "Would you mind just seeing my sister to the turning, Lydney?" he continued; "I don't care to go further myself, and will wait for you here."

Thus unceremoniously disposed of, Maria could only hasten away. Mr. Lydney followed her.

"Let me share your distress," he began in low confidential tones. "Perhaps I may be able to alleviate it, whatever it may be."

It brought back all her fears and she was too agitated to speak.

"You are ill—or agitated," he resumed, perceiving the fact. "Which is it?"

"Both," she replied, turning her face to him. "Oh! do *you* tell me the truth about last night! The suspense is killing me."

"Do you mean the truth about myself?"

"No, no; I have never doubted you. I know that you are one of the firmest friends man can possess: I know that you have been publicly bearing to-day the sins of another in generous silence, so that he should not be suspected. It was Wilfred who came into the Hall last night, and Tiffle mistook him for you."

"No so; Tiffle's eyes are too keen to be deceived. It was myself she saw."

"If you only knew how terrible my fears and suspense are, I think you would not play with me, Mr. Lydney," she faintly said, as if wearied with the contest. "You asked me once to trust you, and I do trust you wholly and entirely, as I would my brother. Will you not bestow on me a little confidence in return? I have learnt that Wilfred was one of those who came in. What was his motive?"

Finding she knew so much, he told her all, describing the facts as they occurred. She listened with a strange sinking of the heart.

"What was his object?" she questioned. "It is impossible that it could have been the plate—unless he has gone quite mad."

"Not the plate, certainly. It was in defending that against the men who were with him that discovery arose. Have you forgotten something else that Wilfred wanted to gain possession of?" he continued: and a sudden light flashed on Maria.

"The deed! It was for that! Did he get it?"

"He did. Mr. Lester has no suspicion of the loss; and

it is well he has not, for it might help him to guess at the real offender."

"I see it all," she murmured. "And you are bearing the odium to shield him! How shall we ever repay you!"

A peculiar smile crossed his lips. "I may be asking for it some time," he said; "but meanwhile let me beg of you to set your fears at rest. There is one quite as powerful as your friend Lord Dane, who has taken Wilfred's interest to heart. His intention is to see him safe out of his troubles generally, including this one, and I am sure he will carry it through."

"Do you mean yourself?"

"No. I am only an agent in the matter. Believe me, things will be made right. Maria, I would not assure you of this lightly."

"But how shall you exonerate yourself? You cannot be *tried* for him! You are only out on bail!"

William Lydney laughed. "I am a great deal more all right than he is; and I am released absolutely, not conditionally. Remember one thing, Maria; that as yet Wilfred is not suspected in Danesheld of having been in this; you must be cautious not to let a hint of it escape you. The best plan will be to forget it yourself. Don't you think you can do so?" he added, turning to her.

"I wish I could."

"Nay, but is it so very difficult, when you have me to trust to?" he softly whispered. "I hope you will have greater things to trust me in than this, as we go through life."

The words called up a vivid blush, a feeling of sadness. Even now, only in walking with him thus, she was all too aware of the scornful reproach that would have been cast on her had Danesheld been by to see. She knew not who or what he was; she had only her own conviction of his worth and honour to guide her. But Maria Lester was not one to throw herself in the face of the world's opinion, and publicly set up a standard of her own.

"In a very short time—it may be in a few hours—I shall have it in my power to speak to Mr. Lester. You will give me permission to do so?"

" To speak to him ? " she rejoined, not understanding.

"On your account. As I hear that Lord Dane would press his claims, I must advance mine, and ask that you may be allowed to choose between us."

He took her hand in his. Her heart, in spite of its doubts and troubles, was beating with a wild sensation of happiness ; perhaps it was this that caused her not to notice footsteps behind them.

They were Lord Dane's. His lordship had made his escape from the dinner, unseen, on the removal of the cloth. He was ill at ease, and chose the quieter road home. The dining-hall, one recently built, was near the new railway station.

But to describe his indignant astonishment when he made out that the man who turned to look at him was the ex-prisoner, and the young lady by his side Miss Lester, would be difficult. Maria, with a sense of the apparent unfitness of things, offered some confused explanation of having just left Wilfred. Lord Dane haughtily expressed his intention of seeing her safe home, and made a movement to take her on his arm, which Mr. Lydney prevented by unceremoniously taking her on his own.

" Your pardon, Lord Dane ; I am quite competent to take charge of Miss Lester."

"Unhand Miss Lester, sir," cried Lord Dane passionately. " Maria, can you be aware how you are degrading yourself ? "

Between the two her position was anything but pleasant, and she grew agitated. She strove to withdraw her arm, but Mr. Lydney held it firmly. It rather vexed her to see a careless smile upon his face. Lord Dane turned his anger on Maria.

" I shall begin to believe the disgraceful report current in Danesheld, that this man, this adventurer, this midnight housebreaker, has gained Miss Lester's ear, when he would cajole her into forgetting social ties and decency, and ally herself to him ! "

"As your lordship has entered on the topic, I may as well avow that the first hope of my life is, so far, to gain

Miss Lester's ear—and heart—and hand," he coolly answered. "Should I succeed, she shall at least find happiness. It may be, that, of the two, I can insure *that* better than your lordship would."

"Maria," cried Lord Dane, his breath half taken away and his eyes flashing, "can you bear this insolence tamely? I cannot. Permit me to remind you that it is a gross insult on you, the future Lady Dane."

"No, it is not," said William Lydney, whilst Maria rather wished the earth would open and extricate her from this position of embarrassment. "As to her being the future Lady Dane—my earnest hope is that she will be."

Maria started. Lord Dane looked on the words as a bit of insolent mockery, and would have liked to fell him to the ground. But the turning was gained now; the entrance to Mr. Lester's was at hand, and Maria, seeing the door open, freed her arm and escaped into it. Mr. Lydney struck across the wood-path, which was the nearest way to the Sailors' Rest, at the risk of keeping Wilfred Lester waiting; but he had somewhat to say to his father, and Lord Dane went on towards home in a fever of passion, registering a vow as he strode along that the morrow should see Danesheld rid of this dangerous man.

CHAPTER XXXIII.

SOWING AND REAPING.

THINGS generally happen by contraries. As Maria dashed into the Hall in blindfold haste, she ran against Lady Adelaide and Mr. Apperly. The lawyer had come with an urgent, if somewhat mysterious, request that her ladyship would accompany him at once to see a gentleman lying ill at the Sailors' Rest. An old friend of hers, he said. Lady

Adelaide complied, and was going forth now with her things on—a suspicion having at once crossed her that the mysterious stranger was her random brother, Lord Irkdale, come to grief.

She spoke sharply to Maria for coming in so late from (as she supposed) Miss Bordillion's, asking who had seen her home.

And Maria had no resource but to say Mr. Lydney: for the question was a peremptory one, and Wilfred's name she dared not mention.

Lady Adelaide lifted her eyebrows in pitying scorn, and went out.

"Were Miss Lester my own daughter, I should know how to treat this matter," she observed to the lawyer. "As it is, I wash my hands of her. If she chooses to lose caste, as her brother has done, why she must do so. How you lawyers and police people can have allowed the man to go out on bail I cannot understand."

"There were grave doubts, I hear, as to his guilt, Lady Adelaide. But in regard to this report—that he is seeking to win Miss Lester for his wife——"

"I think the less you allude to that in my presence, sir, the better," came the haughty interruption.

"I beg your pardon, Lady Adelaide: I was only going to say that Miss Lester might go farther and fare worse."

"She might—what?" cried Lady Adelaide, surprised into the question.

"Go farther and fare worse," was the calm rejoinder. And Lady Adelaide clasped her shawl round her with an impatient movement, disdaining an answer.

"I suspect it is my brother, Lord Irkdale, who is playing me this trick: bringing me out at this unseasonable hour!" she presently said. "It would be just like him to be in some scrape, and unable to show himself." And this time it was the lawyer's turn to make no reply.

The only person Lady Adelaide saw on entering the invalid's room at the Sailors' Rest, was William Lydney. He advanced as if to receive her: indignation flashed from her voice and eye, reproach from her lips,

"Is this your doing, sir? Have *you* dared to call me from my home?"

"It was I who sent for you, Adelaide."

The voice came from behind Lydney, and she started at the sound. There, holding out his hands in greeting, stood Harry Dane, if ever she had seen him in her life—Harry Dane, who was supposed to be lying in the vault at Danesheld. She screamed, shivered, and might have fallen, but that William Lydney hastened to support her. He then quietly retired, and left them together.

Crouching as one in mortal shame and repentance, her face buried on the pillow of the sofa, was the Lady Adelaide, when explanations had partly taken place. In the surprise of the first moments she spoke words which disclosed to Lord Dane—the real lord—what he had suspected from the revelations of Ravensbird and Sophie—that she *had* recognized both himself and Herbert Dane that fatal night, and that the solemn oath she took was a false one.

"My days, for year afterwards, were as one living misery," she wailed in her despair; "the awful terror of discovery was ever upon me. Had I been tried for the crime of perjury, and sent to prison I could not have suffered more than I have suffered; over and over have I lived it again in my dreams."

He sat by, at a little distance, listening.

"And that was not all. I have looked upon myself as your murderer also in a degree: for, had I told at once what I saw, you might have been rescued; and I did not tell it, in my infatuation for Herbert Dane. Ah, how the sin came home to me ere many hours had elapsed! But it was too late then, and I took that oath which has been so fatal to my peace."

"A heavy secret to bear, Adelaide."

"A secret that has made the curse of my existence," was the passionate answer. "In the day's excitement, in the midnight solitude, I have had one awful scene ever before me—the struggle between you and Herbert on the heights, and my false oath following on it. See you not what might have been brought home to me, had the truth come out?—

complicity in the crime. In the daily intercourse, in the conversation with friends, these thoughts have come flashing before my mind's eyes, and I have stopped to shudder. Oh heavens! do you know what secret terror is, Harry? never-ceasing terror of being discovered in some awful guilt? When I did get to sleep in the dark night, it has awakened me, terrified, as from some ghastly dream. They grow to say in the household that I was subject to nightmare; my husband thought it. As a heavy burden on the shoulders weighs down the body, so has the past weighed down my spirit—and I have never dared to tell of it."

"Did Herbert bind you to secrecy?"

"Never. He does not know to this hour that I recognized either him or you. He may have suspected it: I cannot tell. I have held scarcely any communication with him since."

"Altogether, then, my supposed death did not bring you happiness, Adelaide?"

A wail of pain was the only answer. Happiness? Her days had been, as she said, one living misery. The haunting fear, the remorse (it was not repentance), had made her the wretch she was—cold, cruel, indifferent—hateful in her selfishness.

Once more Harry Dane rose and essayed to raise her from her abject position. He succeeded this time, and she sat on the sofa; but she let her brow fall upon its arm.

"But for your own conduct, Adelaide," he said, resuming his chair, "that night's work had never taken place."

Did she not know it—better than he—putting up her hand as if to bar remembrance? "It is past, Harry—it is past."

"Yes, it is past," he assented, "and may bear to be spoken of, now that romance has yielded to the realities of life. I am older than my years, slowly dying of a complaint that is incurable: you are a married woman, and the mother of many children."

She lifted her head. "Who says that you are dying?"

"I say so; the medical men say so; my frame says so. Nothing is more deceitful than my apparent strength: it is deceitful as you were, Adelaide."

She made a deprecating motion with her hands: nothing more.

"Why did you deceive me?" resumed Lord Dane. "Every thought of your life, as I learnt too late, was full of deceit towards me. It came of your absorbing love for Herbert. You refused, after all, to marry him; and I don't wonder, looking on him as a murderer. Did your love for him cease with that night?"

"Can love cease so rapidly?" she asked. "I am not sure that it had quite left me when he came back from his ten years' absence. If I have been false in other things I was at least true in that: I could not help it."

"Yet, in the midst of this love, you married George Lester!"

"What else was left to me? It seemed a more tolerable fate than to be banished to Scotland. He has been an indulgent husband."

"Very much so, I hear," returned Lord Dane. "More indulgent than he has been to poor Katherine Bordillion's children."

The severe, honourable Dane face was bent upon her, and her own flushed, with a burning flush. If the treatment she had pursued towards those children never came home to her before, it came now in all its sin and shame.

"Won't you tell me how you escaped?" she asked, striving to drown the subject.

"And how I discovered the treachery that led to the catastrophe?" he answered, evidently not feeling inclined wholly to spare her. "Can you cast your recollections back to the time?"

"As if they had not always been cast back!—for these ten years."

"I heard that you—Adelaide Errol, whom I so loved—were deceiving me: that, whilst you only professed to care for me, your real love was given to Herbert Dane. I heard that you were in the habit of running out to him on the heights at night. I disbelieved the story, and resented it on my informant. But, as I was going through the chapel ruins with Colonel Moncton, I found a bow of pink ribbon, studded in the centre with pearls. I recognised it for the one you had worn the previous day at dinner, and knew you must have been out with Herbert Dane in the evening. In a moment my eyes were opened, and I determined to watch. Do you remember my coming in unexpectedly to dinner, when my father thought I was dining on board the Pearl? —Do you remember my silence? I had been brooding over my wrongs all the afternoon, and was in no mood even for Moncton's society. Dinner over, I quitted the Castle to go on board the yacht, and say farewell; but I first crossed to the heights, and there I was followed by a man with a tray of small wares on his back. He took it down, and importuned me to buy. I refused—harshly enough, I dare say, for I was in no mood for suavity—and the fellow grew loud and insulting. I promised him if he did not be off I would call forth the servants from my father's castle to convey him and his pack to the lock-up: he hurried away, and I went on to the ruins and stepped inside. I was looking out for proofs of the tale I had been told, waiting for you and for Herbert Dane."

Lord Dane paused and regarded her; but there came only a faint moan by way of answer.

"*He* came. He came stealing up to the ruins; and in my angry emotion I gave some indication of my presence there—not intentionally: I had meant to wait until later to have it out with him; I had engaged to go to his house that evening. He heard the sound and spoke in a whisper: 'Is that you, my dearest?' Can you wonder, Lady Adelaide, that the words goaded my fiery nature beyond control? I sprang out, and reproached him with his infamous treachery: it came to blows; to a struggle; and he pushed me over the cliff."

"Did he do it purposely?" she gasped, showing for a moment her haggard and anxious face.

"No; I think not. In our passion we were both, I fancy, unaware that the edge was so near. I fell, insensible; and he, no doubt, made a speedy escape."

"But how were you rescued?" she asked. "Mitchel, the coastguardsman, left you for dead, and the tide was coming up."

"I was rescued by one of those special interpositions of Providence that come direct from Heaven," reverently replied Lord Dane. "Colonel Moncton, disappointed of seeing me on board, anxious to bid me farewell, caused his yacht to heave-to, when she was abreast of the Castle, put off in the boat with a hand, and came to the very spot where I was lying, intending to seek me at home. Now, mark you: he was not well acquainted with the coast, and he mistook this small beach for the larger one higher up, which I had shown him in the morning: we had gone down the steps to it from the heights together. He found me lying there insensible; and instead of wasting time by trying to find the place, he put me in the boat with the help of the sailor, and they pulled back to the yacht. The motion revived me. Moncton was for putting back to port; but I, smarting under the treatment of the Lady Adelaide, preferred to go on with him, and make the voyage. 'Not back, not back!' I reiterated; 'go on, go on!' My head was confused from its injuries, my arm and side were badly hurt; but they listened to my earnest cries, and sailed gently on. I would not have them put in anywhere; I would not even have Moncton write. 'Let them think me dead,' I said to him."

"But why?"

"Ah, why! You may well ask it. Why do we say foolish things in our passionate tempers? I was feeling that the whole world was against me; that Heaven had turned its eyes from me; and it seemed to my bitterness—my selfishness, if you will—very gratifying to resent it."

"But to go off in that way!" she murmured reproachfully, thinking of the life's pain that might have been spared her.

"That night was the turning-point in my life as well as in yours," was Lord Dane's significant answer. "It opened my eyes to the fact that she for whom alone I cared on earth was but playing a game with me—that whilst her shafts of ridicule and dislike were thrown at me, she kept her heart's love for Herbert Dane. He boasted of this in the scuffle. To become an alien seemed the most sensible thing I could do: perhaps I was romantic enough to enjoy the momentary pang my supposed death might inflict on the

Lady Adelaide: and for myself, England had suddenly become hateful to me."

How hateful the past deceit was feeling to her now, she alone knew—hateful in its shame.

"But now: I never supposed but that the fact of the yacht's picking me up would have been seen, and of course known," resumed Lord Dane. "Thus I was at ease in regard to the suspense of my father and mother; and they could wait for letters from me. By the time we reached the end of the voyage I was in a low fever, a long nervous fever, prostrating both mind and body. 'I will write to them when I get well,' I said to Moncton; and again I forbade *him* to write. It incapacitated me for months, and was the result, I take it, of the blow to my head, combined with the sickness and disappointment of mind. I put off writing from time to time, as one, sick, will put off things; they were not writing to me, and I did not write to them. It was very wrong of me, and I was severely punished. One night, when weeks if not months had gone on, I was dreaming very much of my father and mother. In the morning it struck me that I had been on the wrong tack— that my silence was nothing but unjustifiable ingratitude. 'I'll write to-day,' I said. And I did write. That is I had paper and ink before me, and was in the middle of the first page, when a friend came in with a London weekly newspaper. 'I'm afraid there's something here that concerns you, Dane,' he said, and I took the paper in my hand. These curious coincidences have been known before, Adelaide— home news following upon a home dream. The paragraph told me of the death of my father and mother."

"Of *both*? They did not die at the same time."

"Of both. The real news intended by the paragraph was the death of Lord Dane, my father; but it commented on the short time which had elapsed since the decease of his wife. A concluding sentence—it was only a word or two— mentioned the succession of 'Geoffry, now Baron Dane;' and I of course took it to be my brother. I wrote at once, and I never had an answer."

She looked up quickly.

"No; I received no answer. It vexed me; I supposed Geoffry was nourishing our old brotherly resentment, and I, so to say, *let* him nourish it, and washed my hands of him. Altogether I did not much care whether I ever heard from England again, or whether I did not. I remained away, holding no communication with it, passing the years in visiting remote regions of the New World, travelling everywhere, and never dreaming it was Mr. Herbert who reigned. The remembrance of me cannot have been pleasant to him," concluded Lord Dane after a pause of thought.

Lady Adelaide shook her head. "Others wondered why he went abroad on coming into possession and remained away for years. *I* could have told them—that the sight of the old spot was unbearable to him."

"Yes," responded Lord Dane. "And he may have felt himself safer when beyond the pale of British law. The fear of detection, of the discovery that he was the actor in the night scene, Harry Dane's assailant, must have caused him many a sleepless night: the coroner's verdict was 'Wilful Murder.'"

A pause ensued. It seemed that she could never look up from her agony again.

"Did Herbert receive that letter—the one I wrote to Geoffry? It was addressed to The Lord Dane."

"I know nothing about it. I have held scarcely any communication with him since that night; literally since that night. I should say that he did not receive it."

"Why should you say it?"

"Because—to judge of his feelings by my own—the finding that you were alive must have been the greatest relief that earth or heaven could give him, and he would have hastened to make reparation for the past. At least, it seems so to me. When did you arrive at Danesheld?" she continued. "To-day?"

"Last September, when the troubled sea cast me ashore on my own coast. A curious thing that, was it not? But for your stepson's exertions with the life-boat I had never again seen Danesheld."

"Last September!" she repeated, full of astonishment.

"Was it you who were saved? Is it you who have been lying here since, as the old passenger named Home?"

"Even so."

"But why have you done so?"

"I have had my reasons for it. Possibly—for one thing—from the delicacy of not wishing to deprive my Lord Dane too abruptly of his title and rent-roll."

There was a grim smile of mockery on his face as he spoke. Lady Adelaide Lester slightly started as the full import of the words struck her. She had not thought of it before.

"Why, yes; as you are here, Herbert cannot be the rightful possessor," she slowly said. "You—must—be—Lord Dane!"

"I am. Herbert is not and never has been Lord Dane."

"Then *why* have you not returned to assume your title?"

"I knew not that I had a title to assume. Did you not understand what I said—that I thought Lord Dane was my brother Geoffry?"

"I see, I see: my mind is all confusion. What a blow in that respect it will be for him!"

"Not the least doubt about that. I hear of a rumour abroad that he is seeking a wife in Maria Lester. Pretty child! I can only think of her as she was in the old days."

"How can you have heard that?" exclaimed Lady Adelaide.

"I hear most things," was the careless answer. "Do you favour his hopes?"

"I neither favour nor discourage them. I would not interfere in any project of marriage for Herbert Dane. Maria does not care for him: she is degenerate as her brother, and has fallen into an acquaintance with that Lydney, who must have been your fellow-passenger from America. But you must be cautious, Harry: I saw him in your room when I came in. He has turned out to be a sad character; an adventurer, a poacher, a midnight robber; and he is after Maria for the sake of her money. He broke into our house last night."

"Indeed!" was the composed rejoinder. "Grave accusations to bring against a Dane."

"Against a Dane! Of course they would be; but I am not speaking of a Dane."

"I am. William Lydney is a Dane, and was born one."

Lady Adelaide sat up half stupefied. Lord Dane bent forward and touched her arm.

"You may remember that I informed you of my early marriage. I did not tell you that I had a son born of it, but I intended to acquaint you with it, Adelaide, before I made you my wife. It is he whom you Danesheld people have been mistaking for an adventurer and all the rest of it. He is my own son—Geoffry William Lydney Dane."

"Why then he—he—will be—surely—Lord Dane!" uttered she, when she had gathered her senses together.

"The very moment this fleeting breath shall go out of my body he is lord of Danesheld."

"And he is really your son? But when you entrusted me with the secret of your marriage, why did you not tell me about him?"

"I suppose I thought it better to disclose the facts by degrees. As a matter of course—I may say of necessity—I should have told you before our marriage. In a pecuniary sense he could have made no difference. The boy had his own large fortune, and required no more from me. I never expected then to succeed to the title, and did not give that possibility a thought. My brother, poor fellow, was as healthy a man as I was, and intended to marry some time."

"Your son is rich, then?"

"Very: apart from the Dane revenues. He would be a better match than the cousin Herbert for Maria Lester."

"Shall you proceed against him?" she asked in a low tone.

"What for? Poaching? or housebreaking?"

"O, Harry, don't joke! it seems to mock my misery. I meant—but never mind, never mind!" She had been thinking of Herbert.

"Take it for all in all, then, Adelaide, life has not been to you all flowers and sunshine."

Flowers and sunshine! Take it for all in all—as Lord

Dane put it—it had been a wretched life. The world had spoken of the gay Lady Adelaide; it had more cause to tell of the miserable one. An awful fear of detection had been ever upon her, as it had been on Herbert Lord Dane. And she burst into tears, for the first time during the interview.

"As we sow, so must we reap," said Lord Dane. "Deceit, sooner or later, brings its own punishment."

Suddenly she rose up, and flung herself on her knees before him. She looked up, her eyes streaming.

"Harry, you will keep my wretched secret! You will not betray me! I ask it by the love you once bore me."

"The secret?" he rejoined, scarcely understanding her.

"That I recognised you and Herbert that night. "Oh, I heard some of the words you said, and knew the quarrel was about me! Heaven is merciful; don't you be less so! I would rather die, here as I am, than have the shame and reproach of that oath brought home to me."

Not until he gave her the promise—which he did readily —would she get up, or let him raise her. "From henceforth it should be buried in silence," he answered, "as must other matters connected with the past."

She wound her shawl about her and put her bonnet on to go forth. Lord Dane wondered where his son was, that he might see her home: but she shook her head and put up her hands to wave off the suggestion; she would go forth alone.

"Will you oblige me in one thing, Adelaide?—For the next few hours keep these matters wholly to yourself. I prefer to make myself known in my own way: until then I am Mr. Home."

She bowed her head, and went down the stairs with her veil drawn tightly before her disturbed face, haggard enough then. Mrs. Ravensbird met her at the foot of the stairs.

"Oh, my lady! I would have warned you had I dared," she whispered. "I hope it did not overwhelm you!"

"Have you known it all along, Sophie?"

"Since the second night he was here, my lady. He took off the shade, which was nothing but a disguise, and disclosed himself to Ravensbird. Of course it could not be kept from

me, as I should have known him for myself. And to think
I was ransacking my memory for some face in France that
young Mr. Dane's was like, when I might have found it
nearer home in my late lady's."

Lady Adelaide turned from the gossip and went forth
alone—alone with her humilation and her pain.

CHAPTER XXXIV.

A MAN MAY NOT MARRY HIS GRANDMOTHER.

LORD DANE—meaning Herbert, but we must give him the
title a little longer—sat in the breakfast-room at the Castle
with his sister. The meal had long been over: but he
seemed in a doubtful, reflective, undecided sort of mood. He
had work on his hands that day—the getting rid of Lydney;
and he did not altogether see in what way to set about it.
Miss Dane, airily attired as usual in gay colours, pink pre-
vailing, was playing Bo-peep with a canary-bird, whose cage
hung in the window. She was in a little dilemma on her
own score; for she had done something that might not be
pleasant to her brother, and had now to confess it.

"Geoffry, dear, I want to tell you something," she began.
"You won't be angry?"

"When am I angry with you, Cely?" was the answer.

"Well, then, I've written to ask Mr. Lydney to call
here."

Lord Dane turned sharply round. "You have written
to ask Lydney to call here?" he echoed in incredulous
surprise.

"Well, yes, it was last night, Geoffry. When I heard
that the police had released him from that horrid charge, I
wrote and asked him to call upon me the first thing this
morning. And, Geoffry, dear, if they had kept him in
custody, I should have gone in the carriage to the station,

and paid him a morning visit, just to show my respect to him, and to let Danesheld know how very much I resent the opinion taken up about him. I asked him, one day, whether he was rich—rich enough to keep a wife; and he laughed, and said, 'Yes, and a gilt coach-and-six for her.' He is entitled to consideration, Geoffry, and I shall show it him."

She had delivered all this very quickly, and Lord Dane's attempt to interrupt her had failed. But he spoke with determination now.

"You will certainly not receive him in my house, Cecilia."

"Ah, but I must, Geoffry, dear, for he's coming up the road now," she answered, with a laugh of simplicity. "You'll hear his ring in a minute."

And in truth a ring was speedily heard. Lord Dane went out of the room, muttering a speech not at all complimentary, in which he told her she was a "little fool," and strode downstairs. William Lydney was already in the large hall, and Lord Dane was just in time to see Bruff bowing to him. Bowing to a housebreaker !

"What do you do here, sir ? " he asked, confronting the intruder.

"I came in obedience to a request of Miss Dane's," replied Lydney, courteously. "My visit is not to your lordship."

"I am the master of this house, sir; and there's the door," was the haughty retort. "Go out of it."

He raised his hand as if to enforce the mandate. Bruff hastened between them, full of excitement.

"Oh, my lord, don't, don't ! " he pleaded, in an agitation he could not suppress. "You may be sorry for it later. This gentleman may have as much right as your lordship—to—to enter castles."

Before Lord Dane could fling Bruff aside—if he had a mind to do it—Mr. Blair entered, having followed Lydney to the Castle. He took in the scene at a glance, and advanced to Lord Dane.

"Sir," he said in a low tone, "will you grant me an interview before dealing further with this gentleman ? "

"Sir! *Sir !* " repeated Lord Dane, astonished at the style

of address. For some ten years now he had left the " sir "
behind him.

"I speak advisedly," was Mr. Blair's answer. "I have
strange tidings to communicate to you."

Lord Dane glanced around him—glanced waveringly
from one to the other, as if seized with some inward terror.
The detective officer stood calm and impassive; Lydney
dignified, yet with somewhat of pity in his countenance;
Bruff terribly troubled, but testifying much respect to the
young man. Lord Dane noted it all, and for once his self-
possession deserted him. The prevision of some impending
calamity was upon him, but he did not guess its true
nature.

"Pass in here," he said to Mr. Blair, motioning to Bruff
to open the door of the dining-room ; and, as the old butler
hastened to obey, he saw the same livid look on his master's
face which it had worn the night he passed him in the gateway. They were shut in, and Lord Dane motioned to the
officer to take a chair.

"I have come here to prepare you for a most unwelcome
surprise," began Mr. Blair, somewhat at a loss for words in
which to break the strange tidings; "and I have but a
minute or two to do it in, for one is following me close at
hand whose appearance may startle you unpleasantly. But
you are ill ! "

"No," replied Lord Dane, biting his quivering and rebellious lips. "Proceed."

"You were surprised at my addressing you as 'sir,' and
naturally so. I am sorry that it should have fallen to my
task to inform you of the change hanging over your head ;
but I must do my duty, unpleasant as it. When I released
William Lydney from custody, you questioned my motives,
my right—I believe my good feeling. I could not explain
matters to you then, but I have come to do so now ; and I
can only ask you to *bear* it as a man."

Lord Dane made no reply. He stood with his arms
folded, and his pale face turned on the speaker. That he
only controlled himself to calmness by a very great effort,
was evident.

"Some ten years ago," proceeded Mr. Blair, "a catastrophe occurred in the Dane family. Captain the Honourable Harry Dane met his death, as was supposed, in falling from the heights, struggling with an assailant. Until a day or two ago, it was neither known nor suspected who the other was; but it is at length discovered to have been yourself."

Mr. Blair paused, alarmed at the appearance of Lord Dane, whose agitation was growing painful.

And well it might be! All that he had secretly dreaded for years had come at last. Lady Adelaide wailed over her burden, but hers was light compared with his. One perpetual nightmare had lain upon his soul. In his visions by day, his dreams by night, the racking terror of DISCOVERY had ever been present in all its torment; when he should be dragged from his high pinnacle to answer for the murder of his cousin Harry; perhaps to suffer for it a felon's punishment, death upon the scaffold. That the officer now speaking was about to arrest him, and was thus preparing him, in his humanity, for the blow, he entertained no manner of doubt. The perspiration broke on his brow in great drops of anguish, and he threw up his entreating hands to Mr. Blair.

"It was not wilful murder," he gasped, in tones of the sharpest pain. "If you arrest me for it, you will do me a foul wrong, for I am innocent. We were quarrelling, and it came to blows; he struck the first, as I have a soul to be saved! It was he who attacked me. We approached too near the edge of the cliff in our strife, and he went over, but I did not mean to push him: I swear I did not. I was as guiltless of intentionally causing his death as I am of causing yours. Could Harry Dane speak to you from the next world he would say so."

"Nay, but there is no cause for this violent agitation," interposed Mr. Blair. "Had you heard me to an end——"

"I have thought that something of this unpleasant nature was coming upon me," continued Lord Dane, in a dreamy tone, never so much as hearing the interruption. "A few nights ago Harry Dane appeared to me."

"Oh, he did, did he?" cried Mr. Blair. "His ghost, I suppose? Where?"

"Ay, ridicule it! As I have always ridiculed such tales, deeming them worthy of the veriest mockery. Ghosts! visions! supernatural appearances! they might do well enough for children and women, but not for men. Nevertheless I tell you, in the broad light of day, and in full possession of my senses, that I saw the apparition of my cousin Harry. I was passing through the ruins opposite, and I saw, at one of the apertures, gazing in upon me, the form of Harry Dane. It was bright moonlight. I recognized the features as plainly as ever I had recognized them in his lifetime."

Lord Dane's words concluded abruptly. A stir in the hall, as of much bustle and many voices, was heard. He supposed that the officers of justice were come to apprehend him; and, before Mr. Blair could explain, he opened the door about an inch, and peeped out.

Not much like officers of justice, however, did the group look that met his view. Standing in the hall, his left hand affectionately laid on the shoulder of William Lydney, was a tall, upright figure, whose high and handsome features it was impossible to mistake for any but Harry Dane's. "In the body or in the spirit?" crossed the thoughts of the one who was stealthily looking on. Ravensbird was there; Lawyer Apperly was there; and Bruff's tears were openly running down his cheeks.

"Do you understand it?" whispered Mr. Blair. "It was not your cousin's spirit you saw the other night; it was he himself. He did not die in that fall over the cliff; he was saved by a friend's yacht, Colonel Moncton's, and he has been in the States ever since, the true Lord Dane, though he knew it not. You are not about to be arraigned as a murderer, Mr. Dane, but you will have to put up with the loss of state and station, for he, Lord Dane, has come back to enter upon his own."

Herbert Dane drew a deep breath.

"And he?" he pursued, pointing to Lydney, when his scared senses allowed him to speak, as a conviction flashed over his mind that he had been all along labouring under some extraordinary delusion as to the young man's doings and character.

" His son: the Honourable Geoffry William."

Herbert Dane wiped the drops from his brow. He went forth, and they stood face to face, gazing at each other.

" Herbert ! "—" Harry ! "

In a moment their hands were locked together, and alone they retired to the dining-room, Lord Dane leaning upon Herbert.

" First of all, Herbert, let me say that I forgive you——"

" It was not purposely done," interrupted Herbert Dane, with emotion. " I did not send you over intentionally; I knew not that we were so near the edge until you fell. Harry, I swear it."

" Not for the encounter," explained Lord Dane. " I have as much need of your forgiveness for that, as you have of mine, for I believe that I was the aggressor. But you might have come to see after me or sent assistance to me when I was down."

" I never supposed but that it must have killed you, and in my cowardice I dreaded detection and punishment. As for assistance, I saw that one of the preventive-men was underneath."

" What I would forgive you for is the *provocation*— the deceit practised towards me by you and Adelaide. Do you realize what it must have been to me ? I forgive you, as I have forgiven her."

" She was worthy neither of you nor me, Harry; I have lived to learn it. She jilted me afterwards just as she had been ready to jilt you. Many a thousand times have I wished, in my pain and remorse, that I had let you win her. It would have been well for us all."

" Did you know or suspect that I was still in existence ? " asked Lord Dane.

" Never. How was it possible ? "

" Did you receive no letter from me ? I despatched one to ' Lord Dane,' after he came into the title, supposing, of course, that the Lord Dane was not you, but my brother Geoffry. *That* would have testified to my existence."

"I never received it, or heard of it. No such letter came to the Castle to my knowledge. After I went abroad there was at first some irregularity in forwarding my letters, and I knew that two or three were lost; I was vexed with Cecilia in consequence, and she laid the blame on Mrs. Knox. Harry, had any intimation come to me that you were in existence, and I not a slayer of man, I should have hailed it as a boon from heaven."

The words bore their own earnest of truth, and Lord Dane could doubt no longer. "But you played me a shabby trick, Herbert, about that box," he resumed. "What induced you to take it, and conceal it?"

"I can't tell you," was the prompt answer; "I don't know myself. When I saw the box on the beach--*your* box--it oppressed me with a nameless fear. What I dreaded, I knew not. I have feared detection in every leaf and sound these ten years, and in the panic that came over me I had the box taken to the Castle, and concealed it. When the fuss arose about it I thought I had been a fool for my pains; but it was too late to give it up then. Neither did I believe that young Lydney had a right to claim it. You shall have the box, Harry; it is safe in the Castle."

"I don't fancy it is," thought Lord Dane. "But now, Herbert, comes another question: Why have you so persecuted my son?"

"I did not know him for your son. I no more supposed him to be your son than I supposed him to be mine. I believed him to be altogether what he appeared—a suspicious character, consorting with poachers——"

"Consorting with poachers!" interrupted Lord Dane, scorn in his tone. "He was searching for the box—that's what brought him first of all into the poachers' company; and he stayed with them to look after Wilfred Lester, who was going headlong to ruin. Who but Wilfred Lester, do you suppose, broke into his father's house? My son William went there to get him out of it."

"Wilfred Lester!—broke into his father's house! *He* did?"

"He, and no other. Not for ordinary robbery : to get some deed that his father denied him."

Herbert Dane made no answer. Little by little the past was becoming clear to him.

"Herbert, I don't suppose you like moralizing any more than I do," said Lord Dane ; "but I must ask you whether such a thing ever crossed your mind as RETRIBUTION. Have you remarked how surely our doings bring forth their own fruit? We plant an acorn, and it springs up an oak-tree ; we sow a grain of wheat, and it ripens into corn ; we set a noxious weed, and it comes up tares. Just so it is with the moral world : as we plant, so must we gather. You and Adelaide Errol did me a bitter wrong. It was not the injury of a moment—that which may be committed in a moment of passion, without premeditation ; but it was a concerted, long-continued wrong—a deception that you carried on through months of time, one day planning how you should best blind and deceive me the next. What has that conduct borne for you in the end? Adelaide would not have you. She entered on *her* penance, and married George Lester, driving, by her ill-treatment, that fine son of his and Katherine Bordillion's to desperation. Thanks to that, I and my son were saved, for none but a man whose life was valueless to him would have launched the life-boat on that awful night ; and here we are, I to dispossess you of your estate, William of your bride ; for that Maria Lester will choose William, there can be no doubt. See you not how it has been working all along, under Providence ?"

Herbert Dane did see it ; and a recollection flashed over him of young Lydney's expressed hope that Maria might yet become Lady Dane. He felt bewildered.

"I have come to remain, Herbert," resumed Lord Dane. "The Castle from to-day must own me for its lord, and you will be my honoured guest. We shall be closer friends than of old, Herbert. But now let me present my son to you in his proper character."

Lord Dane opened the door as he spoke, intending to call in his son. But what he saw induced him to change

his intention, and go forward himself. Nearly all the
retainers of the Castle were gathered there. The elder
ones recognized him, and a murmur of joyous agitation
arose.

"I said you would know me again," he smiled, his eyes
full, and his hand grasping those of his father's faithful
servants. "I should have been with you all along, but
that I thought my brother Geoffry reigned here."

The hall was rent with a shout. "Long live Lord Dane!
Long live the true Lord Dane!"

"Not for very long, I fear, my dear old friends; for that
grim enemy of us all is already gripping hold of me. But
I shall leave one to replace me," added Lord Dane, placing
his hand upon his son's shoulder, and standing with him
side by side. "My friends, who is he like?"

"He is like a Dane," came the answer.

"Yes, he is like a Dane. You have known him only as
plain William Lydney; you may have heard him traduced
as an adventurer. My old friends, Danesheld little knew
whom it was accusing. He is my only son, your future
lord, the Honourable Geoffry Dane."

Geoffry Dane held out his hand, and they clasped that as
they had clasped his father's. "But my name is William
Lydney, too," he said, with a laugh. "I have not been
sporting altogether false colours."

"There is nothing false about him," interposed Lord
Dane, with emotion. "He is a genuine Dane of the old
stock: honest and upright. Serve him truthfully in all
good faith, as he will be faithful to and protect you.
Herbert"—and Lord Dane wheeled round—"here he is!
How is it you did not know him?"

"Cecilia said he was like Lady Dane," observed Herbert,
as he took Geoffry Dane's hand, and tried to put on a good
grace. "I laughed at her, but I hope we shall eschew
mistakes for the future."

"You will let me go up to her now, won't you?" asked
the young man, with a merry laugh.

They were interrupted by Miss Dane herself. She put
her head timidly in to reconnoitre. Whilst she sat up-

stairs, trembling over the quarrel that might be taking place between her brother and Mr. Lydney, Bruff had bethought himself of her, and carried her the wonderful news.

"May I not come in?" she pleaded. "I don't think I shall ever have my proper understanding again; it seems to be turned upside down. They tell me that Harry has come back as Lord Dane. Harry, is it indeed you?"

He met her with outstretched hands; he gave her a few hearty kisses, and she burst into tears. She and Harry had been as fond brother and sister—and would be so again.

"And William Lydney?" she said, recovering herself, and looking round. "Bruff said that he—but I don't understand it: I think old Bruff must have been dreaming."

"That William Lydney is not himself, but somebody else," he said, advancing to her, with his pleasant smile. "I must introduce myself as your cousin, Miss Dane."

"Oh, dear! Cousin?" she exclaimed, a blank look rising to her face. "Why, to be sure, you must be, if it's true what Bruff said—that you are Harry's son. Is it a second cousin, or what?"

And making some indistinct excuse about having left her canary out of the cage, Miss Dane ran upstairs, caught up her prayer-book in a flutter of doubt, and opened it at that page which begins, "A man may not marry his grandmother."

But meanwhile you may have missed Mr. Blair. In truth, that gentleman, who had previously carved out his little plans of action with Lord Dane, disappeared from the Castle as soon as he had prepared its pseudo master for what was coming upon him, took his way to Danesheld Hall, and asked to see Squire Lester.

Squire Lester assented readily enough. He was in his study, moodily dwelling upon the cross and contrary nature of things in general, and was rather glad of the interruption that took him out of them. The release of the prisoner Lydney from custody, and the refusal of the police to account for their authority, had given him great offence;

all the more because he did not understand it. The chronic state of vexation in which he lived in regard to his son, was also beginning to tell upon his spirit. He *could not* deaden all natural feeling for Wilfred ; and there were moments when he wondered what his wife could be made of, to expect it.

"Lord Dane's banker !" cried he, briskly repeating the words the servant used in announcing him. "Yes, I'll see him. Show him in."

The permission seemed not to be required, for the banker was already within the room, and the servant left them together.

"I am disturbing you early, Mr. Lester, but business must be my excuse. Before I enter upon it, allow me to set you right upon one point. I am not Lord Dane's banker, or any banker at all; nothing half so important in a commercial point of view. I am one of the chief detective officers of the police force."

"Bless my heart !" ejaculated Mr. Lester.

"I came down to watch certain business in Danesheld, and it is convenient to us at such times not to be known for what we really are. Let that pass : I only mention it to convince you that when I ordered young Lydney's release from custody, Bent, whom you are so angry with, had no resource but to obey me."

"Did *you* discharge him ? What could possess you to do it ?" continued Mr. Lester sharply. "The man is as great a villain as ever walked. Did you do it to screen him from the consequences of his guilt ?"

"Hardly. My office is to bring offenders to punishment, not to screen them from it. I released him because he was not guilty. Listen, Mr. Lester. In the attack made on your house, there was a ringleader who planned it, and induced the others, poor poaching fellows, by bribes, to join him; on him, in my opinion, nearly the whole guilt rests."

"It is precisely my opinion," interrupted Mr. Lester. "The ringleader is the one sole guilty man, and that was Lydney."

"Mr. Lester, give me credit for being assured of my facts ;

otherwise I should not have come to you. The ringleader was *not* Lydney."

Mr. Blair's voice had dropped to a low, solemn key, and in his countenance, as he sat, his hands on his knees, his head bending forward, there was a look of severe compassion. The Squire did not altogether relish these signs.

"The ringleader was Wilfred Lester."

Up started Mr. Lester, overturned the inkstand on the table beside him, loud and angry in his son's defence, and hardly knowing what he spoke. Mr. Blair sat with professional coolness until the outburst was over.

"I am not sorry to hear one admission from your lips, Mr. Lester—that it is being under the cloud of your displeasure which *drives* him to be wild. It was your son who broke into your house; it was his own expedition, planned and executed. You can have ample proof of it if you wish; but you may be sure, knowing now who I am, that I should not come to you with an unsubstantiated story."

There could no longer be any holding out against conviction, and Mr. Lester sat down in his chair, an abject man, the father of a midnight housebreaker.

"But what was his motive?" he gasped. "There was no robbery?"

"There was no robbery in the ordinary sense of the term; and the pistol you heard discharged, was raised by him at one of the men who seemed inclined to effect a little on his own private score. There was, however, something taken."

"What was it?" asked Mr. Lester, glancing about him, as if to make sure that the chairs and tables were in their places.

"Have you examined your iron safe?"

"No." But Mr. Lester turned short round and examined it then. That is, he stared at the outside.

"I fancy his object was to get into his possession a certain deed relating to some money he believes he is entitled to, but which you withhold. And I think he succeeded."

After a pause of astonishment, Mr. Lester hastily drew

some keys from his pocket, and unlocked the safe. The deed was gone.

" You now perceive your son's motive," resumed Mr. Blair. " I don't defend him ; mind that ; but some people may deem he had a right to peruse his own deed, which you denied him."

" Are you going to apprehend him ? " was the rejoinder of Mr. Lester, who was cutting rather a sorry figure, as most men do when convicted of dishonour ; and he *knew* he had been all along dishonourable to Wilfred.

" To apprehend him is not in my department. If you choose to do so, you can hand your warrant and instructions to Inspector Bent. Your son might receive the punishment, but I do not think the odium would fall upon him. There's not a judge upon the bench but would recoil from sentencing him."

" I am not going to give him into custody," said Mr. Lester, tartly. " You need not preach." ·

" But that I felt convinced Squire Lester was a good man at` heart, and had been led away (he knows best by what influence) to act harshly, I should not have disclosed to him the true culprit," observed Mr. Blair, looking him steadily in the face. " I knew he would shrink from bringing public punishment on one who is his son, and ought to be his heir, thereby furnishing further food for scandal in Danesheld."

" Further food," retorted Mr. Lester. " I have furnished none yet."

" My good sir," returned the officer, " if you only knew the hard words bestowed upon you from one end of the place to the other, you would not say that. Wilfred, with all his ill-doings, is popular and respected, compared with you."

" You are bold," chafed Mr. Lester.

" It is the fault of my trade," was the answer. " But if you will consider the past with less prejudice than you have probably been in the habit of doing, you may arrive at the same conclusion as myself—that had Wilfred Lester been treated differently by his father, he might never have forfeited his good name."

Mr. Lester gave his brow a rub. It was growing hot.

"And now I come to William Lydney's share in the night's exploits——"

"Yes, William Lydney?" was the fierce interruption, as if Squire Lester found a vent for his anger in the name. "You cannot palliate *his* conduct. He had no deed to get at."

"Pray listen, Mr. Lester. It came accidentally to William Lydney's knowledge on Sunday night that your son was then in the wood with two or three companions, the convoy engaged in the respectable employment of tacking black crape to their hats. Circumstances led him to believe that they were about to attack the Castle. Yes, you look surprised, Squire, but I've no time to explain. He, Lydney, waited on in the cold damp air, hoping to intercept them and to save your son. At the eleventh hour, he found they had attacked the Hall—were in it—and he rushed on here; but not in time to be of much service, except that he got Wilfred home in safety. He allowed himself to be taken into custody because he would not betray him; he has had his character taken from him for Wilfred's sake; whilst Daneshild reproached him with consorting with bad characters, he was only looking after and shielding Wilfred Lester. A friendship had arisen between them."

"Wilfred always had a hankering after low company," was the slighting remark of Squire Lester.

"If he never gets into lower company than young Lydney's, he won't hurt," returned Mr. Blair, bursting into a laugh.

Something in its tone upset Squire Lester's equanimity. "Why, who is Lydney?"

"Oh, as to that, you can ask him when you next see him. But it is not every man who would quietly bear the opprobrium that another merits, even to going to prison for him."

"Lydney must have had his motive for it," scoffed Mr. Lester.

"Or motives—true. Wilfred Lester saved his life, and he may have been actuated by gratitude. A feeling is abroad that he would undergo a great deal for one so nearly related to Miss Lester."

The allusion upset the remainder of Mr. Lester's temper.

"Lydney is a villain, that's what he is. He has been stealthily undermining my daughter's principles. Can you defend him in that, sir?"

"I think I had better leave him to defend himself," said Mr. Blair, as he rose to depart. His mission to Daneshold was over.

"Were I Lord Dane I would shoot him."   •

"Were you Lord Dane, I do not fancy you would," laughed Mr. Blair. And again there was that in his tone and manner which was incomprehensible to Squire Lester.

CHAPTER XXXV.

SALLY'S STEP-UNCLE.

ALMOST as Mr. Blair left Daneshold Hall, three gentlemen, who had just descended from a carriage entered it. As the servant admitted them, he looked askance on one, William Lydney; the second was Apperly, the lawyer; the third was a commanding looking man of attenuated features, a stranger.

"I wish to see Mr. Lester," said the latter.

The servant bowed and led the way to the study. He laid his hand on the handle of the door, and turned.

"What name, sir?"

"Lord Dane."

"I—I beg your pardon, sir," stammered the man in his surprise. "I asked what name."

"Lord Dane," was the distinct repetition; and the servant wondered what old madman had got in, as he announced it. Mr. Apperly followed, but William Lydney had disappeared when the man looked round for him.

Squire Lester, pacing his study in perturbation—for Mr. Blair's communication had been anything but a pleasant one—heard the announcement and saw a stranger enter. He supposed some mistake had been made, or that Lord Dane was following. He scanned the bearing and features of the stranger, and felt strangely startled.

"I—I thought he said Lord Dane," broke from him in his embarrassment.

"So he did," was the stranger's answer, as he held out his hand. "Don't you know me, George? Who else, but myself, should be Lord Dane?"

Mr. Lester staggered back against a chair utterly petrified.

"Harry Dane did not die, George: and he has come back at the eleventh hour to claim his own. I should have been home ten years ago, had I dreamt that it was *Herbert* who was representing the Dane peerage; I never supposed but it was my brother Geoffry."

Mr. Lester, feeling that there was nothing but surprise upon surprise happening, sat down in a whirl, and prepared to listen to the explanation. It was given in a very cursory manner. Lord Dane was anxious to call in his son.

"Has your son accompanied you home? Is he in Daneshold?" asked Mr. Lester.

"He is here, in this house. I sent him to the drawing-room whilst I came to you. The truth is, Lester—though I suppose it's premature to say it—he has seen your daughter, and fallen in love with her."

"Where can he have seen her?" wondered Mr. Lester.

"I am agreeable," continued Lord Dane. "Perhaps you will be—although report goes that you have promised her to Herbert. The Castle will still be her destination, you see; the only difference being that her husband will be the true peer, not the false one."

Strange to say, Mr. Lester never thought of the truth—of *Lydney*. He might have done so at a more collected moment; but the step from a poacher and suspected house-breaker to a future peer of England, was altogether too great for his mind even to glance at. Lord Dane rang the bell, and desired that the gentleman who came with him should be requested to appear.

The servant went to the drawing-room and gave the message. Mr. Lydney had been sitting there alone, having found it untenanted. But, even as the man spoke, he saw Maria enter the conservatory from the lawn, and went out to her. Ah! how lovely she looked in her pretty morning dress of delicate lilac muslin.

"Oh, Mr. Lydney!" she exclaimed, in her confusion and dismay dropping some late flowers she had been cutting, "what brings you here? How could you dare to venture? Papa will only order you out again."

"I hope not. He might turn out William Lydney; he will not, I think, turn out Geoffry Dane."

She raised her eyes to him in surprise. As well she might.

He took her two hands in his, and held her before him, rather persistently. His dark grey eyes, dancing with love, smiled down on her blushing cheeks.

"Lord Dane is now with Mr. Lester, asking—at least, I think it likely that he is—asking for you. Will you promise to be the future Lady Dane, Maria? Promise it now to me."

The soft blush deepened, and she strove to draw away from him. But he held her all the tighter.

"Or would you rather promise to be *my* wife?" he continued, in triumphant tenderness. "Maria, it is of no use; I will not let you go without an answer. My darling! I shall never tease you or deceive you again. You trusted the unknown William Lydney. He was obscure, he was under a cloud, and he could not explain or declare himself. I told you the trust was not misplaced. I am Geoffry Dane. My father, Captain Harry Dane, did not die in that fall. He has come home to his own. He is Lord Dane. It is he who is with your father. Maria, will you give me your promise *now?*"

She did not understand at all; but there was a ringing sound of truth and power in his voice, and Maria closed her eyes, and sighed with a feeling of some intense happiness. He gathered her in his sheltering arms, taking from her lips, as of right, the kiss he had so long yearned for—all unconscious, both of them, that Mrs. Tiffle's green eyes were peering in at the outer door of the conservatory.

It did not last a minute; these stolen snatches of bliss rarely do: Fate must be envious of them. Lady Adelaide was coming forward, and Maria vanished behind a towering tropical plant, ready to die at the scene of anger that might be approaching. If anything could have added to her state of wonder, it was to see Lady Adelaide advance with outstretched hand to her lover, and call him " Geoffry." They went forward then to obey the summons to the study, he holding his hand back for Maria. Lord Dane, impatient at the delay, was ringing again.

" What is keeping Geoffry? " he was asking, tartly enough. " I want you to see him. In point of wealth your daughter will be better off with him than she would have been with Herbert. Geoffry inherits an immense fortune from his mother, and I have not been spending half my income. So that, apart from the Dane revenues, my son will be rich."

" It is a most flattering, munificent offer for her," cried the gratified Mr. Lester. " And if Maria will only hear reason—We have had a bad, insidious character about the place lately, and——Halloa! " again broke off Mr. Lester, starting up angrily as he saw Lydney coming in. " You here! You audacious man! How dare you presume to ——I beg your pardon, Lord Dane, but this is the fellow I was just speaking of, Lydney——"

Mr. Lester stopped—for Lord Dane had linked his arm within the " audacious man's," and was leading him up.

" An instant, George Lester. You shall tell me about Lydney when I have made the introduction. My son, Geoffry Dane."

The consternation of Mr. Lester was something ludicrous. " *He* your son? " he gasped.

" My own and only son; Geoffry William Lydney Dane. Ah, Lester! you and Danesheld have been abusing him, have been laying all sorts of outrageous sins to his charge; but Maria saw him for what he was—a man of worth and honour. I think you will have to give her to him, in spite of the prior claims of Mr. Herbert Dane."

Mr. Lester paused. He looked at Maria, who had been drawn into the room almost against her will; he looked at Geoffry Dane. How could he ever have mistaken that noble face? Truth to say, he had from the first been favourably impressed by it, until circumstances and Herbert Dane rose up to bias him.

"Maria shall choose for herself," he said, in a kindly tone. And some of us do become kindly, in our stubborn hearts, when humility is forced upon us.

Geoffry Dane smiled; Maria drooped her head: and Lord Dane began talking to her in a whisper, which brought the brightness back again. Presently he rose, saying that now all was right he must be going.

"Where?" asked Mr. Lester.

"Where! why to show myself abroad with my son; to make a call or two, as I have made one here, previous to holding my levée at the Castle this afternoon," answered Lord Dane. "I shall go about it rather charily, Lester, lest timid people should take me for a ghost. Herbert thought me one the other night. It was the only time I have ventured out: but I felt pining for a breath of fresh air, and I went as far as the ruins. There, as I looked in at one of the windows, I saw Herbert, and I know he took me for an apparition. Whilst he was coming out, I stole round to the nearest aperture and got in. But for having shown myself to him later in flesh and blood, he would have believed in the ghost for ever. Are you ready, William? We will go first to Wilfred Lester's."

"To Wilfred Lester's!" involuntarily repeated that misguided young man's father.

"Yes, sir, to Wilfred Lester's," replied Lord Dane, turning round and speaking in a stern tone, perhaps unconsciously. "If his own flesh and blood have abandoned him to the mercies of a cold world, it's time the world took him up. I intend to carry him and his wife to the Castle to-day, and I shall keep them there, my guests and William's, until some one sees about a provision for them. Daneshold shall see that Wilfred has one efficient friend, at any rate. Pretty Edith! who used to be more ready with her kisses for Captain Harry Dane than you were, Miss Maria. I have heard of *starvation*, George Lester; I have heard of —— but I had better not go on," broke off Lord Dane. " Thank God, I have come home to remedy it ! "

He went out in a suppressed storm. At the door, as he was stepping into the carriage, Miss Bordillion came up : the wonderful news, spreading fast over Daneshold, had penetrated to her.

" It is really true, then ! " she exclaimed, the tears rising in her gentle eyes, as the once intimate Harry Dane clasped her hands. " I thought people were relating a dream."

" I told you the time might come when you would welcome me to your house again," said William, when she had leisure to turn to him. " Your door will, I hope, be open to Geoffry Dane, Miss Bordillion, though it was closed to William Lydney."

" And what about Maria ? " she asked, her senses rather scattered just then.

" Oh, I had serious thoughts of running away with Maria," laughed he ; " but Mr. Lester has obviated the necessity. He tells me I may take her without it."

Miss Bordillion gazed after the carriage as it swept away ; at the smiling face of the new heir, as he sat in it opposite to his father.

" I *never will* be persuaded out of my senses again," said she emphatically. " My judgment trusted him, my heart spoke for him ; I knew he was no adventurer."

Lady Adelaide had not appeared. No, her courage failed her. Shame was rife in her bosom ; fear still ; and she had stolen away to the solitude of her own chamber. Tiffle, who was watching an opportunity, came in with an interruption—

" And grieved I am to have to disclose it, my lady ; but my duty to the family is paramint," she began with her soft sly tones. "I was stepping into the conservetry just now; wanting the gardener about them sparagrass-tops for the glasses, and thinking he might be there, when I saw—but it's a barefaced thing to repeat to your ladyship, and I vow I've been red ever since to my fingers' ends."

"Do go on Tiffle, without nonsense. What is it?"

"My lady, that Lydney was there, he was; him and Miss Lester. And he had her all scrambled to him like, and was—if your ladyship will excuse my saying the word —kissing of her. Kissing of her lips with his own, my lady, like—like anything."

Lady Adelaide languidly raised her eyebrows. "Very sad, of course. But as Miss Lester is to be his wife, Tiffle, I don't know that it matters."

"His wife!" cried Tiffle, her green eyes wide with amazement. "What, and go out with him—excuse me, my lady—a Botany Bay convic!"

"Tiffle!" spoke Lady Adelaide, in a sharp tone of reprimand, as she pointed to the door with her haughty finger. "Have the goodness to recollect that you are speaking of Miss Lester."

Tiffle backed out subdued, not to say thunderstruck, and came against a maid-servant, who said Shad was asking to see her.

"To see me?—the oudacious little reptile!" responded Tiffle in a great amount of wrath. "That Granny Bean is always wanting a fresh supply of stuff for her rheumatix."

She went out, however, and Shad, gathered humbly against a dirty brick wall, accosted her in an under-tone:

"Granny said I was not to mind calling at the house for once, but to cut right off and tell ye. Lord Dane's come back."

"Come back from where?" demanded Tiffle. "Where has he been?"

"Not him at the Castle: he ain't Lord Dane no more. T'other's come to life again—him that fell over the cliff years agone. He have took up his footing at the Castle, and this 'un's got to turn out. Granny said I was to tell ye as Lydney——"

" Well!" said Tiffle, impatiently, staring with all her eyes. " Get on quicker."

" As Lydney have been here in disguise, a-looking after what folks did wrong, but not helping of 'em, as was thought. He's t'other's son, and his name's Geoffry Dane ; and he'll be Lord Dane after him."

Tiffle gathered in the sense of the words, gathered in a summary of her own past policy, and fell back in what was nearly a real fainting fit.

Never, sure, was such a levée seen or heard of. It had no parallel in social history. Modern courts hold their levées, but the crowds flocking to them are of the class who bask on the sunny side of life ; no Lazarus must dare to enter. The levée at Dane Castle was all different.

The news of Harry Dane's resuscitation had gone forth to Danesheld, together with his assumption of the home and honours of his forefathers, and of the reception he was about to hold. It was his pleasure that all should come to it, high and low, rich and poor. The fishermen were bidden as well as the gentry ; the poachers and smugglers were especially invited. The lower end of the hall was lined with the Dane servants, in their handsome livery of white and silver and purple. Bruff and Ravensbird stood behind Lord Dane ; it was hard to say which of the two looked the proudest.

How fast the visitors flocked in, it were a tale in itself to tell, all pushing eagerly to welcome and do honour to Lord Dane. Had he been made of hands, there would not have been sufficient to satisfy the ardent crowd. He stood with them outstretched ; he had a kindly look ; a low, heart-felt word for all. His son stood at his right hand, and he presented him individually to every one. Herbert Dane was there, Wilfred Lester was there, both treated by him with marked esteem and distinction. It would not be Lord Dane's fault if poor Wilfred's escapades were not over ; and it must be remembered that the public knew nothing of his share in the doings of the past Sunday night. The audience, ever ready to be led away by a straw in popular feeling, saw that Squire Lester shook hands with his son, and they at once elbowed each other in hastening to do the like.

When the hall was full, and people had done coming in, so far as could be judged, Mr. Dane—no longer Mr. Lydney—left his father's side to mingle with the crowd. The first face his eye lighted on was Inspector Bent's, and the face did not look altogether at ease. Had he known that young Lydney the suspected would turn out to be the Honourable Mr. Dane, he had certainly treated him less familiarly.

"I hope, sir, you'll not bear malice to me for the past. I'm sure if I had had any idea——"

"Malice!" interrupted young Dane cheerily. "What an idea! I . gave you credit for better sense, Bent; or, at least, believed you would give me credit for better. I think I have a great deal to be obliged to you for: you might have made things worse for me, and did not."

The gratified inspector took the hand held out to him. Mr. Blair, it may be mentioned, had left by the mid-day train, and Bent felt important again. Mr. Dane went on, and came up to Ben Beecher, who was in an obscure corner behind the servants, not daring to advance into notice.

"Is it you, Beecher, come to pay me a visit in my own house?" he exclaimed, in the same hearty tones; and, in point of fact, he had been looking for the man. "More space to welcome you here than I had at the Sailors' Rest. Why don't you come forward to my lord? Your father has already had his confab with him."

"Sir, how could you go on deceiving us and blinding us in that way?" returned Ben Beecher, in a tone of reproach. "If we had dreamt that you were the Lord Dane—or as good as the lord—should we ever have let you into our secrets? Why, there's not a thing about us but what you know, even the very worst."

William Dane burst into laughter. "I'm glad I do, Beecher. It is the very best calamity that could have happened to you."

"Yes, sir, it may be fun for you; but you may just have us all transported to-morrow upon your sole evidence."

"And do you think I am likely to do it?"

"Look here, sir," cried the man, dropping his voice; "I'll swear that we were led into that bad job by young Lester. He——"

"Hush, Beecher!" came the quick and solemn warning. "That is of the past, never to be alluded to. It has been agreed on all sides that bygones shall be bygones."

"Is that to apply to *all* the past, Mr. Lydney?"

"Mr. Dane," corrected William, half jestingly, wishing to put the man at his ease.

"Dash my memory! I wish it never had been Mr. Dane, though. Why, you know all about our poaching, sir!— and the haunts!—and—you know everything."

"I don't intend to remember anything, Beecher. The past is past. But I want you to promise me to keep straight for the future."

"To keep straight?" returned Beecher, dubiously.

"In our first encounter in the wood, which you may not have forgotten, I told you that it was no business of mine did you prowl about the Dane preserves all day, a gun in one hand and snares in the other, seeing that they were not mine. Virtually they were mine, at least my father's, but actually they were in possession of him who was then called Lord Dane. I told you also that, if they were mine, the affair would be very different. You must see that it is, Beecher. It is my duty now to protect the lands, and I shall do it. I care more for one man's well-doing than for all the pheasants in England: nevertheless, I respect and shall uphold the Game Laws. Cannot you and I contrive to remain friends, Beecher, in spite of them?"

"Friends!" echoed the man, with deep feeling.

"I said friends. It will be your fault if we are not. You cannot suppose I shall take advantage of the past in any way, unless it be for your good. You once said, Beecher, that had you and your companions been dealt with in a kindlier spirit, you might have been different men. Begin to be different from this day, and I will help you."

Beecher made no answer: his face was working.

"You shall have suitable work found for you, and good

wages. I shall get my men to give me their best service, and on my part I shall ever be to them a considerate friend. Yes, Beecher, I mean it. I intend that we shall be friends in the best sense of the word, identifying our interests one with the other. Will you promise, Beecher?"

The man shyly held out his hand. "Ay, I will, sir; I'm almost tired of the life I lead, and so are others; and this last business has frightened the lot of us. I'll do as you wish me from this day."

"A bargain," said William Dane, as he shook the hand heartily. "And we will never, I hope, go from it, Beecher."

The one who seemed most anxious of all to accept the position that day and make the best of circumstances, was Mr. Herbert Dane. He was wise to do so. It is true he was suddenly thrown from state and fortune, but, in reality, he had never had a right to either, and had been an unconscious usurper. Lord Dane was not going to talk about mesne profits: on the contrary, he was intending to settle a handsome income upon Herbert. Altogether, things might have been worse for the ex-lord; and oh, to have that awful nightmare lifted from his soul. That of itself seemed heaven.

"You must have been astonished when you found who it was the life-boat brought ashore," he remarked, during a desultory chat with Ravensbird in the course of the afternoon.

"Astonished is not the word for it, sir," replied Ravensbird. "It's not strong enough; there's no word that is. My first thought, after I got over the surprise, was that I had been a regular idiot to mistake that drowned man for my master. He began upon all sorts of questions the night after he was saved from the wreck, and he learnt that it was you, sir, at the Castle, and not his brother, Mr. Dane. Presently he pushed the purple shade off his face and sat up in bed, and asked me if I knew him. You might have knocked me down with a feather. Then there was a consultation between us whether Sophie should be told: my lord was afraid of her letting out the secret; but I saw there was no help for it, for she'd be sure to know him.

How she suceeded in keeping it and mortifying her gossip will always be a joke against her: but my lord threatened her with unheard-of penalties if she disclosed it."

" Ravensbird," said Herbert Dane, awaking from a reverie into which he had fallen, " did you witness the struggle on the heights that night?—for I presume that Lord Dane has told you the truth respecting it."

"He has told me, sir; but not for me to mention it again," answered the man with considerate respect. " I did not witness the struggle; I was not on the heights that night."

"And yet you would not disclose where it was you had been when you were absent from the Sailors' Rest."

" That was my obstinacy, sir; I had no other reason. I was only doing a bit of courting. Sophie had promised to come out and meet me, and we were walking about at the back of the Castle."

" What was your suspicion at the time?"

" Well, sir—if I must say it—-I suspected you. Of course, I wasn't sure; my opinion was on the balance, as it were. I thought it almost certain that you had been the one quarrelling with him; but, on the other hand, you seemed positively to suspect me, and then there came up the suspicion of that packman. I was never sure about it, one way or the other, until my lord came home. Sophie, she also at first suspected you, and thought my Lady Adelaide would have screened you at my expense; but I did all I could to put her off the scent—it might have led to mischief; and I was not sure myself."

" And I, on my part, got to suspect that you had been on the heights at the time, Ravensbird, and saw the scuffle. Let it drop. I am more pleased to see him back, in life, than ever I was at coming into the inheritance."

The levée over, there was a dinner gathering at the Castle; a family party only—the Danes, and the Lesters, and Margaret Bordillion. Unpleasant topics were not alluded to; but William contrived to give Mr. Lester and his wife a hint of the doings of Tiffle. Even Lady Adelaide might not have been so inveterate in her persecution of

William Lester, but for the never-ceasing tales, the insidious promptings of that woman.

The first thing Mr. Lester did on the following morning was to send for Sally. He was an early riser, and the woman made her appearance, in answer to the summons, before the breakfast was well over at the Hall. Sundry reminiscences had been rising up within Mr. Lester, convicting him of a great deal that he felt bitterly ashamed of, now that it was brought home to him. He could not undo the past; but he might, perhaps, help to stop the scandal from henceforth, if he could screw out a little ready money for Wilfred's tradespeople. As a preliminary, he must learn from Sally what the debts were. Mr Lester received her alone in the breakfast-room.

She came in with her uncompromising face, and he entered upon the subject in a cold, distant tone, the better to disguise his feelings—as if it were a wondrous favour and condescension for him to notice the matter at all. Sally mentioned what debts there were, so far as she had cognizance of them; but they did not appear to be recent ones.

"You have been getting in things—as I hear—without stint, of late," observed Mr. Lester. "Even wine, I have been told of. I cannot think how you obtained the credit."

"I didn't have credit," spoke Sally, bluntly.

"Not have credit?"

"No, sir. I paid ready money."

"But where did you get the money?" he asked, staring at her.

"From one that folks were pulling to pieces as a thief and a vagabond," was Sally's answer; "and I used to wish, as I listened, that I could tie the whole lot together and pump on 'em for it. He made friends with me, and told me I must join him in a little bit of deceit for my master and mistress's sake—Mr. Wilfred being proud and refusing to be helped straightforward. He found the money, and I invented a step-uncle, and said I had it from him. And as true as I'm here, sir, I believe that it's thanks to him Miss Edith is alive this day."

" And he was——" Mr. Lester stopped in hesitation.

William Lydney. Knowing now that his father was Captain Harry Dane, I'm not surprised : of course the plot was made up between them. But it isn't many would have carried it out as that young man did. Mr. Wilfred was just going to the dogs as fast as he could go—yes he was, sir ; you are his father, but I'm not going to eat my words ; and William Lydney saved him, and bore scorn and suspicion for his sake. People talk of the noble Danes, but there never was one as noble as this young one !"

Before the words had well left her lips, a violent noise, as of fighting and angry words, was heard outside the door. Mr. Lester pulled it open in displeasure, supposing it to be his children. To his excessive astonishment, there stood Shad and Tiffle, engaged in a pitched battle, scratching, biting, tearing, and shrieking at each other.

The cause was this : Shad had presented himself at the back-door, apparently in a state of much excitement and fear, and demanded to see Mrs. Tiffle. The girl, who answered it, ungraciously told him to " Go and look for her : " for the fact was, Tiffle, who had got up in a most vile temper, had been making several of the servants suffer, and this girl more particularly. Shad, bold as he had never been before, in the terror that was upon him, went into the passages, peeping here and there, until he reached the hall, and there he saw Tiffle, with her ear glued to a keyhole. In truth, Tiffle had a mind to know what her master's business could be with Sally, she feeling rather disturbed at the aspect of affairs in general. Shad stole softly up behind and laid hold of her. Tiffle, startled beyond measure, fearing she was caught at last, turned round ; but when she saw who it was, her temper broke out beyond control, and she began to pay the boy off by sundry tingling slaps on the cheeks. Shad, unprepared for the reception, retaliated in kind, and the result was a contest.

" What is the meaning of this ? " demanded Mr. Lester. " Tiffle ! "

Tiffle softened down to meekness, her sly eyes flashing

out a glance at Lady Adelaide, who appeared on the scene. Shad only howled.

"I'm sure I beg pardon, sir, and my lady," quoth she: "This wicked ragamuffyan of Granny Bean's came startling me to throw me over, just as I was going into the breakfast-room in search of my lady. Little Miss Ada——"

"You wasn't going in," raved Shad, smarting under the late correction; "you was a-stopping at the door, listening."

"The ready lies that these young creatures invent!" ejaculated Tiffle, turning up the whites of her eyes. "I would not have cared for his startling of me, but it vexed me to see him, all bold, in a gentleman's house. Be quiet, you young rep——"

"*You* be quiet, Tiffle," interposed Mr. Lester's voice of stern authority. "How did you get in, Shad?"

"I come to the door and I asked for Mrs. Tiffle," sobbed Shad; "and the young woman she told me to come and find her——"

"Asked for *me—you!*" interrupted Tiffle, in a glow of indignation. "The impidince of that!"

"What be I to do?" howled Shad. "Granny's dead, she is, and I'm afraid to stop there. Who be I to tell?"

The words caused a lull in the storm. Mr. Lester questioned the boy.

"I'm sure on't," sniffed Shad. "She's a-sitting back in her chair, with her face all blue, and her mouth open, and her eyes staring. I wondered as she didn't screech at me to get up; so I lay a-bed, and when I went to her she was like that. And because I comes and tells, I'm kicked at and my hair tored out."

"Please, sir, hadn't I better go back with him, and see what it really is?" asked Tiffle, as mild now as milk, and speaking in quite a confidential tone.

"You can do so if you choose," replied Mr. Lester. "But —step in here for a minute, Tiffle. Shad, sit down," he added, pointing to one of the hall chairs.

Safely inside his study, where he motioned her to enter and Lady Adelaide followed, Mr. Lester shortly told the woman that he and her lady had come to the resolution of parting with her : she could leave them in a month's time.

"To pa—pa—part with me !" gasped Tiffle, turning her dismayed face to Lady Adelaide. " What have I done ? "

Mr. Lester would not enter into particulars ; and Lady Adelaide maintained a haughty silence ; the truth was, she herself shrank from this task, and had left it to her husband. He gave Tiffle a hint that her ferreting propensities had been discovered, together with her falsity, and, therefore, she would no longer suit Danesheld Hall ; and then, passing from the subject as if it were over, he quietly asked her whether there was not some relationship between herself and Shad.

What little temper had been left to Tiffle by the communication, this bold question completely took away. It drove her wild. Having no ready answer at hand, except a vague denial raved out in indignant words, she burst out of the room and seized upon the unhappy Shad, drawing her nails down his face to begin with. Mr. Lester himself came to the rescue ; opened the front door, and sent Shad out of it—howling piteously.

CHAPTER XXXVI.

WRONGS MADE RIGHT.

THINGS and people subsided by degrees into their proper places. Lord Dane strove to make the happiness of all. Herbert Dane chose Paris as a residence. He was fond of the gay city, and Danesheld no longer held claims on him, or had attractions for him. Miss Dane returned to the ivied house with Mrs. Knox, and was intensely happy directly, planning out the most charming dress that could be worn by an assistant at the marriage ceremony. Wilfred Lester, partly through interest, partly through a good sum advanced by Lord Dane privately, was appointed to a post in London, which he would enter on in the spring, and meanwhile he and his wife remained the guests of Lord Dane. Mr. Lester had refunded the twelve hundred pounds to which the deed related, unable to shelter himself under the false excuse that it had been paid.

"I should make Apperly insist on interest as well, Wilfred, were I you," was the remark of Lord Dane, who was inclined to regard the whole matter with severity. "He shall keep Maria's fourteen thousand pounds; William does not want it; but he ought to pay you in full."

Wilfred laughed. He could afford to be generous now; and he did not take the advice about claiming interest.

The marriage was pressed on. Lord Dane's health declined daily, and he wished to see his son settled before he died, Maria made no objection: the day on which she quitted the Hall would be a red-letter one.

It dawned—that day—a clear bright morning early in the new year. Sophie Ravensbird dressed the bride: there was no one else capable of it in Daneshcld, she said, with national vanity. Lord Dane went to church, but was not equal to being present at breakfast.

A grand breakfast was held at the Hall. All friends and relatives were present, except Herbert Dane, who did not come from Paris for it. Squire Lester presided, wearing the subdued, weary manner latterly characteristic of him; Lady Adelaide was gay with a gaiety that seemed more false than true. She had learnt that her life had been a sad mistake, and wondered where comfort would be found.

The breakfast went on to its close. The feasting was over, the wedding-cake had gone round, and the Rev. Mr. James was on his old-fashioned legs, making a speech to the bridegroom and bride, when the door slowly opened, and a tall, spare stranger, with a military air and bronzed features, came in, and stood still, leisurely surveying the company. The company, in their turn, surveyed him. He seemed to strike upon their senses somewhat after the fashion of Banquo's ghost.

"Which is Edith?" he asked, without moving.

Curious words to come from him, and the sea of faces stared in blank consternation, Edith's not less blank than theirs. Suddenly there was a faint cry, and Miss Bordillion rose and hastened to him.

"You must be my brother. Oh, Henry, how you are altered! I am Margaret."

She was right: it was Colonel Bordillion. He had just landed from India, having come home without apprising any one.

Congratulations ensued: all pressing forward with their eager welcome. Edith held aloof in confusion: she had parted from him a little girl, and did not believe that old-looking man was her father. Colonel Bordillion looked round—perhaps seeking the youngest and fairest—and went up to Maria.

"*You* are Edith!"

"Oh papa, papa, no—it is I!" said Edith, as the smile on the face awoke a chord in her memory. She suddenly realized the fact that it was her father, and burst into tears of emotion. "*I* am Edith."

"And you?" asked Colonel Bordillion of Maria, when he had given a few moments to his daughter.

"I am Maria Lester."

"No, you're not," said the bridegroom, "you are Maria Dane."

There was a laugh at poor Maria. Colonel Bordillion did not seem to understand. "Are you Wilfred?" he asked of the speaker.

"No, sir. I am Geoffry Dane, Lord Dane's son."

"I see; it is the face and form of a Dane," observed the colonel. "But I did not know there was a son. And what is the cause of this festive assemblage? Your dress looks like a bridal one, my dear."

He touched Maria's veil and wreath; he looked at the flowing white silk that glittered as she turned. Many tongues hastened to enlighten him, and Wilfred came up to be noticed and received.

"I can understand what they said to me at the station just now—that I should be 'late,'" observed Colonel Bordillion. "So I should have been had I come to give the bride away, or to be best man."

He sat down at the table with them. He was of an exceedingly guileless, open nature, and he entered without ceremony upon his own affairs before every one.

"I have done with service," he observed, "and have come home to rest during the remainder of my days. You and I can live together, Margaret."

"Oh, yes, yes!" she answered: but there was a little sob of the breath as she remembered how very poor a home hers was to welcome him to.

"A sad affair that bank going," exclaimed one of the guests. "Quite ruined you, did it not, Colonel?"

"I thought so at first. It .was believed there would not be a shilling for any one, but it has turned out differently. We have got back more than fifty per cent. of our losses. Over thirty thousand pounds they have refunded to me."

"Over thirty thousand pounds!"

"Yes; that's the first dividend."

Over thirty thousand pounds. The poor, ruined Colonel Bordillion! Margaret stole a glance at Wilfred and Edith, and laid a hand upon her own beating heart.

"Why, you must have been a sixty-thousand pound man, Colonel!" exclaimed an elderly gentleman, who had known Henry Bordillion in early life. "A good fortune, that!"

"What do we wear our lives out in India for, but to make fortunes?" asked the Colonel. "I assure you, the very instant I could draw my dividend, I did so, and made arrangements for returning home to relieve my honoured friend and connection, Squire Lester. It has fallen to him to supply his son and daughter-in-law with an income hitherto, and I thought it high time I took my turn at the cost."

If ever a flush of shame dyed a man's countenance, it dyed at that moment George Lester's. How had he supplied them? Left them to starve: almost allowed Edith to drop into her grave from absolute want: suffered Wilfred to go to ruin as fast as he pleased! An uncomfortable feeling pervaded the room, and Lady Adelaide glanced at Edith, a pleading look on her burning face. It seemed to say, "Do not in pity expose me." So •Edith understood it, and a sweet, reassuring smile went back to her. But Cecilia Dane came unconsciously to the rescue.

"You don't remember me," she said, suddenly approaching him.

"N—o," said Colonel Bordillion, rather puzzled. "Unless you are—Miss Harkaby."

Cecilia Dane gave a genuine scream of mortification. Miss Harkaby had been an elderly young lady of thirty-five when Lieutenant Bordillion went away: she was quite sixty now. The Colonel had not been calculating the lapse of time.

"Oh, how cruel of you! And you were so nice and kind as Henry Bordillion. I remember you well, though I was only a little girl. I didn't think you had forgotten Cely Dane."

Not very many evenings after this—they might have been counted by seven—the setting sun, lighting up the west with floods of gold, illumined a busy scene. Idlers, dressed in their best, had gathered along the road in front of the Castle; children were sporting on the heights. Silly people! attracted as much by curiosity as by affection, they had assembled there to see the return of the bride and bridegroom, who had been recalled thus early from their wedding tour by the increased weakness of Lord Dane.

The carriage came in view, a travelling chariot and four, with the Dane arms on the panels. As it turned the corner of the road, the gathered people became visible to William Dane, who sat in it with his wife.

"What can this mean?" he exclaimed in the surprise of the moment. "Look, Maria!"

Whilst she was looking and wondering, a lovely bouquet of hot-house flowers was thrown in at the window on her lap. She turned to see Mrs. Ravensbird.

"Thank you, Sophie; thank you," she said, leaning forward and laughing. "William, they have assembled to give us an ovation, I am sure."

"Yes; and I never was more thankful to see anything."

"Thankful; for this! I would rather have come home in peace and quietness."

" It is an earnest, I hope, that my father is better," he quietly continued. " At least, not so ill as I have been fearing."

" Ah, yes! Forgive my thoughtlessness, William. Look! there is your friend Ben Beecher."

William Dane's eyes went searching out until they caught Ben Beecher's. He gave him a smile and a nod all to himself, and Ben reddened with pride.

Standing somewhat apart from the rest, were two people : one, a woman in smart attire—a scarlet shawl, and pink bows in her yellow bonnet — and a young gentleman smothered in a new suit of corduroy, ornamented with a great many fancy metal buttons. William Dane took his wife's hand and pointed to the spot.

" See there, Maria ! "

" Shad and Tiffle ! " exclaimed Maria. " How she is decked out ! I wonder she should have that boy with her ! "

" As to that, I have a strong suspicion that Shad has more right to be with her than with any one else," said Mr. Dane.

" What do you mean, William ? "

He only laughed, giving no explanation. The carriage drew slowly to the gates, and Tiffle pushed forward to be ready for the descent. Granny Bean had left a letter, bequeathing Shad to Tiffle's tender care; and the friend who wrote the letter for Granny disclosed a fact confided to her : that Shad was—not to put too fine a point upon it— related to Tiffle. Danesheld had just got hold of the news ; and Tiffle, after a day and a night of abusive denial, now brazened it out.

As Mr. Dane was handing his wife from the carriage, Tiffle's yellow bonnet intervened. Never had there been a falser smile on that false countenance than disfigured it now.

" Here's wishing of your lordship every happiness in life, and the same to your lordship's lady ! " curtsied Tiffle, with a great amount of boldness. " Though I have been shame-fully used and abused, I'm not one to bear malice, and I says to Shad, we'll put on our things and go up and offer our kingretilations with the rest on this ouspicious occasion ;

which I am now doing of. . Long life and happiness to my
Lord and Lady Dane ! "

"Houray ! " put in Shad.

They were the first distinct words William Dane had
caught, and he started at their significance.

"I am not Lord Dane yet," he sharply said, in his fear.

"'Twon't be long first, by all accounts," rejoined Tiffle,
"but I might have said the future Lord and Lady Dane.
We wish 'em every health and happiness."

"The future Lord and Lady Dane beg to thank you," was
the response, coldly spoken, as he turned from her. But
Tiffle was not to be repulsed.

"And I've taken up my residence in the cottage which
was Granny Bean's, having accumulated enough for a small
indepindince," pursued Tiffle. "And if I can serve your
lord or ladyship in any way, I shall be grateful to do it."

"Have you taken to Shad as well as to the cottage ? "
asked Mr. Dane.

"Yes, sir, I have. Not being ashamed to acknowledge in
the face of inemies that he's a connection of mine," was the
assured response.

"The best thing for Shad would be to put him into a reformatory," said Mr. Dane ; " the next best would be to send
him to a strict, plain, industrial school. I promised the boy
I would do something for him, and I will. He must be
rescued from his present vagabond life."

"And it's with thanks for your intentions, sir, but I don't
wish to do myself the pleasure of excepting them," spoke
Tiffle, in wrath at the word reformatory, while the boy
broke out into something like a howl. "Shad's no more a
vagabond than other folks, and I've adopted him for my—
my nephew and heir."

Suppressing a laugh at the concluding announcement,
waving the woman and. the subject away for future consideration, William Dane stood facing the crowd, his wife on
his arm, bowing his thanks before the gate closed upon him.
It was a scene worth depicting. The stately old Castle and
its waving flag ; the group of humble friends gathered there,
tendering their homage and affection ; and the fine young

chieftain standing to receive it, bare-headed, free and noble, his face lighted up by the setting sun. A fine face! with its kind, earnest, thoughtful eyes, its calm, keen sense, and its unmistakable expression of goodness stamped on every line. As they gazed, those people, they felt that for them henceforth Danesheld in its lord would possess a *friend*. Maria leaned on him, her cheeks blushing; and very glad indeed when they could take shelter in the Castle.

Lord Dane was better that evening, free from pain, upright almost as ever, as he advanced to meet them. It seemed that nature had rallied all her powers for the welcome home. But William was startled—so great a change had the last few days made in him. Death could not be very far off now, and a pang of self-reproach darted through the young man's heart for having remained away even those seven days.

Lord Dane had assembled guests around him to join in the welcome: the Lesters, Miss Dane, Colonel and Miss Bordillion. Lord Dane, exerting himself beyond his strength and feeling consequent fatigue, withdrew to his room, intending to lie down for a few minutes before dinner.

"I thought his lordship was here," said Bruff, looking round, when he came to say that dinner was served.

"He has not come down yet, Bruff," observed William. "You had better tell him."

Bruff went and came back again, beckoning William out of the room.

"I can't get into my lord's chamber, sir," he whispered. "The door's fastened, and he does not answer."

William was before it in a moment. As Bruff said, the door was fastened; bolted inside. William put his lips to the keyhole.

"My dear father, are you ready?" he asked in a clear, distinct voice. "We are waiting dinner."

There was no response. William Dane turned his face, growing so pale with emotion, on the servant.

"He does not usually fasten his door?"

"No, sir, never. Perhaps he slipped the bolt now, not to be disturbed while he rested. He might have thought you or his servant would be going in."

The rest, to whom some vague fear had spread, came flocking up. Miss Dane grew rather excited.

"Do pray just speak one word, Lord Dane, if only to assure us you are not in a fit," she called out in coaxing and trembling accents. "Harry, then! *won't* you speak?"

"I shall break open the door," said William hurriedly. "Had you not better"—he looked at Maria and the rest—"go back to the drawing-room?"

The door was forced, and Lord Dane was found lying upon the bed in a fainting fit. Medical men were summoned, and he revived to speech and consciousness. But the end was at hand.

Perhaps they did not suspect it, however; and he grew quite cheerful as the evening went on. Lady Adelaide Lester knelt by the bed in deep sorrow and emotion, her haggard face pressed on the counterpane : and a haggard face it was at all times now. That confession did not appear to have brought her either peace or security; it seemed a question whether she would ever gain either. Worn, weary, miserable, she lived on, finding life good neither in the present nor the past. As that past deceit and that awful oath had lain upon her conscience then, so they lay on it still : and she could not feel secure that some chance fate would not betray her. In truth there was little, if any, probability of it; but the terror of a guilty conscience is like jealousy—as given to us by that masterhand—"making the food it feeds on."

It happened that they were alone for a moment, she and the dying man. She looked up suddenly, speaking a word to him in her terrible despair : telling of the unrest that was upon her, the miserable disquietude of her mind and heart.

"Ah, Adelaide," he replied, gently and compassionately laying his hands upon hers. "You ask for peace—peace; but you have not sown it. Adelaide, my dear, you must begin again : it is not yet too late ; you have been all on the wrong tack, and you must change it. Oh, child, how will you dare to hope for peace in the next world, unless you seek to shed it in this?"

"If I could, if I could! Oh, Harry, if I only could!"

"You can set out from to-day. There will be a struggle at first—there will be need of much patience; but you will find the good end at last if you bear steadily on. Throw aside your hard selfishness, and take up instead the sweet spirit of loving help and pity; you will be no longer miserable. Adelaide, it is my dying charge to you."

A few hours, and the Castle flag was floating half-mast high: William Henry, seventeenth Baron Dane, had gone home to his ancestors.

They laid him in the family vault, by the side of that unknown stranger who had been buried for him. Herbert came over to the funeral. Never was there such an attendance seen at any burial in Danesheld. They walked to the grave through the crisp white snow, the blue sky smiling overhead. Geoffry William, eighteenth Baron Dane, walked alone in right of his position. Herbert followed him with Squire Lester, and the rest as chance led them.

Mr. Apperly produced the will on their return to the Castle. All had been remembered. Herbert Dane had a large sum bequeathed to him absolutely, equal to twelve hundred a year; Cecilia had three hundred a year in an annuity. A remembrance was left to Lady Adelaide, and five thousand pounds to Wilfred Lester, as "a thank-offering for having saved my life, and that of one far more precious to me—my dear son, Geoffry William." A thousand pounds were left to Bruff, and two thousand pounds to "my faithful friend and servant, Richard Ravensbird;" a like sum—two thousand pounds—was directed to be equally divided between the Castle servants; and the rest of his private fortune went to his son.

"What a wealthy man he died!" quoth Mr. Wild in an undertone, who had also been remembered.

"He died something better than that—a good one."

Mr. Wild had not thought he was overheard, and turned at the words, which came from the young lord, whilst the tears shone in his earnest eyes as he gave them utterance.

THE END.

LONDON: PRINTED BY WILLIAM CLOWES AND SONS, LIMITED, STAMFORD STREET AND CHARING CROSS.

MRS. HENRY WOOD'S NOVELS.

Sale nearly Two Million Copies.

EAST LYNNE. 400th Thousand.

THE CHANNINGS. 140th Thousand.

MRS. HALLIBURTON'S TROUBLES. 120th Thousand.

THE SHADOW OF ASHLYDYAT. 77th Thousand.

LORD OAKBURN'S DAUGHTERS. 77th Thousand.

VERNER'S PRIDE. 65th Thousand.

ROLAND YORKE. 100th Thousand.

JOHNNY LUDLOW. First Series. 50th Thousand.

MILDRED ARKELL. 68th Thousand.

ST. MARTIN'S EVE. 60th Thousand.

TREVLYN HOLD. 40th Thousand.

GEORGE CANTERBURY'S WILL. 50th Thousand.

THE RED COURT FARM. 44th Thousand.

WITHIN THE MAZE. 85th Thousand.

ELSTER'S FOLLY. 50th Thousand.

LADY ADELAIDE. 50th Thousand.

OSWALD CRAY. 50th Thousand.

JOHNNY LUDLOW. Second Series. 23rd Thousand.

ANNE HEREFORD. 35th Thousand.

DENE HOLLOW. 35th Thousand.

EDINA. 25th Thousand.

A LIFE'S SECRET. 38th Thousand.

COURT NETHERLEIGH. 26th Thousand.

BESSY RANE. 30th Thousand.

JOHNNY LUDLOW. Third Series. 13th Thousand.

THE MASTER OF GREYLANDS. 30th Thousand.

ORVILLE COLLEGE. 33rd Thousand.

POMEROY ABBEY. 30th Thousand.

JOHNNY LUDLOW. Fourth Series. New Edition.

LONDON:

RICHARD BENTLEY & SON, New Burlington Street, W.

(Publishers in Ordinary to Her Majesty the Queen.)

www.ingramcontent.com/pod-product-compliance
Lightning Source LLC
Chambersburg PA
CBHW052339110726
47901CB00005B/1294